FIVE KINGDOMS

TIME JUMPERS

BOOK 5

Brandon Mull

ALADDIN
NEW YORK LONDON TORONTO SYDNEY NEW DELHI

This book is a work of fiction. Any references to historical events, real people,
or real places are used fictitiously. Other names, characters, places, and events are
products of the author's imagination, and any resemblance to actual events or
places or persons, living or dead, is entirely coincidental.

ALADDIN

An imprint of Simon & Schuster Children's Publishing Division
1230 Avenue of the Americas, New York, NY 10020
First Aladdin paperback edition May 2019
Text copyright © 2018 by Brandon Mull
Cover illustration copyright © 2018 by Owen Richardson
Also available in an Aladdin hardcover edition.
All rights reserved, including the right of reproduction in whole or in part in any form.
ALADDIN and related logo are registered trademarks of Simon & Schuster, Inc.
For information about special discounts for bulk purchases, please contact
Simon & Schuster Special Sales at 1-866-506-1949 or business@simonandschuster.com.
The Simon & Schuster Speakers Bureau can bring authors to your live event. For more
information or to book an event contact the Simon & Schuster Speakers Bureau
at 1-866-248-3049 or visit our website at www.simonspeakers.com.
Cover designed by Jessica Handelman
Interior designed by Mike Rosamilia
The text of this book was set in Perpetua.
Manufactured in the United States of America 0419 OFF
2 4 6 8 10 9 7 5 3 1
The Library of Congress has cataloged the hardcover edition as follows:
Names: Mull, Brandon, 1974- author.
Title: Time jumpers / Brandon Mull.
Description: First Aladdin hardcover edition. | New York : Aladdin, 2018. |
Series: Five kingdoms ; book 5 | Summary: Trapped in a world where magic is powerful
and dreams are real, Cole and his friends are pushed to the limit as they make one final
attempt to restore magic to the Outskirts and find their way back home.
Identifiers: LCCN 2017056574 (print) | LCCN 2018001615 (eBook) |
ISBN 9781442497146 (eBook) | ISBN 9781442497122 (hardcover)
Subjects: | CYAC: Fantasy. | Adventure and adventurers—Fiction. | Magic—Fiction. |
Dreams—Fiction. | BISAC: JUVENILE FICTION / Action & Adventure / General. |
JUVENILE FICTION / Fantasy & Magic. |
JUVENILE FICTION / Legends, Myths, Fables / General.
Classification: LCC PZ7.M9112 (eBook) | LCC PZ7.M9112 Tim 2018 (print) |
DDC [Fic]—dc23
LC record available at https://lccn.loc.gov/2017056574
ISBN 9781442497139 (pbk)

For my dear friend Amy,
forever admired and beloved

CHAPTER
—✦— 1 —✦—

PRISONERS

Cole could not see anything.

He lay stretched across the rough wooden planks of a wagon bed, the hood over his head somewhat dampening the impact as the boards rapped against his skull. Judging from the sound of the hoofbeats and the rattling of the vehicle, they were moving briskly along a dirt road. His hands were bound together behind his back with strong, slender cords. Iron manacles encircled his ankles, biting into his skin when he tried to pull free. The coarse material against his face threatened to induce a claustrophobic panic, though he could breathe reasonably well.

Unpleasant sensations assailed him—hunger, thirst, soreness, exhaustion.

Having just returned from the echolands, he found ownership of a physical body startlingly unfamiliar. He had not felt hungry in a long while. Or sore.

Cole had been warned before returning to his body. He knew he had been captured, along with Destiny, Honor, and

Desmond. Their bodies had been left behind at the Temple of the Robust Sky when they had departed for the echolands, and their defenseless physical forms had fallen into the power of Enforcers.

The prelate Elana had placed their bodies in a secret room for safekeeping. Clearly something had gone wrong. Wherever Elana was now, Cole hoped she was all right.

"Hello?" Cole called, not at full volume but hopefully loud enough for any other prisoners sharing the wagon to hear.

"Cole?" a voice answered, slightly muffled.

It was Destiny. Tessa. Mira's youngest sister, who he had just rescued in the echolands.

"I'm here too," Honor said, her voice clearer and louder, though somewhat dampened as well. Strong and independent, Honor was Mira's second-oldest sister and had helped in the search for Tessa. "Desmond?"

There came no reply.

"Anybody else?" Honor tried.

"It may just be the three of us," Cole said. "Are you tied up too?"

"Manacles on my hands and feet," Honor replied over the creak and rattle of the wagon. "Hood over my head."

Cole wondered if he should be insulted that only his feet had actual manacles.

"I can't see either," Destiny said. "My hands are tied. My legs are chained."

"Me too," Cole said, deciding that he was considered a lesser threat than Honor.

"Can you spring us, Cole?" Honor asked.

It was a fair question. In the echolands, Cole had finally unlocked his power. His shaping ability had become inaccessible after being mangled when he fought Morgassa in Elloweer. Once his power had become active, Cole found he could awaken the shaping power in others, and he had learned to transform objects in the echolands with his will, as if he were a gifted shaper in Sambria.

Cole could still feel his power smoldering inside. It had been absent for so long, the presence was unmistakable.

In the echolands, he had recently used his power to throw down castle walls. The manacles should not stand a chance. Let alone the fabric of the hood covering his face.

Mustering his focus, Cole willed the unseen manacles cuffing his ankles to dissolve.

Nothing happened.

Cole tugged with his legs against the restraints. The unforgiving iron dug into his skin just as before.

Cole willed the fabric of the hood to split apart. He drew on his power with all of his effort.

Not a single thread popped.

"I don't know," Cole replied. "I can feel my power. But it doesn't seem to be working. I can't make it connect."

"I worried it might be different back in a physical body," Honor said.

"Why should it be different?" Cole asked.

"The echolands are made of a whole different kind of matter," Honor said. "You didn't have a physical body there, and you weren't affecting physical material. I've never heard

3

of anyone developing their power as quickly as you did in the echolands. You have the same abilities here, but using those skills in the physical world may take more time to develop."

Cole relaxed his mind. Without straining, he tried to push his power at the iron cuffs gripping his ankles. Again he got no result. He refocused on the hood, to no avail.

"I'm sorry," Cole said. "I can't even tear the hood. But my power is with me."

"They're probably taking us to Owandell," Honor said. "Once we reach Junction, I should be able to access my power. I'll set us free."

"No," Destiny said, her voice calm and certain. "Going before Owandell will lead us to the paths we must walk."

For a long moment Cole listened to hoofs clopping and scuffing against the dirt. The wagon jerked, swayed, and creaked.

"That settles it," Honor said, resignation in her tone. "No escape attempt. We wait."

"What paths?" Cole asked. "Where are we going?"

"I don't know," Destiny said, sounding like herself once more.

"No hints?" Cole asked.

"I'm sorry," Destiny said. "It just comes. I never know more than what comes."

"No apology needed," Honor said. "Any guidance helps."

In the echolands, Cole had seen Destiny's power in action. Separate from her, in the form of a horse, her power had played a key role in helping him find Destiny, save his friends, and prevent the return of Nazeem, who was really a torivor named Ramarro. Before leaving the afterlife, Destiny's power had been restored to her. And now it was speaking through her.

"We let the Enforcers take us to Owandell?" Cole checked.

"Yes, if we have any sense," Honor said. "No good comes from trying to avoid Tessa's prophecies."

"We don't resist at all?" Cole asked.

"We can try whatever we want after we meet with Owandell," Honor said. "Until then we use patience."

"It's hard to be patient with a bag over your head," Cole observed.

The wagon slowed to a stop.

"Are we there?" Cole asked.

"I don't think so," Honor said in a tone so hushed, Cole could barely hear her. "I'd have some access to my power if we were in Junction. They're probably changing horses."

Cole heard the clink and jangle of chains at the rear of the wagon.

"Play possum," Honor suggested quietly.

Cole went limp as he heard doors open. The unsteady glow of torchlight flickered up through the bottom of his hood. Somebody was checking on the prisoners. Breathing softly, Cole stayed limp.

"Still there," a gruff voice affirmed.

The door closed.

Harnesses jingled and hoofs clopped. A horse whickered. Shortly the wagon lurched forward.

"They're in a hurry," Honor said.

"I don't want to see Owandell," Tessa said in a voice nearly too small to hear.

Cole almost replied that her own power was to blame for their decision to go submissively before the head of the High King's secret police. But since Owandell had used shapecraft—the ability to tamper with the shaping power itself—to take Destiny's power when she was only nine and give it to her father, Cole decided sensitivity was required.

"You must hate him," he said.

"Owandell scares me," Tessa replied.

"He'll hurt you again over my dead body," Honor promised.

"That doesn't comfort me," Tessa said. "I don't want to lose you."

"Trust your power," Cole said. "It helped save us in the echolands."

"Knowing we should talk to Owandell doesn't necessarily spare us from harm," Honor said. "Terrible consequences could follow. Destiny's prophecy could simply mean that any efforts to escape would fail. Or it could mean the encounter with Owandell will produce outcomes that need to happen for some higher purpose. But serving a higher purpose is no guarantee of safety."

"You're not very comforting," Cole said.

"Does our situation seem comfortable?" Honor challenged. "We all need to face reality."

"What do you think they did with Desmond?" Tessa asked.

"He wasn't a high enough priority to transfer him to Junction," Honor said. "Hopefully, he's just imprisoned back near the Temple of the Robust Sky."

"What is our reality?" Cole asked. "Does Owandell want your powers again?"

"Perhaps," Honor said. "Or else he wants us as hostages."

"Can he take your powers?" Cole asked.

"He proved he has the ability," Honor said. "We didn't surrender them willingly the first time."

"Is your father behind this?" Cole wondered. Assisted by Owandell, the High King had used shapecraft to steal the powers of his five daughters several decades ago. The absence of their shaping abilities had stopped the princesses from aging. Miracle, Honor, Constance, and Destiny all had their powers back now. Only their eldest sister, Elegance, still lacked her stolen abilities.

"Hard to say," Honor said. "Though Owandell still works for Father, he doesn't collaborate closely with him anymore, and is clearly carrying out his own schemes with Ramarro. We won't know how much Father is involved until this unfolds."

Cole frowned at the mention of Ramarro. Under the name Nazeem, the torivor had introduced shapecraft into the five kingdoms. Ramarro had just escaped his prison in the echolands, but with help from Cole, the torivor had been diverted to a prison in Creon when he reentered mortality.

"Owandell stole our powers for Father in the first place," Honor said. "I expect Owandell will want to take them again. But I'm not going to resist Destiny's foresight. When she speaks under the influence of her gift, I have never known her to be wrong."

"How many of the Enforcers are loyal to your father?" Cole asked. "Could they be taking us to him?"

"Owandell has recently proven that he controls the majority of the Enforcers," Honor said. "I'm sure there are some exceptions."

"Where do we go if we escape him?" Cole asked.

"In the capital?" Honor asked. "We try to find Mother."

Cole had met Harmony. She had helped him escape Junction the last time he visited. "Do you think she can help us find Mira?" Cole wondered.

"Probably," Honor said. "I hope Mother can also direct us to Elegance. Our highest priority is to stop Ramarro, and we'll need help from Wayminders. Mother has contacts in that community."

Cole felt smothered by more than the hood covering his face. There was so much to be done! The prison where he had helped deposit Ramarro would not hold the torivor forever. It might only restrain him for weeks. Or even days. And if the torivor got free, the Outskirts would fall under his complete control. Not to mention that the torivor wanted revenge against Cole and his friends. The ancient shapers who had created the Outskirts had barely managed to contain Ramarro, and nobody was left who could defeat him. Cole had to find a way to prevent his escape.

And he needed to find his friends, especially Mira, Jace, and Dalton. And his brother, Hunter.

And he needed to rescue Jenna and the other kids who had been kidnapped into the Outskirts from his neighborhood in Arizona.

And he needed to restore Elegance's power and defeat the High King.

And he was currently tied up in a prison wagon.

And his power didn't work right anymore.

"Let's survive Owandell first," Cole said.

"He's a powerful shapecrafter," Honor warned. "He can block the shaping of others. And we know with enough time he can strip away their powers and give them to another."

Cole temporarily wished he could return to the echolands, where he had gained so much power. Nobody in the echolands could chain him up and cart him around. Of course, it was also the last stop before moving on to the next phase of existence. Most people in the echolands were dead.

Cole was back in the living world, and he had to solve his problems here. Or at least try.

"I guess we just have to be patient for now," Cole concluded.

"Save your strength," Honor suggested. "We'll need it before long."

CHAPTER
2

OWANDELL

As the journey wore on, Cole had few options to improve his comfort. He rotated between lying on his stomach, his right side, his left side, and his back. He could not endure resting on his back for long because, with his wrists bound behind him, the position placed too much pressure on his arms. He tried sitting or kneeling from time to time, but that never felt very comfortable.

Cole tried to picture his home.

He had visited a realistic dream version of his room shortly before meeting She Who Stands at the Summit in the echolands. Some of those details still felt pretty fresh.

But riding his bike down his street? Eating breakfast at the kitchen table? A typical day of school? Those memories seemed like remote visions of another life.

A life far from prison wagons, and spiritual realms, and advanced robots, and magical powers. Far from exiled princesses and life-or-death combat.

Would he ever make it home?

Would he see his parents again? His sister?

Would he go to bed without wondering if enemies would capture him while he slept? Or kill him?

Maybe.

If he could survive this current predicament.

There had to be a chance. If Owandell simply wanted him dead, that would have happened while his spirit was in the echolands.

If Cole survived this, then he could work on the next problem.

And the next one.

He had survived a lot. Maybe he could keep on surviving.

One day at a time.

One crisis at a time.

But maybe at some point he wouldn't survive.

Would that be so bad? He had seen there was life after death. He knew something about where he would end up.

And he had heard the call of the Other—the realm beyond the echolands. The call had been inviting.

Someday he would answer that call.

Hopefully not today. Or tomorrow. Or anytime soon.

He had too much to do.

How long had their unanimated bodies traveled in the wagon before he, Honor, and Tessa returned from the echolands? How many times had the teams been changed?

The road seemed smoother, the hoofbeats crisper. The wagon barely rattled.

The road must be paved. Or something similar.

"Are we nearing the capital?" Cole asked.

"We're in Junction," Honor replied. "I felt my powers go active half an hour ago."

"Mine faded a little as we left Necronum," Tessa said.

"Mine feel the same," Cole said.

He tried to will the cords on his wrists to dissolve. Nothing happened. He could sense his power, but he couldn't push it into the physical objects around him. Doing so had felt perfectly natural in the echolands!

Before long the wagon slowed and rounded a corner. The pace remained slow, and turning became frequent, until the wagon descended a short, steep incline, leveled out, and stopped.

Chains clinked at the rear of the wagon. Then the doors opened.

"On your feet," the gruff voice ordered.

Staying limp, Cole held still. He heard no sound from the princesses.

"Come off it," the voice said. "I heard you gabbing off and on for the past twenty miles. On your feet unless you want to be dragged."

Cole heard the princesses stirring, so he stood up as well. It took some extra effort without the use of his hands. He wondered how much the man had heard. They hadn't spoken loudly, the wagon was enclosed, and the horses made noise. Hopefully, the driver had just caught an occasional murmur of conversation.

What if the driver had heard everything? Had they expressed anything compromising?

Cole heard someone approach. An iron collar clamped

around his neck, fitting over the hood and drawing the cloth tighter against his face. Cole tried to keep his breathing calm. Air seemed to pass through the material well enough.

Near his feet, a key clicked inside a lock, and a manacle unfastened from one ankle. Then the other was removed. At least that was a relief.

Cole was suddenly tugged forward by the collar. It guided him forward, sideways, and then to a stop, suggesting that the collar was connected to a pole rather than a rope. Cole felt helplessly angry. Did they have to treat him like an animal? Were they afraid he would bite?

"Drop to the ground," a hard voice commanded.

Probing ahead with his foot, Cole felt nothing but empty air. He must have been at the back of the wagon, and they wanted him to jump down. His inability to see made the prospect uncomfortable.

The opportunity to choose was taken from him as he was yanked forward by his collar. Hands bound behind his back, unable to gauge the arrival of the ground, Cole fell for an alarming moment and then stumbled upon impact. The collar pressed up against the underside of his jaw, stretching his neck as it kept him on his feet.

Cole didn't hear anyone ordering the princesses to jump, so he assumed they were helped down more gently. Did they have collars too? Until now, Cole had been too distracted by what his captors were doing to him to heed any clues about Honor and Tessa.

The unrelenting collar pulled him forward. Others walked nearby. Cole stamped his feet. The level ground and the acoustics of his footfalls made him suspect he was in a room rather than outside.

He halted as murmured words were exchanged. A door opened.

"Honor?" Cole tried.

"Silence," a harsh voice demanded. Whoever held the pole attached to his collar gave it a jolting shake.

"We're here," Honor answered from not far behind him.

"No more words or I start really hurting the boy," the harsh voice threatened.

For a moment Cole forgot the plan to go quietly. He could feel his power inside. Using his anger and frustration to sharpen his focus, he tried to push his power into the collar around his neck. In the echolands, when engaging his power, he could feel the target object without touching it. Here, though he could feel the weight of the collar around his neck, he could not touch it with his power.

He was tugged forward again. Cole walked in brooding silence.

He passed through another door. And another.

Then he was brought to a stop. "Wait here," the harsh voice demanded. "Don't move."

Whoever held the pole connected to his collar set it down.

Footsteps retreated. A door closed.

Cole waited. He could see nothing.

"Honor?" Tessa asked. "Cole?"

"Yes," Cole said.

"Here," Honor said.

"Anyone else?" Tessa tried.

There came no reply.

"Where are we?" Tessa asked.

"Underground," Honor replied. "The bowels of some building. Maybe Hakrel's Castle."

"Where?" Cole asked.

"Headquarters for the Enforcers," Honor replied. "Don't assume we're alone just because nobody answered."

"Indeed," a confident voice replied.

The unexpected male voice startled Cole.

"Owandell," Honor said.

"Good memory," Owandell replied. "Guards, remove the hoods."

Fingers tugged the bottom of Cole's hood out from the iron collar and then removed the coarse covering. He blinked beneath the glare of multiple lanterns. The windowless room was made of mortared stone. Honor and Tessa stood off to one side. They wore no collars, and their hands were free.

Owandell paced before them, hands behind his back, wearing a brown robe, shoulders stooped. His hairless head and fleshy features looked much as Cole remembered them from the ceremony at the Founding Stone beneath the First Castle.

"You guards are dismissed," Owandell said. "Please stay alert."

Looking over his shoulder, Cole saw four guards dressed as Enforcers exit the room. The far end of the pole attached to his collar rested on the floor, as if to prop him up.

"Does our father know we're here?" Honor asked once the door had closed.

Owandell shrugged. "Difficult to be sure. Stafford has many spies. I have not informed him, if that is what you mean. The High King is a scant shadow of the leader he once was. I withhold much from him, for the good of the kingdoms."

"What do you want with us?" Honor asked.

Owandell stopped pacing and smiled. "Is this how it works? Are you conducting an interrogation?"

"You abducted us," Honor said evenly. "I want to know why."

"How authoritative of you," Owandell said. "How absolutely royal. Do you grasp that you are my prisoner? Do you understand that your monarchy is at an end?"

"I understand that you work for my father," Honor said.

Owandell scrunched one eye and looked upward with the other. "In theory, perhaps. According to certain documents, I owe him my allegiance. Ceremonial vows were made. In practice it has been some time since anyone of consequence took Stafford Pemberton seriously."

"This castle, this city, and the five kingdoms all belong to him," Honor said.

"Officially, yes, for the moment," Owandell said, pacing again. "I despise empty words. Listen. You two princesses currently have political value, but not for much longer. All conventional metrics will soon be outdated. The deck will be reshuffled. Serving boys and milkmaids might outrank kings and queens. All that will matter before long is where you stand with Nazeem."

"You mean Ramarro?" Cole asked.

"Very few know that name in connection with Nazeem," Owandell said quietly. "None who do dare utter it."

"Ramarro?" Cole repeated, happy to bother him.

Owandell gave a very brittle smile. "I'm aware you interacted with my master shortly before he departed the echolands. It is part of the reason I wished to consult with you three. That and the novelty of your shaping powers. Your power looks different, Cole. Much more serviceable than when we last met. I take it the echolands agreed with you?"

"I learned a few things," Cole said vaguely.

The smile changed to a baring of teeth. "Hearken to my words, boy. The order of the world is changing. Many will suffer. Many will perish. An elect few will rise. Above most others I have encountered, your power could be of interest to Nazeem."

"It was," Cole said. "Ramarro tried to recruit me."

Owandell drew near him. "You resisted?"

"Good guess," Cole said.

"You are an alien in a dangerous land," Owandell said. "Do you comprehend that his generosity is your only hope?"

"I'm going to stop him," Cole said. "You should help us."

Owandell chuckled. "Do you realize who you're talking to?"

"Do you get who you serve?" Cole challenged. "You'll be a slave."

Owandell grinned. "Even if that were true, Nazeem's slaves will possess more power than kings. He can effectuate shaping potential that exceeds our greediest fantasies."

"And he'll use it to control everyone," Cole said. "You'll

be at his mercy. And he is not merciful. Surrendering to Ramarro is not winning."

"Young," Owandell spat. "Naive. Foolhardy." He turned to the princesses. "There is no sense in resisting the inevitable. No sense in demanding certain destruction. Your shaping power could interest my master as well."

"Do you want us to join you?" Honor asked bitterly. "To trust you? You took our powers! You destroyed our family."

"We've met Ramarro," Tessa said. "We won't be joining you."

Owandell smiled. "I feel you trying to engage your power, Honor. Not in my presence, my dear. I could shut down ten of you, especially here in Junction. Doesn't come as easily as in Elloweer, does it?"

Eyes intent, sweat beading on her brow, Honor grunted in reply.

Owandell shifted his attention to Tessa. "I can even block your squirmy ability. No cryptic babblings will issue forth in my presence."

His gaze moved on to Cole and showed a flicker of concern. "And you . . . are most unusual."

"Let us go," Cole said. "If you won't help us, just let us go. Wouldn't it be better if we stopped Ramarro? Even if it's a long shot?"

Owandell shook his head. "My master is no longer in the echolands. He has already returned."

"Then where is he?" Cole asked.

Owandell narrowed his eyes. "Something interfered. Perhaps some ancient fail-safe built into his prison."

"Maybe it was me," Cole said.

"Impossible," Owandell whispered.

"Then he must have arrived without any problem," Cole said. "Where is he?"

Owandell brought his face right up to Cole's. "What happened? Where is Nazeem?"

"I sent him home to the magical land of the torivors," Cole said.

Real anger flared in Owandell's eyes. "I know that isn't so. It would take an unimaginable amount of power for a torivor to escape this realm. Start speaking truth. Where is Nazeem?"

"Don't explain," Honor cautioned.

"I know," Cole said.

Owandell inched closer, furious eyes unblinking, warm breath unpleasant, until his nose almost touched Cole's. "You will tell me, boy. Or I'll leave your power twice as mangled as it was before."

The threat rattled Cole. He had barely healed his power in the echolands, and the ordeal had stretched him to his limits. With all the troubles ahead, the last thing he wanted was to lose his power again.

But he couldn't lead Owandell to his master. Cole knew some details of the imprisonment. The vault was called the Void, where Ramarro currently floated at the center of a vast, empty space, reliving the same looping millisecond, unable to move, and drawn back to the center if he did. The torivor had been deposited there with help from the consciousness of Dandalus imprinted on the Founding Stone.

Cole knew the Void was in Creon but had no idea where exactly. And he knew the prison, strong as it was, would probably not hold Ramarro very long. If Owandell found Ramarro, the escape would almost certainly come more speedily.

"Ramarro couldn't take me down," Cole said. "Let's see what you've got."

Owandell huffed incredulously. "Nazeem had his considerable powers focused on returning from the afterlife—a nearly impossible feat. You encountered him at a rare moment of vulnerability and proved an inconvenience."

"And I'll do it again," Cole said. "You should help."

"Last warning," Owandell said. "Explain what happened. I know Nazeem crossed over. Tell me where he is."

"Never," Cole said.

Owandell backed up a step, glancing at the princesses.

"You know what I'm about to do to him," Owandell threatened. "Tell me what I want to know."

"We have no idea," Honor said. "Cole doesn't either. He had help diverting Ramarro."

"I believe that," Owandell said. "But the boy knows more than he is telling. Very well." Standing before Cole, Owandell seized his shoulders.

Suddenly Cole could sense Owandell's power, roiling and dark, tainted but mighty. That corrupt power surged at Cole, sliding across the surface of the energy inside him. Gritting his teeth, Cole pushed Owandell's power away.

And Owandell staggered, landing flat on his back. Round eyes stared up in shock and dismay.

Cole felt a flash of similar surprise at how naturally it had come to him, then smiled. It felt good to access his power and feel a reaction. He could still perceive Owandell's power but could no longer connect to it.

Honor laughed. "You're out of your depth, little man."

Without a response, still looking startled, Owandell got to his feet, absently brushing at his robe. His gaze shifted between Honor and Cole.

A knock came at the door.

"All is well," Owandell snapped. "Give us time."

The knock was repeated more insistently.

"Give us time!" Owandell shouted.

A key jiggled in the lock, and the door opened. An Enforcer poked his head inside. "Begging your pardon, we're under attack," the guard said.

"Attack?" Owandell asked, bewildered.

"The royal guard," the Enforcer said. "The legionnaires. The Junction City Militia. Royalist Enforcers. We're being overwhelmed. Commander Ratcleff gave the evacuation order."

Owandell stroked his chin. "Stafford sent his forces against us. The old goat is finally making a move. After all this time, I honestly didn't believe he had it in him."

"A decisive move," the guard said. "Quick. Unexpected. They had help from the inside. The upper levels have already fallen. We can still get you out, but we have to go."

Owandell started laughing.

"Is everything all right?" the guard asked.

"I'm sorry," Owandell said, waving away the comment. "The king has no idea what is coming. He is playing politics while the sky is falling. He is fretting about pests in his garden when the volcano next door is about to erupt."

Cole edged over toward Honor. They needed to escape, and the contact with Owandell had given him an idea. Neither Owandell nor the guard seemed to notice his movement.

"Be that as it may," the guard said, "the king is successfully taking Hakrel's Castle. We must away or surrender."

"Commander Ratcleff had it right," Owandell said. "This castle is meaningless. Cole, you and your peculiar powers? Pointless! You princesses? Irrelevant! Nazeem is coming. All unrelated currency will soon be worthless."

"And yet the castle is falling," the guard reminded everyone. "Leave the prisoners?"

"No," Owandell said. "They won't get off that easily. And I will not hand Stafford that minor victory. Bring the prisoners."

The guard fully opened the door, and three other Enforcers tromped in.

Cole closed the last of the distance between himself and Honor, twisting so he could touch her hand with his hands tied behind his back. He immediately sensed her power, steady and strong. More important, as he had hoped, his own power connected easily to hers. It felt natural and simple, like it had in the echolands.

He could also sense power from Owandell shrouding the energy inside her like a dark, filmy cocoon. Clenching his jaw, Cole used his power to feed energy into hers. Her energy blazed brilliantly, and Owandell's cocoon evaporated.

With a roar, Honor expanded into a huge, shaggy bear, at least three or four feet taller than Cole. Lunging forward, she clamped her fierce jaws down on the shoulder of the nearest guard. She shook him brutally, making his limbs flop, then heaved him off to one side, where he slammed against the wall and dropped to the floor in a savaged heap.

The bulk of the bear made the room seem much smaller. Cole and Tessa fell back behind her. Though Cole was no longer touching Honor, the connection to her power remained, and he kept feeding her energy.

The Enforcer nearest Honor assumed a fighting stance. Thornlike spikes sprouted from his armor, and his sword elongated into a spear. The Enforcers who Cole had encountered usually had shaping powers. This guy was no exception.

The other two guards ushered Owandell toward the door.

"No," Owandell griped. "Not without the prisoners."

"We have no time for a fight," the guard who had first poked his head in cried. "The king's men will be upon us shortly."

The spiky guard lunged forward with his spear. Honor batted the spearhead aside and raked him with her claws. The guard went down, and Honor pounced, wounding her forelegs on his spikes as she tore his armor apart.

The other two guards ushered Owandell out of the room. The door banged shut, and a lock immediately clicked.

Roaring, Honor charged the door, blubber and muscles in motion beneath her golden brown coat. She swatted the door and leaned her bulk against it. She snarled and slashed with her claws. The door held against her assault.

Backing away a pace or two, she faced the door and sat down. The two guards she had mauled lay still.

Owandell did not return.

A RADIANT DEED

Honor had changed back to her human shape by the time the legionnaires encountered them. The smartly uniformed soldiers appeared astonished by the discovery. They abandoned the room once they realized who they had found. When a higher-ranking officer returned, he had Honor and Destiny put on brown robes with cowls.

Cole got the same claustrophobic hood back over his head and was led out of the room by the same iron collar. He proceeded along a winding route to a wagon that carted him away. When he tried to strike up a conversation, Cole found he was alone. He tried to sense Honor's power, only to find that whatever connection he had established no longer remained.

They had survived Owandell for now. Might Stafford be worse? Cole had met the High King before. At the time, Cole was posing as an errand boy. Would the High King remember him? Would Cole even get an audience with him? What would be the fate of the mysterious kid discovered alongside two of the lost princesses?

Execution seemed like a realistic possibility.

After the wagon stopped, Cole was taken on another excursion. He could tell he was indoors once again. The air eventually grew cooler, damper, smelling of stone and rot. He descended many steps. Several doors opened and closed. He was finally unhooded by a surly guard inside a dank cell. The pole was detached from his iron collar, and a chain was threaded through his collar and locked to the wall.

When the guard closed the cell door, the torchlight departed with him. The cell was almost too small for Cole to lie down. He thought he remembered seeing a little hole in the corner for relieving himself. The chain seemed just long enough to let him reach it.

Cole was sad to lose the company of the princesses. He hoped they had better accommodations than he did. He wondered if their father would try to take their powers again. Could he do that without Owandell?

Sighing, Cole sat down. The stone felt uncomfortably cold, even through his clothes. Being locked in a dungeon seemed like an appropriate symbol of total failure. Could he sink lower than this? Maybe a torture chamber. Or a coffin.

The longer Cole sat, the more he began to appreciate the quiet and the darkness. One thing about languishing in a dungeon—it put your other responsibilities on hold. He tried to push his power into the collar again, and into the chain that attached him to the wall, but to no avail. He had felt strong connections with Owandell's power and Honor's power, but everything else remained unreachable.

Cole discovered some relief in the lack of responsibility.

If Ramarro got free in the near future, Cole could do nothing about it from prison. He thought about Jenna at the Temple of the Still Water, awaiting rescue. He pictured Jace, Joe, and Mira, back in their physical bodies somewhere in Necronum. He wondered about Dalton and Hunter, who had avoided getting drawn into the echolands. All were most likely facing their own troubles.

And there was nothing Cole could do.

It might be up to his friends to rescue him this time. The iron collar, the chain, and the locked cell door meant he wasn't going anywhere for a while.

Leaning against the chilly wall, Cole fell asleep.

Cole awoke when his cell door opened. A pair of guardsmen stepped inside, taking up most of the remaining space. One held a torch.

"On your feet," one of the guards ordered gruffly.

"Yeah, okay," Cole said, trying to fully awaken.

The guards leaned close, looking at the collar. He held a tiny key. "I don't see where to put this," he said.

The torchbearer stepped nearer, squinting. "The jailer could have been more specific."

"The chain is just looped through my collar," Cole offered. "I think the lock is on the wall."

The guards studied where the chain was affixed to the wall, undid a lock, and slid the chain from Cole's collar. The guard with the torch stepped out into the hall. The other motioned for Cole to follow.

The guard without a torch slid a hood over Cole's head.

"Really?" Cole asked. "Isn't it dark enough?"

"You're a top-priority prisoner," the guard said. "We're escorting you to a high-ranking official. We'll be using some secret corridors. We have to keep the way secret."

The guard took Cole's arm and led him forward. The guard did a good job warning Cole about upcoming obstacles and steps. For a long time they headed upward. Cole heard a couple of quick interactions with jailers. Then he sensed brighter light seeping through his hood. They walked for a time before it became dark again. More stairs. Endless stairs. Then several twists and turns and doorways.

When the hood was finally removed, Cole stood in a spacious, opulent bedchamber. The huge four-poster bed had a canopy and velvet covers. Through the parted curtains, Cole beheld an aged man propped up on pillows, his complexion an unhealthy gray. Upon recognizing Cole, the man's expression sharpened with sudden interest. "You."

Though they had met not too long ago, it took Cole a moment to recognize the man in the bed as Stafford Pemberton. With less hair, deeper wrinkles, slighter shoulders, and looser skin, the High King looked at least twenty years older.

"Hello, Your Majesty," Cole said.

The king's eyes darted to the guards. "Thank you. I require a private audience." He might be old and sick, but he seemed alert.

The guards immediately departed.

A lone guard remained in a corner of the room, holding a crossbow. He was not one of the guards who had brought Cole from the cell.

"No funny business," Stafford warned. "Or Tuteo will put a quarrel in you. He is deaf and mute, and thus the perfect escort for private conferences." Stafford began coughing, small at first, then louder and longer and wetter. As the fit wound down, he wiped his lips with a handkerchief. "Come closer. I cannot afford to shout."

Cole approached the bed.

Stafford studied him. "I remember you. The errand boy. Rod, was it? What subterfuge is this? Why were you being held by Owandell with two of my daughters?"

"I've been helping them," Cole said. "Protecting them. My real name is Cole."

Stafford coughed again, eyes shut, chest heaving. He spat into his handkerchief and opened his eyes. "I am weary of the many schemers seeking personal advantage through my offspring. The Unseen want to justify a revolution. Owandell wants a coup. The hour has come to——" He became lost in another fit of coughing.

Cole listened uncomfortably to the wet hacking.

Stafford wiped his lips again and took several shallow breaths. "The hour has come to take action. I have remained dormant too long as my foes plot my demise. You are a member of the Unseen?"

"Not a member," Cole said. "I'm just helping your daughters."

"You misrepresented yourself, Cole. You offered a false name. To my face. Lying to the king is punishable by death. Why should I refrain from enforcing this law?"

"Because a radiant deed shines forever," Cole said.

Stafford paled, his eyes widening. "Impossible. Where did you learn that phrase?"

"You told it to me," Cole said.

Stafford's eyes hardened. "My father spoke that phrase to a handful of people. All are long in their graves. Over my lifetime, I have uttered the phrase to three persons. None of them were you. And you would have been born long after the last of them died."

"You told me in the Cave of Memory," Cole said.

Stafford covered his mouth with a hand that was all tendons, wrinkles, and liver spots. "Intriguing. Plausible. An imprint of me resides there. An imprint left years ago. A secret portion of my history. A younger self, but me, and mentally sound. In some ways more than I am now. My imprint shared the phrase?"

"You told me it could bring a reward," Cole said.

"I must have trusted and appreciated you immensely," Stafford said. "Baffling. Unexpected. My daughters vouched for you. They warned that I needed to treat you kindly. Honor spoke of a rising threat, one only reported to me as a rumor so far. Nazeem. And a new name: Ramarro. The master who taught Owandell shapecraft."

"I met Ramarro," Cole said. "In the echolands. I tried to keep him in prison. He got free. I slowed his return, but not permanently."

"Honor shared similar . . . shared similar . . ." Stafford turned away and began coughing again, frail shoulders heaving. He hawked up phlegm and spat into a handkerchief. "She expressed similar concerns." His eyes looked watery. "Could you pass me the tonic on my nightstand?"

A single stoppered vial rested on the bedside table. Cole handed it to the king. Stafford unstopped it, sniffed the contents, and winced. "Vile stuff. Meant to scare the sickness away, I suppose." He took a long sip, swished it around his mouth, then swallowed. A sour grimace followed.

"Nasty?" Cole asked.

"Dreadful concoction," Stafford said. "I should lend it to my interrogators. They'd have every secret out in no time. It eases the coughing, but the royal stomach and bowels pay a price. I was saying?"

"Honor had similar concerns," Cole reminded him.

"A torivor of legend about to commence a reign of terror with the help of Owandell," Stafford said. "Frankly it sounds absurd. Like fairy tales invented to frighten children. Or perhaps propaganda devised by Owandell to inspire awe." He handed the vial to Cole, who replaced it on the nightstand. "You saw this torivor?"

"Honor did too," Cole said. "And others. In the echolands. He's real. Send spies to the echolands. Lots of people there know about Nazeem."

"You believe you can stop this torivor?" Stafford asked.

"Somebody has to," Cole said.

"Indeed," Stafford said. "When you met me in the Cave of Memory, I take it you liked me?"

"Yes," Cole said.

"What did you do for me? Why did I share the phrase with you? I intended to be supremely cautious as an imprint."

"The imprints can't hold new memories," Cole said.

"Your imprint only recalled what he knew up until you left the cave."

"I'm aware how imprints function," Stafford said.

"I used rocks to spell out that you end up with Harmony," Cole said. "So the imprint could remember."

Tears filled Stafford's eyes. One took a crooked path down his wrinkled cheek. "I see. Clever boy. You found a weak spot. Yes, at the time, that would have meant everything to me. Why?"

"What do you mean?"

"Why the act of kindness? You have been protecting my daughters. You must have unfavorable feelings about me."

"You could say that."

"Then why?"

Cole thought for a moment. "I liked the Stafford I met in the cave. He seemed like a good person."

Stafford shifted against his pillows. He coughed gently. "He was, Cole," he whispered. "I was." He stared at Cole uncertainly. "Would you believe that man is still inside me somewhere? Would you?"

Cole shrugged. "I guess he has to be, right?"

Stafford looked away. "I don't know either, sometimes."

"I'm sorry," Cole said.

"I'm dying, Cole. You can see that."

"You look a lot older than the last time we met."

"The powers I borrowed prolonged my life," Stafford said. He cleared his throat. "The shaping powers I stole from my own flesh and blood. They prolonged a certain youthfulness. As I lost my hold on those powers, the stolen years

31

began to catch up with me. The aging accelerated the more power I lost. Now I only retain a small portion of Elegance's power. I don't know whether I will hang on until it departs. I have tried to keep my waning health a secret. My rule has grown unstable enough without my enemies knowing I am bedridden."

"Have you had success?" Cole asked.

"Probably not," Stafford said. "I had eleven spies executed this year. Spies caught right here in the First Castle. If you catch eleven rats, how many more are still in the walls, raiding the pantry?"

"Maybe a lot," Cole said.

"I've lost spies too," Stafford said. "This year, no less than thirty, right here in Junction City. The majority taken by Owandell, no doubt. Hard to be sure. He is crafty. Cole, I am High King of the five kingdoms, I am dying, and there is not a single person I fully trust."

Cole winced. "That sounds terrible."

"And along you come with your radiant deed."

Cole said nothing.

"You witnessed me as I was, Cole," Stafford said softly. "I never meant to become who I am. I went on from that cave to win Harmony. And it was wonderful. And so intimidating. Children were born. All the unrest and problems and strife of five kingdoms and one capital flowed to my doorway. If you ever want to ensure your worst enemy never again enjoys a good night's rest, make him a king. I was daunted, Cole. Overwhelmed. I was not up to the challenge. Owandell offered critical support."

Cole nodded to show he was listening.

"Owandell gradually moved from the background of my life to the forefront," Stafford continued. "Under his guidance I made the necessary connections to win Harmony. When the crown came to me younger than anyone expected, he quietly became my right hand. He reduced my burdens. He fixed problems great and small. He showed no interest in acclaim. I came to rely on him as I had never relied on anyone. And then, as my five daughters grew, and their abilities flourished, one day he made a suggestion."

"Take their powers," Cole said.

"Borrow them," Stafford clarified. "The word was always 'borrow.' I had no idea borrowing shaping power was possible. Owandell assured me it could be done. Just for enough time to firmly establish my rule. To provide Harmony the strong husband she deserved. To grant my daughters the protection they needed. To give my subjects a monarch worth heeding. So many selfless reasons to commit a supremely selfish act." Stafford shook his head. "I was struggling to lead Grand Shapers and councillors and other governors who were so much more powerful than me. I was insufficient. I had married into much more than I merited. Owandell offered a chance to become the man I should have been."

"And you took it."

Stafford gave a small nod. "And that marked the end of the man you met in the cave."

Cole stared at Stafford solemnly.

"I did not know I would lose my daughters instead of

protect them," Stafford said. "I did not expect to destroy the trust of my wife. And . . . I never anticipated how much I would adore the power."

"Wow," Cole said, surprised by the candor.

"I have lived many years," Stafford said. "I consolidated power as no other ruler of the Outskirts has done before. And . . . I lost my way. I see it now, as I wane. It's like awakening from a delirium. I lost my way, Cole."

Cole gave a nod.

"A king, even a High King, even a High King with astonishing powers, is just a man. Only a man. Subject to weaknesses and foolishness. He longs for the same basics any man longs for. He suffers from many of the same insecurities that torment other men. A king has resources, yes, and those resources can quench certain longings, but they can also be used to hide frailties. Those resources can conceal flaws. They can prevent certain wounds from being tended and healed. They can . . . Look at me! I'm rambling!"

"It makes sense," Cole said. "It's so sad."

Stafford harrumphed. "I'm not looking for sympathy. I lived large, Cole. I threw an enormous shadow. Few ever lived larger. Whether feared or loved, my name was known in every corner of the land. My voice was heard. My presence was felt. None of the five kingdoms would be the same without me." Stafford sniffed. "No man lives up to his ideals. No man. Not if he reflects deeply and honestly. We all have our failings. I lived very large, Cole. My failings were magnified. They became enormous."

Cole didn't know how to respond.

"The bitter truth? The starkest reality? If I could redo it all . . . I would have never taken their powers. I long to pretend it was worth it. I wish I could claim it was difficult but necessary—a brutal obligation of governance. The truth is I understood too late what my decision really meant. I would have rather been a mediocre king and a good husband, a good father. But I cannot go back. And I cannot repair what has been lost. Despite my regrets, when I felt the power leaving, I fought to keep it. Fought hard, Cole. It was torture to feel the power slipping away. The damage to my relationships had been done. And so I wanted to at least enjoy the spoils of my folly. They were all I had left."

"Maybe you can still help your family," Cole said.

"I never wished them harm," Stafford said. "Through my darkest hours, my love remained constant. I realize that my actions shout louder than any words I can pronounce, but I never wished them harm. Not Harmony. Not my girls. They ever remained part of my calculations. I would help them now, if I could. Unfortunately, in this hour of gravest need, my capacity dwindles."

"Ramarro is real," Cole said. "He is coming. You command a lot of people."

"I've engaged my forces," Stafford said. "I turned Owandell into a fugitive to take my daughters from him. I know he is no longer my ally. I've known for years. I was not sure I could survive a war with him, even with my full powers. Now our precarious stalemate is broken. He will try to make me pay."

"Owandell is focused on his master," Cole said.

Stafford coughed softly. He sat up a little straighter. "You are more than I expected you to be, my boy. And I owe you a favor. Ask. You have the High King's attention."

"Where are Honor and——"

"Leave my daughters out of it," Stafford interrupted. "They are quite safe. Including from me. I have neither the ability nor the inclination to disturb their powers again. And I will not have them drawn into more danger, regardless of their protests. Leave my daughters out of it and request your favor. I have many resources at my disposal. I have no objection to you pursuing the issue of Ramarro."

"I came here from Outside," Cole said. "A place called Arizona."

"The latest group?" Stafford asked. "Did Ansel bring you?"

"He brought a lot of my friends," Cole said. "I slipped through to help them and got caught too. I'd like to find my friends."

The king frowned thoughtfully. "I do not know the locations of those slaves. None were powerful enough to be of serious interest to me. I have no objection to you finding them. The slaver Ansel would know. I received a report on Ansel. We had him in custody for a time. He has returned to Five Roads. I believe he is organizing another slaving excursion. Would you like to visit with him?"

It made Cole sick to hear about another slaving excursion—another batch of innocent kids would be ripped from their homes and forgotten by their loved ones. And for Stafford it was just business as usual. Cole did not understand how anyone could permit slavery. And it was utterly incomprehensible to think of how a leader could let kidnapped children serve as the supply. But this was not the moment to fight this battle. "I can't go to him yet," Cole said. "I need to stop Ramarro first."

"Then what is your request?"

"You don't fully trust anyone who works for you," Cole said.

Stafford frowned, wrinkles sagging farther. "I do not."

"Will you free me?" Cole asked. "Let me go to Harmony for help?"

Closing his eyes, Stafford took a couple of measured breaths. "Yes." One eye opened. "And I will do better than that. I will make you my personal agent and give you my royal seal. You will outrank any general you meet. For as long as I wear the crown, you will speak with my voice, command with my authority. I will cover any expenses you incur. How does that suit you?"

"I can hardly believe it," Cole said honestly.

"Don't be too grateful," Stafford said. "You will be swimming in dangerous waters. Starting now, you are one of the few people I doubt will outlive me. Please prove me wrong."

"I'll do my best."

CHAPTER
4

VIOLET

Cole entered Harmony's private chambers clothed like a young lord. After assembling his outfit, a small team of servants had only let him dress himself at his insistence. Eight guards had escorted him to Harmony's tower, and then the same old woman he recalled from a prior visit had admitted him to her chamber.

The queen looked much as he remembered, tall and graceful, with some streaks of white in her auburn hair and a few worry lines on her lovely face. Hints of darkness under her eyes and a few stray hairs made her appear a little more tired than he had seen her. She looked Cole up and down suspiciously.

"I see you are wearing the king's seal," Harmony said. "Are you the most fantastic spy of all time? Have you changed sides?"

"The sides are shifting," Cole said, fingering the medallion on his chest. "The High King knows I've been protecting your daughters. And he knows that won't change."

"I am happy to see you are well," Harmony said. "What news of my children?"

Cole explained that as far as he knew, Constance was safe back in Zeropolis. He told how Mira, Honor, and Destiny had all made it out of the echolands. Then he related some details about the fight with Ramarro and how he, Honor, and Destiny were captured by Owandell.

"That clarifies why Stafford sent his forces against Hakrel's Castle," Harmony said. "I wondered if he had finally lost all reason. But to retrieve Honor and Destiny . . . it makes sense. Do you know where Mira went after the echolands?"

"Back to Necronum somewhere," Cole said. "She was with some of our other friends. At least she's not alone."

"And you are certain this Nazeem is actually a torivor?" Harmony asked. "Like Trillian?"

"Yes," Cole said. "And incredibly powerful." Only two torivors had ever come to the Outskirts. Trillian was imprisoned in Elloweer within the Lost Palace. And Ramarro had been trapped in the echolands. "I had help diverting Ramarro into another prison, but it probably won't hold him for long. We have to find another way to stop him. Owandell is convinced that when Ramarro arrives, the torivor will easily conquer the five kingdoms."

Harmony sighed and covered her eyes with one manicured hand. "If torivors live up to their reputation, I expect he's right. This keeps spiraling from bad to worse. First I was primarily protecting my girls from Stafford. Then Owandell loomed larger, and civil war became a serious possibility. And now . . . an unthinkable evil from the darkest annals of our history threatens not only my family but the lives of everyone we govern."

"Ramarro was behind so much of the rest," Cole said. "Ramarro trained Owandell, who then recruited your husband. Ramarro taught Owandell how to steal the shaping power. Without Owandell, your daughters would never have lost their abilities."

"Stafford has Honor and Destiny?" Harmony asked.

"Yeah," Cole said. "He refused to free them, but promised to keep them safe."

Harmony rolled her eyes. "That provides little comfort. According to Stafford, everything he has done has been to protect the girls. Including taking their powers and driving them into exile. He has gotten much too comfortable with falsehoods and distortions. Even if he meant what he said, Stafford has a very crooked way of viewing his familial duties."

"Have you seen him lately?" Cole asked.

"Not since before the last time I saw you," Harmony said. "Stafford and I haven't been close for decades, after I had to hide our daughters, but he has been growing even more reclusive lately, conducting all his business through spokespeople."

"He looks older," Cole said.

"How much older?" Harmony asked.

"Like your father at best," Cole said. "Maybe even your grandfather. He looks like a feeble old man, and coughs like crazy, and can't get out of bed."

"I heard the rumors he had taken ill," Harmony said, swaying a little. "I hadn't guessed the full extent." Her voice dropped to a whisper, pensive eyes staring away from Cole. "I have wished him dead so many times. So many times." Eyes finding Cole again, she smiled unconvincingly, and her voice returned to conversational volume. "The brute brought it on himself. The gifts he robbed from his daughters prolonged his youth. As he loses those powers, he is paying the price."

"He acts like he may not have much time," Cole said.

"He may be right," Harmony said, eyebrows knitting together, pain filling her eyes. "If he wished to live longer, there were places we could have gone, techniques we could have used. But Stafford desired power at any cost. And it has burned him up in so many ways. Why did he give you his seal? Even from his deathbed, that surprises me."

"I met a younger version of him in the Cave of Memory," Cole said. "I did his imprint a favor, and he told me a phrase that had a lot of meaning to his family."

"I know the phrase you mean," Harmony said.

"That convinced the king to listen to me," Cole said. "He gave me the seal to help me as I try to stop Ramarro."

"I see," Harmony said. "He was willing to sponsor your suicide mission."

"You think I don't have a chance?" Cole asked.

"You're noble to try, Cole," Harmony said. "I'm not sure if success is very realistic."

"But worth trying, right? I mean, how much success would I have running from Ramarro? Or hiding? Those aren't very realistic options either. Might as well try to stop him. I've already won some other fights I probably should have lost. Dandalus encouraged me."

"*The* Dandalus?" Harmony asked. "As in the chief architect of this world? When we spoke before, you mentioned a semblance of his consciousness associated with the Founding Stone."

"Yeah," Cole said. "I met his actual echo in the echolands. He was watching over Destiny. And he helped me learn to use my power. It worked better in the echolands."

"Cole, I will help you however I can," Harmony said. "I just want to be sure you understand the risks."

"I understand enough," Cole said. "Speaking of the Founding Stone, could you help me get to it? I could use more information."

"The Founding Stone resides under Owandell's tower," Harmony said. "Stafford's men have seized it. With my husband sponsoring you, a visit should be simple to arrange. For now, you deserve to rest. How can I make you comfortable?"

Cole shook his head. "I can't rest. Not now. Not when I know who's coming. And not without knowing how long it will take him to get here. I don't have any idea how to stop him yet. I don't even know where to find his prison."

"You have no clue?" Harmony asked.

"Well, can you keep a secret?" Cole asked.

"Absolutely," Harmony said.

"Good," Cole replied. "Because Owandell really wants to know this one." Cole took a step closer and lowered his voice. "Ramarro is inside a vault in Creon."

Harmony arched an eyebrow. "Creon? I may be able to help you. What sort of assistance are you looking for?"

"The best you can offer," Cole said. "Transportation for a

start. Advice. Helpers. I'm also hoping you can help me find Mira. And Elegance. You stopped putting stars in the sky. Can you still sense where your daughters are?"

"With an effort I can always sense them," Harmony said. "Except those who were in the echolands, while they were separated from their physical bodies. That was distressing. I stopped marking Elegance with a star years ago. No need. She hasn't left her current position in more than thirty years."

"Is she all right?" Cole wondered.

"She found a safe haven," Harmony said. "I have my suspicions why. I can reveal exactly where Elegance is located. I don't believe she has any intention of leaving."

"Not even to find her power?" Cole wondered.

"Perhaps," Harmony said. "She's been responsible from a young age. But is Elegance relevant for you now? Won't you be looking for Nazeem?"

"If Elegance's power is loose in Creon, it will be stirring things up," Cole said. "It might be trying to take over the place like Mira's power in Sambria or Constance's power in Zeropolis. It might be going rogue like Honor's power in Elloweer. Or it might help us like Destiny's power in Necronum. But it won't be sitting still."

Harmony folded her arms, hands cupping her elbows. Her gaze became remote. "I don't suppose I can spare my girls from the coming trials."

"There won't be anywhere to hide them once Ramarro gets loose," Cole said. "Owandell knows them. And Ramarro has met three of them. Your enemies are powerful,

Harmony. They'll find whoever they want to find. The time to fight is now. Before Ramarro gets free."

Harmony gave a quick nod. "Elegance is at the Iron Fort—the most exclusive retirement community in the Outskirts. Time can be manipulated in Creon. Some who wish to prolong their lives take shelter in the Iron Fort. Protected by soaring walls, powerful Wayminders, and an elite mercenary army, it's a place where those who can buy their way in spend their waning years in safety and comfort."

"Retirement community?" Cole wondered. "Elegance didn't age, did she?"

"Not any more than my other daughters," Harmony said. "Elegance was the eldest when their powers were stolen—nearly a grown woman on the verge of her eighteenth birthday. She has not aged more than that. She simply sought shelter at the safest haven in Creon. Since she took refuge there, I have worried about her least of all my daughters."

"What about Mira?" Cole asked. "Do you know where I can find her?"

"She returned from the echolands," Harmony said. "I felt it and pinpointed her location yesterday. The undertaking requires some time and effort. She was at the Locked Shrine." Harmony closed her eyes. Her brow furrowed. "Strange . . . I no longer sense her."

"Is that normal?" Cole asked.

"No," Harmony said. "My attention shifted to Honor and Destiny when I felt them coming this way."

"She's not . . . ," Cole said.

"I would have felt her death," Harmony assured him. "It's as if she returned to the echolands."

Cole frowned. That didn't sound good. Why would Mira go back? Their business in the echolands was done. "Are you sure?"

Harmony opened her eyes. "I'm not in Necronum. It takes time for me to muster sufficient power to really investigate."

"Maybe I can help," Cole said. "My power could give you a boost."

Harmony raised her eyebrows skeptically. "Indeed?"

"Just take my hand," Cole said, holding one hand out to her.

With some reluctance, the queen extended her hand, longish nails carefully polished. A delicate ring held a brilliant blue stone. When Cole took her hand, he immediately felt her power, misty and less easily defined than any power he had felt before. He pushed energy into her power, and the mist brightened.

"Oh!" Harmony exclaimed, sounding flustered. "I see! How extraordinary! One moment." She closed her eyes again. "Yes, she must be in the echolands. In fact, I believe she embarked for the echolands from the Locked Shrine. Or very near there."

Cole released Harmony's hand and let the connection break. "I don't know why she would have gone back," he said.

"Perplexing," Harmony said, rubbing her hands together. "You can augment any power like that?"

"I can help people use their power in any kingdom," Cole said.

"Any kingdom?" Harmony asked. "Here in Junction all powers work a little."

"I made weapons like my Jumping Sword work in the wrong kingdoms," Cole said. "I guess I haven't fully tested it with people yet. But I'm pretty sure."

"Interesting," Harmony said. "You explained a little about using your power to revive the powers of others in the echolands. I didn't understand how fully you might be able to do that here among the physically living. How singular. Now I understand why Owandell wanted you brought along with my daughters. Your power would have fascinated him. So much potential."

"I'm still getting used to it," Cole said. "My power was blocked for so long. In the echolands I could change reality, kind of like a shaper in Sambria. I could affect whatever I wanted. It doesn't seem to work like that in the physical world."

"Activating abilities outside their corresponding kingdoms is plenty incredible," Harmony said. "I wonder . . ."

"What?"

"If you were partnered with a Wayminder, you might be able to travel anywhere," Harmony said.

"Can't they already go pretty much anywhere?" Cole asked.

"Within Creon they can," Harmony said. "And from Creon they can open a wayport to just about anywhere in the five kingdoms. Getting back is another matter. Some can manage a wayport from Junction to Creon. But not anywhere else. Ways can be opened to Earth from Junction or Creon, and some have managed it in Zeropolis. Unless the starting point is inside of Creon, Wayminders can't just open ways from one kingdom to another. Or even from one place in a kingdom to another location in the same kingdom. But partnered with your ability . . . who knows?"

"Know any Wayminders?" Cole asked.

"The School of Minding in Junction City is the only serious school for Wayminders outside of Creon. When you mentioned Ramarro could be incarcerated in Creon, I had already begun to think of partnering you with a certain Wayminder. She's young but highly talented, and new to Junction, so she isn't embroiled in the politics yet. Meaning I befriended her first."

"You think she would help me?" Cole asked.

"On my recommendation?" Harmony asked. "Absolutely. I am her sponsor. She pledged fealty to me. Let alone after she learns how you might be able to augment her abilities. Go downstairs. I'll send for her. Greta will bring you a meal while you wait."

Cole had not yet finished his roast duck in a sauce that tasted sweetly of apples when the air in the parlor began to shimmer. Alone in the room, Cole stood up just before a young woman stepped out of the rippling disturbance and the room returned to normal. She looked a few years older than Cole, maybe fourteen or fifteen. Her brown hair had a few small ribbons in it and looked fairly messy and perhaps unevenly cut, but it still kind of worked. Her crimson robe was a little too big and loose, and the striped scarf around her neck didn't match. She blinked at Cole.

"The queen's tower?" she asked.

"Right," Cole said.

She wiped her brow. "Phew. I was a worried for a second. I'm supposed to meet an adventurer named Cole."

"That's me."

She froze. "You're a kid."

"So are you."

She made a displeased face. "I prefer prodigy. Especially from people way younger than me."

"How old are you?" Cole complained.

"I'm practically fifteen."

"Which means fourteen," Cole said. "Older than me. I guess I look young if you were expecting an adventurer. I'm a prodigy too."

"A prodigy at what?"

Cole shrugged. "Adventuring."

She clenched her fists and stamped a foot. "This is what the queen thinks of me? I opened a wayport to get here quickly and impress you. I had no idea she just needed a nanny."

A door opened and Harmony entered. "Excellent. Hello, Violet. I see you've met Cole."

Violet whirled to face Harmony and dropped to one knee, head bowed. "Yes, Your Highness. He's . . . less mature than I imagined."

"I told you he was young in my missive," the queen said.

"You did, Your Highness," Violet said, head still bowed. "My mistake. When you called him a young adventurer, I was picturing under thirty. Maybe with muscles and some stubble."

"Rise, Violet," Harmony said. "This is an informal meeting."

Violet stood.

"Was I supposed to kneel?" Cole asked.

"He wasn't kneeling?" Violet cried, looking over her shoulder at Cole. "He doesn't even know to kneel when royalty enters?"

"I thought I was supposed to bow!" Cole maintained.

"Did you even bow?" Violet asked.

"It's a lot to remember," Cole said.

"Cole is relatively new to our customs," Harmony said. "And he has perhaps grown overly familiar in the company of royalty. He has been aiding my daughters."

"Your daughters?" Violet exclaimed in astonishment. "Then the rumors . . . ?"

"They live," Harmony said. "In fact, they have hardly aged since their supposed deaths. They have survived in exile all these years. I have watched over them from afar. But dire threats have arisen. I need a Wayminder to help Cole on his mission."

"Will it involve the princesses?" Violet asked.

"Yes," Harmony said. "But first you must swear secrecy."

"Nobody can keep a secret like me," Violet assured her. "I can't prove it, though. Nobody knows what secrets I know. Only the people who told me."

"Do you swear?" Harmony asked. "It's a matter of life and death."

"I promise," Violet said.

"Your mission is of the utmost importance," Harmony said. "I do not exaggerate by saying the fate of the entire Outskirts hangs in the balance."

Violet glanced over her shoulder. "And you're sending . . . him?"

"I thought you would be the last person who would judge another based on their age," Harmony chided. "Aren't you the youngest candidate to be admitted to the School of Minding in a hundred years?"

Violet scrunched her brow. "What are the chances of lightning striking twice? He's a lot younger than me. And he's shorter than me. And he must be really good at . . . something."

"The mission will be incredibly perilous," Harmony said. "There is a high risk of fatality. Of course, should the mission fail, we will all face our demise."

"What can he do?" Violet asked. "Does he have radically weaponized shaping powers? Maybe he wields fire effortlessly? Or summons weather?" She gasped. "Can he kill with his mind?"

"None of those things," Harmony said. "He does have extraordinary powers, though. You heard me express that the mission will be dangerous?"

Violet gave a little bow. "I'm yours to command. And pleased you thought of me! I have sometimes wondered whether you take me seriously. I'll keep the secrets! And I'll assume the risks! When do we leave?"

"Now," Cole said.

"Wait, now?" Violet asked. "I just opened a wayport! Your Highness, your missive told me to come here through a way. You know a lot about wayminding. I'm talented, but I'll need a fair amount of rest before opening another."

"I told you to come here through a wayport precisely so your power would be depleted," Harmony said. "I want to demonstrate what Cole can do. And to test a theory."

"He opens wayports too?" Violet exclaimed. "Then why do you need me?"

"I can replenish your power," Cole said.

"Nobody can do that," Violet said.

"Cole is extraordinary," Harmony explained.

"Ah," Violet said, finally looking at Cole with real interest. "I see why people might ignore your age. Where are we going?"

"Necronum, first," Cole said.

Violet turned to Harmony and held up a finger. "You know that nobody can—"

"No Wayminder has ever opened a wayport to Necronum from Junction City," Harmony said. "Only from Creon. We're testing another theory."

"I can help your power work anywhere," Cole said. "We should be able to go from anywhere to anywhere."

Violet looked from Cole to Harmony and back. "If we weren't with the queen, I might suspect you were teasing."

"It's no joke," Harmony said. "You know your geography?"

Violet gave a cocky chuckle. "If you can stump me, it's more than the instructors can do. I baffle them all the time."

"Then you know the location of the Locked Shrine?" Harmony inquired.

"In Necronum, near Dobson," Violet said. "Not far from the infamous Gamat Rue."

"Sounds right," Cole said.

"Can you open a wayport to the Locked Shrine?" Harmony asked.

"No problem from Creon," Violet said. "It would be fun.

I've never gone to Necronum. I opened a way to Zeropolis for my trial. It's a popular destination since you can take the train back to Junction City. Such tall buildings!"

"Can you attempt to open a way to the Locked Shrine from here?" Harmony asked. "It's to check on my daughter Miracle."

"I'd need a lot more power," Violet said. "At full strength I can't even feel for a location in Necronum from Junction."

Harmony looked to Cole. "Ready to give it a try?"

CHAPTER
5
THE LOCKED SHRINE

I have to hold your hand to establish the connection," Cole said.

"I bet you use that on all the girls," Violet replied.

Cole noticed Harmony turning away to cover a laugh. Violet held out her hand.

"Try not to fall in love," Cole said, gingerly touching a couple of her fingers.

Her power was not as brilliant as some, but steady and strong. Cole focused and forced energy into her power.

"No way!" Violet exclaimed. "I can see Necronum easier than I could ever see Creon from here. Unreal."

"I've never encountered anyone like him," Harmony said.

"I see the Locked Shrine," Violet reported. "I can open a wayport. I've never felt this . . . ready."

"Please do," Harmony said.

A shimmer appeared in the air in front of Violet, somewhat indistinct, but basically oval in shape, taller than her and almost touching the ground. "I feel like I could hold it open all day," Violet said.

Cole was no longer touching her, but he maintained the connection and continued to energize her power. "You could if I keep helping you."

"Are you sure your ability will work the same in Necronum?" Violet asked. "If not, it's a long walk back here. And an even longer trek to Creon."

"I'm pretty sure," Cole said. "It's untested. We're about to find out."

"Are you wearing the High King's seal?" Violet asked. "How did I miss that?"

"I probably shouldn't wear it openly," Cole said, tucking the medallion under his shirt.

"Wait, who does he work for?" Violet asked Harmony.

"Stafford and I both support Cole in this mission," Harmony said. "Every now and again our interests align in a manner that allows cooperation."

"We should go," Cole said.

"If you find Mira, bring her back here," Harmony said. "I wish to see her."

"Will you want to keep her here?" Cole asked.

"That is between my daughter and me," Harmony said.

"Okay," Cole agreed.

"Don't worry, Your Highness," Violet said. "We'll be back. I'm the one taking us places."

"How do we use the wayport?" Cole asked.

"Step through," Violet offered.

After giving a little wave to Harmony, Cole stepped into

the rippling oval. A sensation of focused pressure swept across his body as he passed through the wayport. Immediately he stood on a grassy slope. A series of terraced ponds were arrayed before him, overflowing into one another down the incline, fed at the top by a stream. Beyond the lowest pool, the stream flowed away. In the midst of the tiered ponds, about halfway up, smoldered the charred remains of a building, thin tendrils of smoke rising from the debris.

Violet stepped through beside him. "I still felt the energy from you after you stepped through," she said. "Good thing. If waywalking to Necronum had cut off the connection, you could have been stuck here alone."

"I still feel the connection," Cole said. "I'll break it."

The shimmering wayport vanished.

Violet gave a little gasp. "That was abrupt. I went from full to empty in an instant. What happened here?"

"Was that our shrine?" Cole asked.

"I'm afraid so," Violet said.

"I thought you saw it before we came," Cole said.

"I saw the area," Violet said. "I don't see a perfect picture. It's not like looking with your eyes. I get a general sense of an area. I was focused on the locks."

"I'm pretty sure it's unlocked at this point," Cole said.

"Calling it the Locked Shrine is wordplay," Violet said. "The locks are the surrounding ponds connected by gates and sluices so the water levels can be adjusted."

"You sound like a travel guide," Cole said.

"I read a lot," Violet replied. "We're looking for Miracle Pemberton?"

"Mira," Cole said. He turned around. There was not another person in sight. "I guess everyone got scared off when the place burned down."

Violet shook her head. "There's water all around it. Buckets, people!"

"It was probably an attack. Plenty of enemies want my friends captured or dead. Harmony told me Mira isn't dead. But she is in the echolands."

"Then her body has to be somewhere," Violet said.

"Maybe somebody snuck off with it," Cole said. "Should we take a closer look?"

"My power feels dead now," Violet said. "Completely drained. I can't see Junction or Creon. I can get no read on opening a wayport. Aren't you curious to see if we'll be able to get back?"

Cole took her hand and forced power into her. It felt no more challenging than it had in Junction.

"Amazing," Violet said. "Never leave me, Cole. You're my new best friend. I feel superb. Like I haven't opened a wayport in a month. And now I can see other kingdoms better than I could in Creon. I could open a way back to Harmony's tower right now. From this same spot! It's usually tough to open a new wayport in a place where another wayport was recently established. Not with you around."

Cole released her hand and let the connection to her power lapse.

"And I'm spent again," Violet said, slumping a tad. "Like I should be. It should take days for me to open another wayport in an ideal spot. And even with a year to rest, opening a wayport in Necronum would never happen." She grabbed Cole by the shoulders. "Do you realize all we could do together?"

"Open ways?" Cole tried.

Releasing him, Violet looked around, eyes blinking rapidly, hands waving like a conductor. "We could travel the five kingdoms! We could fearlessly explore remote corners of the world, knowing the return trip would be easy. The far reaches of Necronum, Elloweer, Zeropolis, and Sambria have not been properly mapped. Wayminders won't often open wayports to the distant corners of the world because the journey back is too long and arduous. Only the bravest explorers attempt those kinds of expeditions. We could do it whenever the mood hit us!"

"True," Cole said. "And being able to teleport around will help us on our mission."

"We can travel as no Wayminder has traveled before," Violet continued. "We can open ways whenever the desire strikes. Breakfast at the Prismatic Falls in Sambria, lunch at a marsh town in Elloweer, and dinner on top of Skybreaker Tower in Zeropolis."

"Except we have a mission," Cole reminded her again.

"We have to find Mira," Violet said.

"That is only the beginning," Cole said. "Have you heard of torivors?"

"Only two torivors ever came to the Outskirts," Violet said. "The Lost Palace in Elloweer is one of the forbidden destinations. It holds Trillian. The other torivor, Ramarro, was lost from history."

"Ramarro was trapped in the echolands," Cole said. "I fought him with some of the princesses and some friends. He is coming back."

"An actual torivor?" Violet asked.

"So powerful he can bend reality just about however he wants," Cole said. "You'll keep all of this secret?"

"I swear," Violet said. "And I believe you, by the way, even though it sounds absurd. If Queen Harmony is backing you, and you really have been helping her lost daughters, I might be ready to believe anything."

"I promise I'm not kidding," Cole said. "Or wrong. Ramarro is locked in a vault in Creon. It's really powerful. A guy named Kendo Rattan built it."

"Of course he did," Violet said. "The most famous Wayminder of all time. The father of our shaping discipline. The first and greatest of Creon's Grand Shapers."

"Strong or not, the vault may not hold Ramarro for long," Cole said. "We have to find a way to stop him before he gets free."

Violet scratched her head. "That sounds impossible."

"All part of the fun," Cole said. "First we need to find Mira and my friends. Let's have a look."

Cole started working his way around the terraced ponds toward the scorched remnants of the Locked Shrine. He had to hop little channels of water, walk along the tops of wooden dams, cross little footbridges, and climb a variety of stairs and ladders. As he neared the ruins, the reek of charred wood grew stronger.

"Think whoever burned down the shrine is still watching

the place?" Violet asked. She followed a few steps behind Cole.

Cole paused to look around. "I hope not. I don't see anybody. If trouble shows up, we open a wayport and scram." He started walking again. "I just realized I don't have any weapons. Do you?"

"Wayminders don't carry arms as a rule," Violet said.

"Why not?"

"We offer transportation services to any who will pay," Violet said. "We work hard to stay politically neutral. By not carrying weapons, we generally don't get attacked."

"Spend time with me, and you're going to get attacked," Cole said. "You might want to think about getting a weapon."

"Our order has norms."

"Does it really matter? Are you even a full Wayminder yet?"

"Of course I'm a full Wayminder!" Violet exclaimed. "I'm young, not incompetent! Do you think Harmony would give you a trainee?"

"Aren't you a student?" Cole asked.

"The School of Minding in Junction City is for graduate studies," Violet said. "Only true Wayminders can attend. The training happens back in Creon. Junction would be a difficult place to learn. Our shaping is so much weaker there. But it allows for interesting studies."

"So no weapons for you," Cole said.

"Not likely," Violet replied.

A small moat surrounded the circular jumble of smoldering debris, the water dark and still. It was too wide to jump.

"There must have been a bridge," Cole said.

"Not anymore," Violet said. "Do you really think we'll find anything in the ashes? Your friends can't be in there. Not if they're alive."

"Probably not," Cole agreed, staring at the fuming timbers. "Maybe we'll find a clue? Some sign? Where else can we look? If Mira went to the echolands from nearby, her body has to be in the area."

"The closest town is Dobson," Violet said.

"If the shrine was under attack, it probably means Mira was discovered," Cole said. "I doubt they could have made it to the town."

"Unless they had an early warning," Violet said. "Mira could have slipped out before the attack started."

"Harmony felt like Mira went to the echolands from this shrine," Cole said.

"Maybe she meant from the vicinity," Violet said. "Or maybe her body was smuggled to Dobson. Getting to the town is no big deal for us. Normally I wouldn't open a way to travel a short distance, but with you around, why not? Actually, I could open a wayport to the other side of the moat if you want to poke around."

"Sure," Cole said. "Let's go across."

He took her hand and infused her power with energy, and the air nearby became distorted. Cole could see another shimmer on the far side of the moat.

"Go ahead," Violet said.

Cole stepped into the near shimmer and came out the other one. He looked back at Violet and watched her come through.

Holding his hand over his nose and mouth to help with the potent odor, Cole roamed the burned rubble. He didn't climb where blackened timbers had piled up, choosing instead to skirt the fringes. He saw no bodies or bones. Maybe everyone had evacuated? Or maybe the attackers had carted them away?

"Hey!" a voice called from the far side of the moat.

Cole spun around to find a young boy staring at him. He had black hair and faint freckles and was perhaps seven or eight. Cole walked to the edge of the moat. "Are you here alone?"

"No gold or nothing over there," the boy said. "I already checked."

"How'd you get across?" Cole asked.

"Used a board," the boy said. "Skinny one. I have good balance."

"I'm not hunting for gold," Cole said.

"What are you looking for?" the boy asked.

"Some friends," Cole said.

"Maybe I can help," the boy said. "I came here a lot."

"Did your parents work here?"

"I don't have parents," the boy said. "The shrines are good about giving orphans work and food. A little schooling, too. What's your name?"

"Cole. What's yours?"

"Arie," he said. "You're really named Cole?"

"Yeah. Why?"

"I'm supposed to check," the boy said. "Have you ever been a slave? Answer true."

"Yes."

"What was your first slave job?"

The kid clearly had knowledge of him and was vetting him. "Sky Raider."

"What do Sky Raiders say before a mission?"

"'Die bravely,'" Cole said. "To avoid getting jinxed."

"What was the name of the little robot in Zeropolis?"

"Sidekick."

"Who is your brother?"

"Hunter."

"Okay," Arie said. "You pass. Who is the girl?"

Cole looked over his shoulder to find Violet standing behind him. "My friend Violet."

"Wink if she's trouble," Arie said more quietly.

"She's on my side," Cole assured him.

"Looks like it's just the two of you," Arie said. "I'm supposed to fetch somebody who wants to talk to you. Somebody who knows about your friends. Wait here?"

"Is the person far?" Cole asked.

"Not too far," Arie said. "We were keeping watch for you."

"Who burned this place down?" Cole asked.

"Enforcers," Arie replied. He spat disgustedly into the moat.

"Are they gone?" Cole asked.

"I think so," Arie said. "It was quiet all afternoon until you came along."

"When did it burn down?"

"Last night," Arie said. "I'll be back." He scampered off.

"If he'd tell us where he's going, I could open a way," Violet said.

Cole shook his head. "It might scare him. He's acting as a scout. Plus, it would give away our secret advantage. We better just wait."

"Should we go back across the moat?" Violet asked.

Cole scanned the fuming ruins. "Yeah. I didn't find anything useful."

"Not unless we can find a use for burned wood," Violet said.

They joined hands, and she opened a wayport back to the other side of the moat. Cole stepped through, and she followed.

"It doesn't tire you out?" Violet asked. "Giving me all that energy?"

"Not really," Cole said.

"You used to be a slave?"

"When I first came here," Cole said. "I'm from Outside. A place called Arizona. My friends were taken by slavers. I came through and tried to help them but got captured too."

"If you're from Outside, a Wayminder must have helped the slavers."

"The first person I met here in the Outskirts was a Wayminder."

"You have a freemark," she observed.

Cole held up a hand to look at the mark. "The Grand Shaper of Sambria changed it for me."

"Naturally," Violet said. "You know Miracle Pemberton. Why not the exiled Grand Shaper of Sambria?"

"I've had some adventures," Cole said.

"Some Wayminders have helped slavers," Violet said. "I don't agree with slavery."

"That's something we have in common," Cole said.

"Plenty of us don't," Violet said. "Wayminders, I mean. We're not supposed to get too political, though. We aren't noisy about it."

"Sometimes you have to get loud," Cole said. "Even when you're not supposed to."

Violet nodded. "I agree. It's all about finding the right moment."

"Wait, you're a Wayminder," Cole said as something occurred to him.

"You're catching on!" Violet said with a little grin.

"I mean, can you open a way to my home?" Cole asked. "To Earth? To Arizona?"

"In theory," Violet said. "I've never opened a wayport to the Outside. That's very advanced. I'd need more instruction. I've never found a connection to Earth. Where in Arizona?"

"Have you heard of Mesa?" Cole asked.

"Phoenix area," Violet said. "Are you sure you wouldn't prefer Gilbert? Or Chandler?"

"How do you know those places?" Cole exclaimed. Plenty of Americans who lived outside of Arizona hadn't heard of those cities!

"I told you I'm good at geography," Violet said. "Can't get enough of it. Earth is the main place Wayminders visit outside of the Outskirts. There are rumors of other worlds, but I've never heard specifics."

"I hope to get home someday," Cole said.

"A visit wouldn't be too hard," Violet said. "I know some

Wayminders who could get you there. A few could even do it from Junction."

"I want to get home and stay home," Cole said. "I want my family to remember me."

Violet sucked in air through her teeth. "That could be tough. Getting there could happen. But you would be drawn back to the Outskirts before long. And those who know you best will have forgotten you. Casual acquaintances might remember you a little."

"I know how it works," Cole said. "But I'm going to find a way to change it."

"Now that would be a project!" Violet exclaimed. "Talk about testing the limits of the possible."

"Just you wait," Cole said. "I'll figure it out."

"I hope so." Sighing, Violet looked beyond Cole. "When will that kid come back? I'm getting sick of this smell."

DEENA

After some time, Cole spotted Arie and a tall, bony woman making their way between the ponds toward the burned shrine. She had long, graying hair and waved at Cole when she saw him.

As they drew near, the woman came directly to Cole and took his hands in hers. He noticed her short fingernails and dry skin. "Welcome, young Cole. I am Deena. Your friends told me to watch for you. They mentioned others as well, but you especially. And here you are." She glanced at Violet. "Well met, young woman."

"Good day," Violet replied with a small bow.

Holding her hands, Cole could sense Deena's power, fairly strong, and somewhat murky. "Do you know where I can find my friends?"

"I better know," Deena said. "I hid them." She looked around. "I don't believe any of the Enforcers lingered. But who knows for certain? Those jackals can be subtle."

"Burning down a shrine is subtle?" Violet asked.

"They can be harsh, too," Deena said. "Though they have never gone so far as to directly attack a shrine before. Unprecedented boldness."

"Almost like they suspect the world is ending," Violet murmured.

"Are my friends hidden nearby?" Cole asked.

"Yes," Deena said. She held up a small golden strand. "First, if you are indeed Cole, Jace told me you could turn this little string into a rope."

Seeing the rope made Cole happy. It was almost like seeing Jace. He accepted it, found his shaping power could connect easily, and forced some energy into it. The little string expanded to the size of a bullwhip.

"Excellent," Deena said. "We should waste no time."

"Wait," Violet said. "How do we know we can trust you?"

"Because I haven't attacked you, and I'll bring you right to your friends," Deena said.

"Fair enough," Cole said.

"This way," Deena said, leading them around one of the nearest ponds along a squishy embankment, and then down a ladder to a small wooden platform beside another pond, this one larger and partly covered with lily pads. She started turning a crank. "Arie? Would you go close the other intake?"

"Completely?" the boy asked with relish.

"Yes," Deena said. "Then open the outflow gate all the way."

"You got it," the boy said, running along the edge of the pond to another platform, where he started turning a crank of his own.

"What are we doing?" Cole asked.

"Draining the pond," Violet said.

Deena winked. "Funny thing about traveling into the echolands. The body left behind enters a hibernation state. Whole metabolism slows to a crawl. Keeps a person from wasting away. Slow heartbeat. Minimal breathing."

"They're underwater?" Cole asked.

"Inside sealed capsules," Deena said. "I sent them back to the echolands so I could use my best hiding place. In hibernation, they would last at least a week down there, even with the small amount of fresh air trapped with them."

Deena hustled along a narrow path bordered by tiny, dense clover to the dam at the other side of the pond. There she turned another crank. On the far end of the dam, Arie cranked as well.

"How'd you put them down there?" Cole asked.

"We have weighty boxes for the purpose," Deena said. "They look like coffins. An echo warned us of the approaching Enforcers. It was too late for conventional fleeing. We sank Joe, Jace, and Mira before our enemies arrived. The Enforcers demanded we give up the princess. When we refused, they set fire to the shrine. Some who worked here were slain. Several of us fled. I was chosen to linger and awaken our sunken guests after the Enforcers departed. Before they went into the water, your comrades charged me to keep watch for you. And for Dalton or Hunter. They gave me questions to verify your identities, in case of deception. If nobody showed up, I would have extracted them in three days."

"The water level is falling," Violet observed.

"It doesn't take long," Deena said. "Ingenious design. Different waterfalls come and go depending on how the flow is managed. Not all the ponds can be completely emptied. This one is the deepest pool designed to be fully drained."

Arie rejoined them. "I've never seen this one dry," he said.

"We don't empty them often," Deena said. "Not entirely." She closed her eyes, breathing slowly. When she opened her eyes, she smiled at Cole. "Your friends are nearby. Their echoes have found their way here. I began summoning them as soon as they crossed over. I should be able to rouse them with little difficulty."

"Why summoned?" Violet asked. "Didn't they cross over here?"

Deena shook her head. "They had all been to the echolands before, so their lifesparks joined their existing echoes. They had some distance to travel before I could restore them to their physical bodies."

Cole watched the water level drop. Eventually, three bronze coffins were revealed. As the pond finished draining, Cole followed Deena down into the resultant depression, avoiding puddles as they picked their way among slimy rocks and stranded lily pads.

"These containers are airtight," Deena explained as she approached one of the coffins. She unfastened some clasps along one end of the lid. "They have seldom been used."

Deena grabbed one side of the lid, Cole the other, and, pushing upward, they raised it on surprisingly smooth hinges. Inside rested Mira, still as death, and completely dry. Cole couldn't resist a shudder at the horrifying sight.

Deena closed her eyes and extended one hand, lips moving soundlessly. Mira sat up with a gasp, her eyes fluttering open. She looked disoriented for a moment, but when she recognized Cole, her face lit up, and he felt a rush of relief. "You found us! Good job!" Her gaze switched to Deena. "Hurry with the others. Some troublemakers just showed up."

"I saw how she opened it," Violet said from behind Cole, grabbing his shoulder. "Come on."

Cole ran to one of the other coffins with Violet, while Mira and Deena raced to the third. Violet moved along one side of the container, undoing clasps. Cole had not paid close enough attention to learn the trick, but he helped Violet lift the lid when she had finished.

Jace lay inside, frowning in hibernation.

Deena ran toward them, slipping on the greasy stones but somehow keeping her balance. Joe clambered from the other coffin, soaked and dripping.

"Quick," Joe called. "We're right by a slipstream. They're trying to force him in."

Deena reached the coffin and closed her eyes. Jace flinched, rolled over, and then stared wildly up at Cole. "Took you long enough!"

"We're doing our best!" Cole said.

"At least I made it," Jace said, swinging out of the coffin. "You couldn't have cut it any closer. I was getting chucked into a slipstream when I woke up in the box. I'm not sure if our echoes are going to escape. I may have to skip the echolands when I die."

"Who are they?" Violet asked, pointing.

Cole turned to see two men standing in the middle of the empty pond. The bald one was tall and broad. The shorter one was heavyset with a long brown beard. Both glared. Both had a hint of transparency to them.

"Echoes," Deena said.

"They were both there," Jace confirmed. "About ten others as well. Some of them were rushing away, talking about reinforcements." Jace raised his voice. "Nice try!"

The bald echo pointed at him. "Your echo rode the stream. You will never return to the echolands."

"You can keep your lousy land!" Jace cried, crouching to pick up a slimy stone. "All of it! I'm happy to go straight to the Other when my time is up!" He threw the stone, and it passed harmlessly through the echo's chest.

The bald echo smiled. "That will be promptly arranged, I'm sure." His stare shifted to Joe and Mira. "We have your echoes in custody. When you return here, you will be ours."

In the distance a horn sounded. A second horn answered from another direction.

"Enforcers!" Arie called down from the platform where he stood watch. "Lots of them!"

The two echoes in the pond grinned.

"See you shortly," the bald one said to Mira.

Deena stretched a hand toward the echoes. "You dare materialize and threaten in my presence?" she sang out. "I bind you!"

The two echoes went from gloating to alarmed. They held still, trembling, eyes fearful.

"I call you home!" Deena yelled. Then her voice became

71

gentler. "Luxuriate in the homesong. Submit to the tranquility. Answer the summons. Away with you!"

The two echoes disappeared.

"Did you get them?" Jace asked hopefully.

"They didn't stand a chance so near to a slipstream," Deena said. "In they went. It's not much consolation. My deepest apologies to all of you. I didn't know the Enforcers were so near. This has been a trap, sprung simultaneously in the physical world and in the echolands."

"No problem," Cole said with a big smile. "We have a Wayminder."

Mira rolled her eyes. "It doesn't work like that, Cole. She can't open a way in Necronum."

"She can with me around," Cole said, taking Violet's hand.

A glimmering oval appeared nearby.

"Yes!" Jace said, raising a clenched fist. "Cole, you're the best!"

"Hurry," Cole said. "Deena, you and Arie should come too."

"Arie!" Deena shouted. "Come down here immediately!"

The orphan scrambled down the steep side of the pond, falling part of the way. Clothes and skin streaked with mud, he dashed toward them across the pebbly ground.

"We have company!" Jace warned.

Cole looked up to see an enormous bird of prey swooping toward the pond. An Enforcer dangled from the talons.

"Through the wayport," Cole urged.

Deena stepped into the oval and vanished. Then Arie.

"My rope?" Jace asked.

"I have it," Cole said, fishing the golden strand from his

pocket and making sure it was still connected to his power.

The huge bird screeched and dropped the Enforcer, who rolled to a stop at the edge of the pond and produced a crossbow. He raised it and took aim.

Cole passed the golden rope to Jace.

Joe stepped in front of Mira as she entered the shimmering wayport. When he turned to follow her through, a quarrel pierced his thigh. Joe stumbled into the wayport and disappeared.

The Enforcer produced a second quarrel as the golden rope reached him and snaked around his waist. The rope heaved him high into the air and then smashed him down against the glossy stones of the emptied pond, armor clanging violently. As Jace retracted the rope, the broken body remained motionless.

"Go," Cole ordered

Jace lunged through. Cole followed.

Suddenly he was back in the parlor inside Harmony's tower. Arie turned slowly, staring at the room with astonished eyes. Deena and Mira crouched over Joe, examining the quarrel that jutted from his thigh. Cole winced at the dark red stain spreading across the wet pant leg from the wound. He couldn't help thinking about the time Sultan had bled out and died from a wounded shoulder.

"I can yank it," Jace offered, his golden rope twirling above him like a magical lasso.

"Don't you dare," Joe growled through gritted teeth.

Jace's rope shrank back into a small golden strand. Violet came through the way, and it disappeared behind her.

"There must be a healer around," Mira said. "Where are we?"

"You mom's tower," Cole said.

Mira glanced at him. "Really?" She looked around. "She didn't use to live in a tower."

"Your dad lives in another one," Cole said.

Mira turned back to Joe. "Did you hear that? We're with my mother. We'll get you the best healer in the Outskirts."

His expression strained, Joe gave a nod. "Some painkiller would do."

"Why are your clothes all wet?" Jace asked.

"His container must have sprung a slow leak," Deena said. "Some air remained when we opened it. But not much."

"Thanks for shielding me," Mira said. "You shouldn't have."

"I was trying to get away too," Joe replied modestly.

"You probably saved my life," Mira said.

"Who's that?" Arie asked, pointing to Queen Harmony, who had just entered the room.

She stood staring at her daughter.

Mira ran to her mother and embraced her.

Harmony hugged back, her expression stunned. Tears filled her eyes, and she tightened her embrace.

Only Violet knelt.

"We need a healer, Mother," Mira said. "Our friend Joe was shot while protecting me."

"Of course," Harmony replied, her lips finally parting in a huge smile. "Right away, my darling Miracle." Harmony held Miracle away from her and looked her up and down. "You haven't aged a day."

"I barely started again once I got my power back," Mira said.

"You're unhurt?" Harmony asked.

"Mother—Joe!" Mira insisted, almost whining. Cole had never heard that particular tone from Mira before.

"Right away," Harmony said, bustling out of the room.

Deena was using a frilly doily stolen from a nearby table to apply pressure at the source of the bleeding. Sweat slicked Joe's face.

"Those Enforcers will wonder what happened," Jace said.

"What about the one with the great raptor?" Deena asked. "Didn't he see our escape?"

"I took care of that one," Jace said. "No living Enforcers saw how we got away."

Queen Harmony returned.

Violet knelt again.

"My personal physician is on his way," Harmony said. "Rise, Violet. Formalities end when people are bleeding." The queen crouched beside Joe and placed a hand on his shoulder. "Thank you for protecting my daughter. You have my lasting gratitude. Rest assured that you will soon be in some of the most capable hands in Junction."

"Thanks," Joe said.

"Who are our other guests?" Harmony asked, straightening.

"This is Deena," Mira said. "She took care of our physical bodies when we were in the echolands the first time. Then she sent me, Joe, and Jace back to the echolands and hid our bodies when the Enforcers attacked."

"You also have my deepest gratitude," Harmony said, inclining her head. "And this young man?"

"Jace has traveled with me and Cole since we escaped the Sky Raiders," Mira said. "I owe him my life many times over."

"Thank you, Jace," Harmony said.

"We have more to do," Jace said. "Right, Cole?"

"Yes," Cole said. "And this little guy is Arie."

"I found Cole and drained the pond," the boy said. "You don't have to thank me."

"If you helped my daughter make it home, I thank you nonetheless," Harmony said. "You will all be rewarded."

"Spend it quickly," Jace muttered. "There's a torivor coming."

A short, narrow man entered the room, his mostly bald head offset by a gray goatee. He hurried to Joe and placed both hands on his leg.

"What did you do?" Joe asked. "The pain just . . . stopped."

"A minor changing," the physician said. "I'm from Elloweer. Not a pretty wound. The quarrel was designed to wreak havoc. But I'll get you patched up."

Jace was looking around the room. "So this is the First Castle."

"Not the best part," Mira said. "You should see the parade grounds. And the stables. And of course the main residence."

"I make do here," Harmony said.

"Sorry, Mother," Mira said. "I didn't mean . . ."

"Do not speak of sorrow, dear one," Harmony said. "You belonged here these many years, and instead you lived like a hunted trophy. My sorrow is an ocean without shores. Where do we begin, my child? I want to hear about your time away from me! Tell me of your sisters! I understand you have seen all but Elegance. I want to know everything!"

Deena bowed. "I imagine you would prefer some privacy."

"You all deserve to be made more comfortable," Harmony said. "My head of staff is on her way!"

"Did you figure out how to get me to the Founding Stone?" Cole asked.

Harmony gasped. "I meant to tell you! The Founding Stone is gone!"

"Isn't that impossible?" Deena asked.

"Legend has it the stone cannot be moved," Harmony said. "And yet it is clearly missing. Not a fragment remains."

"Owandell must have moved it somehow," Cole said. "He used shapecraft to break off a piece and send it to the echolands. He must have used shapecraft to move the whole stone."

"It's unsettling," Harmony said.

"I wonder what he's going to do with it," Cole said.

"Maybe he just wanted to keep it away from you," Mira suggested.

"I'm not sure it can do much unless I power it up," Cole said. "But maybe they can energize it somehow through shapecraft."

"I will do my best to find it," Harmony promised. "What would you like to do now?"

"I kind of want to keep moving," Cole said.

"Where to next?" Jace asked.

"Well, with Violet, we can go anywhere," Cole said. "I need a good weapon. I couldn't bring my Jumping Sword back from the echolands. The Sky Raiders had a bunch. I thought maybe we could go there and resupply."

"The Sky Raiders?" Jace exclaimed. "Are you trying to give me a heart attack? Do you know how many nights I contemplated my death in that place? And how many days I barely dodged it?"

"No scouting missions," Cole said. "Just buying gear."

"Adam won't sell anything cheap," Jace said. "Who is paying?"

Cole pulled out the king's seal. "The High King gave me unlimited credit."

Jace stared openmouthed. "Unlimited credit? Of course he did! Because the world is about to end. Life is always torture."

Cole tucked the medallion away. "At least it should get me a Jumping Sword." He turned to Violet. "Can you take us to Skyport?"

"I've always hoped to go there!" Violet gushed. "I want to look off the Brink! Endless sky up *and* down? I have to see it!"

"You'll come back here before heading to Creon," Mira said.

"We can," Cole said uncertainly.

Mira turned to her mother. "You won't try to stop me?"

"We should talk," Harmony said. "Cole, absolutely come back before you go after Elegance."

"Okay," Cole said. He glanced at Jace. "Coming?"

Jace held up his hand. "I've never been to Skyport with a freemark. Freaky memories or not, I wouldn't miss it." He bowed to Harmony. "Nice to meet you, Your Highness."

Violet joined hands with Cole, and a shimmering disturbance appeared.

"The pleasure is all mine," Harmony said. "Good luck."

Jace gave a lopsided smile. "That doesn't work where we're going right now."

"Die bravely," Mira said.

"That's more like it," Jace said. "Off we go."

CHAPTER 7

JUMPING SWORD

Constructed from stone and heavy timbers, the sprawling main building of Skyport clung to the edge of the Brink. Several porches and balconies projected out over the endless drop. Beyond the Brink, in a bright sky decorated with puffy white clouds, several castles floated at different altitudes, one of them close enough to allow Cole to make out details like the battlements on the walls and towers. A single skycraft floated serenely near the closest castle.

Cole stood on a slope looking down at Skyport. Jace emerged from the quivering disturbance beside him, and then Violet came through as well. The wayport closed behind her.

"That has to be the Brink," Violet said, staring out at the vista.

"Brings back awful memories," Jace said.

"Should we head into Skyport?" Cole prompted. "You could go out on the porch and look down."

Violet clapped her hands. "Let's go!"

"Couldn't you have put the wayport a little closer?" Cole asked. "Or inside the common room?"

"Slightly closer maybe," Violet said. "I thought coming in on the side of the valley would grant a better view. And Wayminders never open a way into a building uninvited. Don't you know that?"

"I did," Jace volunteered.

"I didn't," Cole admitted. "Why not?"

"We don't want to be hated," Violet said. "At the beginning of our discipline, some Wayminders opened ways to spy or steal. Very soon we were all despised and hunted. Certain rulers vowed to exterminate us. Our leadership made a pledge never to enter a building without written permission. All Wayminders agreed, most voluntarily. Eventually we earned back the public trust. A Wayminder who violates that rule is immediately stripped of all rights and banished."

"Harmony gave you written permission to enter her tower," Cole said.

"Exactly," Violet said. "In the missive she sent."

"Come on," Jace said, trotting down the slope toward Skyport. "We're wasting daylight."

Cole and Violet caught up, and together they descended to Skyport and entered the mostly empty common room. A few men played cards in one corner. Adam Jones, a burly man with a grayish beard and long curly hair, sat on his cushioned throne of translucent jade.

"This is a surprise!" Adam bellowed when the three kids entered. "I didn't expect to set eyes on you two again. Should I prepare for an invasion of legionnaires?"

"The legionnaires were after Mira," Cole said, approaching the elaborate throne.

"Have they nabbed her?" Adam asked.

"Almost," Cole said. "Not yet."

"You boys ready to get back to work?" Adam asked. "I still own both of you."

"Nobody owns me," Jace said, showing his freemark.

"Me neither," Cole agreed, doing the same.

Adam leaned forward. "Come here." He inspected both freemarks. "Who did this work? You keep him away from here. The scoundrel will drive me right out of business. And who is this young maiden? A Wayminder, I see."

"I'm Violet," she said with a small curtsy.

"I gather you brought her to me as a peace offering?" Adam asked.

"No," Cole said. "She's with us."

Violet held up her freemark.

"Those legionnaires did plenty of damage when they tore through here," Adam said soberly. "I lost three of my scouts when you ran off, plus Mira. And I had to bribe the interlopers to leave us in peace after we slowed their efforts to arrest you."

Cole pulled the royal seal from under his shirt and showed Adam. "The High King will cover the expenses."

"You now speak for Stafford Pemberton?" Adam exclaimed. "Somebody has risen in the world! Are you here on official business? Should I set the table with my bestmost utensils?"

"No meals," Cole said.

Jace elbowed him, then stepped toward Adam. "What are you having?"

"If the High King is paying, we can supply just about whatever you want," Adam said. He looked intently at Cole. "Is this some sort of stunt? Where did you get that seal?"

"From the High King," Cole said. "It's legit."

"Aye, it appears authentic," Adam said. He raised his voice. "Bennett! Prepare an invoice for the damage done by the legionnaires, the bribes paid, and the value of three scouts." Adam leaned back in his throne and drummed his hands on the arms. "Now . . . what else are you after? Or did you just come here to settle up accounts?"

"I lost my Jumping Sword," Cole said. "I need a replacement. The High King will pay for that, too."

Adam winced. "We used to have several Jumping Swords. Then we lost the shapecrafter who made them."

"Durny," Cole said.

Adam gave a nod. "We still haven't found an adequate replacement. Scouting is dangerous. Only one Jumping Sword remains. We don't let the scouts use it. We keep it in the armory in case of emergency."

Cole stepped closer to the throne and lowered his voice. "This is a major emergency. The entire Outskirts is in danger. We're trying to stop a torivor."

Adam laughed. "What is that supposed to mean?"

"Don't you know about torivors?" Cole asked.

"Vaguely," Adam said. "Fearmongering spooksters from the ether or some such nonsense. Isn't there one in Elloweer? I'm not a mythologist."

"There are only two in the Outskirts," Cole said. "One is about to get free. If he does, the Outskirts ends. No more salvaging. No more Skyport. No more Brink. No more Sambria."

"Sounds awfully dramatic," Adam said. "In my experience, boasts that grand don't tend to pay what they promise. I don't understand the witchery of torivors, but I am a merchant. I'll sell you the Jumping Sword if the High King will cover it."

"Good enough," Cole said.

"Funny you should mention torivors," Adam said.

"Why?" Cole asked.

"One of our teams found a talking castle yesterday that promised an important message about a torivor called Ramarro."

Cole stiffened and leaned forward. "What was the message?"

Adam shrugged. "The scout who entered the castle never returned. That means we abort."

"Is the castle still out there?" Cole asked. "Has it entered the Eastern Cloudwall yet?"

"Wouldn't take long to find out," Adam said. "Are you interested?"

"Yeah," Cole said, his heart racing. "We need to get there as soon as we can."

"Make yourselves comfortable while you wait," Adam said. "I'll send for the sword."

Violet cleared her throat. "Do you mind if I look off the edge? I've never been to the Brink."

"Be my guest," Adam said. "I'll have a scope brought to you."

* * *

"No way am I returning to a sky castle," Jace said. "Not if you tied me up and dragged me. Especially one that already killed a scout."

They sat beside each other in rocking chairs, tilting lazily. Violet stood at the railing peering through a small telescope.

"But Dandalus created the cloudwalls that make and destroy the castles," Cole said. "What if he's sending a message?"

"Then he should have found a delivery method that doesn't kill scouts," Jace said. "I used to be sure I would die in a sky castle. I even managed to make peace with the idea. We're all just prolonging the inevitable, right? And then we got away. And I gradually accepted that I wouldn't die in the sky. Don't make me do this, Cole."

"You can stay behind with Violet," Cole said. "Too much depends on stopping Ramarro. We have no real leads. I have to look."

Jace sighed miserably. "I'm braver than you. If you go, I have to go. Let's just take the sword and get out of here. Who knows? Adam could be messing with you."

"You think?"

"Why not? He could just want you to give him a free scouting mission."

"I'd check the castle before I went inside. Ever heard of a talking sky castle?"

"Nope," Jace said.

"Which one talks?" Violet asked, her telescope aimed at one of the castles.

"We don't know," Cole said. "Probably not one to the west. They're created in the Western Cloudwall and drift

85

east to the Eastern Cloudwall, where they vanish into a huge vortex. The talking one was explored yesterday, so if it's still around, it should be in the east."

"So much to see," Violet said. "Are you sure you don't want to borrow the telescope?"

"We've seen them a lot closer," Jace said.

"But not *these* castles," Violet stressed. "A person could spend a lifetime studying this phenomenon."

"Or lose a lifetime," Jace said. "Really quickly. I've seen too many people die in those pretty castles."

"They're not all pretty," Violet corrected. "They all have presence, though. Character."

"And death traps," Jace added. "Most of them have death traps."

She pointed the telescope downward. "There has to be a bottom somewhere."

"Nobody has ever found one," Jace said.

"At least nobody who lived to tell about it," Violet said, aiming her telescope straight up. "Who knows what trickery the designers used? Looping space, maybe? Illusions? What is behind this sky? It can't extend forever."

A man came out onto the porch.

"Wenzel," Jace said, rocking to his feet.

Cole recognized the man but had never officially met him.

"Jace," Wenzel acknowledged. He held out a sheathed short sword to Cole. "This is yours now."

"Thanks," Cole said. Drawing it, he found it a tad longer than his previous Jumping Sword, and a little heavier. He would have to experiment with it and make sure it worked as well as his other one.

"The talking castle has not yet departed the sky," Wenzel said. "Only a few hours remain before it passes out of reach. If one of you wants to scout it, Adam gave me permission to take you there aboard the *Vulture*."

"Did you see it?" Jace asked.

"We visited yesterday," Wenzel said. "Strange hearing a castle speak. It promised vast treasures and secrets. We got plenty curious. Never saw the scout again once he went inside. The temperament of the castle changed when we left. It sounded angry. I won't bring the *Vulture* very near. If you insist on a close look, you'll be on your own."

Jace shook his head at Cole.

"We better hurry," Cole said. "Sounds like time is short."

Violet had spent the first part of the flight exploring the *Vulture*, fingering ropes, peeking into lifeboats, and asking the crew questions. Now she stood at the front of the skycraft as the desired castle drew nearer. The Eastern Cloudwall loomed not too far in the distance.

Nearby, Jace adjusted the straps of Cole's parachute. "Do you remember why you have this?" Jace asked.

"Of course I do," Cole said.

"You have it because the horrors inside that castle might be worse than jumping into a bottomless sky and hoping somebody can get under you before you fall forever."

"Unlike you, I've used a parachute to escape before," Cole reminded him.

"I wouldn't brag about that," Jace said. "It's good to survive a close call. But the scouts who have too many close calls end up dead."

"I know the dangers," Cole said.

Jace touched the little vial around Cole's neck. "Remember what this holds?"

"Poison, so I can end my misery if I end up falling and nobody can catch me."

"If you fall below the range where the floatstones work, you will never see anyone else again."

"And poison might be better than starving while falling endlessly."

"Does suicide poison seem like something you should bring along when doing something voluntary?"

"I'm not doing it for fun, Jace. I'm doing it to get info about Ramarro. I'll talk to the castle first. I won't even go inside unless it sounds like what we need."

Jace sighed. "You're determined?"

"You know I am."

"Then I'm coming too," Jace said. He walked away and came back, shrugging into his own parachute.

"You don't have to join me," Cole said.

"I'm going if you are," Jace said firmly.

"Should I wear one?" Violet asked.

"They're for people who are coming," Cole said.

Violet put her hands on her hips. "I'm not coming?"

"It's dangerous," Cole said.

"I heard," Violet replied. "Won't it be less dangerous if you can open a way and escape whenever you want?"

Cole and Jace looked at each other.

"Yes," Jace said. "That would actually be much less dangerous."

"Might also be easier to get to the castle using a wayport rather than a lifeboat," Violet suggested.

Cole swallowed. "True."

"But should I wear a parachute in case you get killed, Cole, and I can't open a wayport?"

"I'll grab one," Jace said, hurrying off.

Cole looked down at the approaching castle. Composed of weathered gray stone, the huge building looked long abandoned. Bulky towers added height to the outer wall, while more artful towers topped the soaring buildings within. "Looks ominous," Cole said.

"Looks empty," Violet replied. "I wonder how it talks."

"Are you sure you want to go down there?" Cole said. "We really could die. It looks quiet right now, but visitors get killed in these castles all the time. Opening a wayport could save us. Or we could get crushed or poisoned or stabbed or shot before a wayport can be opened."

"You're a terrible recruiter," Violet said. "I knew there would be danger when Queen Harmony assigned me to you. Having me along improves our chances for success. I'm part of this mission."

Jace returned with a parachute for Violet and poison to wear around her neck. Captain Wenzel joined them. They all leaned slightly to compensate as the *Vulture* drifted to a stop.

"Jace tells me you can open a wayport to the castle,"

Wenzel said. "And another to get back. Is such a miracle possible?"

"It's a little-known technique for traveling short distances," she replied. "Lets me open many wayports without the usual recovery time needed. Something I am beginning to master."

"I wish we had that talent with us every day," Wenzel said. "If your technique will work, I see no purpose in drawing any closer to the destination."

"The boys will need you if I get killed," Violet said.

"Aye," Wenzel agreed. "We'll linger and keep a lifeboat standing ready in case a rescue is needed."

"Thanks," Cole said, casually touching Violet's hand and energizing her power. "We hope to be back soon. Right away if the castle doesn't seem promising."

"Don't take too long," Wenzel warned. "We won't bring the skycraft too near the cloudwall. You don't want to be in the castle when it gets there. Things quickly get out of control."

"Let's get this over with," Jace suggested.

Violet opened a wayport.

Jace nodded at Cole. "Die bravely."

"Die bravely," Cole replied as his friend stepped through, golden rope in hand.

Gripping the hilt of his Jumping Sword, Cole followed.

CHAPTER
8

CASTLE

Battle-scarred walls loomed imposingly above Cole as he arrived beside Jace. With the massive drawbridge closed, the castle appeared unassailable. The only handholds on the ancient wall were narrow slits for archers that began forty feet up.

Cole could not take his eyes off the colossal structure. Its menacing presence demanded attention. There was no obvious threat—no defenders manned the parapets, no sound issued from within. So why did he suddenly feel like a rodent cowering in the shadow of a hawk?

Cole peripherally sensed Violet emerge from the way-port and close it.

The three of them gazed up at the castle. Was it staring back? Cole could identify no eyes, but he felt seen.

"What now?" Jace asked quietly.

"Not sure," Cole said. It seemed inappropriate to talk. He wasn't even sure he should blink.

They continued to stare.

"Does it know we're here?" Violet eventually whispered.

Without any proof, Cole nodded.

The castle remained still.

"Hello?" Jace called.

Cole flinched at the volume. The word fell flat, swallowed by the silence.

"We're not alone," Jace muttered.

"Could you have transported us into the courtyard?" Cole asked.

"The courtyard is protected by walls," Violet said. "Wayminders don't trespass."

"Does that have to include empty castles made by magic clouds?" Jace asked.

"Didn't we want to make sure the castle was worth entering?" Violet replied.

"Hard to tell from out here," Jace complained.

An enormous voice emanated from the castle, resonant and deep, loud without straining. "ENTER IF YOU DARE."

Cole felt the voice in his chest as well as heard it with his ears. He glanced at his friends. Both appeared uncertain.

"How would we enter?" Cole asked.

The drawbridge swung outward, chains unspooling noisily, until it thudded heavily against the ground. A portcullis behind the drawbridge raised high enough for a person to duck beneath it. Then all became silent again.

"Should we go in?" Jace asked.

Cole studied the castle suspiciously. "I'm not sure about this."

"TREASURES UNTOLD AWAIT," the penetrating voice said.

"What treasures?" Cole asked.

"RICHES BEYOND IMAGINATION," the voice said. "SECRETS OF CREON. MYSTERIES OF THE TORIVOR RAMARRO."

"Tell us about the mysteries," Cole said. "Tell us about Ramarro."

"HE WHO DESIRES THE TREASURE MUST ENTER," the voice asserted.

After drawing his Jumping Sword, Cole touched Violet with his free hand and made sure their connection was strong. "Stay ready."

She gave a nod.

Cole reached for Jace's rope.

"Sambria, remember?" Jace said, expanding his rope slightly and twirling it. "Works fine here."

"I forgot," Cole said.

"Time to die bravely," Jace said, striding forward.

The castle remained still and silent as they approached the drawbridge. Was it actually a bridge if it spanned no moat or trench? When they stepped onto the drawbridge, the voice spoke again.

"TRESSPASSERS NOT INTENDED TO RECEIVE THE TREASURE MUST SURELY PERISH."

Cole paused. The others looked at him. "We're going after Ramarro," he said. "Dandalus knows that. Let's hope this is meant for us."

"And if not," Violet said, "I'll open a wayport back to the skycraft."

Cole, Jace, and Violet crossed the rest of the drawbridge and ducked under the portcullis together. They had not taken more than a step beyond it before the portcullis crashed down. Quick as a mousetrap, the drawbridge slammed shut with thunderous finality.

"This treasure better be good," Jace muttered.

They proceeded into the abandoned courtyard, the vast castle before them, the wall behind and around them. No signs of life disturbed the stillness. And yet Cole felt sure they were not alone. He kept checking over his shoulders, turning as he walked.

"I don't see an entrance to the castle," Cole said.

Up ahead, a flight of steps led to a blank wall. No doors into the castle were in view. The lower levels had no windows.

"I see balconies," Jace said.

"Now that we're inside will you open a wayport?" Cole asked.

"Into the castle?" Violet asked. "I don't feel good about that. In fact, the interior of the building feels shielded from my mind. Somebody took measures to keep Wayminders out. But I could now go anywhere in the courtyard, including a balcony."

"Do it," Cole said, maintaining his connection to her power without physical contact.

"SURVIVE THE TRIAL TO OBTAIN THE REWARD," the voice declared.

An oval disturbance appeared near Cole. He stepped through onto a large balcony high above the courtyard. Jace and Violet promptly joined him.

A door led from the balcony into the castle.

For an instant.

Then the surrounding wall swallowed the door. The portal vanished without a trace, leaving only stone blocks. The wall also filled in the nearby windows.

"This might be harder than it—" Jace began.

Without warning the balcony detached from the side of the castle and plummeted toward the courtyard.

Cole separated from the balcony in the air before he could kick off it with his Jumping Sword. He watched in shocked terror as he plunged toward the ground. Without someplace to jump from, his sword was useless. The golden rope snaked around him, pulling him close to Jace and Violet. While one end of the rope bound them together, the other stretched to the balustrades of a different balcony, and suddenly they were swinging instead of falling.

The detached balcony smashed below them as the threesome swooped sideways, angling downward at first, then curving upward with terrific speed. The golden rope went limp as the balcony to which it was attached broke from the castle as well. Once again Cole and his friends were sailing through the air. Still holding them together, the golden rope spiraled beneath them into the form of an enormous spring that absorbed the impact and deposited them safely onto the ground. Off to one side, the second balcony crashed to the courtyard in an explosion of shattered stone.

"Thanks, Jace," Cole said. "We were goners."

"Don't relax yet," Jace warned.

Statues were detaching from the castle, stepping fully carved out of the stone walls like divers emerging from deep water. The life-size men, women, and children left behind no holes or indentations, and no carvings hinted at their presence before their arrival. Each of the statues carried a stone weapon—mostly clubs, swords, and spears. Cole could not tell whether the stone personages had waited fully formed within the walls and were now passing through the barriers, or if the castle was spontaneously creating them, but all the stone people moved quickly toward him and his friends.

"No fair," Cole said, retreating away from the castle.

The statues went from walking fast to running, stone faces contorting in anger. Cole turned and ran toward the outer wall only to find much larger statues emerging from the soaring fortification, four and five times the height of a man. A bearded giant with a huge war hammer paced toward him, footsteps shaking the ground.

Jace used his golden rope to pick up the statue of a knight and heave it into the statue of a hooded monk. The monk went flying, and the knight lost his head and one arm. Then Jace bashed the damaged knight into a shepherdess with a stone crook. With a resounding crash, she went down as the knight broke in half.

Cole saw that fighting would not solve this problem. They were drastically outnumbered. Running would not work for long either. Dozens of statues were converging on them from all directions. More continued to surface from the ground and emerge from the walls.

"Should we go?" Violet cried.

Jace used his rope to whip the feet out from under the nearest statues as quickly as he could. The disruption was not enough. There were too many. Cole and his friends would be overrun any moment.

Cole still felt a solid connection to Violet's power. "We should probably go."

A wall sprang up out of the ground, dividing him from Violet. Another separated him from Jace, trapping Cole in a narrow alley. Statues closed in from ahead and behind.

He glanced up. The sudden walls were about twenty feet high. Cole pointed at the top of the nearest and shouted, "Away!" He jumped, and the sword pulled him upward. His momentum died at the top of the wall, allowing him to land lightly.

The top of the wall was only about six inches wide. Despite landing gently, Cole lost his balance. Pointing to a spot in the courtyard well beyond the mob of statues, Cole yelled "Away" and kicked off the wall before he lost contact. He streaked through the air toward his destination. The sword decelerated him right before he landed, but Cole still stumbled. Jumping down tended to be more jarring than jumping up.

He had practiced with the new Jumping Sword back at Skyport. The range was similar to his previous Jumping Sword, meaning he could spring to the lower balconies of the nearby castle with a single bound, but the tops of the towers were well out of reach without multiple jumps.

Many of the statues turned to charge Cole. Several of the new statues emerging from the walls came his way as well. A statue of a huge barbarian woman dressed in animal skins detached from the outer wall and stalked toward him, a chain mace in her mighty grip.

Cole saw the golden rope uncoil like a giant spring to propel Jace away from the attacking statues. Jace landed nimbly and used the rope to yank the foot of a giant statue, noisily toppling the brute. A new wall sprang up, blocking his friend from view.

Cole could still feel his connection to Violet and kept pushing energy to her power, but he worried how she was handling the statues. If he felt their connection, she had to be alive. But was she being apprehended or injured? Would she open a way and flee to outside the castle? Had she fled already?

"Over here!" Violet called from across the courtyard. The shimmering wayport beside her vanished, another opened, and one appeared beside Cole as well. Violet stepped into the new wayport and emerged beside Cole.

"Should we go?" she asked.

"We have to get Jace," Cole said.

A wall shot up between them.

Statues were closing in, so Cole sprang to the top of the wall, landing the jump this time. Looking over the far side, he saw Violet disappear into a wayport just before the statues arrived. New walls erupted at unpredictable intervals, partitioning the courtyard into a labyrinth.

Did the castle know Violet was a Wayminder? Or did it just generally try to separate groups?

The female statue with the chain mace stood tall enough to still reach Cole. He jumped away an instant before the spiked ball smashed the top of the wall into fragments. Cole knew he would have too much momentum to land his jump to the top of the next wall, so he shouted "Away" again as he sprang off the next surface he touched, aiming for the ground this time.

As Cole staggered to a stop, Jace yelled, "The castle!"

Unable to see what his friend meant, and with more statues racing at him, Cole sprang to the top of another wall and, pivoting at his waist, arms extended, managed to keep his balance. He promptly realized that a pair of open doors had appeared at the top of the steps at the front of the castle. They had not been there before.

Jace used the rope to slingshot himself in that direction. Cole could feel each time Violet opened a wayport as her power required more energy. For the first time it was becoming an effort to sustain her.

Cole thrust his sword at the top of a wall halfway to the front doors of the castle and shouted, "Away!" He yelled the command again as he landed, skipping onward to the top of the steps.

Jace arrived a moment before him. After Cole landed, a wayport opened, and Violet appeared beside him. Beyond the open doors stretched an empty hall.

"Do we go in?" Violet asked, panting, her hair even wilder than normal.

The walls in the courtyard sank into the ground,

allowing an enormous mob of statues, big and small, to charge directly at them. Cole was unsure what to do. With Violet and Jace beside him, it presented a chance for all of them to escape through a wayport. But did the open doors mean they were passing the test? Was the valuable information about Ramarro down that hallway? Or was the castle simply herding them in that direction to destroy them?

"Come on," Cole said, rushing through the doors.

Jace and Violet sprinted beside him.

"I hope you know what you're doing," Jace said.

"Me too," Cole replied. "Be ready to make a wayport out of here, Violet."

"I can't see in here," Violet said. "Or out of here. Just like how I couldn't see in from outside."

"Try," Cole said, flooding power into her.

"I am, Cole," Violet said. "My mind is blind in here! I'm trying! I can't open a way if I can't see."

Glancing back, Cole saw the mob of statues clattering after them. He and his friends raced up a stairway at the end of the hall, then rushed along another corridor. Statues began to emerge from the walls at either side and behind them. All the doors up ahead disappeared, including where the corridor came to an end.

"No fair!" Cole yelled. This wasn't a trial! This was certain death!

They reached the end of the hall and turned to face the oncoming statues. Instead of running, the statues walked briskly, packed close together, with more pouring from the walls.

"We need a wayport, now," Cole said, feeding Violet all the power he could muster.

"Stop!" Violet shouted, blood leaking from one nostril. "I can't!"

A brawny bald statue with a club in each hand led the attackers. Dozens followed—soldiers, dancers, barbarians, demons, fancy ladies, scholars, and cherubs marched together, weapons ready, expressions confident.

Jace raised his arm, and his golden rope unfurled toward the statues, but before it reached them, a huge hand sprouted from the wall and took hold of it. The rope writhed as Jace tried to wrest it free, but the stone hand held it firmly.

In desperation, Cole summoned his power for a final effort and reached out to the brawny statue at the head of the others. To his surprise, his power connected easily. With an effort of will, Cole blasted the statue into shrapnel that showered the statues in its wake.

The statues all stopped.

Reaching out, Cole could feel all of them. It was like in the echolands. No, even easier than the echolands. He could connect with almost no effort.

Had he been able to do this all along?

Up until now, in the physical world, he had only managed to connect to the power inside other people and to the power within shaped artifacts. He had not tried to connect to anything physical since arriving at the sky castle. He had assumed that he couldn't do it.

He had been wrong.

The mass of statues rushed forward in a desperate charge.

With a growl, Cole threw everything he had at them, and the first couple dozen statues exploded down the corridor in a hail of shattered stone. The surviving statues farther back kept coming, and Cole reached out, feeling them with his power, and then hurling them violently away.

The walls of the hallway began to constrict, closing in, the ceiling descending, the floor elevating. Cole felt the walls, ceiling, and floor with his power and shoved them away, finding them easily malleable. He quickly increased the size of the corridor threefold. The remaining statues melted into the floor and walls.

The corridor became empty. The castle was still.

Jace stared at Cole in amazement.

"Who are you?" Violet asked in an awed tone.

"My power works here like it did in the echolands," Cole said. "I didn't know until I tried in desperation."

A statue emerged from the end of the corridor. Cole reached into it with his power and then paused. The statue carried no weapon. And was smiling.

And looked exactly like Dandalus.

TREASURE

The statue spoke with a smaller version of the voice that had issued from the castle. "Well done. The defenses have disengaged. You're safe now."

"Dandalus?" Cole asked.

"A simplified version of Dandalus, yes, with some specific information. Since you survived, I presume you are Cole Randolph?"

"I am," Cole said.

"I recognize you. From the echolands, the echo of Dandalus created this castle to send you a message. The message is meant only for you, Cole, so Dandalus created defenses that should be able to vanquish any intruder, but that you could easily overcome."

"Easy once I knew how my power worked here," Cole said.

"Was it a challenge?" the statue asked. "This castle was specifically customized to accommodate your abilities."

"Did you miss the falling balconies?" Jace asked with a dark chuckle. "And the horde of statues?"

"Two artificial consciousnesses abide here. One controls the defenses. The other is me. The defenses did not give me access to you until I emerged from the wall."

"I'm glad we found you," Cole said.

"Too bad for the scout who came before us," Jace murmured.

"There is one other living person inside the castle," the statue said. "Could this be your scout? The defenses only kill as a final resort. The primary directive is to capture. The castle is designed to prevent escape. Of course, anyone captured would die with the castle when it enters the Eastern Cloudwall and is unmade."

"The scout is alive?" Cole asked.

"We have a single young human in one of the holding cells. I can take you to him now or after our conversation."

"How about the information first?" Cole prompted.

"The echo of Dandalus became concerned when he realized Ramarro was sent to Creon," the statue said. "There are certain secrets he withheld from the artificial construct of himself residing in the Founding Stone. And many subtle nuances he worried the construct would not understand. One of these secrets is that through their skills in manipulating time, the Grand Shapers of Creon learned the key to everlasting life as long as they never leave Creon."

"I've heard rumors," Violet said. "None confirmed. Wait, we've had many different Grand Shapers in Creon. If they can live forever, why would we need more than one?"

"They retire," the statue said. "Go into hiding. Partly because the duties of a Grand Shaper are taxing, and those who hold the office eventually wear out. Partly so their discovery of a form of immortality can remain hidden. Dandalus knew the secret but didn't want it getting out."

"They can't leave Creon?" Cole asked.

"Time Jumpers can only manipulate time inside of Creon," Violet explained. "Time manipulations can't survive beyond the borders of the kingdom."

"Time Jumpers?" Cole asked.

"Highly specialized Wayminders who can shape time itself," Violet clarified. "I hope to be one someday."

"You can shape time?" Jace asked.

"Me?" Violet asked. "Inside of Creon? Just a little. So I'm told. But a little means I have potential. Not all Wayminders do."

"Can the Grand Shapers of Creon help us?" Cole asked.

"Dandalus wants you to seek out Lorenzo Debray," the statue said.

"He was Grand Shaper more than four hundred years ago!" Violet exclaimed.

"I hope he has a sturdy cane," Jace said.

"You should be able to find him some distance north of the old cache at Shepherd's Grove," the statue said.

Violet looked like she was ready to freak out.

"What?" Cole asked.

"He just told us Lorenzo Debray is alive and where to find him," Violet gushed.

"Lorenzo knows more about the vault holding Ramarro

than anyone but Kendo Rattan, who created it. Dandalus also recommended you seek out Kendo Rattan, though he is unsure where he is hiding or if he still lives."

"Kendo Rattan," Violet said reverently. "The father of our order. The first and greatest Grand Shaper of Creon—a master Wayminder and expert Time Jumper."

"What else?" Cole asked.

"Beware the Ancient One," the statue said. "He has allied with evil across the ages in Creon, and is a probable candidate to support Ramarro."

Violet shivered. "The Ancient One killed one of our Grand Shapers years ago."

"Hard to live forever if you get killed," Jace said.

"No mortal is truly immortal," Violet said. "Some are just really good at stretching it."

"True," the statue said. "The Grand Shapers of Creon are not invulnerable—but they have learned to live indefinitely if nobody interferes."

"How old is the Ancient One?" Cole asked.

"At least fifteen hundred years," the statue said.

"He hides his face," Violet said. "Some people theorize he might be more than one person."

"What do you think?" Cole asked the statue.

"I have no information about the theory," the statue said. "Dandalus primarily wanted me to urge you to seek out Lorenzo Debray. He may be able to help you prepare defenses against Ramarro."

"Thanks," Cole said.

"Dandalus was sorry he couldn't get you this information

earlier," the statue said. "He would have told you this before you left the echolands had he known Ramarro would end up incarcerated in Creon. This was the first castle he sent with a message. He intends to send more, every few days, hoping eventually you would intercept one."

"Lucky that we came to Skyport for a Jumping Sword," Cole said.

"Dandalus thought you might, since you had to leave yours behind when you crossed back to physical Necronum. He also hoped that with multiple castles professing information about Ramarro you would eventually get word of the phenomenon."

"But we found the first castle," Jace said.

"Correct," the statue said.

"Where did Dandalus go to make this castle?" Cole asked. "Where in the echolands do the castles come from?"

"I lack that information," the statue said.

"Can you guess?" Cole asked.

The statue gave a small smile. "I was made to deliver certain information and to have some semblance of a personality. I only know what I know."

"Do you know anything else about Ramarro?" Jace asked.

"Only that Dandalus urges you to hurry," the statue said. "The Void will not hold him very long. You must investigate if a better prison can be devised. Should the torivor get free, there may be no stopping him."

"You mentioned another person alive inside the castle," Cole said.

"Yes," the statue said. "I will take you to him."

The statue turned, and the wall parted, opening into a stairway. Cole, Jace, and Violet followed the statue until they reached a barred cell. A boy perhaps a year or two older than Cole waited inside, skinny with black hair.

"You're a scout?" Jace asked.

"Yeah, with the Sky Raiders," he said.

"I'm Jace. This is Cole and Violet. And a statue."

"I'm Trotter," the boy said.

"I'm a former Sky Raider," Jace said. "So is Cole. Today you get a free pass. Want to get out of here?"

"Really?" Trotter asked. "How'd you beat all the statues?"

"Cole has some shaping tricks," Jace said. "What was your item?"

"A boomerang," Trotter said. "Always came back, no matter how terrible the throw or how much I moved. A statue caught it and broke it."

"Anything else we should know before we go?" Cole asked the statue.

"You have the message," the statue said.

"What message?" Trotter asked.

"Be glad you don't have to worry about it," Jace said.

"Do we need to go outside?" Cole asked Violet.

"I'm not sure," Violet said. "My power went dead when you blasted those statues."

Cole hadn't consciously noticed breaking the connection. "Right," he said, touching her hand.

"I can see our way out now," Violet said. "The defenses are down. Back to the *Vulture*?"

"We should let Wenzel know we made it," Jace said.

The bars of the cell retracted into the floor.

A shimmering distortion appeared.

"Is that a wayport?" Trotter asked.

"She's a Wayminder," Jace said.

"But she can't open a wayport here," Trotter said. "Not in Sambria."

Jace hushed him, a finger to his lips. "Don't tell her."

"Thanks," Cole said to the statue.

The replica of Dandalus gave a nod.

Cole stepped through onto the deck of the *Vulture*. The others joined him, and the wayport closed.

"Is that Trotter?" Wenzel exclaimed. Several other members of the crew shouted welcomes.

"Sorry it took me so long," Trotter said with a wave.

"We assumed you were long gone," Wenzel said.

"I was locked up," Trotter said.

"We should go right to Skyport," Cole told Violet.

A wayport opened.

Jace placed a hand on Trotter's shoulder. "Come with us. I have an idea."

They all went through. This time Violet had placed the wayport not far from the entrance to Skyport. The four of them hurried into the common room.

"Back already?" Adam boomed. "And ahead of the *Vulture*! Bless my beard, is that Trotter? What were chances? Good to see you, lad. Cole, I trust you found what you were looking for?"

"Yes, thanks," Cole said.

"I'm laying claim to Trotter," Jace said.

Cole's eyebrows shot up. He hadn't thought of the idea, but it was a good one—a chance to free another boy from this dangerous life.

Adam sniffed and shifted on his throne. "Listen, pup, I paid good money for Trotter. He has now finished twenty missions even. Thirty remain before he moves up from scout."

"We don't work for you," Jace said. "The crew of the *Vulture* left him behind. We salvaged him."

Adam scowled. "The Sky Raiders had a claim to that castle."

"I didn't see a flag," Jace said. "The claim is lost when a castle is abandoned."

"You got to the castle on one of my vessels," Adam protested, sounding less certain.

"Actually, after the *Vulture* brought us near, we arrived and got home without your skycraft," Jace said. "No claim was made for the Sky Raiders when we visited the castle this time. Not a single Sky Raider set foot on the property. And we had no agreement with you to share salvage."

Adam frowned and nodded. "Valid points. Seeing as how Cole is helping with financial reparations from the High King, I'll concede the issue. Trotter, you are proof that fortune can turn. You now belong to these three."

"And I don't believe in slavery," Jace said. "Adam, can you have his slavemark canceled?"

"I can arrange that."

Trotter looked astonished. "Really? I'm free? Just like that?"

"You're welcome," Jace said.

Cole looked at Jace, impressed. It felt good to know they had freed a slave. Really good. Cole quietly resolved to look for the chance to free more.

Trotter glanced at Adam. "Do you mind if I stay on as a free partner?"

"Partner takes time," Adam said. "But if you want to continue as a free raider or as a hired hand, the door is open."

Trotter raised both fists. "Yes! I can't believe it!" He turned to Cole, Jace, and Violet. "How can I ever thank you? I was doomed. Now . . . I have a brand-new life. I'm forever in your debt."

Jace looked around the common room. "I know this place seems like everything right now, but keep in mind there is an enormous world out there. And you are free to explore it. Enjoy it while you can."

"Thanks for the tip about the castle," Cole said to Adam. "It will help our cause. And thanks for the sword."

"Always happy to do business," Adam said.

"Where to now?" Violet wondered.

"Do you know a village called Kasori?" Cole asked. "In Elloweer?"

"Sure," Violet said. "A grinaldi village. That seems obscure."

"I want to catch up with an old friend," Cole said. He took her hand.

Violet opened a wayport.

Jace waved at Adam. "Stop exploiting children."

Then he stepped through.

CHAPTER 10

TWITCH

From the moment Cole stepped out of the wayport, he could see why Twitch had missed his home. Sunlight shone from a mostly clear sky onto a pastoral blend of fields and groves. The dwellings were simple but tidy—the stone houses on the ground, the wooden ones on stilts or in the largest trees. Neat gardens adjoined the dwellings, many with fruit trees, and one large wheat field was in view.

"What devilry is this?" cried a cranky voice as Violet closed the wayport. "Strangers stepping out of thin air! With the swamp folk, are you? Explain yourselves!"

The complainer was a scrawny old man almost a head shorter than Cole with a sparse white beard and the legs of a grasshopper. Just like Twitch, a pair of antennae projected from his forehead. He shook a knobby walking stick in their direction to punctuate his words.

"We're friends," Cole said, raising empty hands.

"A friend wearing a sword," the old man spat. "Marauders more likely. You better turn tail and magic yourselves away afore our knight gets wind of you. Chop you down to size, he will."

"We like the grinaldi," Cole insisted. "We're friends with Twitch! I mean, Ruben. Do you know Ruben?"

The crinkly scowl deepened. "Do I know Ruben? I practically raised the boy! The lad did chores for me. Mostly paid him in apple butter and sweet cakes. Don't speak that name like it proves anything. Everyone in the region wants to be friends with Ruben. Big hero. Who doesn't want to join a parade? Be part of the fun?"

"We've known him for a while," Cole said.

"Bah!" the man said. "I knew him afore he opened his eyes! Never seen any of you around here before. Especially when times were ugly. I reckon you're scavengers at best."

"We helped him find Minimus," Cole said politely. "The little knight."

"Don't start underestimating little," the old man warned, shaking his stick again. "Is that a jab at me? I can still out-jump any ten humans, big or small."

Jace stepped forward. "Do you know where we can find Ruben?"

"Now we're getting to it," the old man said, taking a couple hops backward. "Assassins, are you? Come to destroy our deliverer?"

"We really are good friends with Ruben," Cole said. "He met us during his wanderings. We helped each other. He'll vouch for us."

The old man shook his head. "Strangers that appear asking questions ought to disappear twice as quickly. Our knight will cut you down faster than a bee sting."

A female grinaldi hopped into view, landing near the old man. Young, slender, and pretty, she looked no older than Violet. "You be polite, Granddad. They answered your questions patiently."

The old man grunted. "Polite? I saw what polite got us with the swamp folk! Got us kicked out of our homes and working our own land like slaves."

"These aren't swamp folk," she said. "You can see that."

"Worse than swamp folk, if you ask me," the old man said, looking them up and down. "Swamp ghosts, appearing out of empty air. Swamp wizards come for vengeance."

"Do you think ghosts would stand there taking all this abuse from you?" the girl asked. "Or wizards? Or assassins?"

"That's how they get you," the old man griped. "Lure you in with honey. You reach out a hand of fellowship, and they stick in the knife."

"Or they are polite friends of Ruben inquiring after him," the girl said.

"Bah," the old man grunted, turning away. "Don't say I didn't warn you."

Looking around, Cole noticed several grinaldi coming out of hiding. They appeared around tree trunks, rose out of fields, and peered out of windows.

"I'm Chuli," the girl said. "First time in Kasori?"

"Yes," Cole said. "We really are just looking for Ruben."

"Look how many there are!" Jace exclaimed, turning around. "Did you all hide when I came through? Or were you already hiding?"

"We took cover when we saw the air turn funny," Chuli said. "Then you appeared."

"That was fast," Jace said. "No wonder Twitch—I mean, Ruben—likes to hide. You guys are experts."

"You can find Ruben at the Wallows," Chuli said.

"We don't know where—" Cole began.

"Down the main village road, past the central storehouse on the left," Violet piped up.

"That's right," Chuli said.

"Really?" Jace asked.

Violet shrugged. "It was on the map."

"You have a map of Kasori?" Jace asked.

"The Wayminder archives do." Violet tapped her temple. "Good memory."

"I can guide you," Chuli offered.

"Okay," Cole said.

She led them to a little lane and turned down it, passing dwellings on the ground and in trees. They saw no other grinaldi.

"Is everyone hiding?" Jace asked.

"We were careful about strangers before the swamp folk took over," Chuli said. "Our oppressors might be gone, but if anything, we're even more cautious than before. You don't have to fight what can't find you."

"Doesn't that leave your homes vulnerable?" Jace asked.

"Minimus has been training us how to attack out of hiding," Chuli said. "It plays to our strengths. Much more effective than direct aggression."

"Are the swamp folk completely gone?" Cole asked.

"Yes," Chuli said. "The big battle happened here in Kasori after Minimus defeated Renford Poleman, their champion. Renford's knights from other villages came after Minimus until none were left. The surviving swamp folk returned to their rafts, and Minimus became champion of all our villages."

"So things are good now?" Cole asked.

Chuli did her best to smile. "So much better than it was." She looked away. "But many of our people were lost in the fighting."

Up ahead appeared a large, low building made of mortared stone.

"The storehouse?" Jace asked.

"The Wallows is just a little farther," Chuli said.

Beyond the storehouse they left the lane for a trail. Cole began to notice a new humidity in the air along with the rich smell of damp earth. As they passed through a stand of trees, several large pools of dark mud came into view. Some had puddles on the surface. Heat radiated from the nearest, and steam rose from a few. Several grinaldi waded or lounged in two of the larger mud pools.

"Hot springs?" Cole asked.

"Mud springs," Jace corrected.

"The Wallows," Chuli said with a smile. "The most relaxing haven in all the villages."

Violet scrunched her face. "It looks filthy."

"Of course," Chuli said.

"What's relaxing about filthy?" Violet asked.

"You'll know if you try it," Chuli assured her. "Ruben

is this way, in the Governor's Wallow. It's reserved for the aldermen."

"Ruben is an alderman?" Cole asked.

"More or less," Chuli said. "As champion, Minimus appoints the aldermen. Ruben is his first knight. In some ways that makes him more powerful than the aldermen. And he's younger than I am!"

"Scrawnier too," Jace said.

"And he's saved our lives more than once," Cole said pointedly.

"Here we are," Chuli said, speaking more quietly.

Broad-leafed plants ringed the mud pool where Twitch reclined. Nestled within a smaller and deeper pit than the others, this wallow had the blackest, slickest mud and the most pungent smell. Twitch rested near the bottom, alone, at the edge of where the mud pool leveled out, pink flower petals over his eyes. Only his chest, arms, and head remained above the muck. A female grinaldi climbed out of the pit carrying an empty cup, grasshopper legs muddy to the thighs.

"Did she just bring him a drink?" Jace murmured.

"This is the fanciest wallow," Chuli whispered.

The woman emerging from the wallow approached them, eyeing Cole, Jace, and Violet uncertainly. "Access to this wallow is by invitation only."

"Twitch is our friend," Cole said quietly. "I mean Ruben. Can we surprise him?"

"The first knight needs time to meditate and relax," the woman insisted. "There is a protocol to—"

"Hey, Twitch!" Jace called, stripping off his shirt.

Rolling over, Twitch wiped the petals off his face and looked up. His eyes brightened. "Jace! Cole! What are you doing here?"

"We didn't want you to be the only one lazing around in the mud," Jace said, unlacing his shoes.

"I'm sorry, Lord Ruben," the woman apologized.

"No need," Twitch said. "These are my friends! Come on in!"

"Looks like you can take it from here," Chuli told Cole.

"Thanks," Cole replied. He turned to Violet. "Want to go in?"

She stared at the dark mud in horror. "Why?"

"Warm and squishy," Jace said, yanking off his pants. Clad only in his undershorts, he jumped from the edge, plunging into the mud almost to his thighs. Scrambling forward, Jace plopped down by Twitch, spattering him.

Cole started taking off his shoes. "Looks kind of fun."

"Yep!" Jace confirmed. "Warm and squishy!"

"I'll just . . . stay dressed," Violet said. "And, you know, relatively clean."

Cole felt a little embarrassed stripping down to his underwear, but Jace had set the example, and he didn't love the idea of ruining his clothes. He waded down into the warm mud, feeling it slurp between his toes, first sinking to his shins, then to his knees. Toward the bottom of the pit the mud got soupier, and he sank almost to his waist.

"Hey, Cole," Twitch said. "Don't go in farther or you might get stuck. Plus, it gets a little too hot out toward the center. Come relax at the edge of the deep part."

Cole settled in on the opposite side of Twitch from Jace, resting his shoulders on an incline of firm mud. The goopier mud covered him halfway up his chest, warm but not hot. "You're missing out," Cole called up to Violet.

"I'm going to let you have all the fun this time," Violet said.

"She's a Wayminder?" Twitch asked.

"Only way to travel," Jace said.

Twitch started blinking and gave a weak smile. "She can't travel from here, though."

"Actually she can," Cole said. "When I energize her with my power, she can open ways anywhere."

Twitch blinked faster, and his lips quivered a bit. "No kidding? So, you guys aren't dead, huh?"

"Lots of near misses," Jace said. "Zeropolis was bad. Necronum even worse. And we just barely survived a sky castle. Made me think of you."

"Sky castle?" Twitch asked. "Why would you return to the Brink?"

"I needed a new Jumping Sword," Cole said. "Then we got talked into checking out a castle. We ended up with some good info."

"And now you're here," Twitch said, still blinking a lot.

"We wanted to check up on you," Jace said. "Make sure you were getting plenty of toasty mud baths while we were off risking our necks."

"I saw some fighting too," Twitch said.

"I heard Minimus defeated Renford, and you guys drove out the swamp folk," Cole said.

Twitch shivered. "It was quite a battle. At least we won."

"Zig told me you helped rally the grinaldi," Cole said. "You dropped Renford's brother."

Twitch jerked in surprise. "Wait, Zig? How did you talk to Zig? He died not long after the battle."

"I was in the echolands," Cole said. "I met his echo and got news about you."

Twitch gave an impressed whistle. "Really? The echolands? You *have* been traveling. How was Zig?"

"Well, you know, dead," Cole said. "But otherwise he seemed well. He was in a place reserved for heroes."

"Was it a mud pit?" Jace asked.

"A little cleaner," Cole said. "Where's Minimus?"

"Wenachi," Twitch said. "He travels between the villages. Makes sure things run smoothly. Trains fighters. He takes his job as champion seriously. Minimus told me the grinaldi feel like the family he never had. I didn't know if he would want to stay on after the trouble was over, but for now he seems really content."

"Not as content as you lounging in the mud all day," Jace said.

Twitch gave a guilty smile. "I don't just do this. I sometimes help Minimus train our fighters. I lead gathering expeditions. Everyone has been really good to me since we kicked out the swamp folk, but sometimes the attention becomes a little much." He lowered his voice. "The Wallows are warm and cozy, but I mostly come here to hide."

"Attention from who?" Jace asked, splashing some mud at Twitch. "The ladies?"

Twitch's antennae quivered, and he hunkered lower in the mud. "A little, yeah, even though I'm too young for all that. Just everyone. I have aldermen asking for my advice. Farmers wanting my opinion. I brought a knight who kicked out the swamp folk. That doesn't make me an expert in harvests or planting or managing a village."

"So you fake it," Jace said. "Leaders all fake it. Why not boss everyone around? Maybe you'll end up king!"

Twitch rolled his eyes. "I don't want any of that. I just want . . . I don't know . . ."

"To nap in the mud?" Jace suggested.

"To live a normal life," Twitch said.

"Weak," Jace mocked. "Boring. Want to come with us to Creon to stop a torivor?"

Twitch cringed and looked to Cole.

"We are kind of here to recruit you," Cole said.

"Did he say a torivor?" Twitch asked. "Like Trillian?"

Cole quietly explained about Ramarro. Twitch listened solemnly.

"You're talking about the end of the world," Twitch said when Cole had finished.

"Pretty much," Cole said. "Unless we do something about it."

Twitch shook his head. "Why us? What are we supposed to do? Isn't there somebody else?"

"Nobody has a power like mine," Cole said. "When I use my ability on a Wayminder, we can go anywhere. We've defeated some tough stuff, Twitch. Dandalus encouraged me to try. The High King sponsored me for the mission as well. Gave me authority to speak in his name and everything."

"The High King helped you?" Twitch marveled.

"He's worried about the end of the world," Cole said.

Twitch rubbed his chin. "What could I do?"

"You're part of the team," Cole said. "You've saved us more than once. We never forgot you. We just didn't know how to find you."

Twitch closed his eyes. His eyelids fluttered. "We could disappoint the whole world."

"We could save the world," Cole said. "We can't count on anybody else to do it. And if we fail, it isn't any worse than doing nothing. We'd fail that way for sure."

Twitch blinked a lot and nodded. "You're right. Not much sense in doing nothing if we have a chance to keep the torivor locked up. Even a tiny chance."

"We'll be trying to find Wayminders who can help," Cole said. "Grand Shapers. We have some clues on where to look."

Twitch sighed. "I was really worried I would never see you guys again. And I was really worried I *would* see you guys again."

"This is worse, right?" Jace said. "Don't you wish we were dead?"

"No," Twitch said. His eyes grew still. "But it's scary."

"Would you prefer a torivor showing up and destroying your people?" Cole asked. "Or enslaving them? Is that less scary?"

Twitch clenched his jaw and shook his head. "No. Scary or

not, I'm willing to protect my village. My family. My people."

"Then what are we sitting here for?" Jace asked.

"Squishy and warm," Twitch said.

Jace nodded. "True."

Twitch stood up. "But I know another pool where we can wash off."

CHAPTER
— 11 —

JENNA

Cole had done his best to wring out his underwear but still felt a little damp beneath his pants when he returned to the parlor in the First Castle. Evening had fallen by the time Twitch finished his good-byes. The fancy room in Harmony's tower was dim and empty.

"I can't believe I'm inside the First Castle," Twitch said. He looked like a human again. Cole had almost forgotten that outside of Elloweer, Twitch lost his grinaldi features and became human unless he used his enchanted pendant. "You guys really know Queen Harmony?"

"She's Mira's mom," Jace said.

"I know," Twitch said. "That's different from actually meeting her."

"Cole is now an agent for the High King," Jace said. "Stick with us—you'll go places."

"Want to do one more trip tonight?" Cole asked Violet. "Just you and me?"

"Do you ever rest?" she asked.

"I don't know how much time we have," Cole said. "We're racing the end of the world."

"Why just the two of you?" Jace asked. "Looking for some romance?"

"No!" Cole said, glancing uncomfortably at Violet. "I thought you and Twitch would rather get settled."

"What are you up to?" Twitch asked.

"I want to find Dalton and Hunter," Cole said.

"Hunter?" Twitch asked.

Cole explained that he had found his older brother, who had been working as a feared Enforcer called the Hunter before changing sides.

"Do you know where to look?" Jace asked.

"They were going to try to check on Jenna," Cole said. "I thought I could try the Temple of the Still Water."

"Mystery solved," Jace said. "You want time with Jenna!"

"Who's Jenna?" Violet asked.

"The girl Cole likes," Jace said.

"No," Cole said, shuffling his feet. "I used to like her. I had a crush on her. It's different now. I'm mostly just worried about her. She was taken from our home by slavers with other kids from my neighborhood."

"She's at some temple?" Twitch asked.

"I saw her at the Temple of the Still Water when I was an echo," Cole said.

"Back to Necronum?" Violet asked. "We did a shrine. I've always wanted to see one of their temples."

"You go romance Jenna," Jace said. "We'll find the queen." He led Twitch out of the room.

"It's not a romance," Cole said.

"Can't be much of one," Violet said. "You don't even have your first whiskers."

"I had strong feelings for Jenna without really knowing her," Cole said. "The crush was in my mind. She was pretty and we were friends. The friend part is the most important now."

"Think the temple will still be standing?" Violet asked, taking Cole's hand and receiving an energy boost.

"I hope so," Cole said. "Owandell wants the princesses. I'm not sure he even knows about Jenna. And I'm not sure how much he cares about Dalton or Hunter."

The wayport opened, a glimmering oval in the dim light. "Ladies first?" Cole offered.

"I'd rather know you're through so I'll be sure I can get back," Violet said. "No offense."

Cole stepped through and emerged outside the temple. The fading sunset had already allowed the brightest stars to appear. The temple was not particularly tall but extremely broad, built with wavy shapes and rounded edges. Violet arrived beside him. The large gate was shut.

"Is that the front?" Cole asked.

"Looks closed," Violet said.

"Let's go see," Cole replied, walking forward.

A guard emerged from a gatehouse as they approached. He wore a breastplate and rested one hand on the hilt of the sword at his waist. The guard tipped his hat. "Good evening, esteemed Wayminder. The temple gates closed at sundown."

"We're here on business from the High King," Cole said, producing the seal.

The guard took a close look, and his face reacted with shock. "That's the royal seal!"

"I'm his agent," Cole said.

The guard saluted. "Can I arrange a meeting for you, sir?"

"How about the prelate?" Cole asked.

"As you wish," the guard said. He thumped the gate. "Open in the name of the king!"

"It's past sundown," a voice replied from above.

"An agent of the High King seeks admittance," the guard called.

"Here?" the voice answered. "Now? Unannounced? Are you sure, Walter?"

"He showed up with a Wayminder," Walter said. "It's the royal seal, jewels and all."

The gate opened.

Walter had another guard take his place in the gatehouse and then escorted Cole and Violet to a waiting room inside the temple. He excused himself, promising to return shortly.

"That seal works wonders," Violet said.

"I was a little worried he might think it was fake," Cole said. "I'm just a kid."

"The guardsmen and legionnaires are well trained in matters of rank," Violet said. "And a Wayminder adds authenticity. We're known for our honesty. Though it undermines us a bit that I'm so young too."

Walter returned and led them to a simple, elegant room, where a slender man in a soft, dark robe awaited them. He greeted them sedately. "Welcome to the Temple of the Still Water. I am the prelate, Harward Aza. I understand you are servants of the High King?"

Cole showed the seal. "I'm his agent, yes—call me Cole—and this is my colleague Violet."

"Greetings, worthy Wayminder," the prelate said. "May I inquire what business brings you to our temple this fine evening?"

"The king has interest in a slave called Jenna," Cole said. "She arrived here from Junction several weeks ago."

"I know the girl," Harward said. "A competent weaver."

"I need an interview with her," Cole said.

"Easily granted," the prelate said. "May I ask what this concerns? Is she a threat?"

"No," Cole said, recalling that some weavers were good at detecting falsehoods. He needed to keep his words true but vague. "She has important connections. If she is willing to work with me, the High King wants her freedom granted."

The prelate's demeanor grew a little colder. "She came at a price."

"You will get twice what you paid," Cole said.

Harward nodded. "A reasonable offer. I foresee no problem with this arrangement. May I ask . . . You seem young to hold so much responsibility. I am surprised I have not heard of your ascension to this office."

"It happened recently," Cole said. "I'm sure you'll hear about me before long." Cole felt tempted to offer his shaping powers as a reason for the instatement but decided people with real power didn't tend to offer big explanations.

"Would you mind if I take a closer look at the seal?" Harward asked.

"No problem," Cole said. He could tell the prelate was suspicious.

Harward leaned forward and shut one eye, fingering the medallion. He nodded, then backed up and gave a slight bow. "You will need accommodations for tonight?"

"No, thanks," Cole said. "We'll leave after we meet with Jenna."

"As you will," the prelate said. "Follow me."

Cole could tell the prelate remained a little skeptical. It also seemed that Harward had been shown enough evidence not to ask more questions for now. Cole hoped the High King would get word around the five kingdoms about his appointment. The seal would hold more power if people actually believed him.

Harward excused himself after introducing Cole and Violet to an older woman named Gilda, who oversaw the enslaved female weavers. Gilda led Cole and Violet through a set of ornate doors to a spacious room with a floor of pale marble. Statues stood about the room. Several chairs and divans offered a variety of places to sit. Silver accented many of the furnishings.

"This late in the evening the silver sanctum is all yours," Gilda said. "You can hold your interview here without being disturbed. While I fetch Jenna, please, make yourselves comfortable." She indicated a bowl of grapes beside a carafe of water and left.

"I don't think Harward trusts us," Violet said, plucking a

grape from the basket and popping it into her mouth.

"I'm young," Cole said. "He's never heard of me. It must look shady."

"*I'm* still suspicious," Violet said with a grin. "Can I see that seal again?"

"Very funny."

"Shouldn't be as big of a problem in Creon," Violet said. "Wayminders get full respect there."

"Even teenage ones?" Cole asked.

"Especially teenage ones," Violet said. "It means I'm gifted."

"People never gave you a hard time because of your age?" Cole asked.

Violet scrunched her brow. "I'm not sure."

"You didn't notice?" Cole asked.

"I can't remember very well," Violet said.

"How young were you?"

"I came to Junction a little more than a year ago."

"That's too long to remember?"

Violet slapped her forehead. "You're from Outside and you've never been to Creon."

"Right."

"You don't know about the mindscreen."

"What's that?"

"When you leave Creon, you forget a lot of what happened there," Violet said. "Especially specifics."

"Really?" Cole asked. "Do you remember your family?"

"You remember people," Violet said. "You remember how you feel about them more than specific things you did or said. You remember vocabulary and how to swim, but you forget stories and accomplishments."

"What about all your geography?" Cole asked.

"I had to relearn it," Violet said. "I was good at geography in Creon, so I relearned quickly."

"Still . . . that must be frustrating," Cole said.

Violet shrugged. "It's the price of being a Wayminder outside of Creon. A lot of what I know about Creon was learned at the school in Junction, not remembered."

"Will you remember when you go back?" Cole asked.

"Yes, everything," Violet said.

"Will I forget stuff?" Cole asked.

"You don't forget coming in," Violet said. "Only going out. We believe the founders of Creon designed it that way so you can't send information back in time and have it leave Creon."

"Because people can time travel in Creon," Cole said.

"Yes. Not frequently, or easily, but yes. The time travel doesn't stick when you leave Creon. If I took you to Creon right now, and you went back in time a hundred years, stayed a week, then left Creon, you would find yourself a week from now. You stay linked to the timestream in the rest of the Outskirts no matter how far back you go in Creon."

"So why would they need to wipe your memory?" Cole asked.

"If you went back in time and gave information to somebody a hundred years ago in Creon, and if that person left Creon, it would still be a hundred years ago for him or her, because the person fully belongs to that time. But because of the mindscreen, anyone you told wouldn't remember the message when they left Creon."

"Write it down," Cole said.

Violet smiled. "Smart. Except the writing in Creon doesn't translate when it leaves Creon. However you normally write outside of Creon, inside Creon, it always comes out in Creonese. And outside of Creon, the same power that translates all languages in the Outskirts into a universal tongue leaves Creonese incomprehensible."

"They planned well," Cole said.

"Some Wayminders theorize that the mindscreen may not have been deliberate. They speculate the mindscreen and the barriers to written communication might have been an unavoidable consequence of placing a kingdom where time travel is possible beside kingdoms where time is inflexible."

"Now my brain is hurting," Cole said.

"It's you!" came a voice from across the room.

Cole turned to find Jenna hurrying toward him. With her hood down, the wavy curls of her dark hair spilled across the shoulders of her silver robe. Gilda had not returned, but an old woman with a kindly face followed behind Jenna.

"Hi, Jenna," Cole said, catching her in a tight hug.

"You're not an echo this time," she said, hugging back.

"Alive and in person," Cole said, releasing the embrace. "This is Violet. She's a Wayminder."

"Hello," Jenna said with a little curtsy. "We don't see many Wayminders here."

"Have you seen any?" Violet asked.

"You're the first," Jenna admitted.

"Who is the lady?" Cole asked quietly.

"This is Granny Helki," Jenna said. "She's the echo I spend the most time with."

"We're like family," Helki said in a sugary voice, smiling sweetly. "And how do you know my Jenna?"

Now that Cole looked closely, he could see that the old woman was faintly translucent. "We're old friends," he said.

Helki's smile suddenly looked more forced. "How charming."

"Did you find Dalton and Hunter?" Jenna asked.

"Not yet," Cole said.

"They're looking for you," Jenna said.

"You saw them?" Cole exclaimed.

"I thought that might be why you came by," Jenna said. "They were just here yesterday."

"Really?" Cole said, then glanced at Helki. He stepped closer to Jenna. "Should we maybe talk in private?"

"No use in whispering," Helki said. "I have superb hearing."

"She knows they were here," Jenna said. "I trust her."

Cole felt uncertain. "I have some sensitive info for you. It could put Helki in danger."

"Then it could put my Jenna in danger," Helki said. "Darling, why not return to our project?"

"What project?" Cole asked.

"She's teaching me to crochet," Jenna said. "I'm working on a scarf."

"Jenna has a golden touch," Helki proclaimed.

"Do you know where Dalton and Hunter went?" Cole asked.

"They didn't get specific," Jenna said. "They thought it could endanger me. But I know they were looking for you."

"Any idea what direction they went?" Violet asked.

"I really don't know," Jenna said. "They promised to come back for me when things are more settled."

Cole rubbed his forehead. "That's frustrating. I was really hoping to find them."

"You can leave a message with me in case they come back," Jenna said.

"Unless you want to leave with us," Cole said.

"She is a slave of this temple, young man," Helki said. "Illegalities are unacceptable. A runaway slave faces execution."

"I don't mean as a runaway," Cole said. "I talked with the prelate. I'm an agent of the High King. I have permission to free you."

"Really?" Jenna said, hope and disbelief at war in her gaze.

"Sounds like a lot to swallow," Helki said. "Jenna, dear, are you sure you trust this ragamuffin?"

"Absolutely," Jenna said.

"It's true," Cole said. "You're free."

Jenna threw her arms around Cole. "Thank you! I can hardly believe it." She released him. "But how did you become an agent to the High King? I didn't think you were exactly on his side."

"We all have a bigger enemy now," Cole said. "Helki, have you heard of Nazeem?"

"Jenna, dear, you don't want to get involved with this scoundrel," Helki said. "I know the type. He's talking about foolishness you don't want in your life."

"Nazeem is incredibly powerful," Cole said. "He escaped the echolands. He's temporarily trapped, but if he gets free, the entire Outskirts is toast."

"Are you trying to stop him?" Jenna asked in wonder.

"Yeah," Cole said. "Your echo friend is right that you don't want to get mixed up in that."

"First reasonable thought of the night," Helki muttered.

"Do *you* have to be mixed up in it?" Jenna asked.

"It's me or nobody," Cole said. "I'm in deep. I have to see it through. The question is what you want to do. I could free you, and you could stay here. It's really easy to get to you now. I have a special way of traveling."

"We see the Wayminder," Helki said. "That can get you here quickly. But it's a one-way journey."

"Not really for me," Cole said. "I have other options."

"Is he talking sense?" Helki asked.

"Yes," Violet confirmed. "We have some unusual methods of traveling together."

"It means you could stay here, and we can come back for you no problem," Cole said. "Or we could take you to the First Castle, and you can wait with Queen Harmony."

"I have heard some whopping tales in my time," Helki murmured.

"All true," Violet verified. "Cole directly serves the High King. I'm with him by request of the queen."

"What do you think I should do?" Jenna asked.

"It depends where you would be more comfortable," Cole said. "We'll be off trying to stop Nazeem. Do you like it here?"

"She loves it here," Helki assured him. "Jenna is an extremely gifted summoner. She belongs in Necronum. She has a future here. It would be cruel to tear her from her home and her loved ones."

"I really do have friends here," Jenna said. "If I wasn't a slave, it would be about as good as I could hope for. Plus, Dalton and Hunter may come back here looking for me. I want to help you find them if I can. I think I should stay."

"Makes sense," Cole said.

"You've got that right, buster," Helki said with a sniff.

"Be nice," Jenna told Helki. "He's my friend." She faced Cole. "She's protective."

"I noticed," Cole said.

"Is Hunter really your brother?" Jenna asked.

"Yeah," Cole said. "I didn't remember him at first. He was taken before us, obviously, so we forgot him. He remembers me, though. He's awesome in a fight. In the echolands a powerful lady helped me find some memories of him."

"He seemed great," Jenna said. "And it was so good to see Dalton. Good job rounding us up!"

"I've been trying," Cole said.

Violet covered a yawn. "Sorry. Long day."

"We should probably get going," Cole said. "There's so much to do."

Jenna hugged him again. "Am I really free?"

"Yes," Cole said. "I'm not sure how much good it will do you if you're just staying here."

"Lots of good," Jenna said. "I can get paid. I can advance. I can come and go when I want."

"I just have to finalize the details," Cole said.

"You're a miracle worker, Cole," Jenna said. "Thank you so much. You're going to be out there fighting Nazeem?"

"Hopefully not fighting him," Cole said. "Hopefully just keeping him contained."

"You're incredible," Jenna said. "Be careful. Keep me updated."

"You bet," Cole said, feeling pleased and a little shy. He didn't feel as giddily attracted to Jenna as he once had, but he still cared about her and appreciated her praise. "We'll confirm everything with the prelate on our way out. I'll see you again soon, unless, you know . . ."

"He visits as an echo," Helki said.

Jenna shook her head. "You can do it. I'll see you soon."

Cole gave a tight smile. "You're the first person who thinks I have a chance."

"Perhaps because she doesn't understand what you're up against," Helki said. "Take care not to drag her further into it."

"I'm glad you're watching out for her," Cole said. "Stay alert, Helki. Scary times are coming. Watch out for Enforcers. Any controlled by Owandell are working for Nazeem."

"We'll be careful," Jenna promised.

"Tell Dalton and Hunter to wait here if they come back," Cole said. "We'll check in again before too long."

"I'll be waiting," Jenna said. "Nice to meet you, Violet."

"Same," Violet said.

"Bye," Cole said.

He and Violet walked away.

CHAPTER
12

THE IRON FORT

"I'm coming with you," Mira announced as she entered the room where Cole sat eating his breakfast.

"Good morning," Cole said, taking another bite of his omelet.

"Sure, hi!" she said with an edge. "Tasty eggs? How's the weather? Aren't we in a hurry?"

"Who knows when I'll get another breakfast this good?" Cole replied.

"Whenever you want," Mira said. "With you around, Violet can open unlimited wayports. We can come back and eat here every morning."

"You're right," Cole said, wiping his lips with a fabric napkin. "I guess I don't have to completely stuff myself."

"Everyone else is ready," Mira said.

"I was hungry!" Cole said. "I slept in. I was up late."

"What about the big race against the end of the world?" Mira said. "Never mind. We'll wait. Want anything else? A soufflé?"

"I worked hard yesterday. I'll work hard today." Cole wiped his lips and chin. "I'm done. I'm glad you're coming with us. Is your mom really okay with it?"

"She tried to talk me out of it. I reminded her that we're top targets if Ramarro gets free. Trying to stop him beats hiding."

"Makes sense to me," Cole said.

"It did to her, too," Mira said. "She's just scared. And worn out from so much worry. I think this has been harder on her than on any of us. In the end I asked if I was supposed to be her prisoner to match Father holding Honor and Destiny."

Cole winced. "How'd she take that?"

"She cried," Mira said. "But I have permission to go."

Cole finished a glass of apple juice and stood. "Then let's go."

Mira led him back to the parlor where they had first entered the tower together. Jace, Violet, Twitch, and Harmony awaited them.

"Hi, guys," Cole said. "Sorry to keep you waiting."

Violet jerked her head toward the queen.

Cole gave a bow. "Hello, Your Highness."

"Greetings, Cole. I trust you rested well?"

"And had a good breakfast," Cole said. "How is Joe?"

"Stable," Harmony said. "It will be a couple of weeks before he should walk on that leg. My physician will keep him in prolonged sleep for the next few days to accelerate the healing."

"He might miss all the action," Jace said.

"How do I get involved in that plan?" Twitch asked.

Everyone laughed, and he smiled uncertainly.

"Can you keep an eye out for my friend Dalton and my brother, Hunter?" Cole asked Harmony. "They'll be looking for me. I missed them by a day when I visited Jenna last night in Necronum."

"How was Jenna?" Jace wondered.

"Very pretty," Violet said. "She appreciates Cole. Not much chemistry, though."

"Ouch," Cole said.

"She likes him," Violet said. "They're friends."

"I will watch for Dalton and Hunter and put out the word to my contacts," Harmony said. "Can I trust you to protect my Miracle? And to be careful with my Elegance?"

"I'll do my best," Cole promised.

"We all will," Jace assured her.

"Then you had better be off," Harmony said. "Come back often."

"We will," Mira promised.

"Violet, do you know how to approach the Iron Fort?" Harmony asked.

"I understand the basics, Your Highness," Violet said, "but I've never done it."

"What makes it tricky to approach?" Twitch asked.

"The walls of iron are not the main protection," Violet said. "The space around the Iron Fort has been shaped so that a Wayminder can't open a wayport into the fort or anywhere near it. If you try to walk or ride there, you will find the distance to it ever increasing."

"So how do we get there?" Jace asked.

"Access must be granted," Violet said. "I know where to go. I'm not sure how it works."

"Nor am I," Harmony said. She held up a sealed message. "This letter asks for admittance in my name. It should suffice. If not, Cole can use his status as an agent of the High King. Don't begin with that, since Elegance would resist anyone coming in the name of her father."

"We should go," Mira said.

"Give Elegance my love," Harmony said. "Return as soon as you can."

"We won't remember much of what happened in Creon when we check back in," Violet said.

"That's right," Harmony said. "The mindscreen. But at least I will know you are well."

"Thank you, Mother," Mira said, giving Harmony a hug. "I'll see you soon."

Violet opened a wayport near Cole.

"Off we go," Cole said.

One step later, he stood on a sandy expanse. Low dunes overlapped into the distance in all directions. Heat poured down from the morning sun and reflected up from the sand. Before him stood an ancient statue of a hooded snake, rising out of the sand as if prepared to strike, four times his height, most of the details worn smooth. Not far from the statue bloomed a large orange-and-yellow-striped tent, a blue pennant hanging limp at the top.

Jace came through the wayport, followed by Mira, Twitch, and finally Violet. Scanning all around, Cole saw no other signs of life—no buildings, no roads, no vegetation, no animals, no fences, no footprints. Certainly no iron fortress.

"Whoa," Violet said, raising one hand to her temple. "I just got a big chunk of my life back."

"Your memories?" Cole asked.

"It's like waking up," Violet said. "I wasn't ready for it to be so sudden. So much so quickly."

"Big snake," Jace said.

"A monument to the Perennial Serpent," Violet said. "Hundreds of years ago, it plagued Creon, unpredictably appearing and slaying whoever it encountered, usually Wayminders. It gets the blame for killing two Grand Shapers."

"Gets the blame?" Twitch asked.

"Witnesses don't tend to survive the Perennial Serpent," Violet said. "A lot of what we know is speculation. Educated guesses."

"Is it still around?" Mira asked.

Violet fished a couple of copper ringers from her robe and tossed them onto the sand near the statue. "Not for a couple hundred years."

"If you have too many ringers, I'll take them," Jace offered.

Violet smiled. "The monuments are used as warnings to intruders. And as superstitious petitions for the serpent to pass by a location." She tossed one more copper ringer onto the sand. "We can use all the luck we can get."

Jace shrugged. "You think it's lucky to throw away money? We were raised very differently."

"What about the tent?" Cole asked.

"That's where we're going," Violet said.

"Kind of flimsy iron," Jace said.

Violet rolled her eyes. "It's not the fort. Hopefully whoever is inside can grant access."

Cole followed Violet over to the tent, feet sinking halfway into the sand with each step. They huddled together near the flap covering the entrance.

"Hello?" Violet called. "We seek the Iron Fort."

"Enter," a voice replied.

Violet lifted the flap, and Cole stepped into the tent, the others right behind him. The coolness inside washed over him in stark contrast to the desert heat. Could it be air-conditioned? He didn't see any machinery.

A man and a woman stood toward the center of the generous space. They wore robes like Wayminders, but iron bands circled their foreheads, and veils hid their faces. Embroidered rugs covered the ground, with large pillows and cushions serving as furniture. Most incongruently, a stone fountain babbled near one silky wall.

"Have you an appointment?" the man inquired.

"No," Violet said.

"Visits to the retreat are handled only by appointment," the man replied swiftly.

"This is an emergency," Violet said.

The woman held up her hands. "What one might label an emergency, another might term a lack of preparation."

"Security is the top priority of the retreat," the man said. "Our protocols must be followed for the benefit of our clients."

"My sister lives there," Mira said.

143

"Many of our clients have relatives," the man said. "They all must adhere to our policies."

"I have a letter from the queen," Violet said, producing her document.

"Queen Harmony?" the man asked. He paused. "Let me see."

Violet approached with the letter. The man took it and looked it over. The woman slid aside her veil and leaned in close. A thin chain curved from one nostril to her earlobe.

The woman whispered to the man. He whispered back, then faced Violet. "My associate will take your document inside. Please back away toward the door."

Violet returned to stand by Cole.

"No hasty movements," the man said. "We're both ready to die and ready to kill you."

A wayport opened up, shining more brightly than any of the wayports Violet had opened. The woman stepped through, carrying the letter. The wayport closed behind her.

"Mind if I get a drink?" Jace asked. "The sound is making me so thirsty."

"Help yourself," the man said. "Use the ladle."

Jace went to the fountain and ladled water into an ornate bowl. He took a sip. Violet and Twitch joined him.

"Where does the water come from?" Mira asked.

"We keep a tiny wayport open to a distant lake," the man said.

"Is that how you keep the air cool?" Cole wondered.

"Two other small wayports to a pair of chilly locations," the man said.

"You have a conduit to the Iron Fort?" Violet wondered as she sipped water.

"As you might imagine," the man said.

"A conduit is like a permanent wayport," Violet explained. "Think of it like an established tunnel versus a temporary passage. The conduit must be the only practical way through the defenses."

"We can collapse it at any time," the man said.

The bright wayport reappeared, and the woman emerged. The wayport remained open.

"The Host wishes to meet them," the woman reported.

"You're not serious," the man said.

"That was an authentic request from Queen Harmony," the woman said. "Urgent undertones. The Host wants to know more."

"All of them?" the man replied.

"The Host is intrigued," the woman said.

The man shrugged. "Not my call." He waved at the wayport. "Go with Renni."

Violet entered first, then Mira, and then Cole. He emerged inside a spacious cage standing on light gray sand. After the cool of the tent, the heat was instantly uncomfortable. Beyond the bars of the cage loomed a gigantic wall of solid iron. Endless sharp-edged dunes extended in all other directions.

Jace came through the wayport, followed by Twitch and finally the woman. The wayport closed.

"Renni—reporting with the visitors!" the woman called out.

A new bright wayport opened up.

"One at a time," Renni said.

Violet stepped through.

Twitch sidled up next to Cole, his eyes on the bars of the cage. "If they didn't like who came through, you'd be in trouble."

Cole nodded. "You'd be an easy target with nowhere to run."

"Proceed," Renni said.

The others had gone through already. Cole passed through the wayport after Twitch and found himself in a windowless iron room lit by torches. Two armored guards faced him. Renni came through, and the wayport closed.

"Leave all weapons here," one guard said. "They will be returned when you exit."

Cole unbuckled his Jumping Sword. Mira gave up her Jumping Sword as well. Twitch turned in his short sword. Violet handed over a small knife, more a tool than a weapon. Jace made no move to surrender his rope.

The guards gave them all a pat down. Cole avoided staring at Jace in fear of making the guards suspicious. His golden rope was currently a small golden strand. It shouldn't even be able to work here. If the guards didn't know about Cole's power, there would be no reason to worry about the rope, even if they could tell it had been expertly shaped.

They all passed inspection, and another bright wayport opened. One by one they went through. Cole hung back until his friends had gone, then stepped through into a fancy office, where a gaunt man with a widow's peak sat behind an iron desk, large hands with long fingers laced in front of him on top of the document from the queen. Renni followed and closed the wayport.

"Queen Harmony endorses your visit," the gaunt man said briskly. "I am the Host at this retreat. My primary job is protecting our clients. Explain who you wish to see."

"My sister Elegance," Mira said.

"Ah," the Host said, leaning back in his chair. "You are one of the sisters."

"Miracle Pemberton," she said.

"You could have all taken refuge here," the Host said. "It would have been sensible."

"The idea was to spread us out," Mira said. "One in each kingdom. I need to see Elegance."

"So I have gathered," the Host said. He attempted a smile. It did not appear natural. "I have never been approached by a group composed entirely of children. Even the Wayminder is young. Was this supposed to appeal to my sentiment?"

"We're on a mission," Cole said.

The Host leaned forward, hands still clasped. "Such unlikely agents. Can it be as urgent as the queen insinuates?"

"It's vital," Mira said.

"You five were entrusted with a matter of supreme importance?" the Host asked. "Is there more to you than greets the eye? What would you do if I attempted to hold you here?"

"Seriously?" Jace asked.

"Seriously," the Host said, his smile looking more natural and a lot less friendly.

Jace held out his strand. Cole touched it and pushed

power into it. The golden rope shot out and snaked around the Host's neck, jerking him to his feet. Cole grabbed Violet, and she opened a wayport. Renni produced a knife, and the other end of the golden rope bound her hands and thrust her back against the wall.

Still smiling, the Host gave a chuckle. "Better than expected. I asked for this. Message received. Please release me."

The rope went slack and retracted. The Host rubbed his neck.

"I'm so sorry," Renni said.

"No apology required," the Host replied. "Would you release her as well? Stand down, Renni."

The rope unwound from her arms and shrank into a small golden strand.

"You opened a wayport so quickly?" the Host asked. "Where could it have led?"

"A lower level here in the fort," Violet said. "I couldn't feel a way out."

"Thankfully," the Host said. "Or else we would have needed to reconstruct our entire defensive scheme. You reached our arrival station by wayport only minutes ago."

"Yes," Violet said.

"What an unbelievably quick recovery from your previous efforts," the Host said.

Renni sank to her knees, head bowed. "I am ashamed. I do not know how——"

The Host held up a hand and interrupted. "No apology required. I still don't understand how they did it. You, boy, your name?"

"Cole."

"Cole, I am perplexed. Your power appears whole and untainted. Are you a shapecrafter? To my knowledge, only they can so flagrantly flout the natural order of shaping."

"No, but my power is unusual."

The Host gave a sharklike smile. "That puts it lightly. I don't suppose you are for hire."

"We really are on an urgent mission," Cole said.

"I believe you," the Host said. "I have a keen interest in world events. Intelligence supports effective security. Your secrets are safe here. Discretion is my specialty. Tell me the urgent matter, and I will grant the access you seek."

Cole found all of his friends looking at him. He saw no big reason to keep Ramarro a secret. The more who prepared to meet him the better. "A torivor is about to break free in Creon."

"There is no torivor in Creon," the Host said.

Cole held up a finger. "There *was* no torivor in Creon. A torivor named Ramarro recently escaped the echolands and was imprisoned here. The prison will not hold him long. In the echolands he went by Nazeem."

"Fascinating," the Host said slowly. "I have heard of this Nazeem. I gather information from all quarters. The name has been repeated in the echolands of late. It never occurred to me the name could belong to Ramarro. These are dire tidings."

"You mentioned shapecraft," Cole said. "The shape-crafters are our enemies. Ramarro taught them, starting with Owandell."

"All these pieces fit," the Host said. "This is the best intelligence I have heard in years. It demands my immediate attention. I not only grant you the access you seek, but I wish you well in your mission, and offer permission to return here if you have information to share or desire employment." He glanced at Renni. "That is all."

A new wayport appeared. Violet let hers close.

CHAPTER
13

ELEGANCE

In a quiet courtyard within the fort, flagstone paths meandered between lawns, flower beds, and shrubs. Led by Renni, Cole and his friends found Elegance near a still pond shaded by numerous trees with sprawling limbs.

Cole had previously seen Elegance in a simulated reality created by the torivor Trillian, but he was struck by her beauty as never before. Maybe it was her current hairstyle, or her flattering dress, or a knowing quality in her soulful eyes, but the sight of her made him secretly thrilled, and a little shy. Elegance had stopped aging around her eighteenth birthday, and she appeared fully grown. Tall and graceful, of all the princesses, she bore the clearest resemblance to Harmony.

Beside her sat an old man in a wheelchair made mostly of dark, polished wood. A blanket lay folded across his lap. What wispy white hair remained was neatly combed. Liver spots showed through on his partially bald scalp.

Elegance glided forward to greet her sister. "Miracle, I'm so relieved to find you well."

Cole didn't think her tone or manner seemed relieved. At best she seemed polite.

"Hi, Ella," Mira said.

"Elegance, dear, among company," Elegance said.

Mira rolled her eyes. "These are my friends, not company. And we're in a hideout, not our castle."

Elegance raised a chiding finger. "I know these are friends. Otherwise, I wouldn't publicly correct you."

"When have you ever resisted a chance to correct anyone?" Mira asked.

The old man in the wheelchair chuckled. Elegance shot him a glance. "Living among the barbarians need not mean living like the barbarians. Social graces matter. We can languish in exile and still live like royalty."

"Until you're being chased by Enforcers," Mira said.

"I've run from my share of Enforcers," Elegance assured her. "And I still behave as my station demands."

"That you have," said the old man in the wheelchair, gazing at her lovingly. "And that you do."

"This is Brogan Holt," Elegance said. "My protector ever since I went into hiding."

"I remember Brogan," Mira said. "I can't believe Mother paired him with you."

"I recall you, too, Mira," Brogan said, his voice a bit frail. "You haven't changed at all. Just like your sister. I've looked better."

"He's also my husband," Elegance said, a touch of defiance in her tone.

"Really?" Mira asked. "Mother is going to faint."

"Mother knows," Elegance asked. "Do you think I'd make a move like that unsanctioned?"

"We were wed twelve years after going into hiding," Brogan said.

"You were thirty," Elegance replied. "Aging while I didn't. We started out the same age. I turned eighteen the week we went into exile."

"Wait," Jace said. "You were put in charge of her when you were eighteen?"

The old man smiled. "We had no idea how young we were."

Cole couldn't help thinking the relationship was fairly strange—Elegance seemed much too youthful to have such an elderly husband. But Cole supposed it made sense since they'd started out the same age, and because, unlike her younger sisters, Elegance was mostly grown-up when she stopped aging. Even with excuses in mind, witnessing the extreme age gap between the couple was still a little unsettling.

"The name Brogan Holt would be known across the five kingdoms had he not become my protector," Elegance said. "He is without question the finest swordsman of his generation. He won the Harvest Tournament at sixteen and seventeen, the youngest to ever win it by five years."

"And by eighteen he was in exile," Cole said.

"Only one other knight ever won in back-to-back years," Elegance said, looking at the old man warmly. "Only two other knights won three times in their lifetimes. None won four. Brogan might have won it ten times. He only got better."

"Isn't sixteen young to enter the Harvest Tournament?" Twitch asked.

Brogan gave a chuckle.

"Unusually young, yes," Elegance said. "Each noble family in the kingdoms has an annual right to one entrant. Each puts forth their best champion—a seasoned knight from the household or an expert member of the family. Brogan's father was a lesser lord of the sort whose champions tend to get knocked out in the early rounds. Brogan showed great promise, and, without more impressive options, he got the nomination and won the most stunning string of upsets in memory. Contender after contender fell to him. Then the next year, with every competitor preparing specifically for him, he won again. He made it look easier the second time."

"It was easier," Brogan said from his chair. "I had grown some."

"My father added him to his personal guard," Elegance said. "But he became close with Mother."

"He became close with *you*," Mira said. "I still can't believe Mother sent you away with him."

Elegance glanced shyly at Brogan. "It was a desperate hour. Mother needed someone she could fully trust to protect me. I lobbied for Brogan and she agreed. And that choice almost certainly saved my life. I can't count how many times he rescued us with his sword."

"We had an adventure or two," Brogan said with a smile.

"You were young back then," Jace said. "But you don't look as old as you should be."

"It's why we came here," Elegance said. "We lived on

the run for years, affiliating with the Unseen. As sixty approached, Brogan was still the best fighter in the five kingdoms, but we were starting to realize he wasn't immortal."

"I never asked you to come here with me," Brogan said. "I wanted you to find a new protector and leave me behind."

Elegance crossed to Brogan and touched his shoulder. "I want all the time with you I can get. Being here has already prolonged your life at least twenty years. I'm hoping for thirty more."

Brogan gave a gentle huff. "Optimistic."

"We're dominating the conversation," Elegance said. "How have you been, Miracle? You look well."

"I have my power back," Mira said.

"In full?" Elegance asked.

"In full. All the sisters do. Except you."

"How?" Elegance asked, looking surprised.

"Have you felt your shaping returning?" Mira asked. "We've all experienced it to varying degrees."

"No," Elegance said. "Nothing. No difference."

"Are you sure?" Mira asked.

Elegance gave Mira a knowing glare. "Believe me, I would notice."

Mira recited how Owandell had conspired to take the shaping powers he had given their father and reshape them for his own purposes. She explained how his efforts had gone wrong in different ways with Carnag, the Rogue Knight, Roxie, and the Mare. She told how their father's health diminished as he lost his connection to their powers.

"Whatever hardships befall that man are too little and

too late," Elegance said. "I can't express how long I've yearned to hear of his demise."

"It could be soon, based on how he looked when I last saw him," Cole said.

"You met our father?" Elegance asked him.

"We spoke not long ago," Cole said, not wanting to go into detail about becoming Stafford's emissary.

"Has there been any strange trouble in Creon over the last year?" Mira asked. "Some way your power could have been manifesting?"

"Not that comes to mind," Elegance said, glancing at Brogan, who gave a vague shrug. "We get briefed by the Host. There are all the usual tensions between the nobles and the Wayminders, but no instances of rampaging shaping power."

"Nothing," Brogan agreed. "You could ask the Host directly."

"I still haven't shared the worst news," Mira said. "Have you heard of the torivors?"

"I know the stories," Elegance said.

Mira explained about Owandell and the torivors in detail. She emphasized that Ramarro was imprisoned somewhere in Creon and that stopping him was the only way to save the world.

Elegance smirked. "And Mother sent . . . children?"

"Mother could have sent anyone," Mira said. "And she chose to send us. These children defeated Carnag in Sambria. We saved Elloweer from Morgassa. We protected Zeropolis from Roxie. And we stood up to Ramarro in Necronum.

When the torivor was making his escape into the physical world, Cole forced him into a new prison. You're not new to the five kingdoms. You know examples of young people with great shaping power."

"Don't be so touchy, Miracle," Elegance said. "It's just peculiar."

"We're it, Ella," Mira said. "We're the last line of defense."

"Elegance."

Mira sighed. "And we need your help."

"What am I supposed to do?" Elegance asked.

"Help us find your shaping power," Mira said. "Owandell wants to help Ramarro. He already abandoned Junction. Sooner or later Owandell will come to Creon. He and his shapecrafters might try to use your shaping power against us."

"Miracle, I don't have any powers," Elegance said. "And I'm not a specialist in combat. You want Honor for that. I need to look after Brogan."

"I'm in the safest stronghold in the five kingdoms," Brogan said. "With servants watching over me. Don't let me hold you back. Ever."

Elegance knelt beside her husband. "You know I'm not a fighter."

Brogan looked at Mira. "Elegance is brave and good and has faced unspeakable danger. And she is little use in a physical confrontation."

"None of us are expert fighters," Mira said.

"Speak for yourself," Jace said.

"We're doing what needs to be done," Mira continued, ignoring him.

"Maybe we could wheel Brogan at them," Jace said. "Can you still hold a jousting lance?"

Brogan grinned. "I'd welcome the chance to try."

"This is becoming absurd," Elegance said shortly. "I am sympathetic to your mission. It sounds heroic and necessary. But I hear no evidence of how my involvement can benefit anyone."

"What if your power is causing harm?" Mira asked. "What if only you can help us stop it?"

"Where is the evidence of my power harming anyone?" Elegance asked. "I hear no hint of my power currently being involved. I am a princess of the Outskirts and heir to the throne. If we discover my power is wreaking havoc, I will do my duty. But right now all you have is speculation."

"What about other kinds of help?" Mira asked. "Connections?"

"I had contacts among the Unseen here," Elegance said. "Those relationships have faded over the years. We've lived in relative isolation for decades. My best connection now is the Host. Perhaps he can offer guidance. He takes a real interest in the welfare of Creon and has serious access to Creon's elite."

Mira looked at Cole.

"Worth a try," Cole said. "We need to find Grand Shapers. People who can help us figure out how the vault holding Ramarro works and how we can make it stronger. People who can help us figure out how to face Ramarro if he gets free."

"I wish I could help," Brogan said. "It's not fair that a man learns and grows and reaches his prime only to enter a slow decline that eventually leaves him helpless as a baby."

"You gave years of valiant service, my love," Elegance said. "You saved my life innumerable times, through your wisdom and your skill. Now is your time to rest. This hour comes to all who live long enough."

"We can handle it," Jace said stoutly.

"Thanks for wanting to help," Cole said.

"Perhaps I should send you on your way," Elegance said. "Your errand sounds urgent, and more talk will only cause frustration."

"Surely they can stay for a meal," Brogan said.

"We are in kind of a hurry," Cole said.

"What about the Host?" Mira asked.

"Remind me your name?" Elegance asked Renni.

"Renni, Your Highness," she replied with a slight curtsy.

"Can you return them to the Host?" Elegance asked.

"It should not be a problem," Renni said.

"Very well," Elegance said. "Miracle, I'm relieved you are well. Thank you for news about Mother and our siblings." Her gaze swept the others in the group. "Thank you for your roles in aiding my family and protecting the kingdom. I'm grateful for your service and your sacrifices."

"Come with me," Renni said.

Less than half an hour later, Cole sat at a table with Jace, Twitch, Violet, Mira, and the Host. Renni stood nearby. Once the food was laid out, the servants departed. Between the delicious meal before him and the shady courtyard where they dined, Cole was almost able to forget they were in an iron fortress in the middle of a vast desert. And that the world could end at any moment.

"I trust your sister is pleased with her stay," the Host said to Mira politely as he gently removed a roasted chunk of squash from a skewer.

"She seems really content," Mira said. "Thanks for guarding her and Brogan so well. She wasn't as helpful as we'd hoped."

"Oh?" the Host asked before inserting the squash into his mouth.

"We need information," Mira said. "Connections. Leads to follow. Ramarro must be stopped. There is so much we don't know."

"The steak," Jace murmured to Cole.

"Huh?" Cole asked.

Jace pointed at a skewer of seasoned beef with his fork. "Try some. So garlicky. Heaven."

"It really is excellent steak," the Host said. "I need to limit my intake, but please, indulge."

Cole jabbed his fork into a juicy hunk of meat and slid it off the skewer. It was almost too hot, and surprisingly tender. Jace was right—it was divine.

"What information do you most require?" the Host asked.

Mira nodded at Cole.

"In other kingdoms we've had help from Grand Shapers," Cole said. "In most cases we wouldn't have survived long without it."

"You would like an audience with the Grand Shaper of Creon?" the Host asked.

"As many as we can find," Cole replied.

The Host narrowed his gaze. "Are you seeking confirmation of the rumor that there is more than one living Grand Shaper in Creon?"

"We know that much," Cole said. "We just want to find as many as possible. We have to keep the vault closed. If we can't, we need a plan to recapture Ramarro. Or maybe even to fight him."

"Very few know that some of the former Grand Shapers of Creon secretly dwell among us," the Host said. "Very few indeed. None know where to find them. Including our present Grand Shaper."

"We have a clue about where to find one," Cole said.

The Host's eyes flashed with interest. "I don't suppose you would be willing to share?"

"Depends what he says after we make contact," Cole said.

"Who is he?" the Host asked.

"We need to keep a few secrets for now," Cole said. "Lots of people want to stop us. We can't risk info getting out about where we are going."

"I am a secure confidant," the Host assured him. "But I admire the caution. What else?"

"Do you have any idea where the ancient vault might be that is holding Ramarro?" Cole asked.

The Host folded his arms and bowed his head in thought. "I do not. If it wasn't made known to the ruling class, a project so secretive and important would have been cleverly hidden long ago. I can have my people research the topic."

"Would you?" Mira asked.

"Life as we know it in the Outskirts is under attack," the Host said. "I'll do all in my power to aid you. If you need help from any of the noble families of Creon, I can open doors. Finding Grand Shapers gets hazy. I don't have the information, and I have no idea who does."

"We appreciate what help you have given," Mira said. "We should get going."

"After we eat some more," Jace said around a mouthful of steak.

"I understand," the Host said. He stood. "Other matters require my attention. Renni will show you out when you're ready." He held out a rolled length of parchment to Mira. "This document contains written permission to access the retreat from the outer tent. Few have such general permission, including residents here. Feel free to visit me as needed. I will continue to investigate the matters we have discussed."

Mira accepted the document, and the Host gave a stiff bow before exiting.

"I can't believe we just received permanent access to the Iron Fort," Violet said reverently.

"Neither can I," Renni added with a sniff.

After the meal, Renni led them through a wayport back to the lonely tent in the desert. The air inside the tent remained refreshing. Two men Cole had not seen yet stood guard.

Upon exiting the tent, the heat struck violently, radiating up from the sand and down from the sky. The bright sun was still an hour or two from sinking into the dunes.

"We're going to cook if we stay here long," Cole said.

"Where to next?" Twitch asked.

"Are you speaking again?" Jace asked. "I almost forgot you were here."

Twitch blinked repeatedly and shrugged. "Maybe I don't want attention from powerful people."

"Might not be bad thinking," Cole muttered.

"First we should check in with Mother," Mira said. "Then . . . I guess we go looking for Lorenzo Debray."

"All right," Violet said. "Back to Harmony's tower in the First Castle." She held out her hand, and Cole took it, then pushed power into her.

A wayport opened.

Mira stepped through first. Violet came last.

The old female servant who had greeted Cole several times stood staring at them with wide, worried eyes.

"Greta," Mira said. "What's wrong?"

The woman looked around as if nervous. "You don't know?" she whispered. "They've all gone missing!"

"Who?" Mira asked.

Greta winced. "Keep your voice down, Your Highness. The soldiers are still investigating."

"Who is missing?" Mira whispered urgently.

"Your mother, your father, your sisters," Greta said. "All of them. You and your little band are all suspects."

CHAPTER 14

IMPLICATED

W hy are we suspects?" Mira asked ardently, her voice rising above a whisper.

"Keep it down, Your Highness," Greta warned, looking around again. "They simply vanished. All of them. While under heavy guard. And you've been popping in and out lately with a Wayminder."

"Maybe they snuck off," Mira said.

"All of them?" Greta asked incredulously. "The king and queen together? Not to mention that word has it your father is in no condition to travel."

"He isn't," Cole confirmed.

Mira looked stunned. "They're all . . . gone?"

"Disappeared right under our noses," Greta said. "I was here when it happened. Never heard a peep. Her Majesty seemed to disappear, just like the others. The captain of the guard has kept it quiet while he investigates."

"It wasn't me," Violet said. "But it must have been Wayminders."

"You told me Wayminders wouldn't enter a private place," Cole said.

"And Enforcers don't burn down shrines," Violet replied. "Owandell expects the world to end. He's breaking all the rules."

"Could be," Mira said.

"Owandell?" Greta asked.

A door to the parlor opened, and a soldier froze, staring at them.

"Time to go," Greta whispered urgently.

Jace held out his rope to Cole, who touched it and flooded it with energy. The rope lashed out and thrust the soldier back as he began to raise the alarm.

Cole grabbed Violet, and she opened a wayport. Twitch ducked through. Jace slammed the parlor door with the rope. Then he used the rope to slide a fancy sofa in front of it.

"To the parlor!" the soldier was calling from beyond the door. "They're here! Greta was in on it!"

"Come, Greta," Mira said, guiding the old woman into the wayport.

The door burst open, toppling the sofa. Multiple soldiers lunged forward and were slammed back as Jace hurled an armchair into the doorway.

Maintaining his connection to the rope and Violet, Cole hurried through the portal. Jace followed. Then Violet. Soldiers were shouting.

The wayport closed.

Cole and his friends stood on the slope outside of Skyport. A light breeze ruffled the brush. Castles drifted in the distance.

"You're quick with that rope," Violet said.

"I liked bashing them with the chair," Jace said. "I need to remember to pick up stuff and use it like a club more."

"Skyport?" Cole asked.

"First place that came to mind," Violet said.

"I really don't miss this place," Mira said, gazing out at the castles.

"That was close," Twitch said. "What now?"

Mira approached Greta. "Are you all right?"

The woman looked shaken. "Well enough, I suppose, for suddenly being a fugitive after decades of loyal service."

"Try being her daughter," Mira said bitterly.

"You children really weren't involved in the disappearances?" Greta asked.

"Not at all," Mira said. "It had to be Owandell."

Greta nodded. "Stafford made his move against him. Owandell would waste little time retaliating if he could."

"No king," Mira said. "No queen. No heirs."

"Who will run the kingdom?" Violet asked.

"Owandell would have had the best chance before the High King discredited him," Greta said. "I suppose the nobles will fight it out once the news goes abroad."

Mira picked up a rock and flung it down the slope. "I shouldn't have left them! We had Violet! We could have stolen Nori and Tessa. We could have brought Mother to safety. I didn't take them, Greta. But I should have!"

"We couldn't see this coming," Cole said.

Mira made fists and closed her eyes. "Seems pretty clear now! We had them, Cole! They were safe. We had them.

Now they're who knows where? And Owandell is playing this like he has nothing to lose."

"We'll save them," Jace said.

"We better," Mira said.

"We will," Jace assured her. "They're too valuable for Owandell to harm them."

"I hope you're right," Mira said. "We don't really know what Owandell is capable of with his master returning." She turned to Greta. "Where would you like to go?"

"Me?" Greta asked.

"We can take you anywhere," Mira said. "Where would you be most safe and comfortable?"

"My sister has a farm outside of Junction City near the border of Elloweer," Greta said.

"Nearest town?" Violet asked.

"Just a little hamlet. Willet."

"I know it," Violet said. "South of Myer's Mill. Does the farm have any distinguishing features?"

"Big farm," Greta said. "Just east of Willet. Two barns. An orchard with concentric rings of trees. That's not usual, at least in those parts."

Violet closed her eyes.

Still connected to her power, Cole fed her some extra energy.

"I think I have it," Violet said, opening her eyes. "Should she go now?"

"The less she hears the better," Twitch said. "For her and for us."

A shimmering wayport appeared.

Wringing her hands, Greta turned to Mira. "You'll come get me if you find your mother?"

"Of course," Mira said. "And I'll come make sure Violet has the right farm."

Greta stepped through the wayport. Mira followed.

"I wonder what kind of fruit the orchard has?" Jace mused.

"Didn't we just eat?" Cole asked. "I feel full."

"Not fruit," Jace said. "Apples sound good."

Twitch approached the wayport. "I can't see through it. Or hear them."

"That's right," Violet said. "Many wayports are soundproof."

"But I can feel connections through them," Cole said. "If I have them established. Even if I can't see or hear the other side."

"I can't explain that," Violet said. "Must work differently than sight and sound."

Mira came back through, and the wayport vanished.

"Good job," Mira said. "It was her sister's place."

Violet gave a pleased smile.

"Remember when the four of us escaped this nightmare in a flying lifeboat?" Twitch asked, gazing down at Skyport.

"Probably the best day of my life," Jace said.

"It was a scary day," Cole observed. "We almost died."

"'Almost' can be a very important word," Jace said.

"Do any of you remember if we saw Elegance?" Mira asked.

Cole turned to her. What did he remember? "I think so. There was an old guy in a wheelchair."

"Yes," Twitch said. "And I remember Elegance."

"Me too," Jace said. "But I don't remember what we decided."

"The mindscreen," Cole muttered.

"I couldn't tell if I was remembering her or imagining it," Mira said. "Now that you mention it, I remember the old guy too. He had been her protector I think."

"Now he is her husband," Violet said. "I recall that much."

"The old guy?" Cole asked.

"They must have gotten married when they were younger," Mira said. "I wonder if Mother knows."

"Wasn't there another guy?" Twitch asked. "Who ran the Iron Fort?"

"He liked us," Cole said. "I don't remember much else."

"I have this," Mira said, holding up a rolled parchment.

"Won't do you any good," Violet said as Mira unrolled it.

"She's right," Mira said. "Gibberish."

"Think it might be a clue?" Cole asked. "Info about Ramarro or the Grand Shapers?"

"We'll be able to read it in Creon," Violet said. "And we'll remember what we forgot."

"I don't even know if Elegance is joining us," Mira said.

"Wouldn't she already be with us?" Twitch asked.

"Probably true," Cole said.

"Imagine your whole life being like this," Violet said. "Remembering people, especially those closest to you, but without so many specifics."

"I wouldn't mind forgetting a lot of my life," Jace said.

"It might feel that way sometimes," Violet said. "I promise you it isn't very fun."

"Should we go to Creon so we can remember?" Twitch asked.

"There is one stop I want to make first," Cole said. "While I still speak for the king. Before news spreads that he's gone."

"Where?" Mira asked.

"The slave trader Ansel is at Five Roads," Cole said. "I can use my authority to find out where all the kids from my neighborhood ended up."

"That could take some time, Cole," Jace said. "And the slaver might not cooperate."

"He for sure won't cooperate if people think I kidnapped the king," Cole said. "This could be my best chance."

"Your best chance is stopping the end of the world," Jace said. "If you find out where your friends are and the world ends, what was the point? If we stop Ramarro, you'll have all kinds of help finding those kids."

"Jace is right," Mira said. "You have lots of people on your side, Cole. We'll find your friends together."

Cole wanted to argue. What if they stopped Ramarro, but the order of the kingdoms unraveled? What if the Pemberton family lost the power to help him? What if Ansel moved on, and they never found him again? But Jace's position was too solid—what was the point of finding the kids from his neighborhood if Ramarro conquered the Outskirts? Locating Ansel and getting the information was risky and could cost precious time.

"I get it," Cole said. "Ramarro first. Where should we go?"

"We'll plan better in Creon," Twitch said. "With our recent memories."

"I know a place," Violet said. She reached out a hand, and Cole took it. A wayport shimmered into existence.

"Someplace safe?" Twitch asked.

"Safe as I know," Violet said.

Cole stepped through, maintaining his connection to Violet until she came through last of all and the wayport closed. They stood in a grove of trees near a huge lawn. A stately complex of buildings stood in the distance.

Memories awakened in Cole's mind.

"We went into the Iron Fort in the desert," Jace said.

"It was comfortable inside," Twitch said. "Except for the strict guards."

"Elegance isn't joining us," Mira said. "At least not for now."

"Should we go tell the Host about the king and queen?" Cole asked.

"We'll tell him when it makes sense to go back there," Jace said. "We're not his errand boys."

"Or girls," Violet added.

"Where are we?" Cole wondered.

"That was my first wayminding school," Violet said. "I grew up in a quiet region of Creon called Twin Lakes. We should be safe here for a moment."

Mira held up the rolled parchment. "I can read this now."

"It's permission to go back to the Iron Fort," Jace said.

"I know," Mira said. "But so weird that it's now perfectly legible. It looked like nonsense hardly a minute ago."

"Should we chase down Lorenzo?" Jace said. "Where was he again?"

"North of the forgotten cache at Shepherd's Grove," Violet said. "I hope those directions are more specific than they sound. How far north? A hundred paces? A mile north? Ten miles? Fifty? How directly north? Straight north?"

"Hopefully, Lorenzo is close to the cache, or Dandalus would have used a better landmark," Cole said.

"We should start at the cache and work northward," Mira suggested.

"What's the forgotten cache?" Twitch asked.

"Certain Wayminders used to transport merchandise, often from Earth," Violet said. "Taking shortcuts across wide spaces can be useful in shipping. The items were stored in caches. A lot of the big caches closed down and were abandoned."

"Did you just say there might be stuff to loot?" Jace asked.

"Old stuff people left behind," Violet said. "The caches are technically off-limits."

"I worked for a salvage operation," Jace said. "Abandoned cargo is fair game."

Violet shrugged. "In school we were told not to visit them. I'll take us to the north side of the cache near Shepherd's Grove. Cole, I'll need a boost so I can see where we want to go."

Cole took her hand and energized her power.

Violet gave a small gasp. "With your help I can see so clearly from here! Not clearly inside the cache. It's shielded. But the borders of the cache are easy to make out. It's big. There is an empty field toward the center of the north side."

A wayport appeared.

Jace stepped through the glimmering portal. The others followed. Violet came through last.

Cole first noticed that it was cooler—almost cold enough to wish for a jacket when the frosty breeze slithered over him. Long grass and wild flowers extended before him, sloping up into a series of low hills fringed with evergreens. Turning, Cole found a tall metal fence topped with spikes. Through the fence he could see a stagecoach, a slot machine, a few department-store mannequins in outdated fashions, and an old biplane that made him think of World War I.

"That stuff is from my world," Cole said.

"I wouldn't know," Violet replied.

"Does that fly?" Jace asked, pointing at the plane.

"If you know how," Cole said. "And if it has fuel. And room to take off."

"Makes me think of Zeropolis," Jace said. "Cool tech. Does your world have good weapons?"

"Actually, yeah, we're pretty good at weapons."

"We have to go in there," Jace said. "Violet, how about a way to the other side of the fence? Just a tiny hop?"

"These caches are off-limits," Violet reminded him. "We're in Creon! Are you trying to get me penalized?"

"If Owandell is playing this like the world is about to end, why can't we?" Jace asked.

"In case it doesn't," Violet said. "And in case we get detained before we can try to stop Ramarro."

"How tall is that fence?" Jace asked, looking up.

"About twenty feet," Twitch said.

"Maybe there's a gate," Cole suggested.

Violet shook her head. "We're in Creon. The caches were built to be secure. No gates. Anybody with permission to be inside would use a wayport."

"And items would be moved in and out the same way," Mira said.

Jace held his golden strand out to Cole. "A little help?"

"Is it smart to go in there?" Cole asked. "Dandalus told us Lorenzo Debray was north of here."

"This was the only place named," Jace said. "We should check it out. There may be clues."

"Or awesome weapons from another world," Twitch said knowingly.

"Is that so bad?" Jace asked. "We're being hunted by Owandell. We're trying to stop a powerful torivor. Nobody wants better weapons?"

"Might be worth a look," Mira said.

Cole touched the golden strand and energized it.

"I need some help," Twitch said. "The ring that lets me take my true form outside of Elloweer only works in Sambria."

Cole placed a hand on Twitch's shoulder. Twitch's shaping power felt dim—suppressed. Cole brightened it, and suddenly Twitch had grasshopper legs and antennae.

"You're good," Twitch said.

"Can you power all of us at the same time?" Mira asked, holding out her Jumping Sword.

Cole touched the flat of the blade and awoke the power inside. He drew his sword and energized it. "No problem. It'll be a big jump over the fence. Don't forget to jump again when you land."

Mira grinned. "Don't forget who introduced you to Jumping Swords."

"How does my rope work again?" Jace asked with a smirk. "Twitch? Do you remember how to hop?"

"I can stand guard here," Violet offered.

"Oh no," Jace said. "If you're too nervous to open a way in, I'll bring you." He turned his back to her. "Climb on."

"Away," Mira said, pointing her sword and leaping well over the fence. "Away," she said again when she landed, taking a smaller jump forward before coming to a stop. Twitch sprang as well, wings fluttering, and easily cleared the fence.

Cole called out the command and enjoyed the rush of soaring up over the fence, including the brief weightlessness at the apex of his flight. With the added elevation, he glimpsed random objects from his world continuing into the distance. A school bus? A long glittery Chinese dragon? A McDonald's?

Cole landed with a second little jump to dampen the impact. Jace landed beside him, the coils of his rope slowing his descent. Violet climbed down from his back.

"Now we're trespassers," Violet said.

"We're not exactly burning down shrines or kidnapping royalty," Jace said.

"I guess if our enemies play dirty, we may need to cross boundaries sometimes," Violet said.

"You trespassed with us into a sky castle," Jace reminded her.

"Yeah, but I'm from here," Violet said. "I know the rules here."

"How long can you keep me in my true form?" Twitch asked.

"As long as I keep sending power to you," Cole said.

"Would it be easier to just charge up my ring?"

"I'd have to maintain that connection too," Cole said.

"And you can hold the connection without touching me," Twitch said. "Does that mean you could form the connection without touching me?"

"Maybe," Cole said.

Cole released his connection to Twitch, who reverted to a human appearance. Reaching out with all of his focus, Cole could sense the shaping power within his friend. It was familiar. But could he touch that power without physically touching Twitch? Could he establish a connection from a distance?

Cole became aware of the others watching him. He closed his eyes and focused more intently on Twitch's power. He could almost feel it. But no matter how hard he pushed, he fell short of connecting to it.

"Not right now," Cole said. "Maybe if I practice."

"My rope went limp," Jace said.

Cole realized that he had broken his connections with Violet and everything else to concentrate on Twitch. "I was giving it my all."

"It would be great if you could learn to do it," Mira said.

Cole nodded. "A lot smoother in a fight if I don't have to touch everything to power it up."

"It's already unreal," Twitch said. "Nobody else can do what you do."

"I bet Ramarro can," Cole said. "And so much more."

"Let's find an incredible weapon from Cole's world," Jace said. "Something undefeatable." He pointed. "Maybe that?"

"That's a tuba," Cole said. "It's a musical instrument."

"I get it," Jace said. "Like a big horn. Who blows that thing? How big are their lungs?"

"Pretty hefty, I guess," Cole said.

"Who is that guy?" Twitch asked, indicating a large reddish statue.

"I think that's Buddha," Cole said. "There are people on my planet who worship him."

They set off through a jungle of random items. Cole noticed an old-fashioned gas pump, a stone birdbath, a bronze statue of a baseball player, a rickshaw, a simple wooden canoe, a tin washtub, and an Egyptian sarcophagus. He showed the others how to wear the Chinese dragon and tried the door of the McDonald's, finding it locked. Putting his face to the glass, he could see tables and the counter and the menu. There was nobody inside and no sign of electricity, but otherwise it appeared an entire McDonald's had been transported to Creon intact.

"This is a restaurant in my world," Cole explained. "Not a fancy one. It's for when you're in a hurry. They serve hamburgers."

"Dalton showed me a hamburger once," Jace said. "An illusion."

"They're good," Cole said. "McDonald's isn't the ultimate, but they're popular for a reason. What's it doing here?"

"Want to break in?" Mira asked.

Cole shook his head. "It must have been here a while. No way is any food inside still good."

"Let's keep moving," Twitch suggested.

They passed more Earth paraphernalia large and small, ancient and modern. Cole noticed that nothing looked quite from his time period. The newest stuff seemed to be from at least thirty years ago. Maybe more.

"What's that?" Mira asked.

Cole looked ahead to a full carousel with horses and other animals on poles. "It's a carousel. A ride."

"Does it turn around?" Twitch asked.

"If it had power," Cole said. "Probably not here."

"You can power it," Jace suggested.

"I don't think so," Cole said. "It runs on a different kind of power called electricity."

They went to the carousel and climbed on. Cole stared at a white horse, head thrown back, motionless mane molded as if blowing in the wind. Fake jewels decorated the fanciful saddle and bridle.

"Your world is strange," Jace said, standing beside a big frog with a brass pole through it.

"Kind of strange, I guess," Cole admitted. "But also pretty fun."

"What do you kids think you're doing?" called a shrill voice.

Cole whirled to find a bony older woman coming toward them. She had frizzy gray hair and walked with a bouncy sway, almost like she was running in place. Cole glanced at the others in surprise and worry.

"Told you," Violet muttered.

CACHE

Y our ride doesn't work," Jace said, yanking on the pole through the frog.

The woman stared at him huffily, hands on her hips. "Shows what you know! Works just fine."

"It's supposed to spin around," Cole said.

Her gaze shifted to Cole. "I know what it does, young man. The question is, why have you hooligans entered uninvited? And with a Wayminder among you? Let me guess—the robes are stolen."

"It was her idea," Jace said. "She dared us."

Violet flushed and opened her mouth, but no words came out.

"We don't mean any harm," Mira said.

"Has all order been overthrown?" the old woman asked. "Are laws only meant for people who mean harm now? How exactly is that measured?"

"Turn it on," Jace said.

"Excuse me?" the woman asked.

"You claim it works," Jace said. "Prove it. Turn it on."

"Stop trying to tangle me, young man," the woman said. "How did you kids get here? There are no settlements nearby. Are you actually a Wayminder?"

Violet turned a shade redder. Cole could tell she wanted to disappear.

"Is she mute?" the woman asked. "I know somebody opened a wayport north of the fence. I've seen a few winters, but not all of my senses have fled yet."

"She's shy," Cole said. "We pushed her into coming here."

"Kidnapped you, did they?" the woman asked.

"I volunteered," Violet admitted.

"What's the punishment for trespassing?" Jace asked. "Do you really care? Isn't this ride going to waste with nobody to play on it? What's the use of all this junk with nobody here?"

"These artifacts were collected over many years," the woman said. "That carousel is unique in all the Outskirts."

"Not as unique where I'm from," Cole said.

"Am I supposed to believe you're from Outside?" the woman asked. "Do you think that gives you a claim on this collection?"

"Maybe," Cole said. "My friends were stolen from our world. How did this stuff get here?"

"The world walkers acquired these pieces over long years," the woman said.

"World walkers?" Violet asked.

The woman waved her hands as if swatting away gnats. "Now you've got me talking about history better left unmentioned."

"You should be glad we're here," Jace said. "Isn't a collection meant to be viewed? This place looks abandoned. Does anyone else work here?"

"I'm alone here sometimes," the woman said. "I have help at times too. I can call security, and they'll be here in no time. Then you'll wish I hadn't."

"Don't get us in trouble," Cole said. "We're just curious. Does the carousel really work? Wouldn't it need electricity?"

"We bring it in direct from Earth using—" She placed a hand over her mouth, then removed it. "You kids are good at getting me talking."

"I bet it doesn't work," Jace said. "I know a bluff when I see one."

The woman pointed at him. "I know what you're doing, and it won't work."

"Jace has a point," Cole said. "What use is a carousel without people to ride it?"

The woman folded her arms. Then unfolded them. "It is a piece of foreign culture."

"Meant to have riders," Cole said.

The woman sighed. "It's been some time since I let it spin. Okay, how about this arrangement? I let you ride, then you leave and swear to tell nobody you came here."

"I can live with that," Mira said.

"Maybe I can as well," the woman said. "You seem all right. First tell me what prompted your interest in this place? We've discouraged interest in the caches enough that few in your generation care they exist."

Cole decided to take a risk. "We're looking for somebody."

All heads turned to him.

"Not me, I take it," the woman said. "Who could you possibly be looking for here?"

"Lorenzo Debray," Cole said.

Her face clearly registered worried surprise before she covered the reaction. She forced an awkward chuckle. "Now you're getting absurd."

"Are we?" Mira asked. "Creon is in danger, and we need to find him."

"What sort of danger?" the woman asked.

"We can't get too specific," Cole said. "But it involves stopping a torivor."

The woman looked perplexed. "Trillian remains safe inside—"

"Not him," Cole said. "Ramarro."

The woman nodded. "You realize Lorenzo Debray was a Grand Shaper hundreds of years ago."

"Yes, and he's in hiding near here," Cole said.

The woman shook her head. "I've never met a crazier troop of rascals. You're all far too fond of nonsense."

"The world walkers collected these things from Outside?" Violet asked.

"No more of that talk," the woman said. "The world walkers were officially disbanded more than sixty years ago. Their unofficial excursions tapered off roughly twenty years ago. Those in charge questioned the ethics of securing these items and the propriety of too much attention fixed outside our world."

"Then this stuff is just junk," Jace said. "Relics from an abandoned project."

"A few of us still find value here," the woman said. "We're allowed to curate the caches as long as we keep them closed to the public. So your presence endangers my life's work."

"Were you a world walker?" Twitch asked.

"I have worked with some of the best of them," the woman said. "And I keep talking too much! I must be lonelier than I realized! One ride, then you depart, lips sealed."

"We'll depart and look for Lorenzo Debray," Cole said.

"Why not find Kendo Rattan while you're at it?" the woman asked.

"We expect to," Cole said. "One step at a time."

The woman threw up her hands as if the discussion was hopeless and teetered over to a shed. She unlocked the door and went inside.

"Did you see her face when you mentioned Lorenzo Debray?" Mira whispered. "She knows something."

"Seemed like it," Jace whispered.

"Think she'll help us?" Cole asked.

"Depends if we can get her to trust us," Mira whispered. "The location of Lorenzo Debray is an enormous secret. She has to be good at keeping it."

Thousands of light bulbs came on all over the carousel. Music began to play, and it slowly started to turn.

"It works," Jace said with a smile. He rummaged in a satchel, pulled out the hat he got in Zeropolis, and put it on.

"Grab something to ride," Cole said. "Make sure your pole connects to the crank at the top or it won't go up and down."

Everyone claimed a mount as the carousel sped up. The old woman exited the shed and watched, a smile on her lips.

Cole looked back at Jace, eyes closed, grinning, his tiger rising and falling. He opened his eyes and took off his hat, waving it in the air.

"You love that hat," Cole called.

"Perfect for holidays," Jace replied.

Cole could not help imagining life as a slave—a life without holidays. He realized he couldn't even begin to understand what it was really like for someone who had spent their whole life that way.

Mira laughed on her horse. Twitch bobbed up and down on a colorful rooster, trying to look in every direction at once, soaking in the experience. Violet contentedly held the pole above her dolphin with both hands.

"Had enough?" the old woman called as they passed her.

"Nobody is waiting for a turn," Cole called back. "Keep it going!"

Something slammed into Cole and constricted around him, knocking him from his horse. He fell short of hitting the floor of the carousel. It took Cole a moment to recognize the crisscross pattern of a net pressed to his face, and enveloping the rest of him as well. He hung, trapped, off the side of his horse, head lower than his feet, unable to do more than barely squirm.

"Run!" Jace shouted over the chiming music.

Cole struggled fruitlessly. The world scrolled by as the carousel spun. In flashes from his awkward dangling position, Cole saw his friends scrambling and Enforcers approaching. They had been ambushed.

Cole had no connection to Violet, Twitch, or any of the

weapons. He reached out but could not get a sense for where his friends were, let alone connect to their powers.

Then Jace was at his side, hatless, thrusting the golden strand against his shoulder. "Quick," Jace said.

"My hands," Cole said.

But both hands were trapped between his chest and the side of the horse.

"Hurry," Jace said, holding the golden strand against his elbow, as close to Cole's hands as he could manage.

Cole fought to make his hands available. He also tried to feel the power of the rope through his sleeve. And then Jace was yanked away. An Enforcer stood in his place.

Cole redoubled his effort to remotely connect to the golden rope. If only he could energize the rope, Jace could probably handle the Enforcers. But Cole could establish no connection.

The carousel slowed to a stop. The music continued, and the lights remained on. Hands detached Cole's net from the horse. Somebody seized Cole's feet, dragged him to the edge of the carousel, and swung him off. Still hopelessly ensnared in the net, he landed in the dust, shoulder first, and did his best to absorb the impact by rolling.

The net shrank around him, constricting so tight that Cole could barely breathe. From his helpless position on the ground, Cole watched the Enforcers round up his friends. Mira wielded her Jumping Sword against an Enforcer with four arms. Without energy from Cole the sword was useless for jumping. The Enforcer outfought her with a pair of long knives and knocked the sword from her grasp.

Another Enforcer moved with supernatural speed, first hurling Jace to the ground, then tracking down Twitch, who had tried to run off. Violet surrendered without a fight.

Soon all his friends lay on the ground as well, hands bound. Cole counted a total of five Enforcers. The old woman seemed to have disappeared. Could she have slipped into the shed?

"Keep them away from Cole," the fast Enforcer said. "Jermaine, where's our wayport? Let's get them to the boss."

"Having a little trouble," Jermaine said. "I tried to hold our wayport open, but it collapsed."

"That's why we have two Wayminders," the fast Enforcer said. "Eric?"

"The cache must be shielded," Eric said. "I can't open anything here. We may have to take them outside the fence."

"Not much of a fight," the Enforcer with four arms said. "Any two of us could have handled this."

"We had good intelligence," the fast Enforcer said. "Isolate Cole. Nice work, Carson. Easy job after that."

"It was a solid plan, Lars," Carson said.

Cole miserably strained against the squeeze of the net. The Enforcers were right. Without him to energize the others, they had been easy prey.

"What kind of net is that?" Mira asked. "Looks really tight."

"Never you mind," Lars said. "No talking. Boys, what is the best way to convey them outside the fence?"

Mira stared purposefully at Cole. She was right! The net was supernaturally tight. Sure enough, he could sense shaping power in it. Pressing his hands against the confining strands, he connected to the power.

How was it energized? The power in the net felt like Sambrian shaping. Could somebody else energize objects to work outside their proper kingdoms? No. The power originated with one of the Enforcers. The guy called Carson. He wasn't energizing power inherent to the net. He was using Sambrian shaping to directly control it. Carson's power had been mangled by shapecrafters to allow his Sambrian shaping to work in Creon.

Cole knew he needed to act decisively. It would be easy to block Carson's power from controlling the net. With the net's embrace loosened, Cole might be able to move. But better if he could shake Carson up along with it.

Using his connection with the power guiding the net, Cole traced the power back to its origin. Gritting his teeth, Cole connected directly to Carson's power. Not to energize it. To tear it apart.

Carson screamed and fell.

The net slackened.

Cole pushed a hand free. Lars stood nearest, and Cole grabbed his ankle. Cole felt his shaping power more distinctly than Carson's. It was marred throughout, tangled with darkness. Without the darkness, it felt Ellowine.

Pushing with all his might, Cole burned away the darkness. Lars cried out and collapsed.

Flailing to free himself from the net, Cole lunged over to Jace. The other Enforcers looked stunned. Cole took the golden strand from Jace's bound hands and forced energy into it.

The four-armed guy charged, but Cole quickly ensnared him with the rope, then used the contact to find the man's power. With a mighty surge of energy, Cole burned away the darkness throughout his power. Two of the man's arms disappeared.

Cole swung the stunned man violently into Eric. They connected with a clang of armor and a crunch of bone. Lars returned to his feet, looking shaky.

Cole drew his Jumping Sword and forced energy into it. "Surrender or you're all going to die," he warned.

Jermaine charged forward, sword in hand. Cole snared his ankles with the golden rope and whipped him into the air.

Crouching, Lars set down his weapon and raised both hands. "This is over. Stand down."

"What did you do to me?" Carson asked with a miserable groan.

"He went right to your power," Lars said. "Went straight to mine, too."

Eric and the other Enforcer remained motionless. Cole flopped Jermaine onto the ground, not gently, and retracted the rope.

"On your faces," Cole said.

The Enforcers who could move complied.

"No shapecrafter can connect to your power that easily," Carson said, his voice still unsteady.

"They warned us he was good," Lars said. "I didn't think of him using the net to get to you. What did you do to me? I can't feel my power."

"I healed you," Cole said. "Took away all the shape-crafting done to you."

"No fooling," Lars said with some admiration. "That quickly? I know shapecrafters who can adjust modifications to your power. I don't know anyone who can simply undo them."

"Seemed like the fastest way to take away your shaping here," Cole said, using his Jumping Sword to carefully cut Jace's cords. "It'll still work back in Elloweer."

"You didn't do that to me," Carson said. "I feel . . . wrong inside."

"I'd say sorry," Cole said, "but you were trying to capture us." The cords fell away from Jace's wrists, and Cole passed him the sword. Jace started freeing the others.

"You followed my power through the net and back to me?" Carson asked. "Who does that?"

"The guy who is going to stop Ramarro," Cole said.

"Who?" Lars asked.

"Ramarro," Cole said. "You call him Nazeem."

"What?" Carson asked.

"You guys don't even know who you're following?" Jace asked.

"Explain," Lars said.

"Your leader is the torivor Ramarro," Cole said. "Going under the name Nazeem."

"You're like those poor suckers who fall under Trillian's power," Mira said.

"Who do you think taught Owandell to mess with the shaping power?" Cole asked. He crossed to Carson.

Crouching, Cole touched the back of his neck. The Enforcer's shaping power was not only marred with darkness but torn, almost scrambled. "I really hurt your power."

"You're telling me," Carson said. "I feel some of the results physically. Like I'm permanently dizzy. It's turning to nausea."

Cole engaged with Carson's power, gently healing it, and then burned away the darkness. It wasn't very difficult.

"You fixed it," Carson said. "All of it."

"You can feel your power," Cole said. "But you can't use it here."

"Yes," Carson said.

"Don't let them maim you again," Cole said. "Jermaine, hold still."

"I'm a Wayminder," Jermaine said, facedown. "My shaping power belongs here."

"I'm going to check you," Cole said, touching the back of his head. His power was mangled, with darkness woven into it. "What did they do to you?"

"Boosted my abilities," Jermaine said. "I can open wayports more frequently than most."

With an effort of will, Cole burned away the darkness. "Not anymore. But your shaping is whole."

Cole went over to Eric and to the Enforcer who formerly had four arms, who was perfectly still. He didn't seem to be breathing. Cole reminded himself that, like the others, that man had been ready to do harm to Cole and his friends.

Eric groaned as Cole approached. "Stay away."

"Hold still or I'll smash you around again," Cole said, touching his neck. He burned away the darkness.

"Enough of this," a shrill voice called.

Cole turned to find the old woman approaching. He held the golden rope ready, just in case.

"Time to send our unwanted visitors on their way," she said. A shimmering wayport appeared. "Sorry if you find the destination inconvenient. Then again, you were never invited to trespass here."

"Does this include us?" Violet asked.

"You were not invited either," the old woman said. "But I wouldn't send children to Outer Yurgo for wanting to ride a carousel. I refer to the Enforcers."

"You heard her," Jace said. "Head through the wayport. Be glad you're alive. Well, except the dead one."

"Wait," Mira said. "Do we want to use a couple of them to spread the word about Ramarro through the Enforcers?"

"There are surer channels," the old woman said. "These men will say whatever they can to get free, then double-cross you in a heartbeat."

"I didn't know we fought for a torivor," Lars said. "And we are an elite unit. If we didn't know, very few know."

"There are better channels," the old woman maintained.

"Into the wayport," Mira said.

"Help Eric," Cole suggested.

"I see that crossbow," the old woman said. "Leave your weapons."

"What about hunting?" Jermaine asked.

"Get creative," the old woman suggested.

Jermaine and Carson carried Eric into the wayport. Lars paused before stepping through and looked at Cole. "If you really are up against a torivor, good luck, kid."

"Like it or not, know it or not, we're all up against a torivor," Cole said.

"Maybe so," Lars said, then stepped through.

The wayport closed.

The old woman crouched over the Enforcer who used to have four arms. "He's not pretending." She raised her voice. "All clear."

A man came out of the shed. Clad in the robes of a Wayminder, he had long hair knotted atop his head and a short beard that followed the edge of his jaw.

"Greetings," he said. "I understand you're looking for Lorenzo Debray. I am he."

HIDDEN

I pictured him older," Jace murmured to Mira.

"I'll take that as a compliment," Lorenzo said.

Violet looked like she was about to pass out. "Are you really Lorenzo Debray?"

"Fair question," Lorenzo said. "You're all involved in some high-stakes trouble. You can't afford to get duped by an imposter."

"Can you prove who you are?" Jace asked.

Lorenzo held up a hand, and Jace became motionless.

"Your friend is unharmed," Lorenzo said. "He is now experiencing time in an unusual way. Not many Wayminders can accomplish this."

"Nobody can do that," Violet said.

"Not many," Lorenzo replied. He waved a hand, and Jace could move again. "Edna informed me that you had come to look for me, and then Enforcers attacked you. I came to survey the situation."

"How did she inform you?" Twitch wondered.

"I opened a wayport to him," the old woman said.

"You're a Wayminder too?" Cole asked.

"Yes, though opening ways here in the cache is easy," the old woman said. "Especially if you belong here. Numberless shortcuts have been established over the years."

"Their unfamiliarity with the protections here hampered the Enforcers," Lorenzo said. "I closed their wayport and prevented them from opening a new one. I thought I would have to rescue you, but then you saved yourselves. I must say, Cole, your abilities are extraordinary."

"Lorenzo Debray knows your name," Violet mumbled in awe.

"I heard the Enforcers use it," Lorenzo said. "And I sensed what he did. So impressive. Are you really trying to stop a torivor?"

"We need help," Cole said.

Lorenzo held up a hand. "Say no more. Come to my lair. We can speak freely there."

A wayport opened.

"We were worried we wouldn't find you," Mira said.

Lorenzo gave a nod. "You have found me. Please, after you."

Jace went first. Then Mira. Cole followed.

He stepped through the wayport into a large, underground chamber, rectangular as the inside of a box, the rock walls, ceiling, and floor unnaturally smooth, the corners perfect. Despite the subterranean appearance, it had been turned into a home. Furniture abounded, and rugs softened the floor. Several lamps lit the space. Taking a closer look, Cole found electric light bulbs inside them.

"These are from my world," Cole said.

Lorenzo had come through after Violet and Twitch and closed the wayport. Edna had not joined them. "This surprises you after riding a carousel?"

"Good point," Cole said.

"How deep are we?" Twitch asked.

"Well below the surface," Lorenzo said. "None will find us here."

"North of the cache?" Mira asked.

"Some distance north, yes," Lorenzo said.

"We had directions to you," she said.

"Who told you this?" Lorenzo asked.

"Dandalus," Cole said.

"Dandalus has moved on," Lorenzo said.

"His echo," Cole clarified. "We worked with him in the echolands."

"Not much can be hidden from Dandalus," Lorenzo said.

"This cave doesn't look . . . natural," Twitch said.

"It isn't," Lorenzo said. "I removed the rock myself."

"With wayminding?" Violet asked, astonished.

"A form of wayminding like the world walkers used," Lorenzo said. "Transporting inanimate matter through spatial manipulation."

"This place doesn't connect to the outside," Jace said.

"Exactly," Lorenzo replied. "I ventilate and regulate the temperature with tiny wayports. This hideaway is heavily shielded against snoopy Wayminders. The best of the best would have a tough time finding it."

"How did Dandalus think we would find you?" Cole asked.

Lorenzo shrugged. "If he somehow knew I was here, he may have assumed I keep an eye on the surface. I do. He may have figured a group of kids out of place would attract my attention. It would have. And it did. Tell me about Ramarro."

"He was imprisoned in the echolands," Cole said. "He recently got loose, but an impression of Dandalus in the Founding Stone helped me redirect Ramarro to a prison in Creon—a vault called the Void."

"You're speaking about legends," Lorenzo said. "Dandalus, Ramarro, and the Void."

"We have to find the Void," Cole said. "Dandalus feels sure it won't hold Ramarro for long. We have to either keep Ramarro in prison, invent a better prison, or figure out a way to defeat a torivor."

Lorenzo sighed. "This is grim. We're probably all going to die."

"We all die anyhow if Ramarro gets free," Cole said. "I've been to the echolands. Death isn't so bad. And whatever lies beyond the echolands feels appealing."

"Fair assessment," Lorenzo said. "Is the torivor as bad as the legends maintain?"

"Seems like it," Cole said. "Dandalus agreed."

"We don't want to face it head-on," Lorenzo said. "But how do you imprison something that can escape the echolands and the Void?"

"Trillian is still bound," Mira said.

"Trillian was mostly defeated when they imprisoned him," Lorenzo said. "If we could defeat Ramarro, it might open up options. But I'm not sure that is possible. And I don't know the specifics of how Trillian was contained. I'm hundreds of years old, but the torivors preceded me by a significant margin."

"Can we find Kendo Rattan?" Jace asked.

"Wouldn't that be nice?" Lorenzo said. "Shouldn't he be long gone?"

"Shouldn't you?" Jace countered.

"Valid observation," Lorenzo said. "But Kendo Rattan predates me by centuries. He helped create the five kingdoms."

"Dandalus told us he might be around," Cole said. "I guess most of the Grand Shapers of Creon gained power over death."

Lorenzo took a slow breath. "You have been told our deepest mysteries, secrets we have killed to protect. In some ways I'm glad. It confirms the gravity of your errand."

"So we can find Kendo Rattan?" Violet asked.

"I cannot be sure of his present location," Lorenzo said. "He has appeared to most, if not all, of the Grand Shapers of Creon after they retire. Never while they remain in office."

"When did you last see him?" Cole asked.

"It has been some time," Lorenzo said. "Kendo could be dead. Wherever he is today, he is beyond our reach unless he wants to be found. But . . . this is an emergency, so we are not necessarily limited to finding him today."

"You mean time travel," Violet gushed.

"I do," Lorenzo said.

"Can you just send us back to one of your previous meetings with Kendo?" Twitch asked.

"Unfortunately, by Kendo's design, all of those meetings

occurred in shielded locations," Lorenzo said. "I can't get you to any of those conferences. I don't know where they happened. But I know my history, and there are a few places where you may be able to interact with Kendo Rattan after he created the Void."

"Why not before he created the Void?" Cole asked. "We could warn him to make it stronger."

Lorenzo smiled sadly. "You are powerful. And so young. You have not traveled through time before?"

Cole shook his head.

"And you know little of Creon?"

Cole nodded.

"You need some fundamentals," Lorenzo said. "First, the past is fixed. You cannot go back in time and change the past. If you do, you will only discover that you become part of the past as it already happened."

"What if I went back in time and killed you when you were a baby?" Jace asked.

Everyone stared at him.

"Not that I would," Jace clarified hastily. "For the sake of argument. I mean, how could you stop me if you were just a little baby?"

"I wouldn't have to stop you," Lorenzo said. "I'm here. I didn't die as a baby. It didn't happen. The past is fixed. You would somehow fail. You could make mistakes. Someone might intervene. You might change your mind. You might even inadvertently save my life. In the end any attempt you made to alter the past would become part of the past as it already transpired."

"But if I went to the past, wouldn't I be a new addition to what happened?" Cole asked. "Couldn't I change the outcome from whatever happened before I went there? I'm just thinking out loud. I want to understand."

"If you visit the past, there is no other past without your visit," Lorenzo said. "The past you visited would be new to you, but it already happened with you in it. You'd just be the last to know. All that already occurred is inevitable. You can't avoid it."

"There's no way around it?" Cole asked.

"People have tried," Lorenzo said. "The theory is sound, but hundreds of attempts have been made to disprove the concept and alter the past. They always fail."

"What if I read in a history book that I died in the past, so I never go?" Jace asked.

"Then either the history was wrong, or you will change your mind and go, or you will somehow get sent to the past," Lorenzo said. "Those of us who journey to the past are few, and we try to do so unobtrusively. We sometimes get caught up in events, but we are there to learn, never to change anything."

"Because you can't," Twitch said.

"No more than I could break any other fundamental law," Lorenzo said.

"Laws get broken all the time in the Outskirts," Cole objected. "You can travel back in time. That seems like breaking a fundamental law."

"You must remember that the Outskirts was constructed in an eternal realm," Lorenzo said. "Many of the laws here are not natural—they were shaped. Certain aspects of those laws are vulnerable to tampering. Some are not. Once you establish sequence, the past is the past."

"It seems like if you can go to the past, you can change it," Cole said.

"It seems that way because you don't understand life in four dimensions," Lorenzo said. "You are imagining multiple pasts. A past with you and a past without you. The past is singular. I already told you, if you go to the past, you were part of it. It's hard to help you see the concept more clearly. It's like trying to explain life in three dimensions to somebody living in two."

"Could shapecrafters warp the fundamental rules and change history?" Jace asked.

Lorenzo shook his head. "If they could, they would have not only surpassed my capabilities, but they would have exceeded what my wildest imaginings consider possible."

"Why go back in time if we can't change history?" Jace asked.

"Like he told us," Violet said. "To learn."

"Yes," Lorenzo agreed. "You could meet with Kendo Rattan and possibly acquire information that you could later use in the present."

"Like where to find the Void," Cole said.

"Or how to strengthen it," Mira added.

"Who knows what you might discover?" Lorenzo said. "Considering the desperate need, I believe it is worth a try."

"Won't it be hard to find him?" Violet asked.

Lorenzo gave a nod. "At least one of you is familiar with Creon."

"Why is it hard?" Cole asked.

"Lots of people would like to meet Kendo Rattan," Violet said. "Or Lorenzo Debray," she quickly added. "Any of the former Grand Shapers, really. So they keep a low profile. They were hard to find when they were alive, and their specific appearances are not recorded in any histories I know about. Their deeds and accomplishments, sure, but not specific dates synced with places."

"The Grand Shapers of Creon are experts at not being found," Lorenzo said. "That includes by time travelers. But I happen to know a place and time visited by Kendo Rattan."

"When?" Violet asked.

"The dedication of the Halbrook School of Wayminding," Lorenzo said. "It was the first school of wayminding in the region, founded by the Grand Shaper Kili Felks, one of Kendo's favorite apprentices. He did not reveal himself to her. But he was in the crowd. After her retirement he told her about it. And he mentioned it to me."

"Can we find Kendo in a crowd?" Cole asked.

"Not if he chooses to avoid you," Lorenzo said. "Kendo is extremely in tune with his surroundings. He can disappear in a blink. He will be aware that you are from another time. He will be intrigued that you are young. And if we can introduce the problem of Ramarro somehow, he will almost surely engage you. He once told me that the two torivors are the biggest threat to the security of the five kingdoms. And Kendo Rattan dedicated his life to protecting the five kingdoms."

"How do we alert him about Ramarro?" Jace asked.

"Would he overhear if we spoke about him? Should we wear signs?"

"Whatever you do needs to work," Lorenzo said. "You can't inhabit the same time in Creon more than once."

"Do you know other times when Kendo Rattan appeared?" Mira asked.

"I could make some educated guesses," Lorenzo said. "The Halbrook School dedication is our best chance. If you fail there, you may never make contact with him."

"Could you come with us?" Cole asked.

"I was already alive then," Lorenzo said. "I was not yet a Grand Shaper. Just a young Wayminder developing my abilities. I cannot return to a time I inhabited. I want to know more about you five. How did you become our defense against a torivor? I understand that Cole has unusual power. It's strange that you are all so young."

"I'm Jace. I used to be a slave owned by the Sky Raiders in Sambria, just like Twitch, Cole, and Mira. I'm free now." He held up his freemark. "The Grand Shaper of Sambria took care of that for me. I've traveled with these guys ever since."

"I'm Miracle Pemberton."

"As in one of the lost princesses?" Lorenzo asked, surprised.

"My father drove me into exile when he took my shaping powers. My friends helped me get them back, and we learned about Owandell and the shapecrafters. We have restored the powers to all of my sisters except Elegance."

"How are your shaping powers?" Lorenzo asked.

"Strengthening," Mira said. "I haven't had much chance to test them."

"As I understand it, Cole could help you try them," Lorenzo said. "Even here."

"True," Mira said.

Lorenzo looked at Twitch.

"I'm Twitch. Ruben, really. I'm one of the grinaldi in Elloweer. I'm basically here by mistake."

"You escaped from the Sky Raiders with Jace, Mira, and Cole?" Lorenzo asked.

"Yes," Twitch said.

"Twitch has saved my life," Cole said. "He's a lot more clever than he admits."

"Not admitting your cleverness is much cleverer than the alternative," Lorenzo said. He turned to Violet. "And what about you?"

"I'm the newest addition to the group," Violet said. "They needed to go to Creon, so a Wayminder was required. Queen Harmony partnered me with them."

"You're young to be a Wayminder," Lorenzo said.

"I passed the trials six weeks after my thirteenth birthday," Violet said.

"Extraordinary," Lorenzo said. "That is younger than I was when I passed them. How old are you now?"

"Nearly fifteen," Violet said.

"So in one sense you are the eldest," Lorenzo said, his eyes straying to Mira.

"Except I have been eleven for decades," Mira said.

"I know the feeling of suspending your age," Lorenzo said. "You are aging normally now."

"Ever since my powers were restored," Mira said.

"And you serve the queen, Violet?"

"I do," Violet said. "I'm worried about her. She was taken, along with the king, and Honor and Destiny Pemberton as well."

"Taken?" Lorenzo asked.

"They disappeared earlier today," Mira said. "Some want to blame us because they know we were working with Violet. But we suspect Owandell used Wayminders willing to break the rules."

Lorenzo nodded. "His Enforcers have grown bolder over the last several years. And recently they seem willing to cross any boundaries."

"They think they're about to take over the world," Jace said.

"They're partly right," Cole said. "Ramarro will conquer the world if he gets free. But the shapecrafters will be his slaves just like everyone else will be."

"Favored slaves, perhaps," Lorenzo said. "I expect a clean death would be much more pleasant. What about you, Cole? What is your story?"

"I came here from Outside," Cole said. "Arizona."

"Phoenix area?" Lorenzo asked.

"Mesa," Cole said. "You know it?"

"Well, after my retirement, I took command of the world walkers for a time," Lorenzo said. "Expanded the operation. I take a great interest in your world."

"So do some slavers," Cole said. "A bunch of kids in my neighborhood were forced to come here. I followed to try to rescue them."

"You came to the Outskirts deliberately," Lorenzo said.

"Yes," Cole said. "Accidentally, but deliberately. And I've been waiting to find a Grand Shaper from Creon."

"You want to get home and stay there," Lorenzo said.

Cole took a deep breath. "Is it possible?"

Lorenzo stroked his mouth. "This world is not designed to allow it. But there are rumors of a way."

"Really?" Violet asked.

"Even Grand Shapers speak of it in whispers," Lorenzo said. "Many with skepticism. We call it the Pilgrim Path. A true way back to temporal reality from an eternal realm. There is no knowledge of it ever working . . . but such knowledge would be difficult to obtain. Any who walk the Pilgrim Path can never return."

"Do you think anyone has walked it?" Cole asked.

"A few Grand Shapers of Creon have died," Lorenzo said. "The rest are in hiding, and most hide extremely well. There are at least two who seem to have vanished. Either they passed away quietly, they hid perfectly, or perhaps they walked the Pilgrim Path."

"Could you do it?" Cole asked.

"I aspire to try someday," Lorenzo said. "I don't have the ability yet. I may never have it. Fortunately, you are trying to find the best man to ask in the history of the Outskirts. Kendo Rattan knows better than anyone if it can be done."

"Should we get going?" Jace asked. "Time is against us."

"Won't it pause time if we go back?" Cole asked.

"A common misconception," Lorenzo said. "You inevitably remain synced to your native timestream. If you go back a hundred years, spend a day there, and return, a day will have passed here. None have found a way around it."

"And if we leave Creon?" Cole asked.

"When you leave Creon, you immediately return to your present point in the timestream," Lorenzo said. "If you go back in time, spend three hours there, and then leave Creon, you will inescapably return to the present to find that three hours have elapsed."

"All the more reason to hurry," Jace said.

"I will do my best," Lorenzo said. "Traveling back in time requires preparation. The longer you want to remain back in time, the more preparation I need."

"How long to be ready?" Cole asked.

"Several days to prepare, minimum," Lorenzo said.

"Too long," Cole said.

"What if you send only one of us?" Jace asked.

"That would help a little," Lorenzo said. "The problem isn't so much the number of travelers. You will all use the same wayport. Opening a way to the past requires an enormous amount of energy. And keeping you there takes additional effort. To be safe, I should send you back for at least six hours. If you want to risk it, I could try sending you for only an hour. But you'll only get one chance within whatever time window we choose."

"We can't return to the same time more than once," Cole remembered.

"Correct," Lorenzo agreed.

"Once our time runs out, we get drawn back to the present?" Mira asked.

"Inevitably, yes," Lorenzo said. "Just like you would get pulled back here if you spent too much time in Cole's home world. Remaining out of sync from where you belong can only be maintained for a limited period."

"Can we get back early?" Jace asked.

"If you were with a Wayminder who knew how to speed up the return," Lorenzo said.

"Could I learn?" Violet asked.

"Have you time shifted?" Lorenzo asked.

"A little," Violet said.

"Then it is possible," Lorenzo said.

"You've gone back in time?" Jace asked, impressed.

"No," Violet said. "Time shifting temporarily alters the flow of time for a person or an object. You can barely tell it has been done unless you're a time-sensitive Wayminder. It's a way to diagnose potential in young Wayminders."

"Our big problem is we don't have several days to wait," Cole said. "We need to get back in time quickly. Lorenzo, what if I help you?"

"How?"

"What if I boost your energy?" Cole asked. "Could it maybe speed up the process?"

Lorenzo paused, looking at Cole uncertainly. "I've mastered the secret of perpetual youth—the skill a Grand Shaper of Creon must acquire to retire. I've improved my abilities for hundreds of years. The power required for time travel surpasses what even the mightiest shapers of other disciplines can imagine."

"Cole is amazing, though," Violet said. "With his help,

I can open a wayport anytime, anywhere, as frequently as I want."

"You should try it at least," Mira said.

Cole held out a hand. "See what you can do with me helping. If it doesn't make a difference, no harm done."

Lorenzo hesitated. "You won't try to alter my power?"

"Have shapecrafters worked on you?" Cole asked.

Lorenzo looked offended. "Of course not. I don't want anyone tampering with my nature."

"I'll just lend you energy," Cole promised. "See if it helps."

Lorenzo took his hand. The Wayminder's power was spectacular—complex and brilliant. Cole started small, then began pouring power into him.

"Whoa," Lorenzo said with wide eyes. "Easy, Cole, easy."

Cole pushed more gently.

"Okay," Lorenzo said. "I see. Yes. No wonder everyone is so interested in you. I expected a lot, but this is . . . unprecedented." Lorenzo released his hand, then cocked his head. "You're still connected to me."

"I can hold the connection without touching," Cole said. "I haven't figured out how to establish it without contact yet."

"I expect you will," Lorenzo said. "The physical contact is just a crutch. Your power touching my power has very little to do with you touching me, as you can currently feel."

"Right," Cole said.

"I can get you where you want to go immediately," Lorenzo said. "Give me one more big push."

Cole flooded energy into Lorenzo, and his ears popped when a wayport appeared off to one side. Cole only had experience with shimmery, delicate wayports. This one was utterly black, like a wound in the fabric of reality.

CHAPTER

—— 17 ——

DEDICATION

"That looks ominous," Twitch said, walking around the dark gash in the air near the center of the room.

"You think baby bunnies look ominous," Jace said.

Twitch blinked multiple times. "They could have germs."

"It should look ominous," Lorenzo said. "Time travel is no trifling matter. I suggest minimal interference in the past. Find Kendo Rattan, if you can, and learn all he will share. You'll have at least twelve hours. I'll talk with Violet about how to get you back early."

"Can we all go?" Mira asked.

"You could, yes," Lorenzo said. "As you please."

"Mira should stay," Jace said.

"No way," Mira said. "If I'm there, Kendo Rattan will be more likely to help us."

"He won't know who you are," Jace said.

"Probably true," Lorenzo said. "Kendo Rattan was actually there when the dedication happened, not visiting the event from the future. But Mira's status as a princess could carry some weight."

"Would it make sense for some of us to stay back?" Cole asked. "If we can each only try this once? So we'll have another chance?"

"If Kendo is going to avoid you, he will avoid you," Lorenzo said. "If any of you could make a difference, it will happen whether you go now or later. I think whoever wishes to try should go together."

"How do we signal him about Ramarro?" Cole asked.

"He'll recognize that you're from the future," Lorenzo said. "It will undoubtedly draw his attention."

"Pieces of parchment?" Mira proposed. "Some could say 'Ram.' Others 'Arro.'"

"Simple," Lorenzo said. "Serviceable. I like it."

"We're all going?" Jace asked.

"We're in this together," Mira said.

"Let me work with Violet for a moment," Lorenzo said. "You see parchment on that desk. Pens as well. Feel free to make your signs."

Lorenzo ushered Violet away while Mira claimed parchment and a pen. "How big?" she asked.

"Small," Cole said. "Just big enough to be noticed. We don't want to draw attention from anyone else."

"What if we get asked about the words?" Twitch wondered.

"Play dumb?" Cole suggested.

"Tell them to mind their own affairs," Mira said.

211

"You could start a fight," Jace said.

"I'll improvise," Twitch said, accepting a slip of parchment from Mira. She handed out pieces to Cole and Jace.

"I guess we'll spread out?" Mira asked.

"Probably," Cole said. "It'll give Kendo a better chance to notice us. And it will keep our paper messages away from each other."

"What if he won't help us?" Jace asked.

"We keep trying," Cole said. "We do all we can."

Jace nodded thoughtfully. "You're right."

"I understand the theory," Violet said, returning with Lorenzo. Mira gave her a slip of parchment.

"With Cole energizing you, an early return could be possible," Lorenzo said. "At the worst, you'll only have to wait about twelve hours. The eventual summons to your proper time will happen naturally."

"If Kendo helps us, he might be able to send us back," Cole said.

"Kendo Rattan is my superior in every way," Lorenzo said. "Let us hope for his aid. Are you ready? Unlike many wayports, once you cross through, you cannot return through the same portal."

"Got it," Jace said. "Time to go?"

"Anything else we should know?" Cole asked.

"A quick departure is better than prolonging this," Lorenzo said. "I'm leaning on Cole's power to hold the timeport open, but the effort remains strenuous. Cole should go through last."

"I've never visited another time," Violet gushed.

"None of us have," Jace said. "Me first."

He stepped into the blackness and vanished.

"Jace?" Twitch called.

"He can't hear you," Lorenzo said.

Twitch jumped through, followed by Violet and Mira.

"Thanks," Cole said to Lorenzo. "See you soon."

It felt to Cole like stepping through a thin, perfectly even waterfall. Instead of getting wet, his skin tingled as the unseen membrane parted to receive him.

And then Cole stood in a narrow, empty ally beside his friends. The sun was much too high in the sky to correspond to the day he had left behind. A trickle of water ran down the middle of the alley before veering into a drain. A pile of melon rinds and wilted vegetables moldered nearby.

Jace took a deep breath. "Does the past smell worse?"

"It does here," Twitch muttered.

"Did it work?" Cole asked. "Are we in the past?"

"Lorenzo Debray sent us," Violet said. "It must have worked." She looked up at the walls with excited eyes, lips parting in a wide smile. "We're in the past!"

"Then it's long before any of us were born," Mira said. "Even me."

"Should we spread out?" Twitch asked.

"Not a lot of room," Jace observed.

"I'm sure he sent us here to disguise our arrival," Violet said. "I bet it's the nearest empty outdoor space to the event."

"Should we leave the alley and spread out?" Twitch clarified.

"Will the school be hard to find?" Cole asked.

"Big granite building," Violet said. "Look for a crowd. Or ask about the dedication."

"I'll go first," Jace said, trotting toward the open end of the alley.

"Meet back here?" Mira asked.

"Unless we find each other elsewhere," Jace called over his shoulder.

Violet hugged herself and looked around. "We're in a different century."

"It seems really normal," Cole said.

"We're in the same kingdom," Violet said. "I've been to the town of Halbrook. Or I will come here someday, if you look at it that way."

"If coming here is in your past, you've been here," Cole said.

"Makes sense," Violet agreed.

"Bye," Mira said, walking away from them.

Cole snapped his fingers. "Jace's rope! I wanted to try and power it up."

"You can connect to me," Violet said, holding out her arm.

Cole extended a hand toward her, then paused. "Lorenzo told me I don't need to touch you." He searched for her power and began to faintly sense it. Reaching out mentally, he tried to connect, but it was slippery.

"Be careful," Twitch said, going down the alley.

Cole grabbed Violet's wrist and instantly made the connection, brightening her power. "I'll try to stay linked to you."

"Do your best," Violet said.

"Want me to go last?" Cole asked.

"Sure," Violet said. She started down the alley, then glanced back. "Soak it in. Few get this opportunity."

Cole watched her pass out of view. The alley failed to impress him. All of the Outskirts except Zeropolis seemed back in time to him. Swords and wagons. He was now further back in time, but there was nothing to emphasize the reality.

He walked to the end of the alley and took a deep breath. There was nothing noteworthy about the air, except that he was away from the moldy vegetables. The street at the end of the alley was narrow, without many people. Cole chose a direction and intersected a larger street with a lot of foot traffic. Many wore Wayminder robes. Most of the others wore tunics. He didn't see anyone with a shirt and trousers like he had on and wondered how conspicuous they made him.

The Wayminders all seemed to flow in the same direction, so Cole followed them. After turning onto another street, Cole found a crowded square filled mostly with Wayminders, everyone facing a huge stone building with numerous fluted pillars. On the far side of the street Cole saw Violet, and up ahead he noticed Mira.

The assembled Wayminders milled and talked as their numbers swelled. Here and there wayports opened, and new Wayminders joined the assembly. No ceremony had begun yet. Cole wondered how early he was.

"Excuse me," a voice said over Cole's shoulder.

He turned to find a short man with reddish hair and Asian features walking behind him. "Yeah?"

"This is an awkward question, but are you bearing tidings about Ramarro?"

Cole stopped walking. "Kendo Rattan?" he whispered.

"I know the name," the man said. "Who sent you?"

"Lorenzo Debray," Cole said.

"I have not met him yet," the man said. "What is the message?"

"Are you Kendo?"

"You came looking for me?"

"Yes."

"How did you know to find me here?"

"Lorenzo."

"May I ask how he knew?"

"I think you told him," Cole said.

"Did I really?" Kendo asked. "That is not how I normally operate."

"He is a former Grand Shaper of Creon. Not yet, though. He will be."

"Perhaps if I had a purpose, I would let such a person contact me in the past," Kendo said. "You are far from your proper time. And you are not native to the Outskirts."

"I have to stop Ramarro," Cole said.

"Why you?" Kendo asked.

"Lots of reasons," Cole said. "I have special abilities."

"Yes, you do," Kendo said. "Glad you mentioned it. I didn't want to be rude. Your power is hard to miss. Unique, I would say."

"Dandalus told me I need to stop the torivor," Cole said.

"Dandalus is long gone in the present day," Kendo said. "Let alone when you are from."

"He left an imprint of himself in the Founding Stone," Cole said. "And I met his echo."

"Fascinating," Kendo said. "What is the threat?"

"Ramarro escaped the echolands," Cole said. "He used a piece of the Founding Stone. The imprint of Dandalus managed to trap him in the vault you made."

Kendo puffed his cheeks and blew out. "You know far too many secrets, young one. Almost more than I do. In your time, my Void is currently holding Ramarro?"

"Yes," Cole said. "Is there any way we can strengthen it?"

"I made it as strong as I could," Kendo said. "I violated some of the laws I established for Creon to do so, bending the rules as far as I knew how. The Void is my ultimate prison. It would hold almost anyone indefinitely. And it is utterly insufficient to contain a torivor."

"How long will it hold him?" Cole asked.

"How long has it held him?" Kendo replied.

"A few days," Cole said.

Kendo nodded. "If it held him for more than an hour, the Void will probably hold him for a few more days. Not weeks. Days. A little over a week maybe."

"You can't make it stronger?" Cole asked.

"Not unless between now and then I learn groundbreaking information about the kingdom I personally designed," Kendo said. "And you are?"

"Cole."

217

"Pardon the bluntness, but is this a trap?" Kendo asked.

"What?"

"A trap to capture or harm me," Kendo said. "I greatly prefer honesty. In the long run it always simplifies matters and saves time."

"This isn't a trap."

"It would be a good one," Kendo said. "A secret issue I desperately care about. Delivered by children."

"You don't die today," Cole said. "You still have to tell Lorenzo you'll be here."

"If you are here because I told him, it will happen," Kendo said. "Of course, you could be lying. I've had misinformation from the future before. Maybe you heard that I die today. Maybe you came to do it. I can't read the future."

"I'm being honest," Cole said.

"What do you want from me?" Kendo asked.

"Information," Cole said. "How do we keep Ramarro imprisoned? How do we stop him if he gets free?"

"Happy to share what I can," Kendo said. "The framers of the Outskirts built the best prisons we could to hold the torivors. Most of the framers are long gone now. Our greatest hope lies in keeping them inside those prisons. If Ramarro gets free, I'm not sure how to recapture him. You came with four others?"

"Yes," Cole said.

"Would you like them to meet with us?"

"Sure."

"I don't mean to be pushy."

"Can you teleport them here?" Cole asked.

"Easier and less conspicuous for you to speak to them," Kendo said. A small disturbance appeared in the air in front of Cole's lips. "Tell them to meet at the corner of the square by the goat statue."

"Guys, I found him. Meet at the corner of the square by the big goat statue." Cole could see the huge goat up ahead.

The disturbance vanished. "Good," Kendo said. "Tell me about your power."

As they walked toward the stone goat, Cole explained how he could make items work outside of the kingdoms where they were designed to function. He also explained how he could energize the abilities of others and burn away the darkness of shapecrafting.

"Truly unique," Kendo said. "I am honored to meet you."

"I'm honored too," Cole said. "You're famous."

"I'm just a man who learned to outlive his time," Kendo said.

"And who helped make a world," Cole said.

"A fair imitation of a world, I'll give it that," Kendo said. "We all have our talents. Human beings tend to hastily decide that if they excel at something, they excel at everything. I try not to be one of them. I have plenty of flaws, and there is plenty I don't know."

Cole waved at his friends, who had all gathered at the goat. Violet looked at Kendo with crazed amazement.

"You are a young Wayminder," Kendo told Violet.

"You're the original Wayminder," she said. "I'm not even worthy to talk to you."

Kendo smiled uncomfortably. "Yet here we stand. As you see, I am only a man. A short one."

Violet shook her head. "A giant. A legend. And you look so young."

"When aging is halted, it halts," Kendo said. He took in the group. "You are facing a terrible threat."

"We've faced a lot," Jace said. "But this tops them all."

"Tell me of the perils of your time," Kendo said.

Cole explained about Owandell and the shapecrafters. Mira told about losing her power. Jace filled in details about some of the fights.

"And now you hope I can help design a way to thwart the torivor," Kendo said. He folded his arms and stared at the ground. "I hate to let people down. Especially when it will cause the end of the world."

"We're feeling the same stress," Cole said.

Kendo grinned. "I suppose so. I have no definitive answer for you now. But I know the day you came from. With knowledge that Ramarro will indeed get free and end up in the Void, I will spend the coming decades preparing. I will devise the best strategy I can."

"What can you tell us now?" Mira asked.

"Can we wait until after the ceremony?" Kendo said. "A former student of mine is involved. Then I can take you to a secluded location where we can speak freely."

"How long until it starts?" Jace asked.

"Less than an hour," Kendo said.

"Can't we just skip ahead?" Jace asked. "You time travel, right?"

Kendo smiled broadly. "It would be convenient. But traveling forward through time is nearly impossible. Particularly if you wish to return." Suddenly he looked shocked. "Oh no."

Cole turned his head, half expecting to see a terrible accident.

"What?" Mira asked.

"The Perennial Serpent is attacking Charlotte Lamb," Kendo said. A wayport opened nearby.

"Who?" Jace asked.

"A former Grand Shaper," Violet said.

"I have warning systems in place," Kendo said. "An alarm just went off. I must go now. I refuse to lose another." He paused, almost spoke, and halted again. "I could use help. Follow if you dare."

Kendo Rattan stepped into the wayport and was gone.

SERPENT

D o we go?" Cole asked.

"And confront the Perennial Serpent?" Violet asked in horror.

"He can handle it, right?" Twitch asked.

"Kendo Rattan lived to tell Lorenzo he would be here today," Mira said.

"What if he lived because we helped him?" Cole asked.

"No way to know," Violet said.

"Might be good practice," Jace said. "We have worse than a snake in our future."

"Does that mean we have to jump into every fight between now and then?" Twitch asked. "If we don't go, Kendo must have survived without us."

"We don't have time to debate," Jace said.

"He's keeping the wayport open," Violet said.

"We need his help," Cole said. "Shouldn't we help him?"

Jace held out his golden strand. "Charge me up."

Cole touched the small rope and infused it with power.

"Nobody has to follow me," Jace said as he lunged through the wayport.

Staring at the shimmering disturbance, Cole drew his Jumping Sword and pushed power into it. He could still feel his connection to the golden rope.

"We're going?" Twitch asked.

"I am," Cole said.

Violet and Twitch held out their hands, and Cole connected to their powers. Suddenly Twitch had grasshopper legs. Mira presented her Jumping Sword, and Cole quickly powered it up. Then he entered the wayport.

He stepped out onto a gentle, grassy slope. Higher up, the slope leveled off, and a wooden palisade enclosed a village. Low fences divided the surrounding fields into sections. At least a dozen cows were running in different directions— away from a giant snake.

Fangs bared, hood spread, a silver-and-white cobra reared up three or four times higher than the man and woman before it. The enormous serpent had a head the size of an anvil and a body as thick as a tree. Cole recognized Kendo as the man. Dressed as a Wayminder, the stocky woman looked well into her autumn years. A long scarf bundled her gray hair.

Jace landed to one side of the serpent, cushioning the impact with the rope. Cole had seen Jace use the rope to propel himself into battle many times. Despite the fearsome appearance of the serpent, Jace had not hesitated.

Pointing his Jumping Sword, Cole aimed for a spot in the field between Kendo and Jace and cried, "Away!" He sprang over the rippling pasture, stumbling as he landed, grass swishing against his shins.

Wielding his rope like a whip, Jace lashed the serpent in the face once, twice, three times. Seeming more annoyed than injured, the snake swiveled to face the new threat.

Mira landed beside Cole. Violet stepped through a way-port on his other side, followed by Twitch. Cole kept feeding all of them power, and his sword as well.

Jace lassoed the huge cobra's mouth shut. The enormous serpent thrashed its head from side to side, then swept Jace's legs out from under him with its tail. Jace lost hold of the rope, and it fell away from the serpent's snout.

Coils writhing into a new position, the Perennial Serpent wheeled and struck at the Grand Shapers. Kendo raised both hands, and the strike slowed almost to stillness. Slender fangs gleaming, the cobra inched forward. Kendo trembled. Cole could sense a massive flood of power emanating from him as he somehow manipulated the speed of the great snake.

The slowness provided an opening.

Cole drew his Jumping Sword, pointed it just below the head of the enormous cobra, and shouted, "Away!" He sprang forward, air rushing over him as he zoomed toward his target. The sword might not have a long enough blade to whack the head clean off, but Cole figured he could deliver an ugly wound. He would plunge the blade deep and let his momentum rip it free. He would need to jump again when he landed to offset the impact. Cole squeezed the hilt tightly. If he lost hold of the sword, it would be an ugly fall.

As the tip of the Jumping Sword neared the silver-white

scales, the serpent vanished. Instead of the expected impact, the sword struck nothing, and Cole sailed through empty space, taking a smaller jump to a nearby spot after landing. Cole saw Mira stagger to a halt some distance away—she had jumped at the snake as well.

"Behind you!" Jace shouted.

Cole turned to find that the enormous serpent had materialized behind him and was rearing up, jaws agape. "Away!" Cole shouted as he jumped back toward Violet and Twitch. In his haste he leaped higher than was necessary—another jump would definitely be needed upon landing.

As Cole reached the apex of his flight, the Perennial Serpent appeared in his landing zone, head turned upward to greet him. Jace had recovered his rope, but the tail of the snake hurled him to the ground again. Cole plunged downward, and the cobra surged up to greet him.

And then Twitch collided with Cole, abruptly changing the course of his descent, insectile wings fluttering. The striking snake missed. With Twitch's arms around him, Cole landed softly.

Twitch dove in front of Cole as the serpent struck again. Sharp fangs plunged into Twitch's thigh, and he disappeared.

The snake tried to come at Cole again, but the golden rope encircled the base of its hood. Moving like a ribbon in a windstorm, the Perennial Serpent thrashed and corkscrewed, but the rope held, and the other end of the rope began to entangle the tail. Jace had lengthened the rope farther than Cole had seen it stretch, allowing him to attack from a greater distance away.

Despite his proximity to the dangerously flailing cobra, Cole looked around for Twitch but could not see his friend anywhere. Cole realized he could no longer feel Twitch's power. What had happened to him? Where had the bite sent him?

Cole saw Mira pointing her Jumping Sword at the serpent and cut power to her weapon. Her mouth formed the word "away" before she took a small, unaided hop forward. He couldn't let her risk an attack!

The snake vanished again.

Still lending power to Violet and the golden rope, Cole aimed his sword at Kendo Rattan and sprang to the Grand Shaper's side. Cole laid a hand on the man's wrist and felt the power blazing within him.

"Stop the snake," Cole said, forcing a massive amount of power into Kendo.

The Perennial Serpent reappeared near Jace, ready to strike. A wayport appeared beside him, and Jace dove through to emerge behind the serpent. Kendo raised both hands, and the serpent moved in slow motion and began to shrink. Jace lassoed the cobra just below the hood again, and Cole could see the rope digging into the scales as it squeezed.

The snake vanished.

Kendo dropped his hands to his knees, panting.

"Stay ready," Cole said.

"It's gone," Kendo said. "Really gone this time."

"Dead?" Cole asked.

"No," Kendo replied. "But it fled through time."

"Should we follow it?" Cole asked.

Kendo shook his head. "I can't track it. And, mind you, I

can track almost anything that moves through space or time. Not the Perennial Serpent. My oldest foe here in Creon."

"What about Twitch?" Cole asked. "The snake bit him and he disappeared."

Kendo regarded Cole with sad eyes. "I'm unsure. Your comrade could be no more. He could be far removed across space or time. I can't sense what that serpent does, or really comprehend how, and believe me, I try."

Cole squeezed the Jumping Sword hard. He wanted to throw it. He screwed one heel into the ground by pivoting it back and forth.

"I'm sorry," Kendo said.

"What can we do?" Cole asked, trying to resist grinding his teeth.

"We can hope," Kendo said.

"What now?" the female Wayminder asked.

"Flee to your safest stronghold," Kendo said. "We're no longer trapped here."

Violet, Jace, and Mira had approached.

"The two of you were stuck here?" Violet asked.

"The fight did not begin here for Charlotte," Kendo said. "The serpent chased her across many locations before corralling her here and blocking all escape. It shielded us from opening wayports to other destinations."

Cole was trying to listen, trying to be interested. He had recruited Twitch for this. And now Twitch was gone. Maybe not for good. Maybe he was all right somewhere.

"I've never felt so helpless," Charlotte said. "My powers utterly failed."

"You did well lasting long enough for me to reach you," Kendo said. "That serpent is so strong. It countered most of the actions I tried to take as well. We would have both fallen had these children not come to our aid."

"Thank you," Charlotte said earnestly. "I'm so sorry about your friend."

Cole gave a nod. Mira squeezed his shoulder from behind.

"Go, Charlotte," Kendo said. "I'll see to the children."

"I'm not sure I can," Charlotte said. "I'm drained."

Kendo glanced at Cole. "Would you mind?"

Cole tried to suppress his feelings. Currently he was needed. Mourning might have to come later. He took Charlotte's hand. Her power was steady and strong but not nearly as dazzling as Kendo's. He lent power to her, and a wayport opened behind her.

"Extraordinary," Charlotte said, gazing at Cole with startled eyes. "Thank you again."

She retreated into the wayport, and it closed.

Kendo absently waved a hand, and a new wayport opened. "Come. Let's converse in a safer place."

"What about Twitch?" Jace asked.

"Kendo isn't sure what happened," Cole said. "The serpent might have sent him far away. Or he could be gone."

"Can't you feel where he went?" Violet asked Kendo, then lowered her eyes. "With respect."

"Ordinarily I could," Kendo said. "This serpent is stealthy. It's like nothing else I've ever encountered, and has been a thorn in my side practically since Creon began."

"Does it always make people vanish?" Mira asked.

"Sometimes," Kendo said. "We have also found corpses. Over the years the Perennial Serpent has slain two active Grand Shapers and dozens of Wayminders, along with many other citizens."

"Were the people who vanished ever found?" Cole asked.

Kendo paused. "Not yet."

"And lots have vanished?" Jace asked. "Some of them a long time ago?"

"The Perennial Serpent has been making people disappear with its bite for hundreds of years," Kendo said.

Growling, Jace picked up a stone and threw it as far as he could. "I'm going to find that snake and tie it into knots!"

Mira approached Jace and hugged him. He embraced her fiercely.

Cole wiped tears from his eyes. He wanted to speak. He wanted to say maybe Twitch was alive and safe someplace far away. Or at worst he was in the echolands. They would all get there eventually. Maybe Twitch had met up with Zig in the Hall of Glory.

No words would come.

Once again Twitch had saved him. And now Twitch was gone.

"We don't know where Twitch went," Mira said. "We can hope for the best."

"Yeah," Jace said. "It seemed like such a nice snake. It probably sent him on a fancy holiday."

"We should adjourn to my hideaway," Kendo said, gesturing toward the wayport.

Violet entered. Mira followed. Cole stepped through after

her into a smallish room filled with walls of clear, overlapping crystals. The smooth floor and ceiling were composed of crystal as well. Trying to stare into the distance gave Cole eyestrain as prism after prism warped and fragmented the view.

Jace came through the wayport with Kendo behind him. The wayport closed.

"I feel like I'm inside a kaleidoscope," Cole said.

"An apt description," Kendo agreed. "Difficult for the eyes. My apologies. Hardly a pleasant room for entertaining guests. Except that it is extremely well shielded against any crooked Wayminders who might wish to visit unexpectedly or spy."

"Have you figured out what the serpent wants?" Mira asked. "Besides killing people?"

"The Perennial Serpent is the oldest unsolved mystery in Creon," Kendo said. "I don't know if it wants anything. For all I know it could have no agenda. It might simply be a predator attracted to strong sources of shaping power. Sometimes it appears with a mysterious figure known as the Ancient One. The relationship between the two is not understood. The serpent has historically attacked Wayminders. Other citizens tend to perish as collateral damage. It will go decades without an appearance, then attack multiple times in a matter of months."

"It has powers," Cole said.

"Strong powers," Kendo agreed. "It shapes in ways I have never seen in Creon. I believe it changes size by some form of spatial manipulation. Or maybe it incorporates elements of shaping from other kingdoms. I try to send it elsewhere, and it blocks me or comes right back."

"It vanished when I jumped at it," Cole said. "I didn't see a wayport."

"Some of what the serpent can do is beyond my understanding," Kendo said.

"And you can't track it?" Violet asked.

"No," Kendo said. "I have set up methods to detect its appearance. And I have given some Wayminders procedures to contact me if it appears. But I can't block an appearance. I can't sense where it goes when it leaves. And I can't tell what it does to the victims it sends away."

"Why not?" Violet asked.

"The shaping it uses is too raw," Kendo said. "I believe it shapes by pure instinct. And it sometimes flouts the laws we established. I'm so sorry about your friend. I wish I could do more."

"Could it be Elegance's power?" Violet asked. "Wouldn't that fit?"

"It's been around so long," Jace said.

"In a world where time travel is possible," Violet replied. "Made of power that allows time travel to happen."

Everyone was silent.

"It fits," Cole said.

"Tell me more," Kendo urged.

Mira and Cole explained how Owandell had been schooled by Ramarro, how he had taken the shaping power from Mira and her sisters, and what it had looked like as they reclaimed the renegade shaping powers across four of the five kingdoms.

"It's a compelling theory," Kendo said when they finished.

"I had not given serious consideration to the Perennial Serpent originating far in the future. But it now sounds plausible, perhaps even probable."

"And we also have the problem of Ramarro," Cole said.

Kendo sighed. "When the torivors first appeared, I knew the seeds of our destruction had been planted. I wish we could have defeated them. Instead we delayed the problem by locking them away. We left an awful catastrophe for future generations to inherit."

"We have to beat Ramarro," Cole said. "Just give us a way."

"I know when you are from," Kendo said. "Allow me twenty years. Have your friend Lorenzo send you to this same location twenty years from today. I will spend the intervening time learning what I can. Hopefully, I can give you better answers after some serious research and experimentation."

"Okay," Cole said.

"For you this is a brief delay," Kendo said. "With your power to help Lorenzo, you will be talking to me again in a few minutes. Shall I send you back and get to work? If I hurry, I can still go catch the dedication ceremony."

"I forgot all about the ceremony," Mira said.

"I want to support my student," Kendo said with a sad smile. "I leave them on their own far too much. So much to do, so little time."

"That's funny coming from a guy who doesn't age," Cole said.

Kendo cocked his head. "Anything finite is over in a blink. No matter how long. Only eternity endures. Trust me—I have investigated thoroughly."

"I have one other question," Cole said. "Maybe it can wait."

"What is it?" Kendo asked.

Cole braced himself. This was it—if Kendo couldn't help him, he doubted anyone could. "I'm from Outside. I hope to get home to stay someday. And to help some of my friends do the same."

"Yes, I see," Kendo said. "The nature of this realm, even before we engineered it to accommodate living mortals, was to accept beings from elsewhere and prepare them to move on. It's a place of transition. This realm separates you from your previous life, your previous world. Distances you. People are not meant to go back from here. They are supposed to journey on toward eternity."

"So a return is impossible?" Cole asked.

"Perhaps not impossible," Kendo said. "But extremely difficult. And contrary to the nature of this place. Among the Grand Shapers of Creon there is talk about the Pilgrim Path—a way back to our home world. By coming to the Outskirts, I gained certain powers and led an interesting life. And I cheated myself out of a truly mortal experience. The longer I live, the more I hope to finish my days with a return to regular mortality."

There it was again, mention of the Pilgrim Path—perhaps a real possibility. Cole didn't trust his voice but had to ask. "Then you might be able to send me home?"

"I'm not sure," Kendo said. "It should not be possible. But many believed it would not be possible to create a place for mortals in this realm. I have defied what is possible before. Allow me more time to work on this as well."

"It's the best news I've gotten," Cole said.

Kendo considered him. "Do you hope to flee before Ramarro gets free?"

Cole shook his head. "I have friends here. No, I just hope there is a way home after we stop him."

Kendo placed a hand on Cole's shoulder. "Quite a boy. I'll work on it. For now—give Lorenzo my regards."

A wayport opened.

CHAPTER
—✳— 19 —✳—

PROPOSAL

"K endo Rattan sent you back with the pathway unshielded," Lorenzo said after Cole, Mira, Jace, and Violet returned. "I could see where you came from. He deliberately let me know how to access the Crystal Asylum."

"He wants us back there twenty years from our previous visit," Violet said.

"I understand," Lorenzo said. "But the Crystal Asylum is the stuff of legend among Wayminders. Even among Grand Shapers."

"Ramarro is a pretty big problem," Cole said.

"What about your friend Twitch?" Lorenzo asked.

Jace explained the fight with the Perennial Serpent. Cole struggled to keep his outward composure.

"What a strange coincidence that the serpent attacked on the very day I sent you back," Lorenzo said. "To my knowledge, the attack was not recorded, perhaps because the Wayminders survived. I'm sorry about your friend. Like you, I hope he is well and simply far away."

"Can I have a minute?" Cole asked. "Do you have a private place here?"

Lorenzo showed him down a hall into a small room with a cot and a writing desk. "Take your time," the Wayminder said, closing the door.

Cole flopped onto the cot and let himself sob. Hot tears flowed.

Why had he brought Twitch into this?

Cole pressed his teeth together. Without Twitch, would *he* have vanished instead? Would he be dead? Or maybe exiled to some distant location? Would his friends be doomed without him? Was it maybe for the best that Twitch had protected him? Was that fair to think?

Cole clenched his fists and squeezed his eyes against the tears. He had to keep it together. He and his friends had to stop Ramarro.

Who was he kidding? Twitch had died. And it was probably pointless. Cole wiped away snot with the back of his hand. He was going to get himself and all his friends killed.

Would it be better to serve Ramarro? They might live. But what kind of life? A life of slavery. A life of becoming like Owandell.

Better to die fighting.

Much better.

But he wanted to live. And he wanted his friends safe.

That meant defeating Ramarro. Was it possible? He simply couldn't know yet. It didn't seem likely at the moment. Hopefully, Kendo Rattan would help them find a way.

Somebody knocked on the door.

Probably Mira.

"Come in," Cole said.

Jace entered.

"Are you all right?" Jace asked.

"Not great," Cole said.

"Twitch might be okay."

"He might be dead."

"We're probably all dead," Jace said, taking a seat beside Cole on the cot. "Ramarro is coming. Think like a Sky Raider. Realize you're probably going to die. And die bravely."

"I'm as ready as I can be," Cole said.

"I know," Jace said seriously. "I've seen. You've changed. Especially since the echolands. You're devoted to this now. You're not as worried about getting home."

"I still want to get home," Cole said.

"But not until you finish what you started here," Jace said. "Not until Ramarro is stopped. Not until the princesses are safe."

"I had a chance to go home," Cole said quietly. "In the echolands. I think it was a real chance, not just a test. And I stayed. I'm committed."

"It shows," Jace said. "But losing Twitch is different for you."

"I went and got him," Cole said. "I brought him into this."

"You gave him a chance to die well instead of cowering," Jace said. "We all have that chance. We should be grateful for it. Don't fall apart. We're all ready for the risks. We're all volunteers. If any of us fall, the rest have to keep going."

Cole nodded. "It's hard."

"Brutal," Jace said. "We have to try to win."

"Right," Cole said. "How is Mira?"

"Honestly? Kind of mad at you."

"Because of Twitch?"

"No. Because you cut power to her sword. On purpose, right?"

Cole winced. "Yeah. She was going to jump at the serpent when it was going wild."

Jace nodded. "She's not happy about it. Feels like you don't trust her. Wonders if you see her as a real part of the team. Worries you might do it again."

"Did she ask you to talk to me?" Cole asked.

"I offered," Jace said. "She complained after you left. But I could tell she didn't want to bring it up with you because of Twitch."

"I was protecting her," Cole said.

"Between you and me, I'm glad you did it," Jace said. "I'll deny those words if you tell her."

"I hear you," Cole said. "Maybe I should have let her jump. Maybe she would have killed it."

"Do you believe that?"

"Not really. I'll talk to her."

"Should we get going? See what Kendo figured out?"

"What if he has nothing?"

"Only one way to find out."

Jace stood. Cole held out a hand, and Jace hauled him to his feet.

The others waited in the main room. Lorenzo was speaking with Violet.

Cole approached Mira. "Sorry for cutting power to your sword."

"Don't try to tell me it was an accident."

"It wasn't," Cole said. "I was trying to protect you."

"I've used Jumping Swords longer than you," Mira reminded him.

"You gave me my first one," Cole said.

"I know you meant well," Mira said. "Please trust me to take care of myself. Let me be part of the team. I need to know you won't strand me in the middle of a fight."

"I'll do my best," Cole said. "I have to do what I think is right. I promise not to do anything like that again unless I have an amazing reason."

"Is that as good as I'm getting?" Mira asked.

"I could lie," Cole said.

"Sorry about Twitch," Mira said.

"Let's hope he's all right," Cole said. "Might as well."

"He could outlive all of us," Jace said. "He might be in some forgotten corner of the Outskirts when the world ends."

"It won't end," Mira said. "We'll stop it."

"Should we go meet Kendo again?" Cole asked.

"I sure hope he has some good news," Mira said.

Cole crossed to Lorenzo. "We're ready. Can you send us?"

"No problem, if you lend me the power. I'll send you back to twenty years after you first met Master Rattan."

Cole took his hand.

A wayport opened.

"Ten hours, if you need it," Lorenzo said. "Otherwise, Kendo Rattan can send you back earlier."

Cole stepped through into the Crystal Asylum. Kendo awaited him, looking much the same, except for different clothes and slightly longer, messier hair. Jace, Violet, and Mira came through behind him. The wayport was not visible on this end, and so they seemed to simply appear.

"Right on schedule," Kendo said. "A quick twenty years for you four, I imagine?"

"Minutes, not hours," Mira said.

"I have refreshments this time," Kendo said, gesturing at a crystal table with five chairs. "I had more time to prepare. Least I can do, seeing as you're trying to save the world against horrible odds. Some quiche. Pies, mostly. Savory on the left, sweet on the right."

"Can we stop Ramarro?" Cole asked.

"I have thoughts on the matter," Kendo said. "More than last time. You realize you caught me off guard. We'll talk as we eat. Come sit."

They gathered around the table. Cole sat beside Violet, across from Jace and Mira. Kendo claimed a seat at the end of the table. He began pointing at various pies with a fork.

"Sausage, beef, lamb, and turkey," he said. "I like the white quiche more than the yellow. And for dessert, peach, apple, or berry."

"Looks good," Jace said, helping himself to a slice of sausage pie. Cole saw cheese in it and bits of vegetables. He went for the beef. It had a layer of mashed potatoes at the base.

"I have only one plan," Kendo said as the kids started eating. A piece of lamb pie sat before him. He spooned mint jelly onto it.

"What is it?" Cole asked.

"It combines the two issues you asked about," Kendo said. "I have come up with no way to strengthen the Void. It will hold as long as it will hold. Probably not very long. I can think of no way to entrap Ramarro once he gets free. And I have no idea how to defeat him."

"Not great so far," Jace said.

"Let me share the plan," Kendo said. "I have explored the feasibility of the Pilgrim Path—a way to go permanently from the Outskirts to Earth. I believe it is possible. I also suspect that if we could lure Ramarro down the Pilgrim Path, we might be able to solve our dilemma."

"What about Earth?" Cole asked.

"There is a chance Ramarro would be powerless on Earth," Kendo said. "And . . . it is possible he would take over your world and rule unchallenged until the end of time."

"We can't let that happen," Cole said, no longer interested in his food.

"Agreed," Kendo said. "And so I must research exactly which alternative would play out."

"Haven't you done that already?" Jace asked.

"As much as I can for now," Kendo said. "The Pilgrim Path remains a theoretical option. I can't be sure it will work until I walk it. And once I walk it, I cannot return."

"So you're waiting," Violet said.

"Yes," Kendo said. "I may have to wait a good while. Walking the Pilgrim Path will strip me of all connection to the Outskirts. I would permanently lose my powers."

"Does that mean Ramarro would lose his powers if he walks the path?" Mira asked.

"I think so," Kendo said. "He would certainly lose his connection to the Outskirts. But torivors are from Outside as well. I'm not sure how his native powers would manifest in Cole's world. I believe Earth would be inherently hostile to his source of power. But I'm not certain."

"We can't send Ramarro to Earth unless we know he won't destroy the planet," Cole said.

"Agreed," Kendo replied.

"Do you think the Pilgrim Path will work?" Violet asked.

"I strongly believe so," Kendo said. "But I'm not completely certain. Nor am I sure what walking the path will do to me. My shaping powers are so much a part of me, I don't know who exactly I will be after I lose them."

"You'll age again," Mira said.

"Yes," Kendo said. "Possibly all at once. I might walk the Pilgrim Path and immediately turn to dust! Though I suspect I will simply return to the normal process of aging."

"How do we find out more?" Cole asked, working on his pie again.

"I have a plan," Kendo said. "Part of me has wanted to attempt the Pilgrim Path for a good while. No man is meant to live forever. At least not as a mortal. And I have borne the burden of protecting the Outskirts for so long. I don't want to bear it eternally. And now I know the day. You children have given me a reason. I can walk away from the Outskirts and protect it at the same time."

"I don't follow," Jace said.

"Hundreds of years from now, ten years before you meet Lorenzo Debray, I will walk the Pilgrim Path. That will allow me to confirm that the path can be walked, and give me time to study the safety of bringing Ramarro to Earth."

"And we will be able to visit you there," Violet said.

"I will continue to research the matter and examine all contingencies. When you return to Lorenzo, he will have information about how to contact me on Earth. And he will send you there to find me."

"Then he already knew you were there when he met us," Cole said.

"Correct, assuming I follow through on this plan. If I do not, he will have other instructions. When you return to Lorenzo, simply tell him I gave you permission to see inside the green box."

"That green box?" Violet asked, pointing to a container roughly the size of a shoe box beside the dessert pies.

"If you have no objection to the container," Kendo said. "I rather like it. I will be preparing for hundreds of years. And you will know my fate in a matter of hours."

"Does this mean I could walk the Pilgrim Path one day?" Cole asked. "And could my friends who were taken?"

"I will leave detailed instructions behind," Kendo said. "If I succeed, yes, it means you could probably walk the Path as well. At the same cost of course. You would lose your shaping abilities, and become so out of tune with the Outskirts that you could never return."

"What about the echolands?" Cole asked. "After I die?"

"I can't speak to those matters," Kendo said. "What happens

after you die is an issue for the Grand Shapers of Necronum. Or, you know, wait and see. I rather enjoy a good surprise."

"There is no other way to fight Ramarro?" Jace asked.

"Not that I can currently imagine," Kendo said. "Not that leaves you a chance to win. I'll keep pondering the matter. If things become sufficiently dire, you could always consult the other torivor."

"Trillian," Cole said. "I've met him."

"And here you stand," Kendo said. "Without his taint upon you. Impressive."

"Talking to Trillian would almost certainly make matters worse," Mira said.

"I agree in principle," Kendo said. "Neither torivor can be trusted. Either would gladly take over the five kingdoms. And yet if defeat ever becomes certain, any chance is better than none."

"It's something to remember," Cole said.

"Dessert," Jace said, reaching for a slice of peach pie.

"So that's it," Cole said. "We go back to Lorenzo and see what's in the box."

"If I come up with new ideas between now and then, I'll adjust," Kendo said. "Otherwise, expect information about how to find me. Hopefully, I will have the answers you need. For now, enjoy the meal."

Cole could not keep his thoughts from straying to Dalton, Hunter, and Jenna as he ate. And the other kids from his world. They would freak out when they heard there was a chance they could truly go home! It had seemed impossible for so long.

If only Cole could live long enough to see them again.

Cole almost didn't dare to hope for success. Though perhaps possible, it remained so distant. And hoping for unlikely but desperately desired outcomes was a fast road to disappointment and pain.

One step at a time.

One victory at a time.

He tried a little of each dessert pie and liked berry the best.

It seemed Jace had about two slices of everything.

"How do you eat so much?" Violet asked him.

"I think the secret is spending most of your life as an underprivileged slave," Jace said. "It also helps when you're pretty sure the world is about to end. And if you don't mind eating until it hurts."

"If you're done, I can send you back to Lorenzo," Kendo said.

Cole looked around the table. The others seemed in agreement.

"Sure," Mira said.

A wayport opened.

"I look forward to our next meeting," Kendo said. "One way or another."

CHAPTER 20

OUTSIDE

Kendo gave us permission to see inside the green box," Cole reported once they were back inside Lorenzo's subterranean lair.

"I knew it!" Lorenzo exclaimed.

"Did you know about us all along?" Mira asked. "And about the box?"

"I very strongly suspected," Lorenzo said. "But I was under strict instructions not to show the box unless you asked."

"How much did you know?" Cole asked.

"I knew about you, Cole, and your power," Lorenzo said. "I knew Mira was a princess. I had heard about Jace and Violet. Kendo Rattan did not want me involving the wrong people. Cole, the extent of your ability still surprised me."

"Have you looked into the box?" Mira asked.

"Never!" Lorenzo said. "I've waited for this day for the last ten years. That was when Kendo confirmed to me that the Pilgrim Path was more than just a fable and left the green box in my care. Then he departed this world."

"Do you know if he survived?" Mira asked.

"He survived," Lorenzo said. "I visited him right after he went. It was a success."

"Did Kendo tell you about the dedication of the Halbrook School so we would find him?" Cole asked.

"Perhaps," Lorenzo said.

"How does that work?" Cole asked. "How could he know to tell you? The first time the dedication happened we wouldn't have been there."

"Remember," Lorenzo said. "Once you go back in time, you were always there. And if you were there, Kendo could have planted seeds to help it happen."

"I don't get it," Cole said.

"You think of cause and effect as linear," Lorenzo said. "You think one has to precede the other. That breaks down when you can move across time. It's hard to think four dimensionally when we typically live in three. Even the best time jumpers only operate as guests in four dimensions."

"The box?" Mira prompted.

"This way," Lorenzo said. A wayport opened. He motioned for them to enter.

Cole went through after Jace and emerged in another large underground rectangular room that looked a lot like the one they had left. Violet and Mira came through, followed by Lorenzo.

"Is this really a different place?" Jace asked suspiciously.

"It's a long way from my other hideout," Lorenzo said. "I'm not much of an artist. I've used the same plan for several hideaways. I almost never come here. It's where I keep the box." He led them to a table. Cole recognized the box awaiting them.

Lorenzo inserted a key and lifted the lid. He removed a piece of lined paper and handed it to Cole.

"This looks like it's from my world," Cole said.

"I'm sure it is," Lorenzo said. "Kendo visited Earth many times before walking the Pilgrim Path. He left the box shortly before he departed the five kingdoms for good."

Cole looked at the note.

Dear Cole, Mira, Jace, and Violet,

I trust you are well. If all goes according to plan, when you read this, we will have recently spoken, though from my point of view it has been a very long time since our last conversation. I will have walked the Pilgrim Path ten years ago. Hopefully, Lorenzo was able to confirm that I arrived to Earth safely. If not, I apologize and encourage you to plan alternate strategies with him.

Come see me, and I will tell you all I can about how we might lure Ramarro to Earth, and whether it would be ethical to try. You will find me in the Miami area. South Beach. A condo high-rise called the Pinnacle on Playa Circle. I'm number 1421. Hit the button. I'll be waiting. See you soon.

By the way, I have encountered the Perennial Serpent a few

*more times and feel it could indeed be an embodiment of stolen
shaping power. I hoped to defeat it for you, but never succeeded.*

See you shortly,
Kendo Rattan

"I've never been to Miami," Cole said.

"It's pleasant," Lorenzo replied.

"You've been?" Cole exclaimed.

"I've visited many places," Lorenzo said. "Miami had delicious stone crab. And wonderful Cuban sandwiches. I can get you near the Pinnacle. You'll have two hours maximum. But I can send you again if needed."

"Our shaping won't work there," Mira said.

"None of it," Lorenzo agreed. "Your powers will be entirely dormant. So be careful." He took out a roll of twenty-dollar bills and handed it to Cole. "Some money . . . just in case."

Cole thumbed through the bills. It was surreal to look at regular money after so long—something that had once felt so valuable and now seemed incredibly small compared to everything else at stake here. Still, his old self would have freaked out to have this much cash in his hands. "This is a lot!" he exclaimed.

Lorenzo shrugged. "Don't be conspicuous about it. You'll have it if you need it." He held out a hand. "Do you mind giving me a little help?"

Cole took his hand and energized his power.

A wayport opened.

It was too bright to stare at directly.

"Are you sure this doesn't lead to the sun?" Cole asked.

"Openings to the Outside tend to be brilliant," Violet said.

"And a little more disorienting," Lorenzo said. "Try to relax. You'll arrive just fine."

"We can go?" Mira asked. "Already?"

"Thanks to my limitless energy source," Lorenzo said, giving Cole a pat on the shoulder.

"I like the hustle," Cole said. "We have no time to waste. I can't believe I'll be back in my world. Even for a little while."

"Me first," Jace said, stepping into the radiant portal.

Cole followed.

When Cole stepped inside, bright whiteness blinded him entirely. His foot did not reach the ground. Instead he floated forward. Or down? He seemed to move and hold still at the same time. Cracking his eyes against the glaring light, Cole could see no details.

He began to feel nauseated.

And then his feet were on dirt, and he could open his eyes just fine. Cole stood beside Jace in a corner where concrete walls intersected. Succulents and shrubs grew all around him, screening him from view. Mira appeared, and then Violet.

Cole led the others out of the patch of vegetation and into a parking lot. Towering white clouds floated in an otherwise blue sky. Art deco buildings crowded an avenue. A row of palm trees stretched high and slender with shaggy tops. Not far away, a white-sand beach spread out with the ocean beyond. Lots of foot traffic moved along a walkway paralleling the beach—a blend of people in touristy attire, scantily clad beachgoers, slackers, and fitness enthusiasts.

"If you get thirsty around here, just breathe," Jace said.

"Hot and humid," Cole agreed. "But look at that beach."

"People in your world don't wear very much when they swim," Jace observed.

"I guess not," Cole had to agree.

"The buildings are huge," Violet said, looking around.

"This is nothing," Cole said. "They get bigger. Like Zeropolis."

"Want to go for a quick swim?" Jace asked, eyes on the water.

"Kind of," Cole said. "Aren't we racing the end of the world?"

"Exactly," Jace said. "What if this is our only chance?"

"Maybe after we talk to Kendo," Mira said. "There may be time."

Cole noticed a street sign. "Playa Circle is right over there. It looks tiny." He pointed to a white building taller than some of the others. "I bet that's the Pinnacle."

"Let's find out," Mira said.

They hurried over to Playa Circle and turned up the little street. An awning over the front doors proclaimed the suspected building the Pinnacle. Cole opened the front doors into a small room with columns of buttons beside four-digit numbers on the wall. The air was markedly cooler. Jace tried the next door but found it locked.

"I think we can call him from here," Cole said. He had seen such devices in movies but had never used one.

"Fourteen twenty-one," Violet reminded them.

Cole found the number and pressed the button. They waited a moment.

"Hello?" asked a male voice, recognizably Kendo.

"Hi, Kendo," Cole said. "We're here."

A pause followed. "Excuse me?"

"It's Cole, Mira, Jace, and Violet," Cole said. "We're here for our meeting."

Another pause. "I'm not sure what you mean. I'm not expecting anyone. There is no soliciting allowed here, young man."

"You're Kendo Rattan, right?"

"That is not . . . what I go by," the man said. "Who are you? Why are you contacting me?"

"You told us to come here," Cole said. "We're from the Outskirts. The five kingdoms. You set up this meeting a long time ago."

A long pause followed. Cole wondered if Kendo had hung up. "Who put you up to this?" the man asked.

"You did," Cole said. "We really need your help."

Violet leaned forward. "Have you forgotten?" she asked.

"There are four of you?" the man asked.

"And we don't have much time," Cole said. "We'll be sucked back to the Outskirts before long. We need to talk about Ramarro."

There came a buzzing sound.

"Come on up," the man said.

Cole pulled the door open and led the way to the elevator. He pushed the button, and they waited until the doors opened. Inside, the buttons rose from L to 18, skipping 13. Cole pressed 14. The elevator started to ascend.

"This will take us up?" Jace asked. "Your world *is* like Zeropolis."

The elevator stopped abruptly enough to make Cole's stomach lurch a little. He walked down a hall until they found the door marked 1421. Cole knocked.

The door opened. Not all the way.

It was definitely Kendo Rattan. He wore a bowling shirt, shorts, and sandals. His hair looked a little grayer and thinner, his face somewhat older, but he was unmistakable.

"Do you remember us now?" Cole asked.

Kendo looked perplexed. He slowly shook his head. "You are not familiar to me."

"None of us?" Mira asked. "You met us a couple of times over the years."

"Have you been working on Ramarro?" Jace asked.

"Where are your parents?" Kendo asked.

"Creon," Violet said.

"Orphan," Jace said.

"Mine don't remember me ever since I was kidnapped to the Outskirts," Cole said.

"And mine were recently abducted," Mira said. "The High King Stafford Pemberton and his consort, Harmony?"

Kendo rubbed his eyes. "I am really losing it."

"You really don't remember?" Cole asked.

Kendo regarded them thoughtfully. He pulled the door fully open. "Come inside."

"Thanks," Cole said.

The front room was nicely appointed. A sliding door led to a balcony with an ocean view. A tiny brown dog yipped at them.

"Hush, Monster," Kendo said. "These are only figments of my imagination." He looked at Cole. "Have a seat. Are you thirsty?"

"We're all right," Cole said.

"What do you have?" Jace asked.

"Water," Kendo said. "Ginger ale. I could make some lemonade."

"I'll try ginger ale," Jace said.

"Anyone else?" Kendo offered.

"Sure," Cole said. "Lemonade." Who knew when he would get his next chance for a taste of home?

The others shook their heads.

Kendo walked into his kitchen. Cole heard an ice machine grinding. Kendo returned with a glass for Jace and another for Cole.

"You came from the Outskirts," Kendo said as if it were unlikely.

"Yes," Cole assured him.

"What did I do there?" Kendo asked.

"You were a Wayminder," Cole said.

"Not just a Wayminder," Violet gushed. "You are Kendo Rattan! Grand Shaper of Creon. The founder of Creon! You helped make the Outskirts."

Kendo gave a little chuckle and tapped his temple. "That I might believe. If I invented it in here. Inside my mind."

"You really don't remember," Mira said.

"This is all very odd," Kendo said. "If it is some kind of joke, please desist. You have no idea how much you could be setting me back. But I'm not sure who would care to make this joke."

"It isn't a joke," Cole promised. "It's the opposite, actually. Desperately real. Life and death."

Kendo rubbed his elbow uncomfortably. "I have . . . journals."

"Yeah?" Cole asked.

"My handwriting. They tell of another place. Another me. An impossible place. An impossible me."

"Creon," Violet said.

"The Outskirts," Jace added.

"You know the names," Kendo said. "How do you know those words?"

"We just came from there," Cole said.

Kendo gave an awkward chuckle. "You can't imagine how absurd this sounds. And how confusing it is."

"Why?" Mira asked.

He gazed at her. "I don't remember my life. My memory goes back eight, nine years. Nothing before then. Only scribblings in journals about preposterous places and incredible dilemmas. As if I wrote an elaborate fiction and became lost in it. As if I broke my mind."

"Why don't you go by your real name?" Cole asked.

"The journals warn me not to use the name Kendo Rattan," Kendo said. "I go by Andy Starnes. Andy Starnes has no history before ten years ago. Neither does Kendo Rattan. No birth certificate."

"Don't you have ID?" Cole asked.

"I have papers," Kendo said. "Andrew Starnes. American citizen. I have a Social Security number. I have a birth certificate. But I did the research. They're fake. Good fakes, but fake."

"How did you get them?" Cole asked.

"I don't remember," Kendo said. "It happened during a hazy period about nine years ago that contains my first flickers of recall. No clear memories. My journal tells me I converted gold to dollars and used it to buy this apartment and a false identity. My journal makes all sorts of wild claims. I have long suspected that I am neither Kendo Rattan nor Andrew Starnes, but rather someone else who lost his sanity. Maybe I had an accident. Maybe it was drugs. I made up a story land called the Outskirts, where I lived. An elaborate farce. Somewhere along the way my true identity perished."

"You're Kendo Rattan," Mira said.

Kendo winced. "Perhaps. Can you imagine how painful that is to hear? I have . . . tattered scraps of the Outskirts in my mind. Like a half-forgotten dream full of gaps and inconsistencies. I can hardly distinguish between what I actually remember and what I read in my journals. My writings are disturbingly coherent. Especially at first. I seemed utterly convinced of this fanciful reality."

"You came here ten years ago," Cole said. "You called it the Pilgrim Path. You knew you would lose your powers. Apparently you also lost your memory."

"I don't remember parents, siblings—any family," Kendo said. "I don't know if I had wives or girlfriends. Children. I don't know if I held a job. I just have words in a book that sound insane. Preposterous. Imaginary."

"Those words are true," Cole said. "And important. In less than two hours, we're going to get drawn back into the Outskirts. You can watch us disappear. Would that help?"

Kendo regarded him in silence. "It would be a comfort to see something concrete. It would also be . . . so distressing. I thought I had this figured out. I thought I had it behind me. If this is some sort of con job, you are unspeakably cruel."

"We're not tricking you," Mira assured him.

"It would seem not," Kendo said.

"You came here to do research about Ramarro," Cole said. "To see what would happen to him if he came here."

"The torivor," Kendo said. "I wrote a lot about him. I was evidently obsessed with the topic. He is dangerous?"

"He's going to destroy the Outskirts if we can't stop him," Cole said.

Kendo nodded. "Wait one moment. Let me fetch my journals." He walked out of the room.

"This is terrible," Jace whispered. "What do we do?"

"We hope he wrote something useful before he forgot what he was doing," Mira said. "Be patient. Part of him wants to believe us."

Kendo returned with a stack of identical hardback journals. He set them on the coffee table and started thumbing through one of them. Cole and the others watched.

"It has been some time since I studied these," Kendo said. "I used to read them frequently. I didn't believe what I had written, but I hoped to find clues about what happened to my mind, what happened to my past." He smoothed his hand over a page. "In these journals, I gave myself instructions. I apparently became aware my memory was failing and shared advice and warnings. It all pertained to an imaginary world." He snapped the book closed. "It has to be imaginary."

"It's not imaginary," Mira said. "Just hard to believe from your current vantage point."

"Do you know how crazy that sounds?" Kendo asked. "How can I possibly believe you?"

"Then where did we come from?" Cole asked. "How do we know what you know?"

"You broke in and read my journals," Kendo said. "Or somebody did. What is more likely? I come from a magical world where I was an important leader? Or I had a mental breakdown, and somebody is now using my journals to exploit me? What do you really want? Money?"

"We want to know how to stop Ramarro," Cole said. "We want to know if it would be safe to lure him here. And we want to know if I can ever get back to Earth with my friends."

"You're from Earth?" Kendo asked.

"Originally," Cole said. "These other kids were born in the Outskirts. But I'm from Arizona. My friends were kidnapped by slavers and taken to the Outskirts. I followed them there, but we can't get home permanently. At least not without your help."

"Yet here you are in the real world," Kendo said. "Asking for nonsensical information about a nonsensical world."

"We need the vital information you recorded before you forgot who you are," Mira said.

"You don't want money?" Kendo said. "You don't want favors? No secrets about my actual past to taunt me with? No blackmail? Come on—don't waste my time. What's the catch?"

"Just info," Cole said. "So we can try to save an entire world."

Kendo folded his arms. "It has been a long time since I looked hard at this stuff. I rambled on and on. But I seem to remember . . ." He picked up a journal and started leafing through it.

Cole watched in silence. So did the others.

Kendo read for a moment. Then paged ahead. Then read again.

"Your names?" Kendo asked.

Cole repeated their names.

Kendo nodded. "It says you would come."

"You told us to come," Cole said. "We're here because of you."

"You're right on schedule," Kendo said. "To the day. I used to wonder if anyone would actually show up. Then I forgot to wonder."

"Here we are," Mira said.

"I left myself a message for you," Kendo said. "If it helps . . . great."

"Let's have it," Cole said.

Kendo started to read. "'I am utterly powerless, and my memory is failing. I could not ascertain what it would look like if torivors reached Earth. I suspect they would be rendered powerless. Perhaps even more powerless than me. Coming here might destroy them. But I have no way to confirm. Please tell Lorenzo to share the location of the Void. And to give you access to the three talismans. It is now the best help I can offer, unless you can find a way to confirm what I could not about the torivors.'"

"You forgot we were coming?" Mira asked.

"I've wanted to forget all of this," Kendo said. "I've mostly succeeded. Talking to you stirred up memories of some things I read."

"Is there more?" Violet asked.

"That was the message," Kendo said. He read it again. "So much in these journals describes how I set up my life here. A lot deals with failed experiments regarding these torivors. I go on and on like a madman. After my message to you, I kept journaling, but my memory was clearly getting worse. Before long I was mostly musing about whether my journal was fact or fiction. By the end I concluded it was fiction. Not long afterward I stopped writing."

"You did your best," Mira said. "It must have been hard."

Kendo looked like he was having difficulty composing himself. "I'm not sure how difficult it was. I lead a comfortable life. Only the words in these journals trouble me. And the huge gap in my memory. I have considered destroying the journals. I expect I would eventually forget them as I have forgotten the rest. Then all I would have is the void in my memory."

"Why haven't you done it?" Cole asked.

Kendo scrunched his face. "I worry that even an insane explanation might be better than none. It's hard not remembering if you have anyone. Not remembering a life or a career. Then again, it's strange reading about yourself being some kind of teleportation wizard in an improbable fairy tale. And it's challenging to meet kids who seem sincere as they seek to confirm your delusions."

"Not delusions," Cole said. "It would be crazy if it never happened. But it happened."

"You gave up a lot," Mira said. "You were so powerful. You could have lived forever."

"Probably not after the torivor got loose," Jace said.

Mira nodded. "Maybe not after that. Do you know about the talismans you mentioned?"

Kendo shook his head. "I allude to them elsewhere. But I never describe them. I assume Lorenzo knows. If he exists."

"Maybe there is hope," Violet said. "Maybe Kendo made another plan before he lost his memory."

"He obviously had some idea," Cole said. "Talismans sound better than nothing."

"Maybe we can still work with Lorenzo to find a way to confirm what will happen to a torivor who comes to Earth," Mira said.

"We can't endanger Earth," Cole said. "We can only try to lure Ramarro here if we're completely sure."

"It is so odd to hear you discuss these matters as if they are real," Kendo said.

"I'm sorry you can't remember who you were," Violet said. "You were amazing."

Kendo took a shuddering breath. "This is overwhelming. You claim that you will eventually disappear before my eyes?"

"Those who stay here," Jace said, standing up. "I'm going to the beach. Who wants to join me?"

CHAPTER

— 21 —

TALISMANS

Cole stood with the salt water to his chin. As a swell came in, his feet left the ground, and he had to tread water to stay above the surface. Off to one side and a bit closer to the shore, Jace tried to catch the wave as it broke around him. What he lacked in skill at bodysurfing, he made up for with persistence.

While Cole kicked with his feet and swept one hand back and forth, he hoisted up the swim trunks borrowed from Kendo. Even with the drawstring pulled as tight as he could tie it, the bathing suit barely stayed on.

Jace turned around after surging shoreward ten or fifteen feet and waded back toward Cole, clutching his own ill-fitting borrowed trunks. Cole let some briny water past his lips and spit it out, finding it too salty to even use as mouthwash.

The sunlight dimmed. The water began to darken. All sound became more remote and developed a slight echo.

As the water receded, Cole's feet reached the sandy

bottom again. He pivoted toward the beach. The water became black, and color bled away from the shore as the day faded to a starless night. The squeal of a young girl reached him slowly, as if through a thick medium and from a great distance.

Cole could feel his power again. No longer in water, he drifted in darkness, nausea curdling in his gut, until his feet touched the ground.

He was back in Lorenzo's underground chamber beside Jace, Mira, and Violet. The Grand Shaper watched them expectantly.

Cole's borrowed swim trunks were gone.

He was no longer wet.

His clothes were back on him.

Jace's were too.

Cole had left his clothes at Kendo's condo along with the two girls. Mira and Violet had decided to remain with Kendo until they were drawn back to the Outskirts so the old man could witness their disappearance.

"Kendo lost his memory," Mira said.

Lorenzo looked disappointed. "How much?"

"All of it," Cole said. "At least about the Outskirts. He forgot over time. He kept journals but stopped believing them. He shared his writings with us."

"Did any key information survive?" Lorenzo asked.

"Kendo could never confirm whether torivors would have powers on Earth," Mira said. "He thinks they wouldn't, and hopes we can research the question more."

Lorenzo sighed. "He should know that is virtually

impossible to do from here. It's a big part of why he walked the Pilgrim Path in the first place. I'll do what I can. Anything else?"

"We're supposed to ask for the location of the Void," Cole said. "I guess you know? And we're supposed to ask for the three talismans."

Lorenzo's expression became grave. He solemnly closed his eyes. "The hour has come."

"What hour?" Violet asked.

Lorenzo opened his eyes. "Centuries ago, the ten most powerful Grand Shapers of Creon united to produce three talismans. Each yields an effect that none of us have learned to replicate on our own. Kendo told me of them before he walked the Pilgrim Path, at the same time when he confided where the Void is hidden. Those talismans were only meant to be used in the event of a crisis that threatened the survival of the Outskirts. Evidently the day has arrived."

"Right," Jace said. "We're all in enormous trouble. It's what we've been trying to tell you."

"What do they do?" Cole asked. "Can they save us?"

"Time will tell," Lorenzo said. "We need to travel elsewhere."

A wayport opened.

"How come I have my clothes back?" Jace asked.

"Pardon me?" Lorenzo asked.

"I was swimming in the ocean," Jace said. "I had left my clothes at Kendo's."

"Your clothes were drawn back to the Outskirts just as you were," Lorenzo said. "They exited as they entered—with you wearing them. It's extremely difficult to move anything from the Outskirts to Earth and keep it there. The Pilgrim Path is the only way we have discovered. Come." He gestured at the wayport.

Cole's stomach had begun to settle. He stepped through the wayport into a room with walls of polished steel. The action made his fading nausea no worse. A round vault door faced him, complete with a keypad and some kind of touch screen. The ceiling and floor were made of glossy steel as well.

The others came through the wayport with Lorenzo bringing up the rear.

"Is that the Void?" Jace asked.

"This is a more ordinary vault," Lorenzo said. "Carefully hidden and shielded by me. This vault comes from Outside." He walked up to the keypad, typed a code, then placed his hand on the touch screen. The background of the screen went from red to green, and a chime sounded.

Lorenzo spun a wheel and hauled the vault door open. It had to be at least two feet thick. Easily bulletproof. Maybe missile-proof too? Lorenzo led the way into a smaller room, again made entirely of steel. This room had drawers in the walls and a burnished metal table in the center.

Lorenzo opened a drawer and removed a flask. From a different drawer came a second flask. Another drawer yielded a third. He set them on the table and sat down.

Cole and his friends sat as well.

"Drinkable talismans?" Cole guessed.

"These three potions are infused with unique shaping capabilities," Lorenzo said. He tapped one. "This will send a single person one hundred years into the future. There is no known way back. It is the least useful for our purposes, unless one of us wants to use it to escape as a last resort."

"If Ramarro gets free, won't he still be running the Outskirts in a hundred years?" Jace asked.

"I imagine so," Lorenzo said. "Unless he grows tired of the experience and moves on to another realm. The only way to know for sure would be to try the potion."

"What do the others do?" Cole asked.

Lorenzo hefted a different flask. "This one can restore youth through time manipulation. Grand Shapers and other advanced Wayminders have learned to use time shifting to slow the aging process. The best of us can essentially halt the process. But none of us have managed to reverse the inevitable. Except with this potion."

"How do you know it works?" Mira asked.

"Kendo is confident," Lorenzo said. "His endorsement is good enough for me. In essence, the potion sends your anatomy back in time while simultaneously keeping you in the present. You get to have the body of yesteryear today. The effect would be destroyed if the subject departed Creon. Otherwise, an elderly citizen of Creon could inherit a second lifetime."

"How young does it make the subject?" Violet asked.

"Around twenty," Lorenzo said.

"Do you have somebody in mind to use it?" Mira asked.

"Nobody in particular," Lorenzo said. "We want someone who could be useful stopping Ramarro."

"I have an elegant idea," Mira said.

Cole immediately thought of the old swordsman sitting in a wheelchair inside the Iron Fort. He met eyes with Mira and nodded.

"And the third one?" Jace asked.

Lorenzo handled the final flask. "The third is the most powerful and potentially the most instructive. Whoever drinks it will gain the opportunity to explore a probable future."

"What does that mean?" Cole asked.

"The potion will fix the subject to the point in the time-stream when he or she drinks it," Lorenzo said. "For the next three days, whoever drinks the potion will seem to move forward in time. It will feel like normal life. But nothing that happens will endure. At the end of three days, the subject will return to the point when he or she drank the potion and proceed forward through time like normal."

"It's like visiting the future," Jace said.

"As near as has ever been managed," Lorenzo said.

"That's not possible," Violet whispered.

"Going into the future and returning is not possible," Lorenzo said. "The subject does not go into the actual future. The subject visits a highly probable future. A possibility. The rest of us seem to be there, but we're really not. None of it is actually happening. To be candid, it sounds unlikely to me as well, and I do not understand how it is accomplished, but Kendo Rattan assured me that it will work as promised."

"What if the person gets killed?" Cole asked.

"I asked the same question," Lorenzo said. "If the subject gets killed, he or she will return to the moment when he or she drank the potion and miss the rest of the three days."

"And if you leave Creon?" Mira asked.

"If the subject leaves Creon, he or she will return to the moment when he or she drank the potion."

"Otherwise, we get a peek at the future," Jace said.

"A probable future," Violet corrected.

"What if we stop Ramarro?" Cole asked.

"At the end of three days, whoever drank the potion will return to the moment when he or she drank the potion," Lorenzo said. "All that seemed to have happened will not have happened yet. Because it was not the actual future. But the subject could then try to replicate what occurred."

"How accurate is the possible future?" Jace asked.

"It's untested," Lorenzo replied. "But it should be extremely accurate."

"We need to wait until the Void is almost open," Cole said. "This will give us an extra chance at figuring out how to stop Ramarro."

"I believe that is what Kendo Rattan intended," Lorenzo said.

"Is there a way to tell when the Void will open?" Cole asked.

"That moment is roughly one day away," Lorenzo said. "Two at best."

The kids all stared at him in stunned silence.

"A day away?" Mira asked.

"How do you know?" Violet wondered.

"When Kendo learned the Void would house Ramarro, he made a few modifications," Lorenzo said. "He included an early warning system that would alert us when Ramarro learned the skills necessary to break down the defenses."

"The alarm went off?" Jace asked.

Lorenzo nodded. "While you were back in time."

"Why didn't you tell us?" Jace exclaimed.

"You've been busy ever since," Lorenzo said. "You needed to visit Kendo before we proceeded."

"So we have a day," Cole said.

"Maybe less," Lorenzo said. "Perhaps a little more."

"Do you know where we can find the Void?" Mira asked.

Lorenzo took a pendant from around his neck. A tarnished sphere dangled at the end of the chain. "This is it."

"Ramarro seemed bigger in the echolands," Jace deadpanned.

"Don't forget that you are in Creon," Lorenzo said. "Space can be manipulated. Enormous areas can be fit into modest confines."

"Ramarro is really in there?" Mira asked.

"The entire vastness of the Void is in here," Lorenzo said. "With Ramarro trapped at the center."

"We shrank him?" Cole asked.

"In a sense," Lorenzo said, flicking the sphere at the end of the pendant. "The Void truly is enormous. If it helps, think of the pendant as the wayport to the Void. The conduit to the Void."

"What if we destroy the pendant?" Cole asked. "Would we break the connection to the Void? Trap him better?"

Lorenzo shook his head. "I wish it could be that simple. Destroying this little sphere would unravel the Void, freeing Ramarro instead of trapping him." He flicked it again.

"Should you maybe not flick it?" Jace asked uncomfortably.

"It's exceedingly durable," Lorenzo said. "I doubt the sphere could be damaged except with mighty shaping."

"Keep it away from Cole," Jace muttered.

"Kendo mentioned that could be a wise precaution," Lorenzo said.

"If we're running out of time, shouldn't we use the potion soon?" Violet asked. "The one that shows the probable future?"

"As soon as possible," Lorenzo said. "Already, whoever ingests it will probably not get to experience the full three days. Unless we defeat Ramarro."

"Who should take it?" Mira asked Lorenzo. "You?"

"Before he left Creon, Kendo nominated Cole," Lorenzo said.

"Why me?" Cole asked.

"Kendo believes your power represents our best hope of stopping Ramarro," Lorenzo said.

"Won't I be in the probable future no matter who goes?" Cole asked.

"Only the person who drinks the potion will remember what happened," Lorenzo said. "To everyone else in the world, the possible future revealed by the potion will have never existed. Kendo wants you to have practice against the torivor. He wants you to remember what works and what doesn't. He wants you to have actual experience facing him."

"Makes sense," Jace said.

"But if you go, could you maybe come up with a way to contain him?" Cole asked Lorenzo.

"I would try," Lorenzo said. "Kendo does not believe I

could succeed. He adamantly felt you represent our best hope."

Cole looked at his friends. "It's a lot of pressure."

"Better you than anyone," Jace said. "You stood up to Ramarro in the echolands. Now do it here."

"What do you think, Mira?" Cole asked.

"I would have wanted you to take it even without Kendo's endorsement," she said.

Cole nodded. It would be nice to let somebody else carry this weight. But he was clearly needed. He looked at Lorenzo. "I'll do my best."

"Then we should hurry," Lorenzo said. "Time keeps passing." He unstopped the flask and handed it to Cole.

"I just drink it?" Cole asked. "Right now?"

"There isn't much inside," Lorenzo said. "A few swallows. Drink it all."

Holding the flask, Cole glanced at Jace, who nodded encouragingly. Mira took his free hand and squeezed it.

Braced for a nasty flavor, Cole put the mouth of the flask to his lips and tipped it. Somewhat viscous fluid reached his tongue, flowing slowly and tasting mildly sweet, like grapes and vanilla. After he swallowed three times he upended the flask until the flow stopped.

CHAPTER

— 22 —

ALTERNATIVES

Lorenzo studied Cole intently. "What did you feel?"

Licking his lips, Cole set down the flask. "Nothing, really. It tasted pretty good."

"No flicker in reality?" Lorenzo asked. "No temporary sense of disconnection? No physical sensation of moving out of sync?"

"I don't think so," Cole said. "I was focused on drinking every drop. It came out kind of slowly."

Lorenzo nodded.

"You look concerned," Mira said.

Lorenzo cocked his head. "I saw none of the indicators I would have expected if Cole had, in fact, detached from his path through time."

"The potion didn't work?" Violet asked.

Lorenzo dragged his fingers through his hair. "I can't be certain. We should proceed under the assumption that it may have failed."

"I thought Kendo made it with the best team ever," Jace said.

"They were attempting something that had never been done," Lorenzo said. "And the potion is untested. It might have worked undetectably. The effect could be active. We can't be sure."

"We'll try to stop Ramarro either way," Cole said.

"Knowing the potion worked would influence our tactics," Lorenzo said. "If it worked, you would emphasize gaining information. If you do return to this point in time, your accomplishments will disappear. All you will have is what you learned."

"But I might not return," Cole said.

"I didn't feel anything out of the ordinary," Violet volunteered.

"You may not return," Lorenzo said. "This might be the only chance we get."

"The focus might be different depending on whether the potion worked," Mira said, "but either way, we need to try to stop Ramarro."

"True," Lorenzo said, holding up the pendant. "If Ramarro gets free, the pendant will be drawn from wherever it is to the Far North Cache. Kendo wanted to control where Ramarro would return."

"Ramarro has to come out at that cache?" Mira asked.

"Think of the pendant as the door and the Far North Cache as the key," Lorenzo said. "As Ramarro forces his way out, Kendo believes the pendant will be summoned to the cache, wrenched across space and time if necessary."

"If you're wearing the pendant, would it bring you with it?" Jace asked.

"Probably not," Lorenzo said. "But I would follow."

"Does it matter where we keep the pendant?" Cole asked.

"We need to keep it from Owandell," Lorenzo said. "Or anyone who might try to aid Ramarro from the outside. And while the pendant remains in our possession, we want it far from the cache."

"Should you keep the pendant?" Jace asked.

"I'm good at hiding," Lorenzo said. "And Owandell is not hunting me."

"What should we do now?" Cole asked. "If Ramarro will be free so soon, what is the next step?"

"Recruit help," Lorenzo said. "I'll see how many Grand Shapers I can gather to our cause."

"We should take the potion to Brogan," Mira said. "What are the chances the Perennial Serpent will get involved?"

"I'm not sure," Lorenzo said. "We must be ready for anything."

"Should we consider approaching Trillian?" Cole asked.

Lorenzo raised his eyebrows. "That path is fraught with peril. And you can't go, Cole. If this is a hypothetical future, leaving Creon will end it."

"I could go," Jace offered.

"How would you get back?" Violet asked. "Without Cole, nobody can open a wayport in Elloweer."

"How could we trust anything Trillian told us?" Mira asked.

"He supposedly can't lie," Cole said.

"My understanding is he absolutely cannot lie," Lorenzo said. "And that he would not hesitate to mislead with carefully presented truth."

"Does he see Ramarro as a rival?" Jace asked.

"The ancient accounts suggest the two torivors worked together against the original Grand Shapers," Lorenzo said. "It's impossible to know whether they would have eventually turned on each other. At worst Trillian would try to completely subvert our attempt to stop Ramarro. At best he would use the opportunity to advance his own agenda to our detriment."

"If we have no way to stop Ramarro, help from Trillian could be better than nothing," Cole said.

"And it might also be considerably worse than nothing," Lorenzo said.

"So for now, gather allies?" Jace said.

"Until Ramarro returns," Violet said. "Will we have any warning?"

"I have a ring for each of you," Lorenzo said. "If the jewels glow, it's time to go to the Far North Cache. Cole, you must be there. Violet, do you know the destination?"

"Of course," she said.

"The cache is shielded," Lorenzo said. "You'll have to come close and then use some established conduits to get inside."

"Can you show me?" Violet asked.

Lorenzo waved a hand, and a wayport appeared. "Come with me quickly. Then we'll go our separate ways."

Violet stepped through the wayport, and Lorenzo followed. It remained open.

"We'll go to the Iron Fort?" Mira asked.

"Yes," Cole said. "Give Brogan the potion."

"Should we tell the Host the world is ending within a day?" Jace said. "See what help he can scrounge up?"

"I wonder where my parents are," Mira said. "And Honor and Destiny. I wish we could get Honor's help in the fight. And Destiny's thoughts about our plan."

"Do you think they're in Creon?" Jace asked.

"The chances are good if they were taken by Wayminders," Mira said. "Some hide out here."

Violet and Lorenzo returned through the wayport, and it closed.

"That was speedy," Jace said.

"Master Debray showed me the pathways they established and how to access them," Violet said. "Not complicated."

"I'm off to recruit all the assistance I can muster," Lorenzo said. "Feel free to use this hideout as a refuge as needed. Watch the rings. Come when they glow. Cole, you must not miss this."

"One last question," Cole said. "Why me? What do you expect me to do against Ramarro? Really."

"That's up to you," Lorenzo said. "Your power is unique and spectacular. If you had time to fully mature, I would wager you could fight Ramarro directly, like the Grand Shapers of old."

"We have less than a day," Cole said.

"Fight him with everything you have," Lorenzo said. "Attack directly. Empower those around you. Kendo Rattan felt you were our best chance. And so do I."

Cole nodded, conscious that he was suddenly sweating. The responsibility was too great. His power was too limited.

He felt sure he would disappoint everyone. "I'll do my best."

"That's the most any of us can do," Lorenzo said. A way-port opened, he stepped through, and it closed.

"Are you all right?" Mira asked.

Cole chuckled softly. "Is it that obvious?"

"A little," she said.

"This feels . . . hopeless," Cole said. "We've survived tough fights. But we've always had some kind of a plan. Some reason to hope."

"We have you," Jace said.

"In the echolands, Ramarro paralyzed us with his mind," Cole said. "And he's supposed to get way more powerful when he appears here. Where do we even start? He'll just snap his fingers and turn us to dust."

"You're talking like we've already lost," Jace said.

"Haven't we?" Cole asked. "Without a plan, won't we just be going to our execution?"

"So we make a plan," Jace said.

"A plan that has a chance," Cole said.

Jace put his hands on his hips. "Use your power."

"Ramarro is way stronger than me," Cole said.

"Are you sure?" Jace asked. "Kendo Rattan had hundreds of years to prepare for this. He could have focused on anybody in the world. And he is betting on you."

"You might be more powerful than you realize," Mira said.

"Attack Ramarro's power," Jace said. "I heard you shook up Owandell that way. You demolished those Enforcers. They had us, and then you scrambled their powers and suddenly they were helpless. Nobody can do that."

"Owandell has some skill at affecting powers," Mira said. "But not like you. And you're just getting started."

"Ramarro is so strong," Cole said. "Do you really think I could hurt his power?"

"He might be overconfident," Jace said. "You won't know until you try."

"If we end up cornered, I'll try it," Cole said. "Feels like a long shot, though."

"What about luring him to Earth?" Mira said. "Kendo thinks he'll be powerless there. How certain do we need to be?"

"We need to be one hundred percent sure," Cole said. "Earth has billions of people, Mira. If there is any doubt, we can't risk it."

"He might go on his own," Jace said. "If Wayminders can find a way there, why not him?"

"If he goes on his own, it's not our fault," Cole said.

"We'll keep planning throughout the day," Mira said. "Learn all you can, Cole. You might get a second shot at this."

"See this through, Cole," Jace said. "Don't expect to lose."

"What about 'die bravely'?" Cole asked. "Aren't we supposed to expect to die?"

"We're guaranteed to die," Jace said. "All of us, no matter how we ignore it. I had to face that with the Sky Raiders. We're all heading for the same destination. Don't let the fear of death rattle you. It's coming, like it or not. Let the fear melt into acceptance. The point becomes how we die. I'm not just going to die, Cole. I'm going to die *bravely*. I'm going to win victories on the way. We've already won some improbable battles. Survived some close calls. Why not more? Try to win. Expect to win. Maybe we'll only live another day. Maybe another fifty years. But whenever we die, go out bravely."

"Thanks," Cole said, eyes stinging with tears. "I needed to hear that."

"Don't cry or you'll ruin it," Jace replied, lightly punching his shoulder.

"We all needed to hear it," Mira said. "And remember it."

"I tell myself all the time," Jace said. "Don't you?"

"Different words," Cole said. "Some of the same ideas."

"Ramarro is really powerful," Violet said. "Guess what he hasn't ever done?"

"What?" Cole asked.

"He hasn't won," Violet said. "Not here in the Outskirts. Not ever. He isn't perfect. He was stopped last time. Let's get him again."

"More good words," Mira said. "If we expect to lose, it's going to happen."

Cole nodded. "Let's find a way to win. Should we go?"

"The Iron Fort," Mira said.

Violet took Cole's hand. He invigorated her power, and a wayport opened.

"Only way to travel," Jace said, stepping through.

The others followed.

The frosty bite in the air startled Cole, who had braced himself for the desert heat. Coming from an underground vault, he was unaware that night had fallen. Overhead in the moonless sky, endless stars decorated the firmament, a cosmic mist of light bejeweled by many brighter bodies of varied colors. Though Cole could feel the sand beneath his feet, the starlight did little to illuminate the darkness around him. Scanning the black horizons, he could have been lost at sea as believably as in a desert.

A pair of cressets flared to life, burning bright in front of the striped tent and casting rippling highlights onto the huge serpent rearing up before him. After a brief jolt of surprise, Cole recognized the statue of the Perennial Serpent.

A figure emerged from the tent, clad in Wayminder robes but with a veiled face and an iron band around the forehead. "State your business," a male voice demanded.

"We are here to see the Host by his invitation," Violet said, producing Mira's document. "May I approach?"

"You may," the man answered.

Violet stepped into the firelight, and the guard examined the parchment. He handed it back to her with a small bow.

"Please, come inside," he offered.

Cole, Mira, and Jace followed them into the tent. The air inside was pleasantly warm.

"The hour is late," the guard said. "Would you prefer lodging for the night before conducting your business?"

"It's urgent," Cole said. "We're hoping to talk to the Host now."

"Highly unusual," the guard said. "But the Host left specific instructions to grant you priority attention. Follow me."

They passed through a wayport into the cage outside the wall, then into a guard room, then, without being searched, into the office where they had met the Host previously. The office was empty except for the four kids and the guard who had accompanied them.

A moment later a wayport opened, and the Host stepped through, wearing long pajamas and a sleeping cap. It looked like he had recently splashed his face with water, but his eyes remained a bit bleary.

"Welcome at this uncomfortable hour," the Host said. "Forgive my appearance. I understand the matter is urgent."

"Ramarro will be free within a day," Cole said.

The Host sobered, his gaze sharpening. "This is certain?"

"Absolutely," Cole said.

The Host's eyes flicked to the guard. "Leave us."

A wayport opened, and the guard exited. The wayport closed behind him.

"Who else knows?" the Host asked.

"Lorenzo Debray," Cole said. "He's trying to get help from other Grand Shapers."

The Host coughed out a laugh. "Do you know how preposterous all of this sounds?"

"Not really," Cole said. "But I've seen Ramarro. And I spent the last several hours with Lorenzo Debray and Kendo Rattan."

"You realize you are wanted for possible regicide?" the Host said. "All of you have been implicated in the disappearance of the High King."

"Already?" Cole asked. "I mean, what are you talking about?"

A smile touched the Host's lips. "I gather information swiftly. I don't believe the accusation. But many will."

"We think it was Owandell," Mira said. "Working with Wayminders. They took my mother, Honor, and Destiny as well."

The Host furrowed his brow. "The princesses were not mentioned."

"Father recently recovered them from Owandell," Mira said.

"So it was retaliation," the Host said.

"Why do you believe us?" Jace asked.

The Host pressed his fingertips together. "Because I learned long ago to see beyond the manipulative lies those who crave power use to advance their agendas."

"What if we're lying?" Jace asked.

"I have corroborated enough of your story to believe you," the Host said. "Now a difficult question—can Ramarro be defeated? Or is Owandell about to become the most powerful man in the five kingdoms? Would we do better to accept the inevitable and align ourselves with this torivor?"

"If we're cowards, maybe," Jace said.

"There is an important distinction between cowardice and prudence," the Host said. "I am charged with protecting the occupants of the retreat. I am the latest in a proud history of successful hosts who accepted this charge. I do not intend to be the last. Ofttimes negotiation can accomplish what strength of arms cannot."

"Ramarro likes to negotiate," Cole said. "If you want to be a puppet, he might give you the chance. But nothing more. He will control this world."

The Host leaned forward. "Yet even he cannot be

everywhere at once. If Ramarro doesn't destroy the world, some of his supposed puppets may gradually return to governing themselves."

"I don't think you understand him," Cole said. "The first Grand Shapers feared him and Trillian for a reason. They really might destroy this place. And if not, we'll all be slaves. Including Owandell, whatever he thinks."

The Host heaved a sigh. "Sadly, this fits my understanding of the torivors. I've been researching them since our previous conversation."

"Any weaknesses?" Jace asked.

"That's a big part of the problem," the Host said. "Ruthless. Brilliant. Incalculably powerful. If the Grand Shapers hadn't imprisoned them promptly, the torivors would have ruled the Outskirts long ago. How much do we know about the upcoming return?"

"He'll be free within a day," Cole said. "We know where he will show up."

"Where?" the Host asked.

"The Far North Cache," Cole said.

"Ah yes, out of the way, shielded, hidden in plain sight," the Host said. "And a torivor will be there within a day. How can I assist?"

"We need to stop him," Cole said. "We need all the help we can get. People to stand against him. Grand Shapers. Warriors."

"What use is an army against a torivor?" the Host wondered.

"Better than no army," Jace replied.

"Yes, I see," the Host said. "Now or never. Try to stop him

when he is most off-balance, while his freedom is new. At worst, die clean rather than inheriting a fate worse than death."

"That's the idea," Mira said. "It's your best chance to protect the Iron Fort."

"It might be," the Host said. "I'll assemble a task force. There are limits to my influence. I have no direct contact with the Grand Shapers, but I can try to signal a couple of them who provide me with information from time to time."

"What about the current Grand Shaper?" Mira asked.

"Kezlyn Vedor is in hiding," the Host said. "It's a big part of why she is still alive. Owandell has a major sympathizer in Governor Vass. He has many Enforcers in his employ. Should you wish to find the abducted king, you may want to look there."

"Who is Governor Vass?" Cole asked.

"The governor of Creon," Mira said. "The acting ruler. Technically a representative of my father."

"Appointed by Owandell," the Host said. "I believe he would abandon the crown for Owandell in a heartbeat. Perhaps he already has."

"It could be useful to find Honor and Destiny," Mira said.

"We'll look into it," Cole agreed.

"If you don't mind me saying, you all look exhausted," the Host said. "If we really have a day before Ramarro returns, you could benefit from some rest."

"He has a point," Violet murmured.

"We can rest for a few hours," Cole said. "We'll want to be sharp when Ramarro arrives."

"I agree," Mira said. "But first, I need to see my sister."

CHAPTER
—◦— 23 —◦—

REJUVENATED

The older woman who answered the door at Elegance's residence looked sleepy and bothered. "Who is knocking at this hour?" she asked, taking in Cole, Mira, Jace, Violet, and the guard escorting them.

"We need to speak with Elegance immediately," Mira said.

The woman looked scandalized. "Her Highness needs her rest," the woman scolded. "This is highly irregular. Next time schedule an appointment through proper channels. I will be speaking to the Host about this."

"We already spoke to him," Mira said. "I am Miracle Pemberton, and this is an emergency."

The woman paled and looked to the guard.

"All true," he said.

The woman became flustered. "Well, that is something else; pardon me, Your Highness. Please come inside while I fetch your sister."

Cole and the others entered a comfortable room with tasteful furnishings. They waited while the servant woman bustled out of the room. A couple of minutes later, Elegance entered the room in a long white nightgown, her hair disheveled, her eyes squinty. Cole thought she looked much younger than when she was all dressed up.

"I wish I could say it was nice to see you," Elegance said, rubbing at her eyes. "Can't this wait until morning? Ethel mentioned an emergency?"

"Mother and Father have been abducted, along with Honor and Destiny," Mira said. "Your power has been terrorizing Creon as the Perennial Serpent for hundreds of years. And the world ends tomorrow."

Elegance blinked. "Are you serious?"

"Completely," Mira said. "Ramarro will be free within a day."

"That all fell apart quickly," Elegance said.

"It's Owandell," Mira said. "He's done with caution because Ramarro is almost free."

"Is my power really the Perennial Serpent?" Elegance asked, almost as if the idea were romantic.

"We're pretty sure," Mira said.

"What can we do?" Elegance asked.

"We have to try to stand against Ramarro," Mira said. "And I want to rescue Mother and our sisters. Maybe they can help us." She held up the flask. "And we want to recruit Brogan."

"Brogan is in no condition—" Elegance began.

"This will make him young again," Mira said.

Elegance stared. "Impossible," she whispered.

"It's one of a kind," Mira said. "Devised by a team of Grand Shapers."

"It performs complicated time shifting," Violet added. "His physical characteristics will go back in time while he remains in the present."

"You're serious," Elegance said, seemingly not wanting to hope in vain.

"It's our understanding," Mira said. "Can we try it?"

Elegance gave a quick nod. "Of course. This way."

She led them into a sumptuous bedroom, where the old man rested on a large bed, propped up by a semicircle of pillows. "Elegance?" he asked. "Is everything all right?"

"It's Miracle and her friends again," Elegance said. "Very little is all right. They want your help. They have a potion that could restore your youth."

"Nonsense," Brogan said.

"It's unique," Mira said. "Made by a group of Grand Shapers."

"And they wish to test it on me?" Brogan asked.

"It was given to us to use on whoever we want," Mira said. "It will mean you can never leave Creon."

"I have no travel plans," Brogan said. "How is this possible?"

"Unprecedented time shifting," Violet said. "It will supposedly give you the body of yesteryear today."

"Last year I didn't look much better than right now," Brogan said. "A decade ago either."

"We're up against the end of the world," Mira said. "The king and queen have been abducted. Two of my sisters as well. And Ramarro returns tomorrow. We need help."

"Give me the drink," Brogan said.

Mira tugged at the stopper and couldn't get it off.

Elegance took the flask from her, gripped it tightly, and yanked it open. She handed the flask to her husband.

Brogan took a probative sip. "Not foul." He drained the flask.

The transformation was so sudden that Cole wondered if he had missed it with a blink. A young man, still holding the flask, looked in astonishment at his hands. He threw aside the sheets and swung his legs out of the bed. A couple of pillows fell to the floor as he stood up.

"I remember what this felt like," Brogan said in a voice that was similar, but fuller and firmer. "I remember like it was yesterday. As if the rest has been a bad dream."

He wasn't just young—he was tall, and his shoulders were broad and strong. His strained nightshirt had clearly been tailored for a frailer man. He clenched a fist, and veins stood out on his solid forearm.

"Look at you," Elegance said.

"How cruel if this is temporary," Brogan said. "How long is it supposed to last?"

"A lifetime," Mira said. "As long as you don't leave Creon, you should age normally."

"Elegance, do you think you could find me more suitable attire?" Brogan asked.

Her eyes wandered up and down his new physique. "It's late. Give me a few minutes."

Elegance ushered the kids out of the room, ordered Ethel to see to their needs, and then rushed away. Jace asked for a sandwich. Cole followed his example. Mira inquired about a restroom, and Violet seconded the request.

"That worked quickly," Jace said after Ethel led the girls away. "I wonder if your potion worked just as well."

"I hope so," Cole said. "It would be nice to have two shots at this."

"Don't count on it," Jace said.

"You know," Cole said. "This might be the perfect time to tell Mira how you feel about her."

"Lower your voice," Jace said, looking around worriedly.

"I'm just saying, none of this might really be happening," Cole said. "Not permanently. I could let you know what she says when I get back. You could know without actually asking."

"And what if this is real?" Jace asked. "Not just a preview."

"You'll still know," Cole said.

Jace shook his head. "It's stupid. It doesn't matter."

"It matters to you," Cole pressed.

"Way too much to risk ruining it," Jace said. "I know she can't love me. I know we're too young. I know she's a princess and I'm a former slave. If I don't say anything, I can stay close. I can protect her and help her. She knows I care. She can see that. It's enough."

"What if she feels the same way?" Cole asked.

Jace shook his head again. "Don't be thick. No way."

"But what if?"

"If she loves me like that, it'll come out."

"Will it? You talk about dying bravely. What about living bravely?"

Jace glared at Cole. "Are you giving me bravery lessons?"

"Maybe when it comes to Mira."

"I'm brave enough."

Brogan opened the door and emerged wearing a robe. It must have been big on him before, because it fit reasonably well, though probably a bit clingier than intended. He held a sword with a polished blade and gilded designs on the hilt.

"Elegance went hunting for clothes?" Brogan asked.

"Yeah," Cole said.

"The others?" Brogan asked.

"Ethel is making sandwiches," Jace said.

"The girls needed the restroom," Cole said.

Brogan swished the sword through the air. "You can't imagine how good this feels."

"Cool sword," Cole said.

"It belonged to my father," Brogan said. "It never collected dust. We kept it in a place of honor. But I have not held it in decades." The blade hissed through the air. "In my later years, I lamented that I knew more than ever but my body was beginning to fail. And then I became an invalid. A dormant repository of combat ability."

"You don't feel rusty?" Cole asked.

"It's a little strange," Brogan said, shifting from side to side. "But rusty? No. I feel more myself than I have in ages. There may be a few kinks to work out." He tossed the sword in the air, let it spin twice, and deftly caught it by the hilt. "Not many."

Elegance entered with a bundle of clothes. "Brogan, don't parade around in that robe! And with your sword? Where is Miracle?"

The comment made Cole notice how the robe hung open

at his chest, and his bare legs extended below the hemline. It wasn't exactly how somebody would normally dress to impress a princess.

"Sorry, Ella," Brogan said. "You found better attire?"

Elegance thrust the bundle of clothes at him. "Go make yourself decent. We have company."

Brogan retreated.

Miracle returned with Violet.

"Success?" Miracle asked.

"He has clothes now," Elegance said.

"And his sword," Jace added.

Ethel entered with sandwiches for Cole and Jace.

"You're not hungry?" Elegance asked Miracle.

"We had oranges," Miracle replied.

"You have oranges?" Jace exclaimed.

"Coming right away," Ethel said, leaving the room.

Brogan emerged again just after the oranges arrived. He looked dapper in a shirt, a vest, trousers, and boots. His sword hung sheathed over his shoulder. "I need armor," he said.

"Are we charging into battle?" Elegance asked.

"Soon as we know where to charge," Brogan replied.

"I like this guy," Jace murmured.

"Is battle the only option?" Elegance asked.

"How sure is your information?" Brogan inquired.

"We got it from Lorenzo Debray and Kendo Rattan," Mira said. "Lorenzo gave us the potion, too."

"Ramarro the torivor will gain freedom tomorrow," Brogan said.

"Within the day," Miracle confirmed. "We have rings

that will notify us when he is about to get loose. Violet will take us to the Far North Cache, where we'll face him."

"What hope have we of success?" Brogan asked.

"Cole's power," Mira said. "He can energize the powers of others to work in any kingdom. And he can directly alter powers."

Brogan fixed his gaze on Cole. "How confident are you?"

"It's a torivor," Cole said. "I'll try not to fail."

"You'll need all the help you can get," Brogan said. "And we'll probably fall." He turned to Mira. "What about your mother and sister? Any leads?"

"We're almost sure it was Owandell," Mira said. "The Host suspects that Governor Vass might know something."

"Vass is certainly controlled by Owandell," Brogan said. "It would be a place to start."

"We think Owandell is working with Wayminders," Mira said.

"Another potential Arthur Vass connection," Brogan said. "And the world ends tomorrow?"

"Unless we stop it," Cole said.

"Who of you can fight?" Brogan asked.

"Jace," Mira said. "His golden rope is from Sambria. When Cole charges it, he's really dangerous."

"Show me," Brogan said.

Jace held out the golden strand, and Cole touched it, pushing power into it.

The rope shot out and picked up a chair.

"Quick," Brogan said, raising his fists. "I'm going to kill you now."

The other end of the rope shot out, bound Brogan's ankles together, and hauled him into the air upside down. Elegance gasped.

"If I believed you, I'd slam you into the wall," Jace said.

"And I'd be trying to slash the rope," Brogan said. "Please set me down."

Jace carefully laid Brogan on the floor, set down the chair, and retracted the rope. Brogan hopped to his feet.

Cole drew his sword. "I have a Jumping Sword," he said.

"A what?" Brogan replied. "I'm not familiar."

"He can make big jumps with it," Mira said. "I have one too. And with Cole's help, Violet can open as many wayports as she likes."

Brogan raised his eyebrows. "Very useful. No limits?"

"We haven't found any," Violet said.

"So without Cole, you all lose your advantages," Brogan said. "Do you need to touch the item and people you're energizing?"

"Yes," Cole said. "To start the connection. Then I don't need contact."

"You can't initiate the connection without touch?"

"So far. I'm working on it."

"How many people can you support at a time?" Brogan asked.

"At least five," Cole said. "Probably more. Maybe a lot more."

"How long before you get exhausted?" Brogan asked.

"I haven't found those limits," Cole said.

Brogan whistled. "Not bad. Incredible, really. Do any of you have authority from the king?"

Cole produced the medallion.

"You speak for him?" Brogan asked in astonishment.

"He authorized me not long ago," Cole said. "I'm not sure if there was an official announcement. And we were implicated in his disappearance."

"The seal could provide leverage with the governor," Brogan said.

"I feel like people don't believe me sometimes when I use it," Cole said.

"Your position has not been publicized?" Brogan asked.

"I don't think so," Cole said. "It barely happened."

"What about your power?" Brogan asked. "Your abilities should command great renown."

"Not too many people know about me yet," Cole said. "I'm just learning how to use my power. The Enforcers are catching on."

"We're going to the governor's mansion," Brogan said. "I'll need Jace, Cole, and Violet."

"What about me?" Mira asked.

"We'll be in his bedchamber," Brogan said. "In those close confines, your Jumping Sword will be largely irrelevant. You have too much strategic value to be risked on this. Stay with Elegance. We won't be long."

Mira looked like she wanted to protest but gave a little nod.

"May I borrow the seal, Cole?" Brogan asked. "We need to bluff this governor. He's smart and tough, but no hero. I think we can get what we need."

"Sure," Cole said, taking off the medallion and handing it over.

"You want me to take us to his room?" Violet asked.

"It's almost certainly how Owandell took the queen," Brogan said.

"Not just into a building," Violet fretted. "Not even just into the governor's mansion. Into his bedroom! I could be more than exiled. I could be executed."

"You could be formally executed," Brogan said. "Or simply killed by the guards with the rest of us. These are desperate times. Our foes are reckless and about to win. They have broken rules. We must break them too."

Violet nodded. "Understood. I know the mansion. I'm not sure how to locate his bedroom."

"Do you know the courtyard with the square fountain?" Brogan asked.

"Yes," Violet said.

"The largest, highest balcony on the east side belongs to his bedchamber," Brogan said. "The room will be shielded. Have you bypassed shielding before?"

"Not yet," Violet said. "With enough power I should be able to manage."

"There are some Wayminders here at the Iron Fort who could probably do it," Brogan said. "I completely trust none of them, and am unsure who would be willing."

"Cole?" Violet asked, holding out a hand.

"You're going now?" Elegance asked.

"Let me feel it out first," Violet said.

"Can you travel there from here?" Mira asked.

"There are too many protections on the Iron Fort for me to open a wayport to the outside from the inside," Violet said. "But I should be able to feel out possible destinations."

Cole took her hand and steadily energized her power.

"I see the mansion," Violet narrated, eyes closed. "I see the balcony. Yes, the bedroom is heavily shielded. I don't know if I can push through. I could try. I bet it would raise alarms."

"What about the balcony?" Brogan asked.

"Shielded too," Violet said. "Not as heavily. Probably anywhere we go will raise alarms."

She released Cole's hand. He took it as a signal to let the connection drop.

"We want to get in and out quickly," Brogan said. "There will be guards. We should take Vass to someplace he won't expect."

"He's a Wayminder?" Cole asked.

"Yes," Brogan said. "And he has guards who will try to rescue him."

"Can we use one of Lorenzo's hideouts?" Jace asked.

"We shouldn't without permission," Violet said. "And we can't come back here."

Brogan shook his head. "No location in Creon is as impenetrable as this fort, but the Host won't want involvement with kidnapping the governor, no matter the reason. Elegance and I have access to a conduit that will take us to the tent in the desert, bypassing security protocols. You can use it with us to get out at our convenience. But we can't come back in with Vass."

"I can use Cole to our advantage," Violet said. "We'll escape through three wayports. They might trace the first.

But I don't know anybody who could follow three jumps. I'll finish at an isolated spot in the wilderness—a high ridgetop. I used to go there to get away and think."

"That should work," Brogan said. "You want to try for the balcony rather than the room?"

"The room is too heavily shielded," Violet said. "Even if I can break through, it will take time. They will have a long warning."

"There are glass doors from the balcony into the bed-chamber," Brogan said.

"I noticed them," Violet confirmed. "How do you know?"

"I remember," Brogan said. "We'll want to smash them immediately. Then cover the door to the bedroom with a wayport so no regular guards can get in. Make them open a wayport beyond it if they want access."

"Clever," Violet said. "Use a wayport as a shield."

"I'll grab Vass," Brogan said. "Violet, once we're in, you open a way out. Jace, cover us with your rope. Cole, keep the sword handy, but your main task is to keep everyone charged up. Feeling good?"

"The plan makes sense," Violet said.

Brogan placed a hand on Jace's shoulder. "Bring something heavy with that rope to smash the doors." Brogan scanned the room. "That end table is made of stone."

Elegance pouted. "I love that piece."

Brogan raised an eyebrow.

Elegance waved her hands dismissively. "I know—it's an emergency, no time; I remember this side of you."

Brogan grinned. "A little like old times."

"The old times were scary," Elegance said.

"At least scary isn't tedious," Brogan said.

"Have I been tedious?" Elegance asked.

"You have been wonderful," Brogan clarified. "Old age is tedious."

"Do you want armor?" Elegance asked.

"Not for this," Brogan said. "I'll want some later." He nodded at Cole. "Do your thing."

"The rope is still energized," Cole told Jace. As the rope extended and curled around the solid stone table, Brogan asked Ethel to open a wayport to the desert tent. The wayport appeared a moment later.

They all went through and gathered on the chilly sand beneath cold stars. Elegance pulled Brogan close and whispered into his ear. Mira gave Cole a hug. "Take care," she said. Cole touched Violet and reestablished their connection.

Violet squinted her eyes shut. Cole felt her drawing a lot of energy and fed her plenty. She trembled and growled a little, and a wayport opened.

CHAPTER
—— 24 ——

GOVERNOR

Hurry after me," Brogan said. "Jace next." He lunged through the portal, sword ready. Then Jace ducked in, trailed by his rope and the table. Mira looked disappointed to be left behind. Cole gave her a wave, energized his Jumping Sword, and went through in time to see Jace bash a pair of elegant doors into splinters and shards.

Making sure he kept power to the rope, his sword, and Violet, Cole followed Brogan and Jace into a spacious bedroom, fragments of wood and glass crunching underfoot. Violet followed closely. A portly man in a white nightcap and long white sleepwear was fumbling out of bed. Brogan charged the man, seized him by the neck, and held his sword threateningly. "Not a sound," Brogan warned.

"I believe your manner of entry will suffice to raise the alarm," the man said. Cole thought his voice stayed surprisingly steady given the circumstances.

A shimmering wayport appeared in front of the doorway into the bedroom, blocking entry. Another trembling disturbance took shape in the middle of the room. A third wayport formed by the tall clock in the corner, and a man with leather armor visible beneath his Wayminder robes stumbled out. Jace hit the newcomer hard enough with the stone table that he flew back through the wayport without touching the ground.

"Call them off, Vass," Brogan warned.

The governor widened his eyes and shook his head. Brogan squeezed his neck.

"No," Vass croaked. "Slay me if you must."

Cole heard shouting from behind the door blocked by the wayport. Apparently the guards were frustrated.

Two other wayports appeared, one near the bed, the other just inside the door to the balcony. Another wayport opened right in front of the wayport by the bed, allowing no space for a person to emerge. Cole realized Violet was probably covering it. An armored guard raced from the wayport by the clock. Jace brought the stone table down on top of the guard with a clangorous crunch. Another guard came through behind him, and the free end of the golden rope wrapped around his waist, slung him brusquely against the ceiling, then slammed him to the floor.

Brogan dragged the governor to the wayport in the center of the room. "This one?" Brogan asked Violet.

"Yes," she confirmed.

Brogan hurled the governor through as a guard emerged from the wayport by the balcony. "Go!" Brogan urged, rushing to intercept the guard. He dodged a swing from the guard's sword and cut him down with a single

301

stroke. More guards came pouring from the wayport by the balcony.

Cole aimed his Jumping Sword at the wayport in the center of the room. "Away!" he cried, leaping forward and soaring low and quick through the wayport.

He emerged with a stumble onto a brushy prairie he had never seen before, the shadowy surroundings barely perceivable on the moonless night. The wayport and the stars shed enough light to see that Vass stood perhaps twenty feet away in a crouched pose. A glimmering wayport opened before him.

"Away!" Cole shouted, streaking forward and lowering his shoulder before plowing into the governor. Cole spun to the ground, and the governor went down too. Hopping to his feet, Cole blocked access to the wayport.

"Out of my way," Vass snapped, lunging forward, one arm raised.

Cole stood his ground and slashed the outstretched arm. The governor cried out and recoiled.

"Stay down!" Cole yelled.

From his knees, Vass dove at Cole's legs and wrapped both arms around them. Cole fell back hard, losing hold of his Jumping Sword. Ignoring Cole, Vass scrambled for the wayport he had opened only to have a golden rope lasso him and yank him to the dirt.

Brogan and Violet came through the wayport where Jace stood, and it closed, making the night a tad darker.

"Quick, Violet," Brogan said, racing forward, sword in hand. "Another gateway."

Cole's power remained connected to Jace's rope, his own sword, and Violet's power. As Cole grabbed his sword and stood up, a new wayport shimmered into existence.

"Send him through," Brogan instructed.

Using his rope, Jace forced Vass through the wayport and followed. Cole saw a new wayport open not far off. An armored guard rushed out.

"Go," Brogan urged.

The guard ran toward them, but Cole hurried through the wayport. Brogan sprang through right after with Violet at his heels, and the wayport disappeared.

They stood atop a dark hill, unseen clouds hiding most of the stars.

"Again," Brogan said.

A new wayport appeared.

"How is she doing this?" Vass asked.

Jace pushed Vass through with the rope. The others followed.

Cole emerged on a rocky ridgetop. Stars were visible again, though not as strikingly abundant as in the desert. The wayport closed.

"Now we're alone," Brogan said.

"You'll hang for this," Vass threatened.

"Be more concerned about your own neck," Brogan said.

"You have broken every—"

"Stop," Brogan said in a hard tone. He knelt beside Vass and seized the front of his nightshirt. "We don't have time to waste. I want to know where Owandell has stashed the king and queen."

"I have no idea what you are——"

Brogan shook him sharply. "Then you are in enormous trouble. Because I believe you do. You are on the wrong side of this, Vass, and it is going to cost you. You're in collusion with an enemy of the monarchy. I am here on behalf of the crown to rescue the High King, his consort, and two of his daughters. They were taken by Owandell using Wayminders. I am happy to employ any means necessary."

"You are speaking nonsense," Vass accused.

"Cole, tell me about his power," Brogan said.

Cole reached down in the dimness and took the governor's soft, plump hand. He could feel the darkness entwined with his considerable power. "He's been shapecrafted."

"I would love some light," Brogan said. He backed away from Vass, took a small oil lamp from a pouch at his waist, clicked an igniter that shed sparks until the wick lit, then set the lamp near Vass.

Blood drenched the formerly white sleeve of the governor's nightshirt where Cole had sliced him. Elsewhere the smooth fabric had been torn or stained with dirt. The governor's face was flushed and sweaty as he lay there panting. He sneered. "Don't pretend to know anything about my power."

"Show him what you can do to his power," Brogan said.

Cole remembered when Morgassa had mangled his power, destroying his ability to use it just as he was first discovering how. He recalled how violated he felt to have those intangible elements within himself corrupted, how exhausted and wounded the ordeal had left him, and how baffled he was to lose touch with the innate abilities he had just begun to understand. He also remembered plunging into the slipstream in the echolands, denying the nearly irresistible summons of the homesong as impurities were scoured from his power, hurricane currents howling around and through him, eventually healing his ability.

Cole knew he had the capacity to mangle the governor's power. He had already done it to an Enforcer in the heat of combat. But could he do it to a captive? Could he do it calmly and deliberately?

They needed the location of the king and queen. If this man collaborated with Owandell, he was an enemy. He was not innocent. He was conspiring to destroy the world.

Cole didn't want to maim the man's power. No matter how good the reason.

He could heal it, though.

Exerting his energy, Cole burned away the impurities from the governor's shaping power. Vass squirmed.

"Hold still," Brogan demanded.

When Cole finished, he released the governor's hand.

"What have you done?" Vass panted. He looked haggard.

"I undid the shapecrafting," Cole said.

"You can't just . . . ," Vass began. Then he closed his eyes, breathing slowly. He coughed. "You're telling the truth."

"Yes," Cole said. "And you're helping to end the world."

"Change the world," Vass corrected, opening his eyes. "Not end it."

"You're handing it over to a being we can't trust," Brogan said.

"The shapecrafting increased my vitality," Vass said,

sagging back to lay flat. "I feel the absence. And I also feel . . . better inside. I had forgotten how it felt."

"They twisted up your power," Cole said. "They injured it. I fixed it."

"He can damage it," Brogan warned. "Leave it in tatters."

"I believe it," Vass said. He raised his head enough to look at Cole. The effort made him tremble. "Will you?"

"I don't want to," Cole said. "We need your information."

"I don't have it," Vass said. "Why would Owandell tell me?"

"The Wayminders who aided him were your people," Brogan said. "Big events are happening in Creon. Owandell would have come to you. You're playing too dumb to be telling the truth."

"You want to talk about dumb?" Vass asked. "What fool would stand against Owandell when his victory is imminent? Find the king. Don't find the king. Does it matter? This is not going to be the same world in a matter of days."

"If it doesn't matter, tell us," Brogan said.

"And cross Owandell?" Vass asked with a tired chuckle. "Now?"

"You're scared of Owandell?" Cole asked. "He'll be as much a puppet as the rest of us."

"That's one theory," Vass said flatly.

"Shred his power, Cole," Brogan said. "Let's see if that softens him up."

"If you would wound my power, how are you any better than the worst of them?" Vass asked.

"Owandell stripped five young girls of their powers," Brogan said through gritted teeth. "Against their will, halting their development and sending them into hiding. One of those girls became my wife."

Vass pushed himself up onto one elbow and looked at Brogan. "Wait, that's not possible."

"I'm Brogan Holt."

Vass scowled in confusion. "You should be ancient."

"I'm not," Brogan said. "And I am going to recover my royal sisters and their parents. Whatever it takes. Cole?"

Vass glanced at Cole. "I wouldn't. Owandell could appear at any moment."

"I'd welcome it," Brogan said.

"Owandell ran away the last time he met Cole," Jace asserted.

"I'm so sorry," Cole said, reaching for the governor's hand, unsure whether the gesture was a bluff and uncertain how much damage he might be willing to inflict.

"Very well," Vass snapped, pulling his hand away. "My best guess is they're at the Island Keep."

"In Sambria?" Violet asked. "The Enforcer stronghold?"

"There is only one," Vass said.

"How sure are you?" Brogan asked.

"Nearly certain," Vass said.

"What if he's lying?" Jace asked.

"Then I give him my word that he will suffer," Brogan said. "And I'm not lying. Any revisions?"

"You now know what I strongly suspect," Vass said.

"You were stalling," Brogan said.

"I knew help might arrive," Vass said. "Evidently it will not. Owandell is very busy right now. May I go?"

"What more do you know?" Brogan asked.

"Broad question," Vass said. "I can tell you what I believe. All of you will be dead before long, no matter what you do with me. You'll be fugitives from the Creonese government and hunted by Owandell. Not to mention his mentor."

"You'll be coming with us until we can verify your claim," Brogan said.

"Then perhaps you'll perish in Sambria rather than Creon," Vass said with a sniff. "Holding me serves no purpose. I have nothing more you need."

"I need your information to be correct," Brogan said soberly. "Violet, open a—"

With a flash, the Perennial Serpent appeared, head rearing up above thick coils as the hood flared wide. Off to one side stood a figure in a black, cowled robe, the hood drawn up to conceal all features. Based on the description Cole had heard, he suspected it was the Ancient One.

Brogan whirled and slashed, opening a long wound in the white scales along the nearest coil. The serpent struck at him and got stabbed in the snout, then vanished to reappear behind Violet.

A large wayport opened between Violet and the overgrown snake, and Violet retreated toward Jace and Cole. Leaning around the wayport, Jace whipped the snake in the face with the golden rope, and Brogan raced around the other side to attack the serpent again. Coils writhing, the Perennial Serpent withdrew from the onslaught. Brogan pursued, and the snake disappeared again, only to materialize near Cole.

The previous wayport closed, and Violet opened a new

wayport, once again blocking the serpent. Jace rushed around the wayport, sharply and relentlessly lashing at the snake's face. The serpent flinched jerkily away from the strikes, gradually retreating.

"Should we go?" Violet asked.

"Maybe we can take it," Cole said, encouraged by how both Brogan and Jace had managed to put the huge snake on the defensive.

The Perennial Serpent vanished again and reappeared behind Brogan, striking immediately, huge mouth closing over the top of his shoulder before he could react. Brogan disappeared.

A wayport opened in front of Cole. "Go!" Violet yelled, shoving him toward it.

Jumping Sword ready, Cole hesitated, but something tackled him from behind, carrying him through the wayport onto cool sand. A dazzling array of cold stars bejeweled the sky. Nearby, cressets burned in front of a striped tent. Jace lay beside Cole, one arm wrapped around him.

As Cole scrambled to his feet, the wayport closed.

When it vanished, Cole lost his connection to Violet.

Cole sprang forward to where the wayport had been. There was no evidence it had ever existed. Cole squeezed the hilt of the Jumping Sword as if trying to crush it. He wanted to leap farther than he ever had, but at what? Panting, he whirled to face Jace.

"We abandoned her," Cole said.

"I thought she would follow," Jace said. "She always comes last."

Cole slashed the Jumping Sword across the sand, sending up a gritty spray. He felt empty, sick, and helpless. "They got her!"

"Who goes there?" called a figure over by the tent.

"Us again," Jace called. "Is that you, Renni?"

"Yes," the guard replied.

"Do you know where this wayport opened from?" Cole asked. "The one we just came through?"

"I'm sorry, no," Renni said.

"Can you figure it out?" Cole pressed.

"That's beyond my ability," Renni said.

Cole kicked the sand in frustration.

"We need to get back inside the fort," Jace said.

"I can help you there," Renni said. "Is your friend all right?"

Cole had fallen to his knees and was stabbing the sand repeatedly.

"We just lost some people," Jace said.

Cole threw his sword down and pressed his face against the cool sand. He squeezed the grains with his hands. It had happened so quickly. Brogan was gone. Violet had been stranded. Did the serpent bite her, too? Or had she been taken prisoner?

Cole sat up and brushed sand from his forehead and cheeks. He looked out at the dark desert beyond the firelight. There was nothing he could do. No way back to Violet. No way to restore Brogan. The fight was over. He was safe, and they were gone.

"We should get inside," Jace said.

"How do you sound so calm?" Cole complained.

Jace shrugged. "One of us should."

Cole picked up his sword. "We could have stayed and fought."

"Not the way that snake was starting to move," Jace said. "Do you think you have better reflexes than Brogan? Violet did the right thing. She knew we had to go."

"You forced me to go," Cole said.

"Now you know how Mira feels," Jace said.

Cole opened his mouth to reply, but nothing came out.

"You had to get away," Jace said. "You have to be there to fight Ramarro. In case we get another chance at this. And in case we don't."

Cole bowed his head. Maybe this was only a possible future. Or maybe not. "Violet. Brogan."

"I know," Jace said, putting a hand on his shoulder.

"What are we going to tell Elegance?"

"How bravely he protected us."

EMPOWERMENT

"Gone?" Elegance asked, tears shimmering in her slightly crazed eyes. "What do you mean, gone?"

"Brogan was bitten by the Perennial Serpent, and he disappeared," Jace said. "The same thing happened to our friend Twitch. He could have been sent far away. He could be dead. He fought so bravely."

Elegance gripped the back of a sofa to steady herself. "I don't need to hear that. Of course he fought bravely. He always fought bravely. But he never fell."

"It wasn't a fair fight," Jace said. "The snake—"

"It was never a fair fight," Elegance interrupted. "I'm sure he fared better than any man could have."

"He got in some good shots," Jace said.

Elegance held up a hand to stop him. "I was already sure of that. You're not certain he's dead?"

"No," Jace said.

"Then he probably survived," Elegance said. "I've thought

him dead several times over the years. Still, this is inconvenient and distressing. I need some time."

"Can we just—" Cole began.

"Children," Elegance said in a harder tone. "Heed me. I need some time."

"Come on," Mira said, herding them out of the room into a different parlor. Renni had brought them to Elegance, and she remained with them. Cole plopped down on an armchair. Jace looked disgruntled, pacing in silence.

"What about Violet?" Mira asked.

"She didn't make it back," Cole said. "The wayport closed before she came through. We don't know what happened to her."

"That's terrible," Mira said.

"And it leaves us without a way to get around," Jace said. "What if our rings signal us to go greet Ramarro?"

"I'm sure Elegance will have solutions," Mira said.

"If she ever speaks to us again," Jace grumbled.

"The Host is sympathetic to your cause," Renni said. "I expect he will assist as needed."

"What do we do now?" Cole asked. "How do we make the most of our time?"

"Maybe we sleep," Mira said. "At least for a few hours. Don't you want to be fresh if we have to go fight a torivor?"

Mentioning sleep somehow gave Cole permission to notice how tired he felt. His eyes were irritated, and his throat was getting sore. When he closed his eyes experimentally, he did not want to open them. "I could sleep right now," he said.

"Not yet," Elegance said, entering the room.

Cole forced his eyes open. She looked refreshed.

"What do we do if you get the signal to fight Ramarro?" Elegance asked.

"We need a way to the Far North Cache," Mira said.

"Ethel will take you," Elegance said. "You may go, Renni." The guard exited.

"Will Ethel know how to get around at the cache?" Cole asked. "Lorenzo Debray showed Violet some secrets."

"She won't know how to access the established conduits," Elegance said.

"We can jump the fence," Jace said.

"Will you be joining us?" Mira asked Elegance.

"What would I do?" Elegance asked.

"The Perennial Serpent could be there," Mira said.

Elegance clenched her jaw. "You see the irony that the distortion of my power may have killed my husband."

"You have to stop it if you can," Mira said.

Elegance glanced at Cole and Jace. "Miracle, Brogan was the fighter. He was the protector. How am I supposed to succeed where he failed?"

"All of your younger sisters have done it," Mira said. "You stand and fight."

Elegance looked at Cole and Jace again. "Perhaps you could give us a moment?"

"No, they're part of this," Mira said.

Elegance flushed a little. "My power is gone. Completely gone. I'm not much use in a fight. How am I supposed to help? What if I just get in the way?"

"Are you sure your power is gone?" Cole asked. "Your sisters all started regaining some of their power as it left your father."

"I'm aware," Elegance said. "I have not had that experience."

"Mind if I check?" Cole asked. "I've had some practice helping with powers."

Mira nodded encouragingly.

"Very well," Elegance said, holding out a hand. "But don't scoff. I was once quite capable."

Cole took her hand and was mildly surprised to discover how empty she felt inside. Emptier than anyone he had ever examined.

"Is it that bad?" Elegance asked.

Cole realized his concern was showing on his face. "Give me a second," he said, composing his expression. Exerting his power and searching hard, he found a dead spot at her center, like a spent lump of charcoal, the inert residue of previous power. "You feel burned out."

"I'm not surprised," Elegance said. "It haunts me."

"Can I try something?" Cole asked.

Mira gave a reassuring nod.

"I suppose," Elegance said.

Cole began pouring his power into the inert spot. At first it felt like shooting sparks at a dead piece of coal. No fuel remained to burn. As he maintained the pressure, the inert spot began to grow warm.

"I feel something," Elegance reported, startled.

In the place that had been dead, Cole could now feel a faint glow of power that was not his own. Seizing that glow,

Cole increased the intensity of his delivery, pushing with all he had, and the glow flared into a blaze.

Cole released her hand and staggered back. He encountered a sofa and sat down hard.

Elegance looked astonished. "I feel it," she whispered. "I feel my power."

"It was so dim," Cole said. "I don't think our powers can ever be fully taken. Not completely. But you were about as close to losing yours as it gets."

"Do you think you can open a wayport now?" Mira asked.

"I . . . I think so," Elegance said. "It has been so long, but I can see again. See far off."

"Open a wayport," Mira urged.

"It will leave me unable to open another if we need it," Elegance said.

"Not with Cole around," Mira said.

Elegance looked to Cole.

"It should be fine," Cole said. "When I woke up people's power in the echolands, it didn't go out again. We won't know unless you try."

Two wayports appeared on opposite sides of the room.

Elegance smiled faintly. "A waste of energy. This only goes from here to there."

The wayports vanished.

"I'm still connected to you," Cole said, feeding her more power.

Elegance raised her eyebrows. "That is amazing. I feel like I could do it again."

"You could," Cole said. "Violet opened wayport after

wayport with me helping. Just a little while ago she opened three at the same time."

"No," Elegance said.

"She did," Cole assured her. "And she was using them as shields against the Perennial Serpent."

"If you have an unlimited power supply, why not?" Elegance said. "It must be taxing for you, Cole?"

"Not too bad," he said.

"Have you found limits?" Elegance asked.

"I feel strained sometimes," Cole said. "It takes concentration. But I haven't really found limits. I think I'm getting stronger."

"Everyone needs rest," Mira said. "You should sleep, Cole. We all should."

"Of course," Elegance said. "You must be exhausted. I'll have Ethel prepare beds for you."

"Good morning," Mira said brightly, startling Cole out of his sleep. He winced as she pulled the curtains aside, and sunlight streamed into the previously gloomy bedroom. Remembering his circumstances, Cole glanced at his ring and felt relieved to see no signal.

"It's bright out," Cole said. "I didn't mean to sleep so long."

"I wanted you to sleep as long as possible," Mira replied. "The Host is waiting at breakfast with the current Grand Shaper of Creon, Kezlyn Vedor."

"The Grand Shaper?" Cole exclaimed, rolling out of bed. "Why didn't you get me?"

"She just arrived," Mira said. "And I am getting you." She walked out of the room.

Despite receiving pajamas, Cole had slept in his clothes, so he only had to put on his socks and shoes. He had considered keeping his shoes on as well, in case the ring had awoken him with a call to action.

Cole wondered if today would be the day. Maybe Kendo had erred on the side of caution. Maybe Ramarro would not make an appearance until tomorrow.

In a way, it would be nice to have it over with. Suspense could be terrible.

But more time to prepare would also be nice.

Unless the only preparation was worrying.

The prospect of meeting a new Grand Shaper gave him hope. In the past, Grand Shapers had played key roles in their victories.

Cole found Jace waiting with Mira outside the door. They escorted him to a large dining room, where Elegance sat with the Host and a woman in plain Wayminder robes. Cole would have guessed the woman was around fifty, with pleasant features and her hair shaved down to short bristles.

They all stood when the kids entered.

"Cole," Elegance said. "You know the Host. May I introduce Kezlyn Vedor, Grand Shaper of Creon."

And then his ring vibrated. Looking down, Cole found it glowing. Mira's ring glowed as well. And Jace's.

"It's time," Cole said.

"The torivor?" Kezlyn asked.

"Ramarro," Cole said. "We have to go to the Far North

Cache. He'll be free any minute. We have to stop him."

A wayport appeared beside Cole as Kezlyn stood. Jace grabbed a muffin and bit into it. Cole figured it wasn't a bad idea and grabbed one too.

"How long do we have?" Kezlyn asked.

"I'm not sure," Cole said.

Elegance walked calmly to the wayport. She turned to face the Host. "Will you be joining us?"

The Host offered a faltering smile. "My post is here, protecting this stronghold." He gestured at Kezlyn. "You are in good hands."

Cole stepped through the wayport. The air was chilly. Jace, Mira, Elegance, and finally Kezlyn joined him.

They stood just outside a tall metal fence topped with spikes. Beyond the fence, assembled curiosities vied for attention, including slot machines, a Viking longship, a cheap swing set, a wooden lifeguard tower, a pool table, a grass hut, a motor home, a row of trash cans, and a large marble statue. Patches of snow clung to the ground, and frost whitened some surfaces, though enough warmth was creeping into the day that Cole thought it might burn off before long.

"No rampaging monster yet," Jace said, looking around.

"Can you take us inside?" Mira asked.

"It's heavily shielded," Kezlyn said. "I'm sure there are established conduits, but it would take time to feel them out."

"Cole," Jace said.

Cole touched Jace's golden rope and Mira's Jumping Sword.

"I can help the others over," Jace said.

"Let me try something," Cole said, stepping beside Elegance. "Grab hold of me."

"You're littler than I am," Elegance said.

"Just try," Cole insisted. She put her hands on his shoulders. Cole concentrated on his connection to the Jumping Sword. With his free hand on her wrist, he found his connection to Elegance's power. Then he tied the Jumping Sword into her as well as himself. He held out the sword. "Away!"

He could feel that the sword required extra energy, so he pushed more power into the weapon as he sprang forward. Elegance rose with him over the fence. He did a little sword-assisted hop as he landed to offset the impact.

"How'd you do that?" Mira shouted.

"He's got skills," Jace said as he deposited Kezlyn over the fence using his rope.

Mira jumped the fence with her sword. Jace launched himself over with the rope.

A rumble came from deeper within the cache. The ground vibrated.

"I don't see Lorenzo," Mira said.

"I don't see anybody," Jace added.

"If he still has the pendant, he'll end up here," Cole said.

"Not Lorenzo Debray?" Kezlyn asked.

"Yeah," Cole said. "He's helping us."

A more serious quake shook the ground, the rumbling becoming thunderous. Again, judging from the sound, the epicenter was farther into the cache. The tremor subsided.

"Hurry," Cole said, running toward the heart of the noise.

"What are we going to do when Ramarro comes?" Kezlyn asked.

"Fight him," Cole said.

"How?" Kezlyn pursued.

"With all we have," Cole said.

Lesser rumbles came and went. The ground trembled.

"We don't generally run toward these kinds of sounds," Jace observed. "Should we hurry?"

Cole gave a nod and drew his Jumping Sword. "Catch up," he said. Then he pointed it forward and shouted, "Away!"

He bounded through the air, then issued the command again when he landed, then again. Up and down he soared, with Mira just behind him to one side and Jace on the other. The cache was cluttered with diverse items large and small, but it was also orderly, with lanes dividing the collection into a grid. Leaping along the lane, Cole focused on reaching the rumbling, only vaguely aware that he was passing an assortment of refrigerators from different eras, or a roller coaster, or an Asian temple, or a putting green, or an Easter Island moai.

Before long Cole reached an open square. The pendant floated at the center, the sphere glowing an intense white. He stopped jumping forward, and so did the others.

"Where is Lorenzo?" Cole asked, studying the empty area. "Wasn't he supposed to be getting a bunch of Grand Shapers?"

"Where is anybody?" Jace asked.

With a brilliant flash and a thunderous roar, the pendant shattered. Cole staggered as the ground shook. Returning his gaze to the center of the square, Cole found they were no longer alone.

CHAPTER
26

RELEASE

A figure stood in the center of the square.

Scary tall.

At least eight feet.

An albino man with long white hair and a lean, powerful physique. A mirthless smile revealed a mouth full of serrated teeth, and his eyes were a blue so pale they were nearly transparent. His lavish robe hung open over a bare chest. Soft moccasins sheathed his feet. He held up a hand, his long fingernails flashing like mirrors.

"Hello, Ramarro," Cole said. The torivor looked different from how Cole had ever seen him.

"Cole," Ramarro answered, his penetrating voice audible to the ears but also somehow piercing directly into the mind. "Of course you are here. And two of your friends. And two I don't know coming along so slowly." He gnashed his teeth, and suddenly Elegance and Kezlyn stood near Cole. "The Grand Shaper, Kezlyn Vedor. Not even an old one. The incumbent. And Elegance, the eldest princess. This is it? Have you come to surrender?"

"We're here to stop you," Cole said.

"I don't like your weapons," Ramarro said, waving a hand. The Jumping Swords and the golden rope turned to dust. "This is insulting. And embarrassing."

The Perennial Serpent appeared off to one side of the square. Beside the huge snake stood a man in a black, cowled robe. He threw back his hood, revealing himself as Owandell. "Welcome, master."

"Owandell," Ramarro said. "You brought a pet. You are otherwise alone?"

"I am here to learn your will," Owandell said.

"You are here unaccompanied in hopes of becoming my mouthpiece," Ramarro said. "Clumsy and presumptuous. But you can be molded."

A wayport appeared on the other side of the square. Lorenzo Debray emerged with a pair of other Wayminders.

"Finally," Ramarro said. "A few of the old guard. But where is Kendo? Ah, he departed at last. A final gesture of cowardice. Very well." He took a deep breath. "I was held captive for a long time. Uncomfortably long—and I'm eternal. Certain types of suspense do not exist in eternity. Well, as was inevitable, your prisons have failed; your chains have broken; your walls have crumbled. Is this to be a fight or a conversation? Who among you is ready to unconditionally surrender?"

"We hope to reason together," Lorenzo said.

Ramarro's smile vanished. "Reason? Now? Where was reason when I was banished to your afterlife? While I was incarcerated, we might have reasoned. A little. To pass the time. Now all that matters is what I want, and who will bow to me."

"We will not bow," Lorenzo said.

"We won't either," Cole added.

"It's too foolish to be admirable," Ramarro said. "Your hearts are only beating because I allow it. I am exercising extreme patience. I am aware that as pathetic as you are, most others are even worse."

Cole wondered if he could somehow get close enough to touch him.

Ramarro's smile returned. "Cole, you wish to confront me directly? None have ever so dared." He motioned for him to approach. "I see your friends believe you may be able to stop me. Shall we lay the matter to rest? By all means, come forward."

"Let me take care of this pretender," Owandell said.

"Are you capable of defeating this child?" Ramarro asked.

Owandell paused. "With your help I—"

Ramarro shook his head. "With my sponsorship anyone here could rule the Outskirts unchallenged for a million years. I am not asking what you can do with my help."

Owandell bowed low. "Please afford me the opportunity to dispatch this foe."

"You princesses remember Owandell," Ramarro said. "Was he this courageous when he stripped your powers?"

"We were chained up," Mira said. "And he had a lot of guards."

"Elegance," Ramarro said. "I believe you and certain

325

elements within this serpent were once acquainted."

"I feel it," Elegance said.

Cole realized that without the weapons, his power was connected to nothing outside himself. He took a step toward Elegance.

"No, Cole, come to me," Ramarro said.

Cole faced Ramarro. If the torivor was willing, did this mean he had no chance? Was the torivor playing mind games, trying to disrupt his confidence? Was it possible that Ramarro was underestimating him?

He started walking toward Ramarro.

"Your power is interesting, Cole," Ramarro said. "Given the chance to mature and develop it, none here but me would be able to threaten you."

Cole wondered if this would be the end of his life. It seemed probable.

"You interrupted my triumphant return," Ramarro said. "I had worked my way free and you delayed me. Few could have accomplished it. Such a cheap, cruel trick. The Void was a clever prison. Imperfect, but clever. Dwelling in the midst of nothingness, locked within a repeating moment. Only I could have escaped it. I have half a mind to put you inside as your reward. Let you hover in an endless stasis as your sanity unravels across the eons."

Cole stopped directly in front of Ramarro, looking up. The torivor was tall and terrifying.

Ramarro held out a hand. "Ready?"

The nails looked sharp, so Cole grabbed his pale wrist.

The jarring influx of power jolted Cole free from all

physical sensation. Power was everywhere. It did not present as something separate. It was not contained. Cole struggled to retain his sense of self. The power blazed above him, below him, around him, within him. It was like he no longer existed. Only the power remained.

Choosing his focus at random, Cole reached out blindly to touch the power, to connect, and raw shaping power sizzled through him. He crashed to the ground, dazed and suddenly detached from the flood of power that had engulfed him. He could not move.

"On your feet," Ramarro ordered. "That was but a glimpse."

Cole discovered he could move again, but his body felt achy. He rose gingerly.

"Allow me, Great One," Owandell said. "This urchin is unworthy of your attention."

"I decide what merits my attention," Ramarro said. He held out a hand to Cole. "Would you care to try again?"

Cole stared at the white hand, long fingers tipped with silvery talons. What was he supposed to do against so much power? It would be like trying to outwrestle the ocean.

"No," Cole said.

"A modicum of intelligence," Ramarro said. "Do you now see the futility of resistance? You have inherited a problem that cannot be solved. I am free. The attempts to contain me have failed. Why perish unnecessarily? Why doom those who stand with you? Submit and survive."

Cole shook his head. "You offered this before. I might not be able to beat you. But I will not join you."

Ramarro gazed at him. "Though it makes you more interesting, it is also disappointing. Defiance will not be tolerated. Our interactions are drawing to a close."

"Wait," Lorenzo declared. He assumed an awkward stance and closed his eyes. The Wayminders with him struck poses of their own.

"What is this?" Ramarro asked. "Not an attack! A demonstration?"

A large, round wayport opened, the edges swirling like an eddying mist.

"We are the protectors of this world," Lorenzo declared. "We may lack the might to defeat you in combat, but we can offer you an alternative." He extended a hand toward the wayport. "This way leads to Earth, a larger, more firmly established world than this one. It has a far greater population and connects to a vast system of worlds and stars and space."

"No!" Cole cried, staring at Lorenzo in shocked disbelief. "How could you?"

Lorenzo turned a sad gaze his way. "I'm sorry, Cole."

"I know about Earth," Ramarro said, stalking over to the wayport.

"Take care, Mighty One," Owandell advised. "They are deceivers."

Ramarro stopped at the mouth of the wayport, studying it. "This would indeed convey me to Earth and permit me to remain there. And you hope it will trap me there."

"We would prefer for the Outskirts to continue as it is," Lorenzo said.

"And to this end you offer Cole's home world," Ramarro said.

Cole was trying to think how he could stop Lorenzo. If he touched him and disrupted his power, would the Pilgrim Path close? How could he get near enough?

Ramarro considered Cole. "You fear for your world. You do not want me to go." He regarded the wayport again. "There is no great complexity here. I could walk this path whenever I choose." He looked at Lorenzo. "A brilliantly conceived prison in the echolands could not hold me. Do you honestly believe an indifferent planet could?"

"Perhaps it would distract you," Lorenzo said. "Amuse you."

Ramarro waved an arm, and the wayport vanished. "I sense much at play here. I will sort out the specifics later. You weary me. Owandell? Do you still wish to engage Cole?"

"If it pleases you," Owandell said, head bowed.

"It does," Ramarro said. "Do not expect aid from me."

"That will not be required," Owandell assured him.

"Wait," Cole said. "Are you leaving me unarmed?"

"If you believe yourself unarmed, you are far simpler than I expected," Ramarro said. "Owandell. I want Cole defeated. Not killed. Not maimed. Not transported else-where. Any of those alternatives would mean you have failed me, with all that entails."

Owandell only hesitated for an instant. "Understood."

Mira appeared at Cole's right. Jace arrived at his left.

Cole was surprised. They didn't have weapons that let them leap there. They must have run.

"If you fight Cole, you fight all of us," Mira said.

329

"Spare Cole," Ramarro ordered. "Do with the others as you wish."

"Peya," Owandell said. "Get them."

The Perennial Serpent slithered forward, head rearing up, hood spreading wide.

"We don't have weapons," Cole whispered. "Back off."

Mira took Cole's hand. "I'm all we've got."

Cole felt the brightness of her power. Her shaping abilities were mostly untested in combat, but he knew she had a lot of raw strength. Maybe Sambrian shaping could help! He energized her with everything he had.

Mira extended a hand, and the ground rippled in front of the snake. A bulbous section of earth arose and took shape, with a pair of crude arms and a trio of slender legs. It reminded Cole of a larger version of the mount Mira had tried to create when they were heading to Carthage from Sambria.

"The mudball?" Jace cried incredulously.

Her impromptu creation toddled toward the snake and swung an arm, but Peya dodged the blow and came streaking at Cole and his friends. Cole ran left. Mira and Jace went right. The Perennial Serpent closed on Mira. Jace jumped in front of her when the serpent struck and disappeared.

Cole screamed.

The snake struck again and Mira vanished.

Then the snake wheeled on Cole.

He had no idea what to do. He tried to run as the snake approached, but within a moment it was encircling him, coils constricting. The thick body wrapped around him twice, pinning his arms to his sides and binding his legs together, immovable muscles clenching beneath smooth scales. Cole suspected the snake could crush his bones to dust if it desired.

"Will that suffice?" Owandell asked.

"Do you yield, Cole?" Ramarro asked lazily.

Focusing on the physical contact with the serpent, Cole connected to its power. Peya's power was impressive, but, unlike Ramarro's, it was comprehensibly finite. Could Cole attack so much power directly? The nature of the energy reminded him of the power he had reignited in Elegance.

Ribs creaking as he peered across the square, Cole saw Elegance watching. If only he could touch her, he could try to link her power to the snake.

Keeping his connection to the Perennial Serpent, Cole concentrated on Elegance. Her power was there. He could sense it. Cole knew he could hold a connection without touching her. Why not make one?

He had failed before. Many times.

Still, he tried, reaching with his power, searching with his mind.

He had a vague, general sense of her power. But nothing he could actually reach.

Cole remembered the dead center he had accessed when he reenergized her. The expired coal he had saturated until it flared to life.

What about that? Where was that?

Suddenly he was no longer just searching for her power.

He had a more specific target. A target he had not known existed.

He was searching for her center.

The heart of her power.

The core.

And he found it, throbbing in the midst of her power, small but intense. He had never noticed the core before. He had not known to look.

Once found, it seemed more tangible than the rest of her power. If her power was light, this was the lantern. Connecting proved almost effortless.

"This is absurd," Owandell said. "Yield. Peya does not have to be gentle."

Peya had sent Twitch away. And Brogan. And Mira. And Jace.

Cole reached into Peya with all he had and heaved her power at Elegance. The transference developed quickly, and suddenly he was not pushing power from the serpent to the princess. It was flowing on its own.

The grip of the snake slackened. And then the serpent began to shrink. Cole felt the power gushing out of the snake as if a dam had burst.

"No!" Owandell cried. "Peya! Attack!"

The spasming serpent offered no reaction. Within moments it lay still, barely a foot in length.

Cole no longer perceived any power in it. He ran toward Owandell.

The robed man looked frightened. "Stay back!" he demanded.

"All right," Cole said, reaching for him with his power. He had touched Owandell's power before. The center had to be in there somewhere.

Finding it proved easier than expected.

Knowing what to look for changed everything.

Suddenly Cole was connected.

"So much darkness, Owandell," Cole said. "Should I brighten it up?"

Mustering all his will, Cole burned away the darkness, untangling the knots and healing the scars. Dropping to his knees, Owandell screamed like he was on fire.

When Cole finished, not much power remained within his foe. But it was untainted.

"Impressive," Ramarro said. "You learn swiftly, Cole. I believe we have a victor."

"No," Owandell moaned, staggering to his feet. "I have served you faithfully. Rebuild me better than before. Empower me, Great One."

"I will decide your fate later," Ramarro said, waving a hand.

Owandell vanished.

"You are a problem, Cole," Ramarro said. "You interest me, and you will not serve me. What is the answer? Destruction? Incarceration? Torture? Perhaps I could use your friends to persuade you."

Jace and Mira reappeared.

"Mira!" Cole exclaimed. "Jace!"

"Whoa," Jace said. "I wasn't expecting this."

"Where were you?" Cole asked.

"Not dead," Jace said.

"The wilderness," Mira said. "The middle of nowhere."

"Not together," Jace said.

"They were far away and back in time," Ramarro said.

"Simple to retrieve. Equally simple to kill. Cole, serve me or the girl dies. I mean now."

"Don't even think about it, Cole," Mira demanded.

"This is over," Ramarro said. "Nothing can stop me. Why not confront the inevitable with maturity? What good will be accomplished by losing your friends? By dying?"

"There is still Trillian," Mira said. "He'll stop you."

"Trillian will never have the chance," Ramarro said. "If you think the founding shapers could build a prison, you have seen nothing yet. Keeping him locked away will be as simple as subduing this absurd little world. Cole?"

Cole's throat was so dry that he gagged when he tried to swallow. "No," he finally managed.

Jace stepped in front of Mira. "You have to go through me first."

"No, I don't," Ramarro said as Mira fell to the ground. "But I don't mind killing you as well. Cole? Want to reconsider?"

"Never," Cole said.

Jace dropped limply, part of him covering Mira.

"Now, Cole, here is an offer," Ramarro said. "Last chance. Your world. Serve me and I promise to leave your world alone for as long as you live. Choose death, and I will oblige, but you get no promise."

Cole glanced numbly at his fallen friends. He had lost them twice now within a few minutes. This felt like the end. Had Ramarro just offered to spare his world? Cole scowled. Could he let that opportunity pass? Wait. No. Ramarro had offered to spare his world for as long as he lived. Under those terms, Ramarro could just kill him and then attack Earth.

"Leave Earth alone forever," Cole said. "Promise that, and we might have a deal."

"You are in no position to bargain," Ramarro seethed. "My offer stands as spoken."

Maybe none of this was really happening. Did his choice even matter?

"What?" Ramarro asked. "How can this be a hypothetical future? It's not possible. . . . No, it could be feasible if they were clever enough. Cole, is this a hypothetical . . . ? You don't know. You're unsure. Just as you were unsure about the wayport they opened. The Pilgrim Path, as they term it. If this is a trick, you will pay dearly. You will all pay."

Ramarro turned to face Lorenzo.

"Go!" Lorenzo called.

Wayports appeared all over the square.

Including one beside Cole.

He leaped into it.

NEW COURSE

I t took a moment for Cole to absorb where he was.

He had leaped into a wayport.

No confusion there.

But instead of coming out the other side of the wayport, he was inexplicably sitting at a polished metallic table with Jace, Mira, Violet, and Lorenzo in an underground vault. There was no wayport in sight.

The transition was so seamless that it was disconcerting. He held a flask in his hand. It felt empty.

Lorenzo studied Cole intently. "What did you feel?"

"No way," Cole said. "I'm back."

"Back from where?" Jace asked. "You just drank it."

"No," Cole said. "I drank it a long time ago. I've been busy. You all died. All but Lorenzo. And he was probably about to get killed."

"You met Ramarro?" Lorenzo asked.

Cole nodded, looking around at his friends, fighting back tears. "I'm so happy to see you."

Mira leaned over and gave him a hug. He pulled her close and held her tightly.

"I wish I could stop time," Cole said. "So much is coming."

"Are you all right?" Lorenzo asked.

"Not really," Cole said. "None of us are."

"What did you learn?" Lorenzo asked.

Cole pointed at him. "You opened the Pilgrim Path. Without permission. You invited Ramarro to Earth."

"He didn't go?" Lorenzo asked.

Cole shook his head. "I think he sensed it was a trap. But we had a deal! You weren't going to risk Earth unless we were sure."

Lorenzo sighed. "I need to come clean. I was conducting an experiment."

"With the fate of Earth?" Cole asked.

"No," Lorenzo said. "I told you I wasn't sure if the potion worked."

"Yeah," Cole said.

"Torivors read minds," Lorenzo said. "I knew the potion would work. I don't remember what I did in the future you experienced, but I know my plan. There were certain things I needed you to believe in order to conduct my experiment. If you were certain you were in a hypothetical future, Ramarro might have sensed it."

"He sensed I wasn't sure toward the end," Cole said. "He was mad."

"He would have been mad," Lorenzo said. "At that point he suspected we were gathering information. I'm sorry he didn't walk the Pilgrim Path."

"You were checking what would happen," Cole said.

"Our last best chance to check was getting Ramarro to walk the path in the possible future you visited," Lorenzo said. "Had he walked it, I would have collected what information I could and reported to you. But the attempt failed?"

"I don't know what Ramarro sensed," Cole said. "But he knew we were up to something with the Pilgrim Path. I was really worried. I thought you were risking Earth."

"None of that was permanent," Lorenzo said. "No matter what happened, it was going to be erased when you returned to this moment. And now you've returned. So we need a new plan."

"We all died?" Mira asked.

"You and Jace for sure," Cole said. "Jace gave his life for you, by the way. Zero hesitation."

Mira gave Jace a tender stare. "Thank you."

"For failing?" Jace asked. "We died. The goal is to keep you alive!"

"I died too?" Violet asked.

"You maybe died," Cole said. "When we kidnapped the governor."

Jace whistled. "You were busy!"

"You kidnapped Governor Vass?" Lorenzo asked.

"We found out where Owandell is holding the king and queen," Cole said.

"Really?" Mira exclaimed. "Where?"

Cole paused. "Good question. Oh no. I know this. It's some fort in Sambria with lots of Enforcers. An island or something."

"The Island Keep?" Violet asked.

"Yes!" Cole shouted with relief. "Thank you. The Island Keep. I would have felt so stupid if I'd forgotten!"

"I may have teased you a lot," Jace said.

"You don't know if I died?" Violet asked.

"The Perennial Serpent showed up and attacked us as we questioned Vass," Cole said. "It's named Peya. Of course I forget the keep but remember that! The snake got Brogan—"

"We made him young?" Mira asked.

"Yes, and he was awesome," Cole said. "But the serpent bit him, and he vanished, like Twitch. You and Jace got bitten later. You vanished, but Ramarro brought you back."

"Then killed us," Jace said.

"He's a jerk," Cole said.

"Where did we go?" Mira asked.

"You told me you were in the wilderness," Cole said. "Ramarro mentioned you were also back in time."

"So Twitch is probably alive," Mira said.

"Pretty good chance he is alive back in time in the wilderness," Cole said.

"Which means he probably died a long time ago," Jace said.

"Not likely," Lorenzo said. "Unless the serpent found a way to keep him permanently back in time."

"I'm still not clear what happened to me," Violet said.

"I was getting there," Cole said. "When Brogan got bitten, you opened a wayport for us to escape. Jace and I went through, but the wayport closed before you joined us."

"We left her?" Jace asked.

"Not on purpose," Cole said. "Things went bad fast. You

were kind of pushy about it, Jace. You wanted to make sure I faced Ramarro."

"Because I'm good in a crisis," Jace said. "Except for getting killed with Mira."

"Maybe I closed it on purpose," Violet said. "To make sure you got away."

"Would you do that?" Jace asked.

"I think so," Violet said. "Or it could have closed if I got killed. Or if the snake tampered with my powers."

"Or Owandell," Cole said. "He can mess with powers."

"Owandell was there?" Mira asked.

"I think so," Cole said. "With Peya. He kept his face covered that time. I think he is the Ancient One. He showed up at the Far North Cache with the same robes when the serpent appeared. We stopped the snake and beat him, by the way, before Ramarro got us."

"But Mira and I got bitten," Jace said.

"Yeah," Cole said. "I stopped the snake, if you want to be specific. With help from Elegance. I connected the serpent's power to hers, and the rest was automatic. Oh! I can connect without touching now!"

Cole focused on Violet, found her center, and connected to her power. He shared energy with her.

"I feel it," Violet said.

Cole turned to Lorenzo. "Why didn't you tell me I just had to reach for the center?"

"The center?" Lorenzo asked.

"Of their power," Cole said. "The core. To connect."

Lorenzo gave a little shrug. "You're teaching me now.

I don't know how to connect to the power of another. I've never felt another's center of power."

"Well, that's the trick," Cole said. "If you can find the center, you can connect."

"What about Ramarro?" Jace asked. "Can we beat him this time?"

Cole sighed. "I don't know, guys. It looks bad."

"Really?" Mira asked.

"He let me touch him so I could try to attack his power," Cole said. "It was like nothing I've ever felt. I had no idea where to begin. His power was everywhere."

"And we can't send him to Earth," Jace said.

"I'm not sure he would go," Cole said. "And no way can we risk it unless we're sure it will strip his powers."

"What else did you learn?" Lorenzo asked. "What should we do?"

"I learned we're in huge trouble," Cole said. "We need to take every risk possible if it might help. I learned if we do the same thing we did last time, Ramarro wins."

"Did Ramarro kill you?" Lorenzo asked.

"Nope," Cole said. "Last minute you opened a ton of wayports. I entered the nearest."

"That was my plan," Lorenzo said. "A plan I may never actually carry out now. If it turned ugly enough, I was going to use the local conduits to open a bunch of wayports. Hopefully enough to temporarily distract Ramarro. Were other Wayminders with me?"

"Two," Cole said.

"Probably the two I have in mind," Lorenzo said. "Grand

Shapers. Anyhow, the wayport nearest you led out of Creon. By going through it, you came directly back to this moment."

"Yes," Cole said. "I went in. But I didn't come out. I just showed up here. As if none of it happened."

"It didn't happen," Lorenzo said. "Even though you remember it."

"With all of you here, it's like telling about a dream," Cole said.

"What's the plan?" Jace asked.

"You and Mira should go to the Iron Fort and give the youth potion to Brogan," Cole said. "That was a brilliant call. Could you take them, Lorenzo?"

"I can take them to the tent before seeking out my associates," Lorenzo said. "Where will you be?"

"Last time I couldn't leave Creon," Cole said. "I need Violet to help me make some visits. The first is the riskiest. I need to talk to Trillian."

"Is that wise?" Lorenzo asked.

"For sure it isn't safe," Cole said. "But I think it might be necessary. We need all the help we can get to beat Ramarro."

"Do you think Trillian will betray his own kind?" Mira asked.

"He might," Cole said. "Mostly because you're really smart. Something you said in the possible future. Look, I know it's risky. I know I might not return. But without help I know we lose. Nobody can help us like Trillian can. It's worth a shot. And time is short. Ramarro shows up tomorrow morning."

"That soon?" Lorenzo asked.

"Count on it," Cole said. "The sun was not very high in the sky. Are you up for it, Violet?"

"Why not?" Violet said.

"You won't remember most of what happened here when you leave Creon," Lorenzo warned.

"Hopefully when I show up at the Lost Palace, I'll get the general idea," Cole said. "Sit tight at the Iron Fort until I get back. I'll try not to take too long. And if I don't come back, I'm so sorry. Do you know where we're going, Violet?"

A wayport opened.

CHAPTER
—— 28 ——

TORIVOR

The sight of the Lost Palace filled Cole with dread. Despite the moonless night, a greenish radiance glowed from the sickly mist eddying across the uneven grounds, all enclosed by a tall fence fanged with barbed spikes. Sagging walls and spindly towers rose out of the luminous haze like the charred skeleton of a castle. Cole remembered all too well who lived there. Contact with Trillian was strictly forbidden for good reason—he turned visitors into puppets. Many who entered his domain never left. Those who did served the torivor with fanatical devotion. Cole had barely survived his previous encounter.

Cole and Violet stood on the Red Road near a wayport. Though surrounded by wilderness, the perfectly maintained avenue stretched behind them to the limits of sight. Ahead, the gate stood open.

"Are you sure this is where we want to be?" Violet asked.

"No," Cole said. His memories from before he emerged from the wayport were cloudy.

"I don't like the open gate," Violet said. "Feels like a trap."

"It's definitely a trap. Nobody should go in there unless they must. But we're probably here on purpose. We came straight from Creon. You opened the wayport?"

The wayport wavered. "Yes. It's mine. Are we really so desperate that we're going to Trillian?"

"We could go back and check, but we won't remember when we return," Cole said.

"We'll remember this moment," Violet said. "If we come back again, it can be a signal that you really want to talk to Trillian."

Cole stepped through the wayport, and Violet followed.

They stood inside the metallic vault. It was empty.

Cole remembered his previous experiences—the possible future he had experienced, his return to his friends, and his decision to visit Trillian. And he recalled going to the Lost Palace and feeling completely confused.

"We want to do this," Cole said, stepping through the wayport. Violet came through as well.

"We're back," Cole said. "I guess this means we need Trillian."

The wayport vanished.

"Should I come in with you?" Violet asked.

"Could you help me teleport out in an emergency?" Cole asked.

Violet held out her hand. Cole took it, connected to her power, and fed her energy.

"It's heavily shielded," Violet said. "Like completely. I can't see anything inside there using my power."

"Don't trust your eyes," Cole said. "Trillian can manipulate reality. It's hard to tell what is real in there."

"I'm not sure if a way out is shielded," Violet said. "Sometimes you can see out of places that block you from looking in."

"Up to you," Cole said. "I don't mind if you wait here."

"I'll come," Violet said, straightening her robes. "I want to see how it goes. Help however I can."

"Then come on," Cole said, leading her through the open gate.

The instant Cole passed the gate, the palace transformed. The castle became a gleaming monument to ingenuity and imagination, miraculously crafted out of pearl and platinum, reflecting warm light from the radiant crystals artfully arranged across the stylish grounds. The colors appeared more rich and vibrant than natural limits should permit, as if Cole had worn a dulling filter over his eyes since birth and it had finally been removed. The luxurious red of the road before them reduced all other reds to halfhearted attempts at pink.

"It's beautiful," Violet said.

"Bait for the trap," Cole said.

A woman approached astride a broad, powerful stallion. She had hair like cascades of molten silver and possessed inhumanly flawless beauty.

"Hi, Hina," Cole said. "We need to see Trillian."

"We are intrigued by your visit," Hina said. "Come with me to the palace."

"It's an emergency," Cole said. "The faster the better."

Hina snapped her fingers, and a pair of saddled horses

galloped up to Cole and Violet. Cole swung up onto the black one. Violet mounted the white.

Cole glanced over at Violet as they rode. She looked nervous and amazed, her hair fluttering in the wind of their speed.

Graceful steps flowed down from the mirrored palace doors. They dismounted at the base of the stairs, and Hina led the ascent. Though there was no hurry evident in her fluid strides, Cole had to jog to keep up.

"We'll go to sleep," Cole told Violet. "Trillian will talk to us in a dream."

Violet held out her hand. Cole took it and energized her power. Violet furrowed her brow and shook her head. "I can't open a wayport here," she whispered.

"No need to whisper," Hina remarked offhandedly. "He hears your thoughts."

They passed through the mirrored doors into a gleaming white hallway decorated with luminous crystals. Hina led them up a sweeping staircase, then invited Violet into a room.

"Alone?" Violet asked.

"We'll meet in our dreams," Cole assured her.

The door closed. A few more steps and Cole received a room of his own. He went straight to the bed and tried to relax. It was not difficult. No beds were this comfortable. Not home, not anywhere.

Soon he stood on a deserted beach, feet buried in the soft, warm sand. A cloud currently hid the sun, but most of the sky was a clear blue. Large waves reared up high before curling and crashing in a foamy tumble. The absence of civilization, together with the tropical air and the ferny shrubs behind him, suggested he might be on an island.

Cole looked around for company. Nobody yet.

He crouched and sifted a handful of fine-grained sand through his fingers. Warm, not hot. Like the air. Ideal. Soothing. Like the bed.

This was a dream.

"More than a dream," a voice said behind him.

Cole turned to find Trillian where he had not been a moment before. An ageless man whose features hinted at mixed ethnicities, Trillian wore a loose golden robe with fur at the collar and at the ends of the sleeves. Light suffused his skin, as if his insides were glowing.

"Hello," Cole said.

"I expected you would return," Trillian said.

"Yeah?" Cole asked.

"If you lived, I knew you would eventually realize you were really fighting Ramarro. I did not believe you would submit to him. And if you wanted a chance to triumph, it would lead you back here."

"I guess you were right," Cole said.

"May I have full access to your mind?" Trillian asked.

"What does that mean?"

"I'm not asking for control or even influence," Trillian said. "Just complete access to your memories."

"I thought you could read minds," Cole said.

"I can see more with permission," Trillian said. "Quicker results. Less guesswork. You've been in Creon. Some of your memories are shielded. I can access them for both of us with permission."

Cole stared as the frothy aftermath of a wave spread flat over the sand. He was here. It was already a huge risk. He might as well get all the help he could. "Go ahead."

A hand softly touched the back of his neck.

"Ah, yes," Trillian said. "You have visited a simulation of the future. I see why you came to me. Let me help you recall."

The events in Creon awoke in Cole's mind as if they had never left. "I remember now," Cole said. "No wonder I came here. Ramarro was going to keep you locked up. He admitted it to Mira."

Trillian stood before Cole and studied him. "I suspected Ramarro would not be faithful to me, given the chance. But knowing is different from suspecting."

"Different enough to help me?" Cole asked.

"Yes," Trillian said. "I predicted you would become embroiled in the events surrounding Ramarro. I did not realize you would be at the center. And I did not realize you would come to understand your power so rapidly. The events in the echolands accelerated the process."

"Can I defeat him?" Cole asked.

"In a direct contest? Not with all the aid I could offer."

"Is there a way?"

"You explored an intriguing possibility."

"Drawing Ramarro to my world?"

"I believe Lorenzo and Kendo were right," Trillian said. "I believe a torivor would be rendered powerless if he followed the Pilgrim Path to Earth."

"Can you be sure?" Cole asked.

"I am nearly convinced already," Trillian said. "I can see the nature of your world through your memories. I know what happened to Kendo Rattan after he walked the path. I must confess it warms my heart to witness him powerless. After all, he did help imprison me here. His condition suggests that many of the principles of power that function in the Outskirts do not function in your world. Torivors are eternal beings. We are suited to eternal places. Your world is much more firmly rooted in time than the Outskirts. Here, time is more of an imitation. Still, to be absolutely sure I would need to investigate."

"Could you investigate from here?" Cole asked.

"If Violet lets me borrow her power, I can replicate a Pilgrim Path," Trillian said. "Now that I understand the possibility, it should not be difficult. The exercise will let me see into your world. I could not walk the path any more than I can leave my castle grounds. I am bound here."

Cole folded his arms and scrunched his toes in the sand. "You can see my worries."

"Sometimes I prefer a conversation," Trillian said.

"How do I know you're telling the truth?" Cole said. "I know torivors supposedly can't lie. What if it's not true, and if you borrow Violet's power, you will escape and destroy my entire world? What if you lie about what you see, and Ramarro destroys my world?"

"You want certainty that a torivor cannot lie," Trillian said. "I understand why. Has anyone ever contradicted this idea?"

"No, people seem to believe it," Cole said. "But what if you're waiting for the crucial moment to tell the perfect lie?"

"I can mislead," Trillian said. "But if I truly lie, my powers will unravel. The control I exert over my surroundings is a reflection of my sincerity. My wholeness of purpose. Torivors are not perfect. If we were perfect, I would work in complete harmony with Ramarro. He is not perfect either. But torivors are unconflicted. He never pledged total loyalty to me, nor I to him. We leave unpleasant matters unresolved. We do not lie about them. We are utterly true to ourselves and to our word."

"What if you're lying now?" Cole asked.

"Some examples from your life will help you glimpse the principle," Trillian said. "In the echolands, you were tempted with the opportunity to go home. Could you have resisted that temptation if you did not sincerely want to save your friends?"

"I don't think so," Cole answered.

"When you fell into the slipstream in the echolands, could you have survived if your desire to rescue your friends was false? Could you have resisted the sweeping force of the slipstream and the bountiful summons of the homesong?"

Cole remembered that arduous moment as the slipstream stripped the impurities from his power. He could have let go and zoomed into the beckoning afterlife of the Other. But he still had work to accomplish. Unfinished business. He had needed to save his friends.

"No," Cole said.

"Heed me, Cole," Trillian said. "I experienced that moment in your mind as vividly as if I had lived it. If I heard the summons of the homesong as you did under those conditions, I would have advanced into the next world. As a caveat, I am not sure that I would have heard the same music you did. I may not have a separate essence as you do. What I seem to be may be all I am. To die in time could be the true end of a torivor. But if I heard that song calling me onward to a superior eternity . . . I'm not sure what desire would be strong enough to anchor me to this one."

"You're saying the slipstream worked like a lie detector," Cole said.

"Among other things, the slipstream proved the sincerity of your desire to save your friends," Trillian said. "Insincerity would not have survived the slipstream. And with a torivor, the power that allows us to bend reality to our wills derives from our integrity. Knowing what I know, being who I am, to lie would be to lose the source of my power. To lie is not enticing. There is no urge to resist. In fact, if for some reason I did not care what it would do to me and I wanted to lie with all my heart, I do not believe it would be possible."

"That explanation is not proof," Cole said.

"Many things that are real cannot be directly proven," Trillian said. "Yet there is evidence. And there is reason. Much that cannot be proven can still be discovered and relied upon."

"But can I risk my world?" Cole asked.

"Search your memories," Trillian said. "Your world is already at risk. If Wayminders can devise a Pilgrim Path to your world, so can Ramarro. You know this. You watched him figure it out. Ramarro will find the way to Earth with or without your involvement. He would likely subjugate the Outskirts first. Perhaps even reduce it to ashes, depending on his desire for vengeance. But if luring Ramarro to Earth could undo him, why not attempt it at the start? Why not give the Outskirts a chance?"

"Can you bring Violet here?" Cole asked.

She appeared beside Cole.

"Welcome, Violet," Trillian said. "We have been talking elsewhere, Cole."

"Should I let him use my power to see Earth?" Violet asked.

"Give me a minute," Cole said, walking away a few paces, enjoying the sand against his bare feet.

His situation was desperate. Without help, Ramarro would take over the Outskirts. If Lorenzo had not opened the Pilgrim Path, would Ramarro have discovered it? Certainly not so quickly. Would he eventually discover it? Seemed likely.

Cole took a deep breath of salty air. Did he believe that Trillian could not lie? He did. But if he was wrong, the consequences could be catastrophic.

"You promise you won't enter my world if you use Violet's power to peek at it?" Cole said. "You promise you won't even try to go there?"

"You have my word," Trillian said. "I cannot break it."

"Okay," Cole said. "How does this work?"

"Connect me to Violet's power," Trillian said. "I'm impressed you learned to reach for the nexus. I could have taught you, but you realized on your own."

"The nexus is the center?" Cole asked.

"Yes," Trillian said.

"Can I reach your nexus?" Cole asked.

"I created a nexus in this version of me," Trillian said, placing a hand over his heart. "It will suffice."

Cole connected to Violet with no problem. Finding the center of the power in Trillian was not complicated either. It didn't feel like the immeasurable ocean of power inside Ramarro. It had boundaries.

"Ramarro felt different," Cole said.

"You met Ramarro in person," Trillian said. "This is a limited version of myself, designed to interact with you."

Cole connected Violet to Trillian.

A huge, round wayport opened, the edges hazy.

"I need to send someone through the Pilgrim Path," Trillian said. "Not you or Violet—you would not be able to return. But if a servant connected to my power goes through, I should be able to feel exactly how going to Earth would affect my power. Any objections?"

"You servant would be stuck there?" Cole asked.

"Cut off from me and from this realm," Trillian said. "That is the nature of the Pilgrim Path."

Cole supposed that going to Earth would be better than staying Trillian's servant. "Do it."

A man appeared on the beach. He was tall and muscular, with a closely trimmed brown beard that followed his jawline.

"Fenrel, I need you to venture to another world," Trillian said. "A world without shaping. You will not be able to return.

But your adventure will provide information that I need."

"You are releasing me from your service?" Fenrel asked, unexcited.

"This great and useful deed will end your service to me, yes," Trillian said. "You will build a new life in a world full of opportunities and conveniences. I trust you will do well."

Fenrel bowed. "It has been an honor."

"Farewell, Fenrel," Trillian said.

Fenrel stepped into the wayport. Unlike other wayports, he did not immediately vanish. He proceeded down it like a tunnel until he faded from view.

Trillian turned to Cole. "We are in what you would consider a dream state. The actual path I opened was on the Red Road. Fenrel's actual body passed into it there. I have lost all contact with him, but not before I got the briefest of glimpses. Your world would utterly strip a torivor of his powers. My only question is whether a torivor would survive."

"You're sure?" Cole asked.

The Pilgrim Path closed.

"Ramarro would be rendered powerless by going to Earth," Trillian said. "As would I. No doubt."

Cole let the connections to Violet and Trillian drop. He watched a curl progress along a breaking wave. "So there's a chance. Last time he didn't want to go."

"Too many people present were hoping for him to go," Trillian said. "Lorenzo and his colleagues wanted it. And though you were conflicted, you also knew Ramarro might be rendered powerless. He sensed the trap."

"And now I know for sure that the path will strip his powers," Cole said. "He'll see it in my mind. Besides, if you can figure out Ramarro would lose his powers, so can he."

"Perhaps he could be persuaded otherwise," Trillian said.

"How?" Cole asked.

"You must understand your foe," Trillian said. "In our native realm, torivors are held in check by one another. We have rulers, but no dictators. Ramarro left home to explore. And to rule."

"You had the same reasons?" Cole asked.

"More or less," Trillian said. "Ramarro views himself as superior to all life he has encountered beyond our home realm. He wants to bend everyone he encounters to his will. If you bow to him, you become largely irrelevant, invisible. He is intrigued by those who defy him."

"I defied him," Cole said.

"I'm aware," Trillian said. "Torivors can read minds. But we cannot see all. Memories are hard to reach unless they are on the main stage of the mind. Your present thoughts are the most vulnerable. We can perceive those as if you are speaking them to us. We will sometimes ask questions to bring thoughts to the foreground. We can deduce and assume much from only a little information. There are patterns."

"I have to try not to think about it?" Cole asked.

"Do not think of a large red lion," Trillian suggested.

"It's all I'm thinking about," Cole said.

"You will not succeed in hiding your thoughts about the Pilgrim Path," Trillian said. "Not on your own."

"You can help?" Cole asked.

"With your permission," Trillian said. "I can hide some memories. I can create new realities in your mind. You will believe them. And I expect Ramarro will too."

"Why do you need my permission?" Cole asked.

"Your will is sovereign," Trillian said. "Your will belongs to you. Others can complicate your circumstances and reduce your options. You can be tricked, abused, intimidated, jailed, and enslaved. But your will, your core self, what you know, who you choose to be, your identity, is yours alone. It can be influenced. It can be surrendered. But not taken."

"What would you make me believe?" Cole asked.

"You would believe that the Pilgrim Path was a temporary opportunity," Trillian said. "Only an option for a very limited time. You would feel sure that the Wayminders wanted to sacrifice Earth to save the Outskirts. And you would believe you had proof that access to Earth would simply allow Ramarro to rule both worlds. You would think you had proof the Wayminders were utterly mistaken in their hopes. It would feel real to you. It would be extremely frightening. And it might mislead Ramarro."

"Wouldn't that be lying?" Cole asked.

"I would help you believe what you tell me you want to believe," Trillian said. "That is not lying. That is executing instructions with permission. Any lies would come from you."

"It could mislead Ramarro," Cole said.

"I mislead frequently," Trillian said. "But I mean every word I say."

"Are you misleading me now?" Cole asked.

"You don't know all of my motives," Trillian said. "But I am telling you the truth."

"Won't Ramarro see other things in other minds?" Cole asked.

"We would need to adjust Violet's mind as well," Trillian said. "The other minds have no certainty. They will appear conflicted. Ramarro would have to see very deeply very quickly. Think of him surrounded by many books. He has the ability to read them, but not the time and perhaps not the desire. He has abundant confidence. The things you believe will shout at him, while other minds are uncertain. It could work."

"And if it fails?" Cole asked.

"You will miss your best opportunity for victory," Trillian said. "At least it grants an opportunity."

"You want to see him fail?" Cole asked.

"It simplifies matters for me," Trillian said. "He would be my only real rival if I ever get free. I knew I did not have his loyalty. After viewing your memories, I know he considers me an enemy. He would kill me if he could."

"But you came here together," Cole said.

"Without ever having dwelled in time," Trillian said. "Without ever risking death. Without ever having weaker beings to dominate. The relationship quickly became complicated and unstable. We had no time for it to play out before we were imprisoned."

"You could have dominated your children," Violet said. "Back home. If you needed to rule somebody."

"No, Violet," Trillian said. "Torivors are eternal. We never began. There are no children in our home realm."

"How can you never begin?" Cole asked.

"Time has beginnings and endings," Trillian said. "Eternity either exists or it doesn't. Only that which is eternal truly exists. You exist. This state is temporary, but your essence is eternal."

"Isn't this temporary for you?" Cole asked.

"I am eternal," Trillian said. "I never had to worry about death. However, when I entered a realm vulnerable to time, I entered a temporary state. My time in the Outskirts began, meaning it will also end. Entering time also made me vulnerable to death. If I die, having come here as an eternal being, will I go elsewhere? This is untested. Unknown. I may be risking not just a temporary life, but my entire existence. Ramarro too. It awakens new insecurities. Confuses relationships. Especially when we were not willing to vow to protect each other. We discovered we both wanted to rule."

"You're dangerous," Cole said.

"You knew that before we met," Trillian said. "I would have offered to help defeat Ramarro in combat if you freed me from my prison. But you know I'm dangerous. And I would have made no promises not to rule. I have time on my side. I am capable of patience. So why waste time with a fruitless conversation? I influence where I can. If you remove Ramarro, you solve a perplexing problem for me."

"And if he won't take the Pilgrim Path?" Cole asked.

"Seek help from all your allies," Trillian said. "Ramarro and I were captured once. It took a group effort. Ramarro will be much more prepared this time. But who knows? Perhaps with enough of the right people involved you could put up a fight."

"Okay," Cole said. "What happens if I let you mess with my mind? Can you change me?"

"Any alteration to your essence can only be accomplished with your full permission," Trillian said. "I can't change you against your will. I can make changes we agree upon. Especially to your memories and your understanding. But that should not happen yet. It would be better for you to remember the reality of the situation as you prepare. Come visit me again shortly before Ramarro will appear, if you like my strategy."

"I will," Cole said. "It's the best I've heard."

"We can go?" Violet asked timidly.

"You have a busy night ahead," Trillian said. "I wish you well."

RESCUE

"That could have been worse," Violet said after they exited the palace grounds through the barbed fence.

"If Trillian didn't want to use us against Ramarro, it would have gone much worse," Cole said.

"Mira got Ramarro to confess he would keep Trillian in prison?"

"Yes," Cole said. "I remember it all now. Having those memories will help."

"I remember Creon, too. I hope all of my memories are real."

"I don't think he can plant fake ones unless we let him."

"I hope you're right. Where to next?"

"The Island Keep?" Cole asked. "Save the queen and Mira's sisters? Maybe even the king."

"Just the two of us?" Violet asked.

"Owandell swiped them with Wayminders," Cole said. "Why not rescue them the same way?"

"You are a tempter," Violet said. "I have already broken

some serious rules as a Wayminder. There is no exception where sneaking into anywhere is acceptable. Not in times of war. Not in emergencies. That includes into a private residence. You are talking about an Enforcer fortress."

"You caved easier for Brogan," Cole said. "You took us to the balcony outside the governor's room to kidnap him."

"I did?" Violet asked.

"Without much hesitation," Cole said. "Except we can't use Brogan for this. If he leaves Creon, he'll get old again."

"They're probably shielded," Violet said. "It may not be a quick in and out. Won't we want Jace?"

"We're always safer with Jace around," Cole said. "But getting Jace will take time. We can't go straight into the Iron Fort, or leave straight from it. Let's just investigate. Maybe all we need is a wayport to the right room."

"Which is why it is so illegal," Violet said.

"Owandell did it to take the king, the queen, and two princesses," Cole said. "He went right into the First Castle and snatched them. We can't use the same method to take them back? We're trying to save the world. Even if this destroys the reputation of Wayminders forever, isn't it better than having all Wayminders destroyed forever?"

Violet's eyes widened with realization. "I'll do it," she said. "Give me a lot of power. I'm going to spy like no Wayminder has spied before."

She reached for Cole's hand, but he waved her away. "I remember how to connect directly."

"All right."

Cole found her nexus and flooded power into her.

Violet closed her eyes. "I'm there. I see it. I don't sense much shielding. I'm too used to Creon. Nobody who broke into the Island Keep from Creon could leave. Unless you were with them, Cole. Only you could help someone open a wayport in Sambria."

"If a wayport opened from Creon to Sambria, couldn't they just leave it open and go back through it?"

"Wayports from Creon to another kingdom do not allow for travel in both directions," Violet said. "Only from Creon to the desired destination."

"Then we have a big advantage," Cole said.

Violet looked at Cole. "If the queen is really at the Island Keep, she must be well out of sight. They can't afford her being discovered. These are Enforcers. At least some would be more loyal to the crown than to Owandell if he abducted their monarch. Until Ramarro reorders the world, Owandell needs to keep this crime quiet. So I need to look in the deepest, most private corners of the dungeon, or else up high in tower cells. With royalty, probably towers. Owandell would want to show respect for the office, and towers would be the most removed from the rest of the fortress. Unless he has some other secret room someplace."

A small wayport opened in front of Violet, no larger than a dinner plate. She leaned close, peering through. Glancing at Cole, she held a finger to her lips. The wayport closed. Another opened.

As they stood on the Red Road, borrowing light from the Lost Palace, Violet opened and closed several small wayports—some as tiny as a coin. Light or sound issued from some. Cole caught fragments of conversation as he kept feeding her power.

After closing the latest little wayport, Violet turned to Cole. "Lots of guards at the base of the second-highest tower. It's full of really sturdy doors, and features a guardroom half-way up with Enforcers inside. Nobody in the third-highest room. Nobody in the second-highest room. And I haven't looked into the top room. It is protected. If I open a wayport there, an alarm will sound."

"Do you have to open a wayport?" Cole asked. "Can't you just look with your mind?"

Violet shook her head. "I can get the lay of the land that way. The shape and position of buildings. But I don't really see. Not like I can with my eyes. And I don't sense living things like people."

"There could be guards inside," Cole said.

"If it goes bad, we could back out and close the wayport," Violet said. "But they might move the prisoners before we can try again."

Cole drew his Jumping Sword. "We can take them, especially if Honor is there. I'll energize her. How many doors to the room?"

"One," Violet said.

"With Brogan, you opened wayports to block doors," Cole said. "Used them defensively."

"I hadn't thought about that," Violet said. "With your help, I bet I could open multiple wayports all at once. How many could I handle?"

"I'm pretty sure you did three at once when we took the

governor," Cole said. "You blocked a door. You also blocked one of the wayports they opened."

Violet nodded. "Okay. You want to try right now?"

"I think we should," Cole said. "Time is working against us tonight."

"It's late," Violet said. "They might be asleep."

"Let's find out," Cole said, energizing her power.

A wayport opened.

"Go," Violet said.

Cole stepped through. He was in a semicircular room. Iron shutters masked the windows. Honor and Harmony sat at a table conversing by lamplight. Stafford rested on one of four narrow beds. Destiny slept on another. There were no guards.

"Hurry," Cole said as Violet stepped through the wayport. "Let's go."

He ran to Tessa and started helping her out of bed. She rubbed her eyes as she sat up. Harmony and Honor joined him.

A key rattled in the door.

A moment later, a wayport blocked the door.

Leaving Destiny with her mother and sister, Cole crossed to Stafford. Looking weary and drawn, the old king shook his head. "I'm in no condition to travel. Leave me."

"We can help you," Cole insisted. "It isn't far. We'll use wayports."

Coughing heavily, Stafford shook his head. "I am still High King of the Outskirts. Do as I command. Leave me. See my wife and children to safety."

Cole still felt conflicted leaving the old man behind, but

then Harmony called from over by the wayport. "Come, Cole." Honor and Destiny had already gone through.

Cole retreated to the wayport as Harmony passed through. He glanced back at Stafford, who waved him away. Cole entered and Violet followed. The wayport closed, leaving Stafford behind. But thankfully everyone else was safely rescued.

"The Red Road?" Honor asked. "Why are we at the Lost Palace?"

Cole understood the edge of hysteria in her voice. She had been held captive here for a long time. "Because we are fighting a torivor in the morning," Cole said.

"Not Trillian," Honor said.

"No, Ramarro," Cole clarified. "And we need all the help we can get."

Honor eyed the Lost Palace uncomfortably. "Do not trust any aid from Trillian."

"He has reasons to help us," Cole said. "I've glimpsed our future. Without help we fail."

"How did you find us?" Harmony asked.

"Long story," Cole replied. "We'll explain later."

"We will face Ramarro in the morning?" Honor asked. "You're sure?"

"I'm sure," Cole said. "I shouldn't share too much. Some of our plans need to stay secret. Ramarro can read minds."

"What should we do?" Harmony asked.

"I was hoping Tessa could give us a clue," Cole said.

"Her power doesn't work on demand," Honor said. "We could go to Necronum and see."

"Maybe if I share power with her here?" Cole asked.

"You can try," Destiny said. "I want to help."

Cole reached out for the nexus of her ability. Although he could sense her power, the center eluded him. He could not connect.

Turning his attention to Honor, he found her center of power swiftly. Harmony as well. The queen gave him a chiding stare as he connected to her nexus.

"I can connect without touching now," Cole said, turning his attention back to Destiny. "Usually."

"My power can be elusive," Tessa said. "Owandell had a hard time with me when he stole it."

Cole took her hand and found he could connect that way. Her power billowed and folded like smoke buffeted by wind from all directions. Even with direct physical contact he could not find the center. He infused the roiling mist of her power with energy.

Tessa gave a small whimper. Her arm trembled in his grasp. She stared at the sky, eyes unnaturally wide. "No," she whispered.

Harmony braced her daughter. "Are you all right?"

Tessa was shaking her head. "A wave," she said, her dispassionate voice incongruent with her quivering frame. "A great and terrible wave of darkness will swallow us. Eternal night. An end to hope."

"Can we fight it?" Harmony asked.

"Where do you hide from a shadow bigger than the world?" Tessa asked. "Can we fight the night? Can we outrun darkness? The wave looms over all, growing as it consumes, engulfing everything."

Tessa's head snapped toward Cole, her eyes dizzily focusing on him. "Find Dandalus," she whispered.

Then she went limp.

Cole stopped feeding Tessa power and helped Harmony lay her down on the road. She stirred slightly.

"That was enormous," Honor said.

"The big visions really deplete her," Harmony said. "That one must have been pressing on her, waiting for an opportunity to manifest."

"Didn't sound good," Cole said.

"Can you find Dandalus?" Harmony asked.

Cole shrugged. "Maybe. I left him in the echolands. He was going to find a new place to hide. I'm not sure where to look. Even with weeks, or months, I might never find him."

"Those were the only hopeful words she spoke," Honor said. "If you're going to ask Tessa, you listen and follow through."

"What about Jenna?" Violet asked.

Cole gave a nod. "I have a friend at a temple in Necronum. I need to go there anyway to see if I can find Hunter and Dalton before the big fight. Maybe I can try to cross over to the echolands briefly. It would have to be quick."

"Should we get moving?" Honor asked.

Violet studied Cole expectantly.

"We'll take you three to the Iron Fort," Cole said. "You can join up with Mira and Elegance. But we won't come in yet. Violet and I have an appointment in Necronum."

REUNITED

Cole and Violet stepped quietly from the wayport into the silver sanctum. They were coming from the tent outside the Iron Fort, where they had left Harmony, Honor, and Destiny. Cole had convinced Violet that it would be better to open a wayport directly into the Temple of the Still Water than to try to talk their way past the guard. He was not sure how broadly word was out that he was wanted as a possible murderer of the king.

"What happens when breaking the fundamental laws of your order becomes routine?" Violet whispered.

"It all depends how it goes," Cole whispered back. "You'll probably end up somewhere between a medal of honor and the death penalty."

"It's quiet," Violet said. "How are we going to find her?"

"I really don't know," Cole said. "We never went to her bedroom. And Jenna is free now. She could be in a totally different area."

"Maybe we should talk louder," Violet said with more volume.

"Get found?" Cole asked.

"Or we can roam and look for somebody still awake," Violet said.

"What if they ask how we got in?" Cole asked, returning to a whisper.

"If we act like we belong, they might not ask," Violet said. "If they do, stay vague—pretend we've been here awhile."

"I'm so thirsty," Cole said loudly, crossing to a carafe of water and filling a glass, making sure to clink them together. He set the carafe down noisily.

"That might be a little much," Violet said more quietly.

"Best water around," Cole said loud enough to make Violet cringe. "Nice and still."

"I thought I heard someone," a female voice remarked from across the room.

Cole turned to find an older woman entering the room. He recalled her from his previous visit, but her name slipped his mind.

"Good evening, Gilda," Violet said warmly.

"Yes," Gilda said. "I remember you two. Isn't it rather late to be up and about?"

"We have an urgent matter for Jenna," Cole said, "or we wouldn't have come by so late."

"We don't know her room," Violet added.

"She's not officially under my watch anymore," Gilda said. "She is now a free woman. But she still tarries in the same quarters. You feel sure she is expecting you?"

"We have news she has been waiting for," Cole assured her.

"Let me fetch her," Gilda said. "Make yourselves comfortable."

Gilda walked away.

"The water is nice and still?" Violet whispered. "At the Temple of the Still Water?"

"Just making conversation," Cole whispered back, pouring more water.

They waited in silence.

"I hope she wants to see us," Cole finally said.

"Maybe she's sleepy," Violet replied.

"What if Gilda called the guards?" Cole whispered. "How fast can you open a wayport?"

"Fast enough," Violet said.

Cole and Violet strolled around the sanctum as they waited, staying close together. At length they heard footsteps coming.

Jenna entered the room, along with Dalton and Hunter.

"Yes!" Cole cried, his voice too loud in the silence. He rushed over to Dalton and gave him a hug, then hugged his big brother. Jenna embraced him as well.

Violet hung back.

"You guys waited for me!" Cole said. "Good job!"

"Just following instructions," Hunter said. "Who is this?"

Cole found Violet staring at Hunter with undisguised interest. Making her attraction even more obvious, she blushed and tried to look elsewhere, but kept glancing back at him.

"This is Violet, the best Wayminder around," Cole said.

"She's our ticket to anywhere we want to go. Violet, this is my best friend, Dalton, and my brother, Hunter."

Beaming from the praise, Violet held out a hand to Hunter. "Nice to meet you. I didn't know Cole's brother would . . . look like you do."

Cole had never seen Violet so delighted to meet someone.

"I went and got them after Gilda woke me," Jenna said. "They were in the guest rooms."

"I'm glad you're all here," Cole said.

"We were so worried about you," Dalton said.

"It's been crazy," Cole said. "I can activate anybody's power now. I don't even have to touch you."

"How about all five powers at once?" Hunter asked.

"You have all five shaping abilities?" Violet asked, as if it sounded much too good to be true.

"I'm proficient in all the disciplines," Hunter said.

"Let's see," Cole said, focusing on Hunter and finding the center of his bright, multifaceted power. Cole connected and shared energy.

"I feel it," Hunter said. He picked up a nearby glass and changed it into a sword. Then he set it down and transformed into a tiger. A wayport appeared. Then he returned to normal, and the wayport vanished.

"Incredible," Hunter said. "Where were you for every fight I've ever had?"

"Cole is why I can take us anywhere," Violet said. "Maybe you can too."

"Probably, if he provides the power," Hunter said.

"And I could reach the dead from outside Necronum," Jenna said, looking as beautiful as ever, dark curls tumbling over her silver robe.

"Oh no," Dalton said. "Granny Helki."

Jenna swatted him. "Granny is darling. But I had someone else in mind. Cole, I had a special visitor not long after you left last time."

"Who?" Cole asked.

"You didn't tell us," Hunter complained.

"I was supposed to wait to tell Cole directly," Jenna said. "It's sensitive information."

Cole wondered who would have reached out from the echolands. "Harvan?"

"His name was Dandalus," Jenna said.

Chills tingled down Cole's back. "Really? He wasn't in hiding?"

"He thought you might be surprised," Jenna said. "He knows you're going to fight Ramarro. He knows where you will be. He promised to be there too. But in order for that to happen, you have to bring me and empower me."

"Sure," Cole said. "Did he mention it might be the end of the world?"

"If it is, we might as well have good seats," Jenna said.

Cole grinned. "That's one of the bravest things I've ever heard. It's going to be bad."

"Dandalus made that clear," Jenna said. "I already decided."

"Destiny Pemberton told me to find Dandalus," Cole said. "It must be important."

"He already found me," Jenna said.

"I would have come here with or without Destiny's help," Cole said. "Dandalus needed to reach me. He bet I would come to you. Can he fight?"

"He can't fight as if he were part of the physical world," Jenna said. "But I know he means to help."

"It must be crucial," Cole said. "Destiny is never wrong."

"What do you know about Ramarro?" Hunter asked.

"He'll break free tomorrow morning," Cole said.

"This coming morning?" Dalton asked.

"It's going to be terrible," Cole said. "I sort of got a peek at the future. He is incredibly powerful. We have a chance. It might be a long shot."

"We knew it would be bad," Hunter said. "Is there no way to keep him locked up? Or to transfer him to another prison?"

"I've talked with some of the Grand Shapers of Creon," Cole said, "including Kendo Rattan and Lorenzo Debray. I don't think we can stop him from getting loose."

Hunter rubbed his mouth. "I'm not sure this could be worse. You really think we have a chance?"

"Ramarro can read minds," Cole said. "I shouldn't say too much. But we do have a chance. And if we win . . . I found a way home."

"Wayminders can go to our world," Hunter said. "But nobody can stay permanently."

Cole shook his head. "Kendo Rattan found a way. He did it himself. It's called the Pilgrim Path. It lets you go to Earth permanently. But you lose all connection to the Outskirts.

After long enough, Kendo began to think he had imagined his life here."

Jenna, Dalton, and Hunter stared at him. Jenna gasped and turned, wiping at her eyes. Hunter looked slightly dazed. A giggle escaped Dalton.

"Really?" Hunter asked. "An actual way home?"

"I've seen it with my own eyes," Cole said.

"Could we take off before Ramarro gets free?" Dalton asked. He glanced at Violet. "No offense."

"I understand," Violet said.

"If we can find Lorenzo, you, Hunter, and Jenna could maybe go home," Cole said. "But I have to stay."

"You *have* to?" Dalton asked.

"I'm the best chance against Ramarro," Cole said. "I won't leave here until we deal with him."

"What if the best chance against Ramarro is still terrible odds?" Hunter said. "Don't forget, home is Mom, Dad, our house, our neighborhood, our world, our future—everything we lost."

"I know," Cole said.

"This ship is sinking," Hunter said. "You don't have to go down with it. Defeating Ramarro is not realistic. If the ship will sink either way, we might as well get off. All of us who can."

Cole nodded. "But what if we can stop it from sinking? What if only I can stop it?"

"There is no way to know," Hunter said.

"The only way to know is by staying," Cole said.

Hunter stood with his hands on his hips. "You get how

dangerous it will be. Last time you met Ramarro he was in a weakened state. He is way beyond anything we've faced."

"I know," Cole said. He thought about how easily Ramarro had bested them in the theoretical future. "Believe me." What if he failed just as quickly again? What if they couldn't trick Ramarro into going to Earth and becoming powerless? What if Cole made a pointless sacrifice? What if he led his brother and Dalton and Jenna to meaningless deaths? Part of Cole desperately wanted to let Hunter take the lead. In some ways, it would be such a relief to run away. To go home. Maybe he would eventually forget the world he had surrendered, the friends he had abandoned. "I just can't."

"Are you sure?" Hunter pressed. "This isn't a game. At best Ramarro will kill us. At worst he could torture us. Maybe forever."

"I might be able to stop him," Cole said. "Kendo Rattan thinks I have the best chance of saving the Outskirts. Dandalus seems to think I have a chance too. We have a plan that could work. It has to stay secret, but it could work, and I can't leave if there's a real chance. I can't leave Mira. I can't leave Jace, or the princesses, or the queen, or any of the others."

"Bring them," Hunter said. "Bring everybody we can. Mira. Jace. Violet. They can start over on Earth. Might be tough, but it beats getting destroyed by Ramarro. Or becoming his slave."

"What about everybody else?" Cole asked. "This is a big place."

"It's not your job to save them," Hunter said. "We don't

even belong here. We were kidnapped. We've been used, Cole. I've been used. I wasn't like you. I didn't come with a group. I was nabbed alone. I thought I was stuck here. I thought there was no way home. So I did my best to get by. I followed the orders they gave me. I trained. I used my powers, became an Enforcer. I was brought here against my will. You were trying to stop a kidnapping. They just wanted us as slaves. Do we really owe them our lives? For a lost cause? Why not go home if we can?"

"Some bad people brought us here," Cole said. "But you know there are good people here too. Just like anywhere. Good and bad. If there is a chance I can save the five kingdoms, I have to try."

"Even when the odds are astronomically terrible?" Hunter asked. "If I thought we had a real chance, I might feel differently. I've seen my share of fights here. This one looks like a sure loss. Why risk it?"

"Because I can't leave this world knowing I might have saved it," Cole said. "I just can't. I'm not scared of dying anymore. Don't get me wrong, I'm not in a hurry, but it doesn't terrify me. We're all going to die. What matters is how we die. And how we live. Leaving when I could have helped—that would kill me more than dying. It just would. Somebody has to fight the hard fights. There are times when somebody else can't do it. Or won't do it. So it's you or nobody. I've had a chance to go home before. And I'm not going anywhere unless I stop Ramarro."

Hunter stared at his brother. "Now *that* might be the bravest thing I've ever heard."

"You guys can go," Cole said. "You guys *should* go. I'm not sure having you there would make much difference."

"Hey, I'm proficient in all five shaping disciplines," Hunter said.

"And you know who we're fighting," Cole replied.

Hunter nodded. "I'm not leaving my little brother. No way. If you're going down, I'll be with you."

"I won't leave either," Dalton said.

Jenna patted Cole on the shoulder. "We'll all do our parts."

"You might not get a chance to leave," Violet said. "We'd need to find Lorenzo. We don't know where he is."

"I know where he'll be in the morning," Cole said.

"That's not good enough," Violet said. "He's central to the plan. We have to find him. He needs to know his part."

Cole thought about that. Unless Lorenzo knew opening the Pilgrim Path to Earth was safe, he might not do it. After his next visit to Trillian, Cole would sincerely believe that letting Ramarro take the Pilgrim Path would destroy the Earth, and Lorenzo might believe his concerns unless he knew the plan. But if Lorenzo knew that the Pilgrim Path would strip Ramarro of his powers, Ramarro might read his mind and learn the truth.

"You're right," Cole said. "We need to find Lorenzo."

"If we take your friends to the Iron Fort, we can start searching Lorenzo's hideouts," Violet said.

Cole gave a nod and rubbed his hands together. He looked at Jenna, Hunter, and Dalton. "Ready to save the world?"

CHAPTER
—— 31 ——

PREPARATIONS

When Cole arrived at Elegance's quarters inside the Iron Fort, he found Lorenzo waiting. Brogan was already a young adult and dressed for battle. Jace, Mira, and Elegance looked ready for a fight as well. Harmony stood near Elegance, like an older version of the same woman. Honor and Destiny sat in a corner playing cards.

"Look who finally decided to join the catastrophe," Jace said.

"We were searching for you guys the whole time," Dalton complained. "And we were getting chased by Enforcers."

"And sometimes we were chasing them," Hunter said.

"Meanwhile we fought Elegance's power," Jace said.

"What is it?" Hunter asked.

"The Perennial Serpent," Jace said.

"Really?" Hunter asked. "But it has been around ever since—right, time travel."

"Are you absolutely sure it's my power?" Elegance asked.

"I'm positive," Cole said. "The snake will be there when

Ramarro returns. If you're with us, Elegance, that part should be an easy fight."

"Then I'll be there," she said.

"And me with her," Brogan added.

"I need to talk to Lorenzo alone," Cole said.

"Ethel," Elegance called. "Please show Cole and Master Debray to a private salon."

Ethel promptly entered and escorted Cole and Lorenzo to a small room. Once inside, Cole closed the door.

"What have you learned?" Lorenzo asked.

"Going to my world will destroy Ramarro's power," Cole said. "Trillian confirmed."

"Excellent," Lorenzo said, pounding a fist into his palm. "That gives us an opportunity."

"You can open the Pilgrim Path without me?" Cole asked.

"I can with the help of two other Grand Shapers," Lorenzo said. "I already recruited them as backup. But why without you?"

"Ramarro can read minds," Cole said. "Right before the fight, I need to go to Trillian and have him program my mind to believe I have sure knowledge that the Pilgrim Path will enable Ramarro to control both worlds. And that the opportunity to take the path may not last very long."

"Brilliant," Lorenzo said. "That could work."

"Except now you know that taking the path will destroy him," Cole said.

"I have some ability at screening my thoughts from scrutiny," Lorenzo said.

"We can't risk it," Cole said. "Everything depends on this.

We should hint to the others that the path is not an option, so they will have that belief. Tomorrow, you come with me to Trillian and let him program you to think Earth is such a tempting world to invade that it will distract Ramarro from the Outskirts. And maybe with a faint hope you can seal him there or something."

"I am very reluctant to open my mind to Trillian," Lorenzo said.

"Does that matter?" Cole asked. "We need to save the Outskirts. This could do it. We can make Trillian promise to only change what we want changed in our minds, right?"

"Assuming he will agree," Lorenzo said.

"He already agreed for me," Cole said. "We almost certainly lose without this. Isn't a real chance to defeat Ramarro worth the risk?"

Lorenzo nodded. "I suppose you're right. You already saw us fail. This is your choice?"

"I think it's our only hope," Cole said.

Lorenzo gave another nod. "Very well."

Cole and Lorenzo returned to the room where the others waited. Lorenzo cleared his throat, and the room fell silent.

"Cole has learned that opening the Pilgrim Path to Ramarro would probably give the torivor control of Earth," Lorenzo announced. "Little would prevent him from returning here and promptly ruling both worlds. We must do our best to fight him as soon as he appears. Perhaps with Cole enhancing all of our abilities, we can catch him off guard."

"I'll do my best," Cole said. "When Ramarro first shows up, I suspect he will destroy our weapons. If we have decoy weapons, but hide the best ones, maybe we can use the good ones in a fight."

"Use a Wayminder," Brogan suggested. "Set the weapons you wish to preserve in a handy location far from the confrontation. Then open a wayport to them when we want them."

The thought had not occurred to Cole. "Perfect. We should sleep. Ramarro will get loose in the morning. I have one last thing to do with Violet around sunrise. Then we should get in place at the Far North Cache."

Violet shook Cole awake the next morning. "The sun will rise soon," she told him.

Cole rolled off the bed, clothes and shoes already on. It felt like he had slept about ten seconds. "Where is Lorenzo?" Cole asked.

"Just outside," Violet said.

Cole and Violet found Lorenzo waiting with a guard. Lorenzo made a gesture, and the guard opened a wayport. They all stepped through to the desert sand near the striped tent.

Color leaked into the sky above the horizon, drizzling the distant dunes with variegated highlights. Cole wondered if this might be the last sunrise he would ever witness. Glancing over at the statue of the Perennial Serpent, he pointed at it. "Whatever else happens, you're finished today."

"We should hurry," Violet said.

Cole connected to her power, and she opened a wayport. They stepped through onto the Red Road in front of the gate to the Lost Palace.

Lorenzo gasped. "I never dreamed I would tread here."

"We're all awake," Cole said, leading the way forward. "Like it or not."

After crossing the gate, Cole found Hina waiting, wearing a gown that glimmered like starlight. There were no horses or other guards, but five canopies stood nearby that had not been there before. Each sheltered an inviting bed.

"It's all so different inside," Lorenzo said.

"Welcome," Hina greeted. "We understand you have need of haste. Please choose a place to lie down." She indicated the canopies.

"He visits in a dream," Cole said. "Go to sleep."

He trotted over to a canopy, walked across an embroidered rug, and sank onto a decadent mattress. Cole worried that, with the urgency of the day, he might have a tough time settling down. Those cares soon dissolved, and his eyelids drooped.

Cole was back home in his bedroom—his bedspread, his books, his jeans on the floor, one pant leg inside out. A cup of water sat within reach on a paper towel. He picked it up and took a sip. He could faintly hear a television in another room.

He went to the window and peered out. The morning sun was too high for a school day. Saturday, maybe?

"Are you ready?" Trillian asked from behind him.

"Is this supposed to relax me?" Cole asked, waving a hand at his room.

"Perhaps," Trillian said.

"Or make me homesick?"

"Perhaps."

"Or show me what I can have if I win?"

"There could be many reasons," Trillian said.

Cole glanced toward the hall. "Are my parents here?"

"They could be," Trillian said. "It would consume time. And it would not be entirely real. We can talk anywhere you wish."

"The beach was good," Cole said.

With no perceptible shift, they were back on the beach. Sizable waves crashed before them. Lukewarm sand greeted Cole's bare feet.

"You enjoyed the beach in Miami," Trillian said. "I prefer more tranquility."

"It's great," Cole said. "Where are the others?"

Violet and Lorenzo appeared.

"I was orienting Master Debray," Trillian said.

"You will only affect my mind so I believe I can send Ramarro to Earth on the Pilgrim Path to distract him from our world," Lorenzo clarified.

"I will leave some hope that taking the path could render him powerless," Trillian said. "I will color it as a vain hope. I think that hope is necessary. I do not believe you could bring yourself to simply give Earth to Ramarro, no matter how I tamper with you."

"And you will do nothing else to my mind," Lorenzo said.

"I cannot alter who you are without explicit permission," Trillian said. "Even then there are limits. I can't tamper with your mind in ways you do not allow. Furthermore, I promise to all of you that I will not even attempt to alter your minds beyond how we explicitly discuss."

"That will have to suffice," Lorenzo said. "All right."

"I will think the Pilgrim Path is a direct route to the conquest of Earth for Ramarro," Violet checked.

"Yes," Trillian said. "If you care for my opinion, I should adjust Lorenzo first. Cole should keep connected to Lorenzo so he can leave the Lost Palace and open a wayport to meet the other Wayminders who will help him open the Pilgrim Path."

"Can I stay connected to him when he leaves the Lost Palace?" Cole asked.

"If he stays on the Red Road, I believe so," Trillian said.

"Very well," Lorenzo said.

"Connect to his nexus, Cole," Trillian instructed.

Cole did so easily.

The torivor touched the back of Lorenzo's neck, and he vanished. Even with Lorenzo gone, Cole's connection to him persisted.

"The transition is smoother if the subject awakens with the false knowledge," Trillian said. "Violet next?"

She nodded. Trillian touched the back of her neck, and she vanished as well.

A large wave roared. Cole wondered if there was something he was not seeing. Some trick Trillian could be playing.

"You're wise to be cautious," Trillian said. "But our interests align here. I would love for you to defeat Ramarro. Be sure to listen to Dandalus as well. He is no fool—he reached out to you for a reason."

"Okay," Cole said.

"Lorenzo is on the road," Trillian said.

Cole could still feel the connection. He fed power to Lorenzo. And then the connection broke.

"He departed through a wayport," Trillian said. "Are you ready?"

"What if the trick doesn't work?" Cole asked. "What if Ramarro doesn't take the bait?"

"You will have a difficult fight on your hands," Trillian said. "Empower your friends. Listen to Dandalus."

"Can you do anything to help me?" Cole asked.

"Any other help I could provide might one day endanger me," Trillian said. "And I will not risk harm to help you. I have been harmed enough in this world."

"All right," Cole said. "Do it."

He felt a hand on the back of his neck.

SHOWDOWN

Cole opened his eyes.

He was on a bed. An unbelievably comfortable bed. Fabric overhead. He was beneath a silken canopy.

No breeze.

Where was he?

Trillian! The canopies all shaded beds!

He was awake! Today was the morning Ramarro would attack.

And then he remembered.

Going to Earth would not strip Ramarro of his powers. The torivor could end up ruling both worlds if he walked the Pilgrim Path! But there was a chance that if they could delay him long enough, some of the Grand Shapers of Creon could take away the opportunity of following the Pilgrim Path.

Cole shivered. He and his friends had no other option but to fight. Hopefully, they could distract Ramarro long enough to give Earth a chance.

No.

They had to do better.

Hopefully, they could defeat Ramarro. No matter how powerful the torivor was, there was always a chance. Maybe if Cole empowered all of his friends, together they could catch Ramarro off-balance and bring him down.

His friends! They needed to know about the Pilgrim Path. Wait.

They were already working under the assumption the path wouldn't work. He had just been here to confirm their suspicions. And to see if Trillian had any extra tips.

There were no tips.

They were on their own.

Cole rolled out of bed. He needed to get back to the Iron Fort.

He found Violet coming toward him.

"The Pilgrim Path won't work," she said.

"I know," Cole replied. "It will just give Ramarro another world to rule. We have to stop him on our own."

"Can we?" Violet asked.

"We have to try," Cole replied.

"But can we win?"

Cole squared his shoulders. "Only one way to find out. Come on."

Violet followed him out the gate to the Red Road. He connected to her power, energized her, and she opened a wayport. Cole stepped through to the sand.

A guard greeted them and brought them to Elegance's quarters. Cole found Elegance, Harmony, Honor, Destiny, Mira, Jace, Dalton, Hunter, and Jenna all seated around a long table enjoying breakfast. The Grand Shaper Kezlyn Vedor was present as well. Ethel and a pair of servants kept food coming and glasses filled.

"Did you sleep in?" Jace asked around the pastry he was eating.

"We just got back," Cole said.

"He knows you did," Dalton said. "How'd it go?"

"Not the best," Cole said. "I got confirmation that we can't rely on the Pilgrim Path. If Ramarro uses it, he'll just add Earth to his conquests. Where is Brogan?"

"He went ahead with a couple of handpicked guards from here to prep the battleground," Elegance said. "And this is the Grand Shaper Kezlyn Vedor. She has come out of hiding to aid us."

"Thanks," Cole said, his mind racing. Having guards from the Iron Fort would be different from last time. Having Brogan would be different too. Last time had been a failure. Differences were encouraging. "What about Lorenzo?"

"We haven't seen him this morning," Mira reported. "Want some food?"

"I'm not really hungry," Cole said. "I'd feel better getting to the Far North Cache."

"The rings are quiet," Mira said.

And last time they had cut it kind of close. It would be smart to help Brogan prep the battleground, using his knowledge from the fight in the hypothetical future. But he didn't want to bring up the possible outcome he had already experienced. Not everyone knew about it. "Might be smart to get there early. Be ready. Who is coming?"

"All of us but Destiny," Harmony said.

"I want to come," Destiny complained.

"We have been over this, Tessa," Harmony said. "Your power has no applications in combat."

"Unless you need to know something," Tessa said. "Like how to stop Ramarro."

"You're too young," Harmony said. "It would disturb me too much. End of subject."

"I can give you some power now," Cole said. "See if your power activates again."

"Yes, please," Tessa said.

Cole moved around the table to her, and she offered her hand. He took it and fed energy into her.

After a long moment, he quit and released her.

"Sorry," Tessa said. "I was trying."

"It never works when you're trying," Mira muttered.

"I was trying last time," Tessa said. "And it worked just fine."

"Eat one of these," Jace said, approaching Cole from behind. He handed him a piece of wheat toast with egg on it. "Everyone deserves a last meal."

"You're going to curse us!" Mira griped.

"I'm trying to help him die bravely," Jace shot back.

Cole took a bite of the toast. It tasted good.

Harmony stood, dabbing her lips with a napkin. "Let's gather our things. Remember your decoys. We need to leave your best weapons where Brogan instructed."

As most of the diners left the table, Cole sat down by Jenna to finish his egg on toast. "Are you all right?" he asked.

"I'm nervous," Jenna said. "I've never been in a fight before."

"This will be a strange fight," Cole said. "It could be over so quickly."

"Well, I could visit some of my friends in the echolands," Jenna said. "I feel bad I didn't say good-bye to Granny Helki."

"We might survive," Cole said, then took a big bite of toast. He set the rest down. "Come on."

The others gathered, then a guard opened a wayport and they went to the sand. Three tables were set up. Some of the group put their special weapons on one table, some on another. Cole went to set his Jumping Sword beside Mira's, but she waved him away.

"Brogan thought you should leave your Jumping Sword on the third table," Mira said. "It's just for you. And Violet could open the wayport for you."

"Sure," Violet said, standing nearby.

Cole set down the Jumping Sword, and his ring started glowing. Mira handed him a short sword. "A decoy for Ramarro to destroy," she explained.

"Time to go," Jace said, holding up a hand to display his shining ring.

"We're still ahead of schedule," Cole muttered to Violet, connecting to her power.

A wayport opened.

"Far North," Violet announced.

Harmony led the procession. Cole watched the others file through, and then went second to last. Violet came after.

He recognized the fence around the cache. Violet had

chosen a different point along the perimeter than Elegance had selected.

That reminded Cole.

"Elegance," he said. "I need to wake up your power. It's important."

"All right," she responded.

Cole found the dead ember at her center and flooded it with energy until it blazed to life. When finished, he kept the connection.

Elegance gazed at Cole in astonishment. "How did you do that?"

"It's part of my ability," Cole said.

Violet gestured at another wayport. "This will take us to the middle of the cache, where Lorenzo expects Ramarro to appear."

Cole had almost forgotten that Lorenzo had taught Violet how to use the conduits at the cache. He went through first this time.

Cole emerged at the square in the center of the cache where he had faced Ramarro before. The pendant already hovered in the middle of the square, shedding white radiance.

"Greetings, Cole," Brogan welcomed him. "Beautiful day to save the world, am I right?"

Cole smiled. As the others came through, the ground began to tremble. Violet stepped from the wayport, and it closed.

The rumbling increased in volume, and the ground quaked harder. The pendant glowed more intensely. Cole staggered along with the others. Dalton sat down, and soon everyone followed his example.

Cole found himself between Violet and Jenna. He focused on connecting to the powers of those around him. He had Elegance and Violet already. He connected to Honor. Then Jenna. Then Mira. Then Harmony. Then Dalton.

Cole realized he had never connected to a weapon like the Jumping Sword or golden rope without touching it. Would weapons have a center like a person? Hopefully. Right now, no shaped weapons were present, so it was too late to experiment.

With a brilliant flash and a thunderous roar, the pendant shattered. Ramarro appeared—a tall, robed albino with a grin like a shark. He looked just as Cole remembered.

The rumbling had ceased. The ground was still.

Cole stood up. His friends followed his lead.

"You got out," Cole said.

"It was only a matter of time," Ramarro said. "Cole, of course you are here. You brought a little entourage." He gnashed his teeth. "The Grand Shaper. Kezlyn Vedor. Not even an old one. The incumbent. And Queen Harmony. Elegance, the eldest princess. Her sisters Miracle and Honor. A few others of lesser consequence. This is it? Have you come to surrender?"

"We're going to stop you," Cole said.

"I don't like your weapons," Ramarro said, waving a hand. The weapons Cole and his comrades held dissolved into dust. "This is insulting. And embarrassing."

The Perennial Serpent appeared off to one side of the square. Beside the huge snake stood a man in a black, cowled robe. He threw back his hood, revealing himself as Owandell. "Welcome, master."

"Owandell," Ramarro said. "You brought a pet. You are alone?"

"I am here to learn your will," Owandell said.

After a moment of effort, Cole connected to the nexus of the Perennial Serpent. He linked the power to Elegance and started a torrential flow. Tail swishing, head flailing, the serpent began to shrink.

"What has he done to Peya?" Owandell shouted. "Stop him!"

"I prefer servants who can defend themselves," Ramarro said.

"Sword," Cole muttered to Violet.

A wayport opened beside him. Reaching through, Cole grabbed the Jumping Sword off the table in the desert. He energized it and flooded the weapon with power.

The hilt was growing warm as Cole overloaded the sword with energy. He pointed it at Owandell and at the last moment tried something new—he disconnected the weapon from the attachment to his body.

"Away!" Cole shouted, releasing the weapon.

The sword flew from his hand faster than an arrow from a bow, streaked through the air, and plunged into Owandell's chest so deep that the hilt disappeared. After staggering back, Owandell stood still for a moment, naked astonishment apparent. He dropped to his knees and extended a shaky hand toward Ramarro.

The Perennial Serpent had shrunk down to barely a foot in length. Ramarro strode forward and crushed its head.

Owandell fell forward, flat on his face, the blade of the

Jumping Sword protruding from his back. A hand twitched, and then he became still.

"That was remarkably efficient," Ramarro said to Cole.

"Thanks," Cole said. "I've never used the Jumping Sword that way before."

A wayport appeared on the other side of the square. Lorenzo Debray emerged with a pair of other Wayminders.

"Finally," Ramarro said. "A few of the old guard. But where is Kendo? I see. He departed at last. A final gesture of cowardice. Very well." He took a deep breath. "I was held captive for a long time. Uncomfortably long—and I'm eternal. Certain types of suspense do not exist in eternity. Well, as was inevitable, your prisons have failed; your chains have broken; your walls have crumbled. Is this to be a fight or a conversation? Who among you is ready to unconditionally surrender?"

"We bring another option," Lorenzo said. He assumed an awkward stance and closed his eyes. The Wayminders with him struck poses of their own.

"What is this?" Ramarro asked. "Ah, not an attack. A demonstration?"

A large, round wayport opened, the edges swirling.

"We are the protectors of this world," Lorenzo declared. "We may lack the power to defeat you in combat. But we can offer you an alternative." He extended a hand toward the wayport. "This way leads to Earth, a larger, more firmly established world than ours. It has a far greater population and connects to a vast system of worlds and stars and space."

"No!" Cole cried, unable to believe what he was seeing

and hearing. How could Lorenzo betray an entire world? Didn't he know the strategy was flawed? Ramarro would now dominate two worlds instead of one!

Cole reached for Lorenzo's center and found it.

And then the connection was severed.

"Leave him be," Ramarro said. "These Wayminders are under my protection."

Ramarro stalked over to the wayport. "The Pilgrim Path," the torivor said, looking down the misty corridor.

Cole desperately reached out for Ramarro, trying to connect to his power, hunting for a center.

"Would you like to contend directly with me?" Ramarro asked, extending a hand toward Cole.

Cole stared. He remembered what it had been like to connect to Ramarro before. There had to be some other way.

Ramarro scowled. "You have done this before. Faced me before. Lived this moment before." He stared intently at Cole. "When? How?"

Cole tried unsuccessfully not to think about it.

"A hypothetical future," Ramarro said. "You had time to prepare for our present encounter." He turned to the wayport. "And this is all suspiciously convenient."

Ramarro stared intently at Lorenzo. Then at Cole. Then at Violet.

"Her too," Ramarro said.

"What?" Cole asked.

"Trillian," Ramarro said, his voice very calm. "Your memories are not genuine, Cole. Would you like the real ones back?"

Suddenly Cole remembered the whole plan. The Pilgrim Path would leave Ramarro powerless if he walked it. Trillian had planted other thoughts to trick Ramarro.

"Oh no," Cole said, realizing their best chance had been thwarted.

"Want your memories, Lorenzo?" Ramarro asked. "Violet? You may as well join us in reality. Can we revisit the opportunity to surrender? I will offer each of you who kneel to me prominent positions in my service."

"None of us will kneel," Cole said.

One of the guards from the Iron Fort dropped to one knee.

"He's not really with us," Cole clarified.

"You cannot stand against me," Ramarro said. "It is a challenge to adequately express your doom. You are little more than figments of my imagination."

"If you're so powerful, bring back Twitch," Cole said. In their hypothetical encounter, Ramarro had retrieved Jace and Mira from where the Perennial Serpent had sent them. He wondered if Ramarro could track down his friend who had been lost for a longer time.

"It would be a simple matter of tracing the history of Elegance's power," Ramarro said. He stared at Elegance for a moment.

Jenna stepped up beside Cole and whispered, "I need extra power."

Cole funneled a larger share of energy into her. He could feel her using what he sent, so he pushed harder.

Twitch appeared a few paces in front of Cole. His clothes

were dirtier than when Cole had last seen him. He looked bewildered until he met eyes with Cole.

"I'm back," Twitch said.

"There is little I cannot do," Ramarro said. "I could kill him quicker than you can blink."

"Oh no," Twitch muttered. "Is that . . . ?"

"Ramarro," Cole supplied.

"Do not be confused," Ramarro said. "This is not really a fight. I could destroy everyone here more easily than taking a step. Your battle against me ended the moment I got free."

"Why not destroy us?" Cole asked.

"Destroying this world would be satisfying," Ramarro said. "Ruling it will be more interesting. You are currently alive because I would prefer interesting subjects to dull ones. But my rule will be absolute. All who will not serve me must perish."

Dandalus appeared beside Violet, not far from Cole, looking almost alive, his form only slightly transparent. "I wondered if I would live to see this day," Dandalus said.

"You didn't," Ramarro replied.

"And yet here I am," Dandalus said.

"An echo," Ramarro said. "I am glad you are here to witness this."

Dandalus held up both hands toward Ramarro, then leaned down and whispered something to Violet. Cole made sure she had plenty of power.

"Secrets are impolite," Ramarro said, an edge of impatience in his voice.

"Listening in is even less polite," Dandalus said, walking

over to Cole. He leaned close and whispered, "Go through the wayport Violet opens. Trust me. You must get away."

"I grow impatient," Ramarro warned. "Don't tempt me, Dandalus, or I will place your echo into a nightmare stasis where—"

"Try it," Dandalus said.

A wayport opened in front of Cole.

"Go, Cole," Dandalus urged.

Ramarro reached toward Cole, and sparks erupted in the air, spreading out across the surface of an invisible wall. Dandalus grunted and trembled. "Go."

"Don't you dare—" Ramarro began.

Cole heard no more, because he sprang forward through the wayport.

CHAPTER 33

COLE

C ole stood in the deserted courtyard of a castle.
He knew this courtyard!

He knew this castle!

"SURVIVE THE TRIAL TO OBTAIN THE REWARD," an enormous voice declared, emanating from the castle itself.

The wayport closed behind him.

All his connections to the others were cut. He had been feeding power so steadily to so many people that the loss felt incredibly abrupt. What would they do without him? He had just stranded most of his favorite people with an angry torivor.

And now he stood alone, drifting on a sentient sky castle, with the Eastern Cloudwall looming not too far away. He had no way off the castle unless a skycraft happened by. Or unless Violet or another Wayminder chose to visit.

He hoped Dandalus had a plan.

Statues great and small began to emerge from the walls

of the courtyard. Some surfaced out of the ground. All converged toward him.

Reaching out, Cole could feel them. Drawing on his power, with an effort of will, he blasted the nearest figures into gravel.

"Stop," Cole ordered. "I'm Cole. This castle was made for me."

The statues came to a halt. All signs of animation departed.

"I haven't been here before," Cole continued. "I went to one just like it. I guess these castles keep appearing?"

Perhaps ten paces away, Ramarro materialized.

"Peculiar destination," the torivor said. "Why flee here? This exhibition of derelict castles did not exist when I first came to the Outskirts. I have heard of it since. Never visited. Did Dandalus think you would escape me here? Did he expect me to follow? It makes sense for us to converse alone."

"Does it?" Cole asked.

"You could save your friends," Ramarro said. "They follow your lead. If you ask them to die, they will. To what end? I will govern the Outskirts with or without your help. If you live, you can advocate on behalf of those I rule. Dead, you can do nothing. This is your last chance. No more stalling. No place left to run. You can order your friends to die. Or you can spare them. It all depends on you."

"I won't kill them," Cole said. "You will."

Ramarro shrugged. "You could stop it. Or not. I am losing interest."

"I'm never going to serve you," Cole said. "Neither will they."

"That keeps it simple," Ramarro said. "Should I just let you drift to oblivion on this castle? I can keep an eye on it, make sure nobody comes or goes. Would you prefer the suspense of a few more minutes? The illusion of hope? Or how about a clean death? Quick and painless. Perhaps I could lock you in the Void. I escaped it. You would not. Should I store you there? Let you hover in an endless stasis as your sanity unravels across the eons?"

Cole looked at the motionless statues spaced around the courtyard. Some had frozen while still separating from the ground or the walls.

"Don't be a fool," Ramarro said.

"Get him!" Cole shouted. In unison, the stone figures charged Ramarro. More issued from the walls and ground. Bearded warriors raced alongside graceful ballerinas—Cole recognized several of them from his previous visit to the similar sky castle.

Ramarro waved a casual hand at the nearest statues. They wobbled but kept coming. He held a hand up as if commanding them to halt. Those directly before him slowed. The others continued toward him at their normal pace.

A statue of Dandalus rose up from the ground beside Cole. "This is your battleground, Cole," the statue said hurriedly, his voice low. "This is the one place you might defeat the torivor. The elements of this island were designed to resist his commands and to follow yours. The island will try to hold him here. It's no sure thing, but perhaps it gives you a chance. Do not let him escape. If you don't win here, you will fail."

Ramarro was now engaging the statues in physical combat. With fluid grace, he moved as if the fight had been choreographed to showcase his excellence. He dodged every attack, disarming opponents and then using their weapons against them. Ruthlessly efficient, he moved much quicker than an ordinary mortal could have managed. With each statue dodged, shoved aside, or destroyed, Ramarro worked his way toward Cole.

"Contain him!" the Dandalus statue cried. "Protect Cole! The enemy is in our midst!"

Walls shot up around Ramarro, shielding him from view. A large slab of stone erupted from the ground and landed atop the walls, forming the top of a huge stone box.

Was this your plan? Ramarro asked, the words searing into Cole's mind. *Lure me into one last trap? None of his traps ever killed me, Cole. And his prisons all failed to hold me. This pathetic trick planned from beyond his grave will soon crumble. If I lay still, nothing here could begin to hurt me. I see that everything here was designed to attack and resist me. And it will. Until I retune it. Until I create it anew. Get ready, Cole. You're about to learn what happens when you choose the wrong allies.*

The front of the stone box exploded outward. Several stone fragments whistling toward Cole turned to dust before reaching him. Ramarro raced from the box, hurling statues aside. More walls sprang up around him, trapping him in another stone box, but it only held for a moment before all the walls exploded outward. Once again, the debris streaking toward Cole evaporated.

Slamming statues out of his way, Ramarro charged forward. Cole was backing up, but Ramarro would soon reach him. Reaching out with his power, Cole grabbed the statues surrounding Ramarro and thrust them at him from all directions. Many of the statues shattered as they collided with Ramarro and crashed into one another. The brutal impact made the torivor stagger.

"Maximum effort!" the Dandalus statue called.

The ground shifted beneath Cole as the entire castle accelerated toward the Eastern Cloudwall. Statues emerged from the walls and ground more rapidly. Other statues merged to form larger ones. Soon none were smaller than Ramarro. Many were bigger. And they were fast. Almost as fast as him.

As Cole kept backing away, he realized that if the castle had attacked him and his friends like this, they would not have lasted more than a few seconds. But though Ramarro was fighting harder, he showed no vulnerability. The occasional weapon that struck him broke apart. And he continued to destroy or dodge statues despite the increased tempo of the brawl.

You will pay for this, Ramarro vowed directly to Cole's mind. *No clean death for you. I will wring agony from you for ages.*

Cole took some consolation from the threats. Ramarro was struggling. Though scary, the threats were also evidence of frustration.

Cole bashed more statues together around Ramarro. The material of the statues felt eager to comply. Those statues shattered by the impact promptly reformed and kept attacking. Ramarro was slowed by the press, and Cole continued to retreat.

The cloudwall filled the sky ahead of the castle, approaching rapidly. As he considered the increased pace of the sky castle, Cole realized the plan.

The vortex within the cloudwall.

Vortex? The word penetrated his thoughts. *What vortex?*

Cole tried not to think of the gigantic vortex behind the cloudwall, and so of course he pictured it vividly. Peering into the whirling maelstrom was like gazing down into a tornado with a mouth as wide as a football stadium. He remembered how the howling experience inside the slipstream in the echolands had reminded him of the violent funnel. Like a cosmic drain, the vortex devoured the endless parade of sky castles flowing into it.

Maybe it could devour a torivor.

How exactly is the vortex like the slipstream? Ramarro asked.

Cole had fallen into the vortex, and he had fallen into a slipstream. In the vortex, he had his physical body. In the slipstream, he was an echo. Still, they sounded similar, felt similar. The silvery material inside seemed somewhere between a liquid and a gas. Cole could remember it rushing around him. The homesong had been loud and clear in the slipstream. Almost irresistible. Had he heard it in the vortex? Not that he recalled.

Cole tried to think about flamingos. He pictured Dalton cannonballing into a swimming pool. He envisioned a guy playing the piano.

He tried not to think about vortexes and slipstreams.

He kept failing.

Let's take this fight elsewhere, Ramarro spoke to his mind.

Nothing changed. Statues kept attacking Ramarro.

Yes, Ramarro thought. *I see. It is difficult to open a wayport here. Even for me. The intent is to hold me here. You are wrong about the vortex. Wrong about this castle. Nothing in this flimsy realm can contain me.*

"That prison in the echolands held for a long time," Cole muttered.

Ramarro roared. Damaged statues went flying.

Cole heaved a flood of statues at Ramarro from one direction, forcing him back and to one side. Though fighting hard against the tide of stone figures, Ramarro was losing ground. More statues emerged. Cole kept hurling them.

I prefer to fight on my own terms, Ramarro conveyed harshly.

Leaping high into the air, Ramarro transformed into a huge eagle and began flying upward. Atop the castle and the surrounding walls, statues slung stones, launched arrows, and hurled javelins. The eagle swerved adroitly. The few projectiles that connected did no visible damage.

Ramarro gained altitude.

He was escaping.

Cole focused on one of the largest statues, a thick-limbed giant with enormous hands. Cole connected with his power and hastily levitated the giant toward the eagle. The giant caught up, but the eagle expertly steered away from the outstretched hands again and again.

Then the eagle seemed to smack against an invisible ceiling. After losing some altitude, the eagle rose again, only to bump once more against an unseen barrier. After the second impact, Cole guided the giant close, and it got hold of a wing.

Cole let the giant fall. The eagle came with it. As the statue and the eagle plummeted, the bird transformed into the robed albino. The impact with the ground blasted the statue to pieces, but Ramarro arose unruffled. Cole wondered if anything could harm him.

I chose an incredibly durable form, Ramarro spoke to his mind.

As other statues converged on Ramarro, Cole focused on one of the towers of the castle. Connecting to it, Cole hurled it down at Ramarro. The avalanche of beams and stone blocks arrived even as statues swarmed the torivor. Billowing dust plumes gusted outward from the tumultuous rubble.

Cole connected to as much of the island as he could mentally embrace and heaved it toward the cloudwall. The pace only increased slightly.

Battered blocks of stone shifted, and Ramarro climbed from the wreckage. Statues continued to attack him.

Vehement words entered Cole's mind like a physical blow. *You will not hold me here!*

Ramarro pointed at Cole and connected to him. Suddenly Cole was submerged in the vast ocean of Ramarro's power. He could not feel or hear or see. He could barely think. The power was all around him, trying to force a way into him. With all of his might, he held it off.

What could he do now? He had not sought this connection and had no idea how to break it. He had reached out to connect to others on many occasions. This time Ramarro was holding him.

Holding him.

Although overwhelming power enveloped Cole, the aggressive power sustaining the connection came from a specific source. Cole desperately focused all of his attention in that direction, and the connection from Ramarro began to feel like a lifeline in a storm-tossed sea. As power surged around him, Cole clung to the connection and traced it back to a blazing nexus.

There was no time for planning. Cole attacked the nexus, determined to rend it apart. The effort proved too great, like trying to pick up an ocean liner while swimming beside it. He began trying to crush it, but the surface felt too dense, as if he were trying to pummel his way into a bank vault with his fists.

Ramarro's power closed in around him, constricting, intensifying. Cole knew that no matter how fiercely he resisted, it would soon overwhelm him. He would be consumed. Ramarro would escape. His friends would die. The world would perish.

But it had not happened yet. This was his only chance. Ignoring the hostile power encroaching from every side, Cole stopped trying to damage the nexus and instead reached into it. The effort was excruciating, but as he pushed with all he had, he felt beneath the surface. Having established that contact, Cole drew upon his hopes, his fears, and his ardent desire to survive, and hit the nexus with everything he had, tearing and shredding with the frantic energy of desperation.

Explosive shock waves quaked through the power around him.

Sharpening his focus like a blade, like a drill, Cole reached deeper into the damaged nexus and savaged it again. Everything around him roared in agony.

The power suddenly withdrew.

Cole stood again in the courtyard, his faculties restored.

Down on one knee, head bowed, Ramarro clutched his chest. Then he looked up, fury in his gaze.

Impossible! The word struck Cole's mind like an explosion.

"Come get more!" Cole yelled, though he could hardly stand.

Fog washed over Cole and Ramarro as the castle entered the cloudwall. The ground lurched, and the speed of the forward motion increased. Cole fell onto his side. He could no longer see Ramarro.

You will die too, Ramarro conveyed.

"I don't care," Cole cried.

Dandalus sent you to your death, Ramarro said.

"At least he gave me a chance to die bravely!" Cole yelled.

Ramarro connected to Cole again. Power washed over Cole, but he immediately followed the connection to the nexus, drove inward, and hit it with everything he had.

Ramarro's power recoiled from Cole. The connection broke. Thick mist gushed across the courtyard as the castle bucked and plunged. Cole sailed into the air as the ground fell away, then smashed against it when it returned.

I'm leaving, Ramarro declared. *This construct cannot resist my full concentration. Die alone.*

Ramarro ducked his head and clenched his fists.

The statue of Dandalus cried out, "Can't . . . hold . . . him!"

Ramarro was about to open a wayport. Or just teleport. He was using his power to dismantle the trap holding him here. At any moment he would vanish. Cole balled his hands into fists.

Ramarro was right. No trap Dandalus had fashioned had ever managed to destroy him.

But this time was different. Ramarro was not alone in this trap.

Cole reached out to Ramarro's power. Connecting to that ocean of shaping prowess, Cole searched the vastness for the blazing nexus he had touched twice before. The area was staggering, but Cole remembered what the nexus had felt like, and as he stretched out with his mental faculties, he caught traces, hints, and followed them.

Until he found it.

Bracing himself as if he were about to use his bare hands to scoop hot coals from a fire, Cole reached deep into the nexus and started twisting and kneading and ripping. Fireworks erupted in his mind, but he held on and kept tearing.

At last he could take no more, and the connection broke.

Ramarro lay sprawled on his face. The torivor looked up, head swaying unsteadily.

How dare you!

"Want more?" Cole yelled.

This will not destroy me, Ramarro warned. *You will pay. This whole world will pay.*

"You're wrong!" Cole yelled.

Even if this leads to the slipstream, I will be fine, Ramarro conveyed. *You survived it. I saw it in your memories. I will escape without a problem.*

"Are you sure?" Cole asked. "I belong in time."

Great fissures opened in the ground. Sections of the walls collapsed, and portions of the castle came down as well. The stones that bounced near Cole kept turning to dust. Several chunks of masonry pummeled the torivor.

For the first time, Ramarro looked afraid.

Suddenly Cole stood on a dark field of volcanic rock. Rivers of lava flowed on either side of him, the searing heat almost too much to bear. The tops of mountains exploded in the distance as lava fountained into a sky saturated with ash.

"We need to talk, Cole," Ramarro said.

"This seems like a nice place," Cole said.

"I'm not in a pleasant mood," Ramarro said. "We have all the time I need. You would be astonished by how long I can make a second last."

"And at the end of it you'll die," Cole said.

"Debatable," Ramarro said. "I can make you suffer."

Pyroclastic explosions erupted around Cole. Lava splashed dangerously close. As the dazzling glare faded and the blistering heat subsided, Cole found he was encased to the waist in warm, black stone.

"I can torture you to death in a million ways, Cole," Ramarro said. "Across a billion landscapes. How long before you break?"

Cole sensed power radiating from Ramarro and realized

the torivor was still trying to get free. He was buying himself time with this conversation.

Once again, Cole reached for Ramarro with his mind and found the increasingly familiar location of the torivor's nexus with little trouble. Penetrating the nexus first, then mangling with all his might, Cole fell out of the dream state. Volcanic rock gave way to the courtyard of the quaking, crumbling castle.

Ramarro finally looked desperate. *You have rattled me,* he confessed, weariness behind the words. *Ludicrous as it seems, you're right—I cannot escape with you harassing me. I don't have time. You don't know what you are destroying. You can't begin to imagine all I am. Spare me, Cole.*

"So you can torture me to death in a million ways?" Cole yelled. "So you can destroy my friends? No way!"

The ground was heaving. Ramarro stretched a hand toward him. *Stop fighting me. Work with me, Cole, and we can both still survive. I don't want to risk ending. I will grant whatever you desire.*

"Dream on!" Cole cried.

The courtyard tipped forward and split apart. Everything was falling. Cole plunged through the mist in a hailstorm of shattered stone. And then all the stone became dust. And the mist parted. And the maelstrom yawned below him, a wild vortex that whirled down toward forever.

Off to one side, Cole saw Ramarro falling, arms and legs flailing.

Unbelievable! Ramarro cried.

They hit the swirling surface of the vortex simultaneously,

perhaps twenty yards apart. Cole tumbled and spun in the hurricane currents, a banshee choir wailing in his ears. He remembered this experience. It was horrifying and familiar.

Somewhere behind all the commotion, Cole could faintly hear the homesong. As he focused on that beckoning music, the tumult seemed to fade.

It was all right.

He could go.

He could die this way.

He had stopped Ramarro.

It had seemed impossible, but he had stopped him.

Cole finally understood the sky castles.

The whole setup had been a trap all along.

A trap set in case the torivors got free.

Dandalus had prepared a battleground that had given Cole a chance.

Cole had made the most of the opportunity. He had fought to keep Ramarro at the doomed castle. And he had won.

He had succeeded.

Now it was up to the vortex. Would it be enough?

Trillian had seen the slipstream in Cole's memory. He had told Cole that he could not have resisted the homesong. And torivors could not lie.

Ramarro would perish. The homesong seemed to promise it.

Cole had saved his friends.

He would miss everyone.

They would miss him.

He was sure they would be proud of him.

He would follow the homesong.

It would lead him to a good place.

A better place than he had ever known.

He was certain. He could feel it so clearly.

Something wrapped around his chest, yanking tight.

He was suddenly hauled free from the screaming currents.

A young man on a flying disk was holding a golden rope. The rope had wrapped around Cole's chest. The young man was Liam.

That couldn't be right.

Cole's vision was fading.

Liam was long gone.

Cole realized he must be dreaming.

And then darkness engulfed him.

CHAPTER
— 34 —

RECOVERY

Cole woke up on a soft bed in an elegantly furnished room. Veins of gray streaked the white marble walls and ceiling. He turned to find Mira seated on a nearby chair, gazing at him tenderly.

"Are we dead?" Cole asked, his throat dry.

"Nope," Mira said.

"Did we get him?"

"You got him."

Cole thought hard. "We fell into the vortex."

"Liam fished you out," Mira said.

Cole propped himself up on one elbow. His body felt stiff. "I remember Liam. I didn't think that could be real. Why was Liam there? We haven't seen him since we fought Carnag."

"The echo of Dandalus sent for him through Jenna."

"That must have happened before I went to get her."

"Yes. She contacted the Unseen in Necronum, who got a message to Liam in hiding. He came here and waited for you. I guess Dandalus expected the fight to end up here."

"Where are we?" Cole asked.

"Inside the castle behind the cloudwall," Mira said. "You know, where Declan lived before he was chased away. It was abandoned until we arrived."

"How did you get here?" Cole asked.

"Lorenzo opened a wayport to here for me, Jace, Twitch, Dalton, Jenna, Hunter, and Violet right after Ramarro followed you to the sky castle. Jace lent Liam the golden rope."

"It didn't need my power to work here," Cole said. "Sambria."

"I've been practicing with my powers since we arrived," Mira said.

"Did you make any walking mudballs?"

Mira broke eye contact. "Maybe."

"How long was I out?"

"Three days."

Cole nodded. His mouth felt dry and tasted funny. "Do you have water?"

She handed him a glass. He took a small sip of the lukewarm fluid. The lining of his mouth seemed to absorb half of it before he could swallow. He took another sip.

"Is your power all right?" Mira asked.

Cole searched inside himself, and his power felt okay but a little unsteady. Cole connected to Mira's power and gave her some energy.

She sat up straighter. "Good!"

"My power felt injured in the fight," Cole said. "Still kind of does. At least it still works. More strained than torn. Ramarro came after me with his power. Since he was reaching for me, I found my way to his center and hurt him back. You're sure the vortex got him?"

"Liam seemed sure," Mira said. "He saw him descending, round and round, deeper and deeper. Ramarro wasn't fighting. He just drifted with the flow. Liam watched until he disappeared. We haven't heard from Ramarro since."

Cole thought for a moment. "You guys can't leave here."

"Not without you. Unless we're ready for a really long walk."

"Violet can only open a wayport here with my help. You were betting on me to survive."

"We bet right," Mira said. "I should get the others."

She hurried away.

Before long, Dalton raced into the room. "I knew it!" he cried, running to give Cole a hug. Cole winced as he hugged back, shoulders aching. He felt a little fragile. "I knew you would be all right. How is your power?"

"Working," Cole said.

"That is a lot more than Ramarro can say," Jace said as he entered with Twitch. "You realize you're a legend now."

Violet, Mira, and Jenna came next, and Hunter and Liam entered last. Cole became the center of smiling attention. He could see they had been worried and were now relieved.

"Thanks for sending Liam," Cole told Jenna. His eyes shifted to Liam. "Thanks for coming to my rescue."

"Least I could do after you saved all of us," Liam said. "It's a little hard to believe when you get a message from one of the long-dead founders of your world."

"I know the feeling," Cole said.

"I guess you do," Liam said. "Thank Jace, too. Without that golden rope it would have been dodgy."

"Thanks, Jace," Cole said.

"Don't you dare thank me," Jace said. "Not after what you did. You took Ramarro in a straight fight. All I can do now is thank you forever."

"The battleground was rigged," Cole said. "The sky castle was set to respond to my abilities and not to his. He tried to figure out how to escape. I did my best to get in the way."

"You fought him," Jace said. "Alone. Dandalus told us where he sent you after Ramarro disappeared. He told us all he could give you was a chance."

"And you did it, Cole," Dalton said.

"I fought him hard," Cole said. "Threw statues at him. Threw the castle at him. I even got to his nexus with my power and hurt him."

"And don't forget that you defeated the Perennial Serpent in seconds," Mira said. "Like it was nothing. Elegance has her power back."

"I had practice," Cole said. "Once I knew what to do, that one was easy."

"And you destroyed Owandell," Hunter said. "You made that look easy too."

"It kind of was," Cole said. "He wasn't too scary. I knew I could take him with my power. The Jumping Sword was just an experiment."

"Style points for the sword," Jace said.

"What do you mean you had practice?" Jenna asked.

Cole explained about the potion that had given him a

look at the possible future. He also explained why he mostly kept that information to himself before fighting Ramarro, since the torivor might have read it in other minds.

"So from your perspective, you fought Ramarro twice," Twitch said. "Brave."

"The first time was a mess," Cole said. "The second time went better. At least I wasn't lost in some forgotten wilderness. We were so worried about you."

"I may never know exactly where I was," Twitch said. "Forested hills, with mountains in the distance. A wet region—lots of ponds and streams. I didn't see another person the entire time. Lots of animals, though. Foraging wasn't too bad—berries and mushrooms especially. I also caught plenty of fish. I was actually roasting a couple of trout over a fire when I was transported to the battleground with Ramarro."

"Sorry," Cole said. "I know it was dangerous to pull you into that fight."

"Don't be sorry!" Twitch said. "It was startling, but it worked beautifully. Here I am."

"I bet your fish burned, though," Jace said.

Twitch laughed. "I might have spent the rest of my days roaming a solitary wilderness."

"I wish I could offer a feast," Liam said. "You all deserve a feast. But the stores were looted by the soldiers who flushed us out of here."

"My mother will provide a feast," Mira said. "All we need is a wayport to the First Castle. I'm sure she went home after Ramarro fell. She'll be trying to set the kingdom in order."

Cole stared at his friends. Worlds were colliding before him—his older brother, friends from back home, and friends made as he adventured in the Outskirts. Because of his preparations to fight Ramarro, Cole hadn't been able to really appreciate having everybody together until this moment.

Cole connected to Violet and energized her ability. "Let's get out of here," he said.

A wayport opened.

"I've got him," Hunter said, nodding toward Cole.

The others started filing into the wayport.

Liam moved off to one side. "I won't join you. I need to get back to Declan, and Junction is the wrong direction. Eat something delicious for me, will you?"

"Violet could send you home by wayport from Junction," Cole said.

Liam paused. "I couldn't have her send me directly to our new hideout. But she could send me kind of close, and it would save time overall." He smiled. "Looks like I'm going to get a better dinner than I had planned."

Hunter helped Cole out of bed. His knees felt sore, and his legs were wobbly. Hunter kept an arm around Cole's shoulders.

"You proved me wrong," Hunter said. "I was really worried. But you saved everybody, and you found a way home."

"Now we just have to track down the other kids," Cole said.

"I bet Queen Harmony will help," Hunter said. "Hopefully Violet will too."

Cole walked unsteadily to the wayport. "How long do you think it will take before we get to walk the Pilgrim Path?"

"We'll know before long," Hunter said.

CHAPTER 35

DEPARTURE

It took three weeks before Cole and Hunter stood in Creon staring at the gaping tunnel of the Pilgrim Path. They were not alone. Under edict from the High Queen, the slaver Ansel had handed over the locations of all the slaves. It might have taken months to collect them under ordinary circumstances, but with Cole empowering Violet, they retrieved every last child within fifteen days. All of the missing kids from Cole's neighborhood stood gathered near the Pilgrim Path, along with Dalton, Jenna, and Joe, whose leg had mostly healed. Little Brady, who had once created his own nightmare playland inside Sambria, stayed beside Joe. Blake, Sarah, and Jill lingered near Jenna.

The High Queen was present as well. When Harmony went to retrieve her husband, she learned he had died the same hour Elegance got her power back. Honor had seemed openly glad about the news. The other princesses had acted torn between sadness and relief. Watching their reactions had reminded Cole that though Stafford had forced them into exile and made their lives difficult, he had been their father. Destiny had wept openly, occasionally muttering "good riddance."

Cole could understand the mixed feelings. Stafford had once been likable. Cole believed the High King initially had good intentions. His relationship with Owandell probably had begun innocently. But the relationship had gotten all twisted, and his choices took darker and darker turns, until Stafford eventually ruined himself and his family. There was plenty of reason to grieve.

All five sisters were in attendance today. Elegance had an arm around Brogan. Desmond attended Honor. Mira stood near Cole. Constance and Destiny held hands. Jace was there as well, and Twitch and Violet.

Lorenzo Debray approached Cole. "All is ready," he said. "Let me remind you that there is no way back from this path if you walk it. Though almost anyone on Earth could be brought to the Outskirts, there is no known way to retrieve any of you who take this path. You will become permanently out of sync with this realm. You will completely lose your powers, and I suspect your memories of the Outskirts will eventually fade."

"You think we'll totally forget?" Cole asked. The prospect seemed ludicrous. How could he ever forget nearly dying? Visiting the afterlife? Saving lives and being saved?

"Consider your own investigation," Lorenzo said. "The greatest Wayminder of all time, who lived more years in the Outskirts than any other person, lost all sense that it really happened. You have been here for months, not years.

You have confronted some very adult problems, but you are young and still growing. I believe the day will come when you will not realize any of this happened."

Cole looked at Mira, Jace, Twitch, and Violet. How could he forget them? They had survived so much together! They were his closest friends. If anything seemed far away, it was his home in Mesa. The Outskirts were present and tangible. He resolved not to forget.

"You don't have to go," Mira said. "You could stay with us. We're all going to miss you, and not just for your unique powers."

"I have to go home," Cole said.

Mira nodded. "I understand. It has been your goal all along." She raised her voice. "None of you need depart if you would rather stay. Your abilities could be of great use here. I will personally ensure that you will have comfortable housing and a job. With my mother's decree to end slavery, we are becoming a much more civilized place to live."

Nobody accepted her offer.

Cole smiled. When Harmony had asked how she could reward him, he had only asked for an end to slavery, followed by help retrieving his friends. She admitted her own conscience had wanted an end to the practice for years and promised to dedicate herself to making it happen.

Jace shook Cole's hand. "You might forget me, but I won't forget you."

Cole hugged his friend. "Keep an eye on Mira."

Jace winked. "Count on it."

Jace moved on to talk to Dalton. Twitch came forward and hugged Cole.

"Have fun in your mud baths," Cole said.

"I don't think I'll be in there so much anymore," Twitch said. "It was a place to hide."

"Take care of the Halfknight," Cole said.

"Thanks for everything," Twitch said.

Violet shook Cole's hand. "Good job, Cole."

"Same to you," Cole said. "Thanks for taking us everywhere."

"Thanks for making it possible," Violet said.

Mira hugged Cole swiftly. After the hug, he stared at her. Was he really leaving her? "Take care of the kingdoms."

"Especially Sambria," Mira said. "I plan to go train with Declan soon."

"Say hi to Liam," Cole said.

"I can never thank you enough," Mira said. "You know that. Without you we would have been lost. You didn't just save me. You saved my sisters, my mother, my whole world. For a long time it didn't seem possible."

"We all worked together," Cole said. "Keep an eye on Jace."

Mira winked. "Have a wonderful life."

The High Queen stood before the entrance to the Pilgrim Path and raised her voice. "On behalf of the people of Junction and the citizens of the five kingdoms, I apologize that you were taken from your homes. And I thank you for helping to save our world. We will forever owe Cole, Dalton, Brady, Joe, Blake, Hunter, Jenna, and all of you our deepest gratitude. May you travel home safely."

She stepped aside.

It was time to go.

"Me first," Blake called, charging down the tunnel. The rest of the kids chased after him, most of them running. Before long only Cole, Hunter, and Dalton remained.

"Ready, little brother?" Hunter asked.

"I guess so," Cole said. He looked back at Mira, Twitch, Jace, and Violet.

If Cole was going to leave, it was time. He had done all he could for the Outskirts. Over the past three weeks, he had burned away the darkness from the powers of more than five hundred shapecrafters. Having their shapecrafted powers healed was the price the High Queen set for amnesty for those who had sided with Owandell. Many took her up on the offer.

Hunter led the way, then Dalton. Cole stepped into the tunnel last.

"Die bravely," Jace called. "But not too soon."

Tears stung Cole's eyes as he walked down the tunnel. A huge part of him didn't want to go yet. And then he was standing on his street, in front of his house, an uncomfortably hot sun not far above the horizon.

The tunnel was gone.

His own house. There it was. Same as ever.

Cole looked at Hunter.

And remembered him.

They used to shoot penalty kicks at each other in the backyard on the bristly lawn. They had home run derbies with Wiffle balls. They rode their bikes around the neighbor-hood and sometimes on trails in the desert. They had shared a bedroom when Cole was smaller——Hunter on the bot-tom bunk, Cole on top. They had played with action figures together and shot baskets on the little hoop clipped to the top of their door.

"I remember you," Cole said.

"About time," Hunter replied with a smile.

"I knew you were my brother," Cole said. "It's just . . . more real now."

The other kids were dispersing. Dalton lingered. Joe pat-ted Cole on the back. Brady stood beside him. "That your house?"

"Am I staring at it?" Cole asked.

"You are," Joe said. "And you should. I'm going to find Brady's home and then make my way to California."

"We can feed you," Hunter offered.

"I'm all right," Joe said. "Lorenzo gave me a lot of money. I'm glad he took an interest in collecting US currency. You guys go see your folks."

Joe strolled off, holding Brady's hand.

"I remember the Outskirts just fine," Dalton observed.

"Me too," Hunter said.

"Let's remind each other," Cole said. "Write it down. Talk about it. Kendo didn't have other people. I bet we can keep from forgetting by talking about it."

"Maybe," Hunter said.

"I should go," Dalton said. "See you guys later."

"See you," Cole said.

"Think it's summer?" Hunter asked as Dalton walked away.

"Feels like summer," Cole said. "I hope the AC is cranked up. Think we missed the school year?"

"Probably," Hunter said. "I wonder what grades you get when your teachers forget all about you?"

"Straight As, I hope," Cole said. "Let's go."

They walked up to the porch and opened the door.

"Cole, Hunter?" their mom called.

"Yeah," Cole replied.

She came to the entry hall, looking just as Cole remembered her. "Where have you boys been?"

"Um," Cole said.

"Dinner was ready an hour ago," she said.

"Sorry," Hunter said.

"Are you crying, Cole?" his mom asked.

"I think I have some dirt in my eye," Cole said. He stepped forward and hugged his mom tightly.

"What's that for?" his mom asked, looking over him at Hunter.

"He's been emotional today," Hunter said. "Little weirdo."

"Mind if I go to my room for a minute?" Cole asked.

"Go ahead," his mom said. "I'll warm you a plate."

"Is Dad around?" Hunter asked. "Chelsea?"

"They're watching TV," she said.

Cole walked away from the conversation and went down the hall to his room. The door was closed.

Behind the door, he found all as he had left it. Exactly.

Same junk on his desk. Same clothes on the floor. A film of dust covered everything. He had been gone for some time.

Cole knew he had to go see his dad and his sister. He knew he had to go eat dinner. He had to fall back into the rhythms of life as if he had not been away for months in a strange and dangerous world.

For a moment he stared at his familiar room.

His old life felt much more real now that he was here.

The Outskirts seemed a little more distant.

But he could not imagine that he would ever forget.

EPILOGUE

Cole sat down on a bench by a sidewalk on the ASU campus, not far from the Hayden Library. He was in an awkward time between classes. In half an hour he would head over to the Memorial Union to meet Dalton for lunch. For the moment he figured he would enjoy the relatively mild day and catch up on some reading.

Glancing up, he noticed a beautiful girl walking toward him. There were plenty of pretty girls on campus, but this one was exceptional—tall and slender, with long brown hair and lovely features. He didn't know her, so he tried not to stare, but when his eyes met hers, she smiled as if she wanted to let him in on a private joke. Cole wondered if he might be sitting in her usual spot. As she approached Cole's bench, he stood.

"Hi, Cole," she said.

"Hi," Cole said, delighted she was speaking with him, surprised that she knew his name. Her expressive eyes hinted at a playful mood. "Do I know you?"

Her smile warmed. "We were friends when we were younger."

Cole did not see how that was possible. Could he have forgotten those lively eyes? Maybe she used to wear glasses? Or dyed her hair? He compared her against the neighborhood kids he had grown up with but came up empty.

"How do you like ASU?" she asked.

"Great so far," Cole said. "First semester."

"Hunter goes here too," she said.

"Are you a friend of Hunter's?" Cole asked. That would make sense. Hunter hung out with some cute girls.

"I like Hunter," she said. "But I'm here to see you."

Cole felt a thrill that an attractive stranger was showing him so much attention. She seemed really personable and open. Was she a little familiar, or was it just that she effortlessly treated him like a friend? "Do you go here?"

She shook her head. "I'm from far away. I'm just here briefly."

"What's your name?"

"Want to guess?"

"It would take a miracle."

Her smile broadened. "You don't remember me at all?"

Cole tried. Maybe a girl in one of his classes? Somebody who moved away? "Not really."

She looked a little disappointed, just for a moment. "You used to talk about the Outskirts."

Cole blushed a little. "That was a game I played with my brother and my friend Dalton."

"A game?"

"You know, sort of a role-playing game. Like Dungeons and Dragons. Except we made it up. Pretty nerdy, I guess."

"Tell me about it."

Her interest mildly surprised him. "We got really into it for a while. We filled up notebooks with stories. I even used to dream about it."

She looked serious. "Do you think any of it really happened?"

Cole huffed. "I'm not crazy."

"You used to talk about it like it might have been real."

"With you?"

"With me."

Cole gave an uncomfortable laugh. "We acted like it was real. That was the point. In the journals we kept, we wrote about it like it really happened. I can't believe I told you so much about it. When did I know you? You never told me your name."

"Mira," she said. "We've met several times, but you don't remember too well."

"Are you teasing me?" Cole asked. "One of the characters in our game was named Mira. One of the imaginary ones."

"That's funny," Mira said, pivoting away. "I'm glad to see you're doing well."

"Are you going?"

"I should," Mira said. "I'll check up on you again. Promise."

"Want to keep in touch?" Cole asked.

"I'll be far away and hard to reach," Mira said. "How are you paying for school?"

Cole was a little surprised by the direct question. "I had saved up, but an anonymous donor is paying for me. The same thing happened to Hunter and my friend Dalton. Some rich relative maybe?"

"Sounds like you have people watching over you," Mira said. "That must be comforting."

"Kind of mysterious," Cole said. "I wish I could thank them." He paused, considering her. "Are you involved in that?"

Mira flashed a smile. "Maybe a little. Have a good year." She started backing away.

"I'll really see you again?"

"I promise. And some of the others, too."

"Others?"

"You'll see."

"I'll remember you next time."

"Don't hold your breath."

"I doubt I could forget you now."

Mira stepped forward and took his hand. The contact felt good. "What matters is I will remember you, Cole. It can be hard to know how you impact people. Somewhere, there might be entire kingdoms that will never forget you, where people young and old speak of you with awe and consider your birthday an important holiday."

"That's a coincidence," Cole said. "Today is my birthday."

"No kidding? Happy birthday."

Cole smiled. "You have a big imagination. I bet we would have been friends as kids."

Mira released his hand. "You have no idea." She backed away.

"Do you have to go?"

"I should."

"See you next time."

"Count on it."

ACKNOWLEDGMENTS

My third major series is now complete! So many people made this book and this series possible. I fell behind schedule writing this final book and am so grateful to the readers and publishing people who have been patient with me.

Liesa Abrams was my editor for this entire series, and once again she elevated the quality of the story and the storytelling with her sharp insights. My agent, Simon Lipskar, offered some keen reactions from his formidable mind as well. I'm so lucky to have them in my corner.

The whole team at Simon & Schuster has my gratitude. Owen Richardson executed another terrific cover image. Thanks go to Mara Anastas, Chriscynethia Floyd, Caitlin Sweeny, Jon Anderson, Jodie Hockensmith, Brian Luster, Chelsea Morgan, Mike Rosamilia, Jeannie Ng, Rebecca Vitkus, Amy Bartram, Jessica Handelman, Julie Doebler, Ian Reilly, Jennifer Rothkin, Gary Urda, Christina Pecorale, and so many others.

Family and friends helped again as well. Thanks go to Tucker Davis, Pamela Mull, Jason Conforto, and Cherie Mull for some early feedback. As always, Mary and my beloved kids were supportive of the time required to write the book and to connect with readers.

Thank you to the teachers, booksellers, and librarians who help bring readers to my work. Without you I would probably end up unemployed!

Finally, I give my thanks to you, the reader. Thanks for bringing this story to life in your imagination. I hope you enjoyed this final volume. Thanks for sharing the story with others. Having readers lets me keep writing stories. I appreciate the opportunity and hope to create a bunch of cool stories in the coming years. More on that in the Note to Readers.

NOTE TO READERS

Five Kingdoms is now complete. Since the Candy Shop War books are not finished and Spirit Animals was a shared project, I consider this the end of my third major series, after Fablehaven and Beyonders. Thank you to all who have waited for this book. It took a little longer than intended, largely because I wanted to get it right. I hope it satisfies.

Now I will return to writing Dragonwatch, the direct sequel series to Fablehaven, featuring the same main characters. Dragonwatch will be a five-book series, and I have a really great story to tell about a worldwide dragon uprising. I also hope to write a third Candy Shop War book before long, as well as begin some brand-new projects.

If you like these books and haven't tried Fablehaven, it is worth a look. The series deals with secret wildlife parks for magical creatures. Beyonders is perhaps my most epic series, about a couple kids who cross to another world and try to help the broken heroes they find there.

To connect with me, look me up by name on Facebook, follow me on Twitter, and check out my Instagram account, @writerbrandon. My website is brandonmull.com. Basically, if you remember my name, you can find me online. Thank you for your interest!

SETH AND KENDRA ARE BACK! READ ON FOR
A GLIMPSE AT THE FIRST CHAPTERS OF A BRAND-NEW
ADVENTURE IN THE WORLD OF FABLEHAVEN:

DRAGONWATCH

BOOK 1!

From the Journal of Stan Sorenson

Could this be the end?

Will I be counted among the last of the caretakers? Could this longstanding trust dissolve during my watch?

I have loved Fablehaven since I first beheld the wonders disguised here. Most in the modern world cannot guess at the splendors concealed within these enchanted refuges, where creatures of legend hunt and frolic. More than fifty years have passed since Fablehaven won my heart.

But it comes with a price.

How far am I willing to go to fulfill my duty? To protect the magical sanctuaries of the world? I made peace with sacrificing my own life long ago. But what about the lives of others? What about my family?

I have longed to share the marvels of Fablehaven with those I love most. But knowledge of those miracles means exposure to the dangers as well. Magical creatures can dazzle. They can also kill. For me, the wonder outweighs the threat. But what right do I have to make that decision for another?

I never forced anyone to discover what is really happening at Fablehaven. Certainly not my grandchildren. But I let their curiosity lead them to the truth. After drinking the milk from Viola, the magical milch cow, Kendra and Seth could recognize that the butterflies here were actually fairies, the goats were satyrs, and the horses were centaurs. That first time is so incredible. And it never becomes ordinary.

I could have prevented it. But I allowed Fablehaven to unfold for them.

Inevitably, it took hold of them. As it always does.

And peril followed.

Kendra and Seth know my real reason for living at Fablehaven. As caretaker, I serve the inhabitants of this preserve and protect the outside world from them. I am fed by experiences that stretch the definition of reality. I behold spectacles known by none except those with access to these extraordinary sanctuaries.

My grandchildren appreciate the responsibility of protecting these refuges. They have shown willingness to sacrifice as well.

I thought we had survived the worst of it. We were pushed to our limits. Our lives were in jeopardy. Loved ones died. Kendra and Seth were almost lost, but in the end, they tipped the scales to save us all.

But now they may be needed again.

I believe I can protect them. But I have wrongly believed that before.

Once again, frankly, I don't know what to do. My responsibility is plain. But how far am I willing to go? How much am I able to risk?

Is it fair to give them a choice?

Is it even a choice, when I know what they will choose?

EAVESDROPPING

Kendra Sorenson jogged through the warm mist, damp gravel crunching underfoot, wondering if the moisture in the air was falling enough to be called rain. Sprinkles, maybe. She glanced up at the gray blur of the sky beyond the treetops, then over at a trio of fairies, each surrounded by a hazy halo of light. Nothing pattered against the hood of her Windbreaker, but it was wet, as were the leafy branches on either side of the long driveway.

This was the murkiest morning of the summer, at least since Kendra had started jogging. The fifteen-year-old typically got up just before sunrise and ran around the perimeter of the big yard three times. Each lap included running up the driveway to the gate and back. Any larger route would either take her beyond the boundaries of Fablehaven, exposing her to threats from outside the preserve, or else make her vulnerable to some of the dangers held back by the magic protecting the yard. Roaming the woods of the sanctuary was not a safe proposition.

There had been no sunrise to watch today. The grayness

had simply grown brighter as she followed her standard path, soles slipping on the wet grass.

The gate came into view up ahead, closed as usual—wrought-iron topped with fleurs-de lis, the only potential opening in the fence that enclosed the entire preserve. Kendra always touched the gate before turning around.

As she approached the black bars and reached out a hand, Kendra paused. She heard a motor approaching, and tires mashing gravel.

That was highly unusual.

The gate to Fablehaven was well back from the main road. A distracter spell helped motorists ignore the nondescript turnoff, and you didn't have to travel far along the driveway before finding several emphatic signs warning away trespassers.

People did not come to Fablehaven by accident.

And when visitors were expected, it was big news. Grandpa or Grandma Sorenson inevitably brought it up ahead of time. Often the gate was left open for the arrival.

So who was approaching?

Who might come to Fablehaven unannounced?

An old friend? A spy? An enemy?

Or somebody really lost and fairly illiterate.

In case the visitor was an enemy, Kendra hurried off the driveway, withdrawing into the trees and crouching behind some shrubs. Leaving the driveway reduced her protection from magical threats, but trouble seldom happened this close to a protected area. The chance to hide seemed worth the small risk.

Before long, a white sedan pulled into view and parked just outside the gate. A cowled figure emerged from the vehicle.

Kendra had a hood herself. The weather called for covering your head. But the hooded brown robe of the stranger looked to have come from a bygone era. It deliberately concealed the face in deep shadow. This was no lost tourist. It might not even be human. This had to be somebody who knew about preserves for magical creatures.

Was the stranger going to try to break in? The gate wasn't visible from the house, but parking on the driveway didn't seem very subtle.

Then Kendra heard crunching footsteps on the gravel from the direction of the house. She remained frozen as Grandpa Sorenson strode into view wearing a jacket and a baseball cap. She held her breath as he walked up to the gate. It didn't open.

"You want to talk?" Grandpa called through the bars to the robed figure.

"Briefly, yes," the figure replied in a raspy voice.

As Captain of the Knights of the Dawn, the organization that policed the magical preserves of the world, Grandpa met from time to time with various individuals who provided information. Those exchanges often happened in his office. Apparently, he also sometimes met informants at the gate.

Kendra felt guilty for eavesdropping, but it seemed more awkward to announce herself at this point. She hunkered lower behind the shrubs.

"The situation continues to deteriorate," the cowled figure

warned. "They will most likely be needed. The boy should settle his affair with the Sisters."

"I understand he has the better part of a year to meet their terms," Grandpa said.

"Owing the Sisters is no small concern," the figure insisted. "Who knows where he might end up over the coming months? What if circumstances prevent him from paying his debt? Why not seize the moment? For how long do you want the sword in his possession? It is powerful, but is it safe? That weapon has a history of corrupting those who wield it."

"I hear you," Grandpa said. "I'll consider advising him. Any word from Soaring Cliffs?"

"No good tidings," the figure responded, taking a step back. "I should depart. We'll be in touch."

"Thank our mutual friend," Grandpa said.

"Thank him by taking the necessary action, Stan Sorenson," the figure warned. "This could quickly become a bigger mess than the previous crisis. Prepare while you have time."

Grandpa glanced down the driveway back toward the house.

"Expecting someone?" the figure asked.

"My granddaughter is out for her morning run," Stan said.

"I must away," the figure said, retreating to his car.

Grandpa started back to the house without a wave.

The engine started, and the vehicle rolled forward and back to make a multipoint turn. By the time the sedan passed out of sight, Kendra could no longer hear her grandfather.

She waited in silence until the sound of the car faded to nothing.

What had she just heard? They had to be talking about her younger brother, Seth. Kendra knew that he had made a deal with some witches to find the legendary sword Vasilis. But why was some shady outsider taking an interest? And what big problem was brewing? Whose help was needed? It sounded like the trouble could involve her and her brother.

Kendra crept back to the road and looked down it carefully. Grandpa was no longer in sight; he had probably entered the house. She jogged back to the yard, then did part of another lap before quitting and going inside.

She found Grandpa Sorenson in his study.

"Good morning, Kendra," he said.

"Good morning," she replied, watching him. He seemed relaxed.

"Strange weather today," Grandpa observed.

"Gray and soggy. Did we have a visitor?"

Grandpa scrunched his eyebrows. "Why would you think that?"

Kendra weighed how much to say. "I noticed you walking down the driveway."

Grandpa smiled. "Just checking the gate. I do that when I get restless."

"Okay," Kendra said. She didn't want to press him. "See you later."

She walked from the room. It wasn't like Grandpa to lie. Part of his job both as a caretaker of Fablehaven and as Captain of the Knights involved keeping secrets. She had no doubt that Grandpa would lie to protect a secret he thought might be harmful to others.

It bothered Kendra to know part of a story that probably involved her and her brother. Should she tell Grandpa she had seen the stranger? Should she relate what she had heard? Should she demand to know the identity of the mysterious figure? Should she ask why she and Seth might be needed?

Her instincts warned her that further probing would yield little fruit. Whatever the details might be, Grandpa wasn't ready to share. And he was a professional at keeping secrets.

Should she talk to Seth about it? Kendra doubted whether her brother could keep this quiet, especially since it involved him directly and there was more to find out. For now it might be best to worry and wonder on her own. Whatever secrets Grandpa and this stranger knew, one thing seemed clear—serious trouble was coming.

A PROMISE KEPT

Seth crept deeper underground, flashlight in hand. Pale roots corkscrewed from the glistening muck of the curved ceiling. Some caves had a rich, earthy smell, full of gritty minerals. This was not one of them. Things were rotting down here. Bugs were breeding and slime was spreading. The uneven floor of the tunnel squelched beneath every step.

The wraith beside him did little to cheer the atmosphere. Not quite alive and not quite dead, it strode silently, disturbingly still even when in motion, the darkest shape in the shadowy tunnel, radiating coldness and an unnerving aura of fear. Some would have stood immobilized in the presence of the wraith, horrified, speechless, struggling to breathe. And the wraith might have crept up to them and temporarily relieved its own iciness by draining their warmth.

But ever since Seth had become a shadow charmer, not only could he endure the presence of the undead, he could even communicate with some of them. The surest way to survive the company of a wraith was to strike a bargain.

Seth had pledged to free this wraith from the dungeon below Fablehaven and deliver it to new owners in exchange for the wraith obeying and protecting him until the transfer was complete.

A few months prior, in order to learn the location of the storied sword Vasilis, Seth had promised to bring the Singing Sisters the sword and a wraith. He had also agreed to fulfill one additional assignment of their choice. If he failed to keep the arrangement, an enchanted knife was ready to hunt him down and kill him. So he had selected the most companionable wraith he could find and set off on a road trip to Missouri with Grandpa Sorenson and the satyrs Newel and Doren. Even with the wraith being transported in a trailer behind their vehicle, its chilly presence had kept the other passengers on edge.

On his only previous visit to the Sisters, Seth had entered through a door in a high bluff. This time, the sentinel who guarded access to this narrow island in the Mississippi River had informed him that return visitors should enter through a low tunnel on the other side. Neither Grandpa nor the satyrs had been allowed to join him. Since arriving on the island and finding the muddy cave, Seth and the wraith had met no living creatures.

Vasilis dangled from a sword belt Seth had slung over one shoulder. Seth was reluctant to part with the legendary Sword of Light and Darkness. He technically had a full year to return the blade after striking the deal that let him find it, and the time was not yet up. But the weapon had served its purpose, helping him and Kendra hold off the demons who had emerged from Zzyzx. Bracken the unicorn had suggested Seth settle his debt with the Sisters early rather than waiting until the last minute—in case something prevented him from fulfilling his promise. Grandpa had agreed and encouraged him to get it over with.

Normally, Seth adhered to a fairly rigid policy of procrastination, but the threat of a knife pursuing him across the globe, intent on ending his life, helped persuade him otherwise. That and the boring months since the demonic apocalypse had been averted. With Grandpa and Grandma Sorenson running Fablehaven alongside Grandpa and Grandma Larsen, life had been woefully uneventful. A road trip had sounded like a welcome relief.

Giving up the wraith was no problem. Early on in the drive, the shadowy form had earned the nickname Whiner. But Seth was going to miss the sword. As souvenirs went, a magic weapon was hard to beat.

The tunnel ended at a corroded door. When Seth knocked, it produced little sound. Though scarred on the surface, the wood was thick.

"You're almost home," Seth told the wraith.

Icy words reached his mind in reply. *There can be no home for me. Only unrest.*

"I felt a little like that in the car," Seth replied, trying to keep the conversation light. "Hard to get comfy. My rear was going numb." The undead tended to dwell on emptiness and yearning. Get them started and it sometimes became hard to shut off. Especially this guy. "Think I knocked loud enough?" He gave the door a couple of kicks.

It swung open to reveal a warty face with bulging yellow eyes. "Who dares rap upon this portal?"

"Good question," Seth said. "You really should wash it."

The river troll blinked in confusion. "This is a domain of perils untold."

"I've been told," Seth said. "I came here before. The Sisters know me."

Leaning forward, the tall troll squinted at him. "Yes, the boy. I suppose you have a right to pass this way. You're not expected for some time."

"I'm early," Seth said. "I brought what they wanted." He touched the hilt of the sword and gestured at the wraith.

The troll took a step back as his gaze shifted to the wraith. "I see. Very well. Since you are returning to fulfill an assignment, you enter by invitation."

Seth glanced at the wraith. "I think you'll like him," he whispered to the troll while stepping across the threshold. "Great roommate. One of the guys."

Long feet flapping against the ground, the troll led them along a corridor that looked like a pale-gray throat. The troll periodically glanced back at the wraith, clearly unsettled. Apparently, even other monsters didn't love the idea of having their lives leeched from them.

The corridor sloped down before opening into a damp chamber cratered with puddles. Huge white maggots stretched and flexed grotesquely, pale flesh rippling, one in each little pool. Several short trolls with puffy builds and oversize heads scuttled away at the approach of Seth and the wraith.

Around one of the puddles, three women stood in a ring. They had no hands. Instead, their wrists were fused together to form a conjoined circle. Seth recalled that the tall skinny one was Berna. The flabby one with the droopy flesh on her arms was Wilna. The shortest, Orna, had acted nicest on his previous visit. The Sisters shifted to better see him. Wilna had to look over her shoulder.

"Seth Sorenson," Berna greeted. "You return well before we expected you."

"Can't you see the future?" Seth asked, trying not to breathe too deeply. The chamber smelled sweet and rotten, like a decaying mix of mushy fruit.

"We don't peer down every avenue," Orna said. "Ruins the suspense."

"We could have sent the covenant knife after you," Wilna said. "You weren't supposed to reveal our arrangement to anyone."

"It wasn't my fault," Seth complained. "Bracken read my mind. He's a unicorn. I didn't tell him."

"She knows that," Orna said. "Otherwise you would already be dead. And such a shame! You're starting out on a path much like the one walked by your great-great-granduncle."

"I have a long way to go before I can compare myself to Patton Burgess," Seth said.

"Don't be so hasty to dismiss the comparison," Orna warned in gentle tones. "It's why I like you."

"We voted two to one against sending the knife," Berna said. "Orna vouched for you because you intrigue her. I joined her because I sense you could be useful."

"Our private agreement leaked to outsiders," Wilna complained with a scowl. "We were within our rights to slay the boy."

"And then we would have no sword and no wraith," Berna said. "That wraith could come in handy."

"The boy still owes us a favor," Orna added. "And don't forget Nagi Luna."

"You heard about that?" Seth asked. He had killed two ancient demons with Vasilis—Nagi Luna and Graulas.

"Why would we need to hear of it?" Wilna snapped. "We can behold such events at our leisure."

"Are you . . . angry?" Seth asked.

The three sisters cackled and swayed, wrists creaking.

"Because Nagi Luna mentored dozens of witches?" Orna asked through her giggles.

"Well, yeah," Seth said. "I guess you heard about Gorgrog, too?"

The witches laughed harder.

"What witch with any right to the title would have failed to note the fall of the Demon King?" Berna asked.

Seth felt confused by the merriment. "Don't witches get their power from demons?"

"That is more or less true," Orna said, using her shoulder to rub away mirthful tears. "But the power comes at a price." She raised her arms, which lifted the connected arms of her sisters. "The demons are our sponsors but seldom our friends. Fear and respect are not the same as love. The fall of a high demon can be . . . delicious."

"To see the king brought low by a child . . . ," Berna said.

"An amusing day for one and all," Wilna concluded.

Seth couldn't take credit for slaying the Demon King. His sister, Kendra, had done it. "You're glad the demons were imprisoned after their escape?" Seth verified.

"Oh my, on the whole, yes," Orna said. "Imagine all the groveling and bootlicking we would have to do with so many powerful demon lords on the prowl."

"It would have shaken things up," Berna said. "No doubt about it."

"We could have found ways to turn an age of demonic rule to our advantage," Wilna asserted stiffly.

"It would have been complicated," Orna said.

"It's always complicated," Wilna replied. "Now we have the dragons to worry about."

"But they have less direct interest in us," Berna said.

"Dragons?" Seth asked.

"No free predictions," Wilna said.

"Did I ask for a prediction?" Seth asked.

"Your future is entwined with the rise of the great wyrms," Orna said.

Berna jerked Orna to one side. "Stop blabbing!"

"Don't pull me!" Orna griped, yanking Berna hard enough to make her stumble.

"You saw my future?" Seth asked.

"We observe many futures," Wilna said. "Not all come to pass."

"Are you going to send me on a mission involving dragons?" Seth wondered.

Wilna narrowed her eyes suspiciously. "You sound hopeful."

Seth shrugged. "I missed some of the dragon stuff at Wyrmroost. I was stuck in a knapsack. The dragons looked really cool at Zzyzx."

"Told you," Orna said. "Patton all over again."

"We have not yet settled on your task," Berna said.

"Are you sure?" Seth checked. "I wouldn't mind getting it over with."

"Why the hurry to repay us?" Wilna asked.

"Things have been kind of dull around Fablehaven," Seth said. "And it doesn't seem like a good idea to owe favors to witches."

"Dullness won't be a problem for long," Orna said.

"Hush," Wilna ordered.

"Why?" Seth asked.

"Turbulent times await us all," Wilna stated.

"You brought the sword," Berna said. "And the wraith appears serviceable."

"It's great," Seth assured them. "Hungry. Cold. Lonely. Everything you could want in an undead servant."

Empty, the wraith thought at them.

"And empty," Seth agreed. "Thirsty, too. Fun at parties."

"You'll serve us?" Wilna asked the wraith.

Seth sensed the answer in his mind. *The boy brought me as a gift. I will serve.*